I0763376

WORKING THE GLASS

A Novel

Andrew Kloak

New Leaf Publishing Team

MOUNTAIN VIEW, CALIFORNIA

Andrew Kloak/New Leaf Publishing Team
Mountain View, California 94043
www.newleafpublishingteam.com

Library of Congress Cataloging-in-Publication Data
Kloak, Andrew

Publisher's Note: This is a work of fiction. Names, characters, places, and incidents are a product of the author's imagination. Locales and public names are sometimes used for atmospheric purposes. Any resemblance to actual people, living or dead, or to businesses, companies, events, institutions, or locales is completely coincidental.

Working the Glass: A Novel/ Andrew Kloak. -- 1st ed.
ISBN 978-0-9970278-0-8

This book is dedicated to my oldest brother Dave. I'm grateful for his guidance and support. Our monthly meetings for breakfast and lunch, both in California and Chicago, inspired and encouraged me when I needed it the most on the journey. He proved to be a leading light that elevated my game and life toward the extraordinary.

CONTENTS

PROLOGUE

CHASING THE CZECH DREAM

My journey began the day after my tenth birthday. My only brother Josef was eight and a half years old. Imre Savek poured cement one afternoon that covered most of our backyard. Later, in his workroom in the basement, he guided his jigsaw across smooth cedar as we held it steady for him. After he blew off the dust, we admired his handiwork: a large rectangle and four smaller squares. The squares, he said, were for later. The next morning, he affixed the rectangle backboard to the side of our brick garage and attached a hoop ten feet from the ground. After he strung nylon to the orange hoop, he began showering us with the fundamentals of ball-handling and shooting. It was always in Czech, the language we spoke in our home in Chicago.

In the winter, when the court was covered with ice and snow, my father sat on the wooden stairs in our unheated basement and watched my brother Josef and me dribble red, white, and blue ABA basketballs around chairs. He pulled out the cedar squares and stapled a thick rubber band on each of them. He helped us put them on like on like mitts with the squares over our palms so we dribbled with only our fingertips. When I put my hands to my face in my grade school classroom, they had the scent of cedar and rubber.

When I graduated from eighth grade, my brother and I were both taller than our father, who was 5'10". We got our height from my 6'0" mother Lidmila. Imre would joke sometimes that he married her for her height.

That summer we always played basketball together in the backyard until my mother called us in for the night.

"Přicházejí do domu, chlapci, " my mother said from the back porch.

About fifteen minutes later she was back on the porch.

"Imre, Imre přicházejí do domu, chlapci," she said, this time with more force and anger. Then she turned off the flood light. It was dark but the city streetlight in the alley provided some light.

"Hey, last play, Mila," Imre said. He called her Mila unless it was a serious disagreement. Then he addressed her as Lidmila.

Imre hit a hook shot from the far corner over the both of us to end the game.

"Štěstí shot," I said, because it was a lucky shot.

"To je talent, tvrdá práce a praxe," Imre said, attributing it all to talent, hard work and practice.

Imre wiped his sweaty forehead. He pulled out two things he always carried in his front pocket: a wad of cash and a black comb. Imre, who had rough hands acquired from his general contractor job, ran the comb through his black hair. Then we went in.

I played on the junior varsity team as a freshman at Mendel High School. Imre liked our high school for two reasons: it was on Cermak Road in the heart of the Czech neighborhoods, and it was named after the botanist Gregori Johann Mendel, who was from Brno where Imre grew up. Josef was good enough to make the varsity team in his freshman year. It was our first time playing together on the same team. At first, our coach Bob Longo matched us against each other in practice, but rivalry spilled out into fights. We shoved and elbowed each other after the whistle blew for a moment and then it was over. Somehow we both had the ability to let go of what just happened and still maintain our friendship.

Josef and I succeeded by working together, and by my junior year we were both good enough to be starters on the first team. We were the tallest players on our high school team. Our ultimate heights reached 6'7" for Josef and 6'5" for me. Our strengths complemented each other. If a team began to concentrate their efforts to stop Josef, then I was freed to pull down more offensive rebounds and score from where I was most effective: close to the basket. If they focused on me, then Josef would find shots in the open seams. If we were down, my job was to help us regain the momentum. I would dive to the hard floor for a loose ball and shovel the ball to my brother streaking toward our basket. Or I would spin around defenders trying to block me out. I'd snare an offensive rebound and put the ball back up for two points.

Our crowning achievement was against Providence St. Mel, our number-one conference rival. St. Mel's, an all-black school on the city's west side, had cold showers and a small visitors' locker room with slits on the sides of the windows that let in wind and snow. St. Mel's was so talented that if you let the locker room situation distract you or the fact that they were listed in the *Sun Times' Power Rankings* as the #1 boys basketball team in the Chicagoland area, they could open the game with a 10-0 lead in the first three minutes. Their *seventh* best player, Dillwyn "Dilly" Jackson, had a 44" inch vertical leap and eventually signed to play at the University of Evansville, a Division I School. St. Mel's had beaten everyone else that season by racing to insurmountable early leads, but we led by two in the final seconds. St. Mel's had a breakaway three-on-one with just me defending our basket. I waited for them to come to me. I focused on the ball and when their point guard passed, I stole it. I stopped their chance to win, dead in their tracks. The final buzzer sounded. I threw the ball up toward the rafters above the court. We had beaten the team that eventually won the Illinois State Championship.

When I graduated from high school I decided to play at North Park College, a small school situated in a tree-lined residential neighborhood on city's northwest side. Josef joined me there after he graduated from Mendel. My basketball success had always come with him along side me. We won three NCAA Division III titles playing together at North Park but our talents developed in different ways. We were completely opposite, as his specialty was scoring and my potency was defense and rebounding. Josef preferred to stay away from inside contact. He relied on smooth movement around the perimeter and slashing drives toward the basket. His quick first step, jumping ability, and long arms helped him develop his scoring prowess. His game was individual flash: rainbow jumpers off the drive, two-handed slam dunks, and occasional rejections into the stands. Josef could send electricity through the crowd but, by itself, his flash didn't help our team play its best basketball or to win.

I was resilient, playing even when I was sick or injured. In fact, that brought out the best in me. After college Josef and I played together in Czech basketball tournaments. Sokols are Czech fraternal orders focused on physical, moral, and intellectual training. They were not just for men but also for women. Every Czech neighborhood in Chicago had a sokol club to preserve the folk customs, keep the language alive, and perfect athletic discipline. The Lithuanians had much larger tournaments and overall club sport organization. But in Czechago, as it was called, Czech basketball was a tradition. Our green-shirted *Ceska Central Park* team played in the Chicagoland Czech basketball summer tournament. There were the two other Czech teams from Chicago and sokols from Brookfield, Berwyn, Cicero and Westchester. *Ceska Central Park* won the Chicago-area tournament every year Josef and I played on the team. At the end of the summer, a North American Czech basketball tournament was hosted that drew sokol teams from across the US and Canada. While there were other Czech-American communities in Texas, Wisconsin, Nebraska and New York, none of them were as large as the one in Chicago and its western suburbs. We played when the North American tournament was held at the Mecca in Milwaukee, Hamilton, Ontario and Cleveland.

After we won the Chicagoland tournament championship when I was 27, our organization lined up an exhibition game at the University of Illinois-Chicago Pavilion against a visiting team of all-stars from across Czechoslovakia. We beat the real Czechs in one of the most exciting and loudest games I ever played in. I'd never seen my father, who attended all our games, happier than that night.

A few days later, Josef announced that he got an offer to play professionally for the *Glasgow Rangers Basketball Club* in Scotland. After two years in Scotland, he signed to play for the *Hemel Hempstead Royals* professional basketball team in North London, where he played for another two years.

Our decade run of playing on the same teams had come to an end.

CHAPTER ONE

THE OFFER

I heard a knock and opened the door. There was Josef. He was wearing a tweed trench coat over his slim frame. His face looked a little gaunter than I remembered it but he still had a full head of wavy brown hair that looked like it needed a comb.

"Dobry den Ferenc, it's great to be back in Czech-ago," he said.
"Josef, good to see you," I said.

I opened my arms and we hugged. He appeared taller than I remember but as I straightened up next to him I was reminded that there were only two inches that separated us.

His eyes had a squint in the corners that revealed that he was tired. As I looked into his eyes, I thought, here is the guy that let four years and four thousand miles get in the way of a once close relationship.

"What happened up there?" Josef said, pointing to my eyebrow.

"I was elbowed in the face in a league game a few months ago."

"You look tougher. Anyway, most of the scar is under those caterpillar eyebrows," he said.

"Let me help you with your bags," I said.

I grabbed his green duffel bag and brought it in.

"I want to figure out my options. I need your place to crash for a while," he said.

"Why don't you stay with Mom and Dad? They have a bigger place."

"I need to stay in a place where I can think," he said.

"I don't have that much room here," I said.

"That's all right. I see you have a couch I can stay on, don't you?"

"As you can see, I live in a loft. One big room," I said.

"That's all right. We can throw up a barrier down the middle."

"A barrier? What are you talking about?"

"Some kind of temporary partition dividing it into two," he said.

"I know what a partition is," I said.

"You didn't answer my question. Can I stay with you here?"

"Yeah, but we're not rearranging the floor plan," I said.

We sat down on my couch. Finally, we took some time to catch up.

"Can I use your phone?" he said.

"Sure, follow me," I said.

On the wall of the kitchen, I had a white phone.

"I've got to make a long distance call to Europe but I'll pay you for it when the bill comes in. Is that okay?" he said.

"Make sure you do. Go ahead, then," I said.

While Josef began the call, there was a knock on the door. My brother shook his head as if he had the situation under control and waved for me to answer the door. I did.

It was Edita, the landlady of my building. In her red robe. She always wore a robe, even during the day. Edita had blonde hair and smelled like moth balls. She liked to bring me food like dumplings or walnut kolaches and sometimes hot cider when she heard me coming up the stairs to my apartment. Edita liked to lean her frame in my doorway and tell me stories in Czech. I always felt like we talked too long, but I still enjoyed her company.

"Dobry den. I bring you a little something, Ferenc. For the rodina," she said. She handed me a pan of Bohemian dumplings. Still warm.

She waved to Josef. My brother partially smiled to acknowledge her, then continued his conversation on the phone.

"Thanks, Edita, I'm sure he'll like it," I said.

"This is big day for you, Ferenc. I'll leave you to your brother," she said. Then she peeked around the corner for one more look.

"He's handsome. Good looks run in the family, I see," she said. Then she turned and ambled back down the stairwell. I walked back to the kitchen.

I tried one of the dumplings. Not bad. Edita, who was in my parents' generation, was an intrusive but kind lady. I looked out my window at Cermak Road, the spine of the Czech community.

My father liked the fact that the Lithuanians had the Marquette Road, the Poles had Milwaukee Avenue, and we had Cermak. There were Czech banks, grocery stores and restaurants that stretched from my parents' neighborhood Ceska Central Park all the way to Brookfield Zoo, although Czech-ago was becoming less defined and had more porous borders. These neighborhoods weren't the same communities that my father immigrated to in 1965 from Czechoslovakia with his two brothers. A good example of this was the Pilsen neighborhood where I lived. My apartment still had the red Hapsburg lion coat of arms inset on the arch over the entrance. The neighborhood was settled and built by Czechs and Slovaks, but ethnic Chicago was undergoing a sea change. There were with supermarcados, bibiolotecas, carenicias and vendors pushing carts selling elotes and aqua fresca on Cermak. Artists and working people of all nationalities also moved in because rent was cheaper than the West Loop core.

I tried to listen in on the phone conversation that my brother was having. He asked whoever he was speaking to about a work visa for his playing on the team.

Then he said goodbye and hung up. I was surprised at how brief his call was.

"Do you want anything to eat?" I said.

"No, I've eaten on the plane. I'd like to go for run with you along the lake. How does that sound?"

"That's great, let's do it," I said.

We put on our running gear and I drove us east along Cermak toward the lake.

"What did that guy from the team say to you when you were on the phone?" I said as I drove.

"That was from Jiri Hasek, head of the Svet Sports club in the Czech Republic. They want me to come and play on their team," Josef said.

"What are you going to do? What's your plan, Josef?"

"I told them I'll be there, ready to go next month."

"That's great. Then you've decided," I said pulling the car up into a parking spot along McFetridge Drive that leads to the Adler Planetarium.

We got out and stretched along a seawall. There was the harbor and beyond it was the skyline of the downtown. A sailboat headed toward where we where we stood, its fully-extended canvas sails rippling in the wind. A man in a polo shirt and jeans, not much older than we were, had a proud look on his face, steered the craft in our direction. Then he turned the boat aggressively at a 90 degree angle. Blue-green turbulence blasted against the hull. The tip of the boat, in turn, serrated the water and the craft maneuvered away from the breakwaters and in the direction of Michigan across the lake.

"I haven't decided," said my brother.

"What do you mean?"

"I had two offers in hand before I left England. A team down in Australia wants me to play with them, too."

"You've got two offers and you've accepted them both?"

"Yes."

I stopped stretching. "Are you crazy?" I said.

"No," my brother said. "I have a plan."

"So what's your plan?" I said. "What are you going to do?"

"I'm going to Australia."

"What about this other team?"

"That's where *you* come in."

"Me?"

"You can go in my place."

"That's crazy. How could I go in your place?"

"Just say you're me. They'll never know. We have the same last name and are about the same height."

"It's insane," I said. "We'd never get away with it."

I finished stretching and looked over to Josef. "Are you ready to go? Let's do it," I said. He nodded yes.

We took off running. Down concrete stairs and then onto a patch of grass. We headed north on the running path along the water in the direction of the Chicago Yacht Club. I felt myself trying to jump-start my body into action. I gauged my brother's stride to be a step faster than I was used to, and I liked the challenge.

I was laid off two months before. A job in public relations was what I placed my hope on but I wasn't finding one as quickly as I had envisioned, much to my discouragement.

"You're nuts to think I'd even want to go," I said.

"You are the best one to do this."

"My basketball days are coming to an end. I don't know if I could play at that level," I said.

"We've played together all these years. It's worth a shot. Plus, they'll pay you 5,000 Kč per month."

"How could it work? There're expecting a scorer, not a defender/rebounder like me. They'll notice that right away."

I ran my hand through my hair to slow the pouring sweat. I began to fall back a few yards.

"Slow down. You're running faster than I can handle," I said.

He looked back at me. "I'm trying to get you ready to go. You'll thank me when you're in Svet."

"Thanks for nothing. It's too fast. How can I go in your place?"

"You'd have three weeks to be ready. They'll be waiting in Vienna and take you across the Czech border to Svet. They're very excited about having me come."

"I'm not you."

"You just have to say you are me, and then you can be yourself."

"I have a future right here. Besides, I don't know what I can do anymore in basketball."

"If you got in the right situation, you could do well for a team, maybe even dominate," said Josef.

"Dominate? That's optimistic," I said.

"You could help a team out. Most of all, you would be helping me out."

I saw that the pace had not slowed at all. We were still running too fast.

It might be a good chance to travel, play basketball and get paid for it. But there was no guarantee it would work.

Still, I could see myself playing basketball in Svet. I loved basketball and this situation could be my final shot.

"What's this about the going to Vienna? What are they going to do, put me in the trunk and smuggle me across the border?" I was barely able to get the words out as I ran. We were abreast of Buckingham Fountain because I could see plumes of water over the small elms that lined our path and Lake Shore Drive.

"No, they said that a border crossing is faster than trying to clear Czech Immigration at the airport in Prague."

"Svet. Where is it?" I said.

"It's a small town in the mountains up near the Polish border. They say they have all the accommodations and excellent facilities there."

"What about the work visa and passport? What happens when it doesn't match with yours?" I said.

"You can use my passport. I'll mail it to you once I get down to Australia. It'll work," Josef said.

"I see—maybe, maybe—is what I say. Did they give you any more information about it?"

"They sent me a letter. It's in my bag back at your place. I'll show you it when we're done."

"What if they find out I'm not you?'

"They don't care who you are if you can play basketball and play well. That's all they care about."

"That doesn't sound right. They've had to have heard about your game and from the minute I get there they'll expect me to play like you do," I said.

"The biggest question is just getting the plane ticket to get to Vienna. How much money have you got?"

"I don't have a lot. About eight hundred dollars."

"That's enough to get you there. All you have to do is liquidate your car and your apartment. That'll help. Give your thirty day notice on the place."

"Wait a minute! What about my life here?"

"What are you talking about? You have nothing holding you back. When did you split with your girlfriend Nancy?"

"Last month, don't remind me," I said.

"Yeah, so that's not happening. Then you're not working and almost broke."

I didn't like hearing his blunt assessment of my life. Humiliating especially hearing my younger brother saying this about me. But it was true.

"Okay, what's your point?" I said.

"Any leads for jobs in public relations? What kind of prospects do you have?"

"Not much hiring right now by firms. It wasn't fun being laid off. At least, I got unemployment coming in."

"Finding a job isn't easy. You'll find something eventually. But in the meantime, you'll make more in the Czech Republic than being on the dole here. That's for sure."

The details were shaky. Go in my brother's place to a small country town up in the mountains where they might find out I'm not the person I say am.

We were reaching the end of our run.

"Let's kick it in," I said, my legs pounding harder in a sprint to the end. Josef was right next to me. My body surged. The wind began to whistle past my ears. Before reaching a green light pole near the entrance to the yacht club that marked the stopping point, my brother put on an incredible blast of energy to finish about five yards in front of me.

"What a slow-ass," Josef said. "You got molasses on your shoes?"

"If I ran every day on the basketball court like you do, I'd have caught you," I said.

I didn't like to lose, but my brother always had a longer stride that made him hard to beat. We took time to wind down and let the sweat dry as the sun began to set behind the lineup of buildings along Michigan Avenue.

When we got back to my apartment, Josef pulled out a letter from the Svet Sports Club. "Here is that letter. Let me read it to you," he said.

17 May 1993
Svet

Dear Mister Josef Savek,

We have heard very positive things about your recent play in the Inter-England league. Congratulations on your fine season! You should be very proud of your accomplishments. This letter is a follow up to your phone conversation on April 30 with our representative Bryan Wexford from Manchester, UK. As the head coach of the Svet Basketball Sports Club I would like to introduce myself to you.

Svet is an idyllic town of 30,000 located in the Czech Republic in the Krkonoše Mountains. We are 125 kilometers northeast of Prague. Our basketball club welcomes a player with your abilities. We think you will be able to help us be more competitive in the ten-team Czech Professional Basketball Superliga. Last season we had a strong team. We play a 28-game regular season and then additional games in the playoffs. Your compensation will be 5,000 Kč per month. Your accommodations will be dormitory style in housing provided by our team owner, Mr. Milos Koliar.

Our season is already underway and the second half starts 10 September. We are beginning our training camp 1 September but we would be willing to have you come seven days prior to our second half opener against Pardubice. The best arrangement would be for us to meet you in Vienna, Austria on 3 September and drive you across the Czech border to Svet.

We think that you will find that Svet is an enjoyable place to live and play in the upcoming part of our season. We hope to speak with you very soon to confirm your intention to join our team.

Sincerely,

JIRI HASEK
Coach/Director Svet Lions Sports Club

Josef scanned my face for a second when I was done.

"What do you think?" Josef said.

"What's 5,000 Crowns per month in U.S. Dollars?" I said

"About $700. It's not great but think of the adventure. Plus you'll be getting out of Chicago," Josef said.

"Any more info on it?"

"Yes, here are the teams in the league," Josef said.

He handed me a league schedule that listed the ten Czech teams on the front.

Brno
České Budějovice
Hradec Králové
Olomouc
Ostrava
Pardubice
Plzeň
Praha-A
Praha-B
Svet

CHAPTER TWO

FAMILY DINNER

The door lock on my blue Chrysler Laser had frozen and I went into the truck for some WD-40. I sprayed into the keyhole and some on my key. That did the trick. When the engine turned over, my recording of BB King at the Blues Fest four years earlier filled the car. I snapped it off at once.

"Hey, I like that song. Keep it on," Josef said.

"Maybe later. I've heard it too much."

Halted at the first stop light, I began to feel the want of a destination. When the light changed I drove on, past the *Stop & Shop* and the fire station and past some Latinos shooting hoops under streetlights at Harrison Park.

Ahead, down Wood Street, I could see the beer signs in the *Bohemian Lounge* window warm and welcoming. We waited at a red light on Cermak Road. In unison we looked over to the *Bohemian.*

I was troubled by a peculiar impatience with it seemed time itself. I was waiting for something. Ceska California Avenue wasn't the place. The old neighborhood made me anxious. I had no desire to go to our parent's home.

When the light changed, I accelerated forward.

"Stop here, Ferenc," Josef said. "I need to get a gift for Mom and Dad."

I swung the car into the parking lot of the *Bohemian.*

"Go on in," I said.

I kept the engine running. He got out but walked over to my side.

"Come. For old times' sake, buddy," Josef said.

We walked in together.

Outside the *Bohemian*, I paused with my hand on the door-knob. When inside, there was an old man behind the counter of the package store. The old man neither knew nor cared who we were. The package store was well stocked with bottles, current magazines and Czech newspapers. Josef bought a half brick of Belgian chocolate and a *Sports Illustrated* and put them in the inside pocket of his jacket.

Passing into the main section of the bar, I could see some familiar faces of the neighborhood. *The Bohemian Lounge* was all dark wood and etched mirrors, a Czech saloon. The place was crowded with men off their shifts at the machine shops and the Inland Steel plant. A few guys actually stood and motioned for us to their stools at the bar. We took them.

"There they are, the lost Bohemian tribe," said one guy named Tomas. He slapped both of us in the back. One of those too hard and aggressive slaps. A crowd formed and all eyes seemed on us.

"Blue Skirt Waltz" by Yankovic was on the jukebox. My favorite polka. I just wish I had someone to dance it with. Nancy did like that Eastern European side of me. If she were here, I could grab her hand and she would swivel into action with me right then. I missed her courage and sense of humor but not her complaints.

The bartender was a club fighter from the Back of the Yards neighborhood named Frankie V. I'd talked to him before when he sponsored our basketball team at Margate a few years back. I gossiped with him about the latest news especially after Josef left. He'd bought our park league team tee-shirts that displayed the name of his bar on the back.

He greeted Josef like we'd been there the night before.

"Say ace," Frankie V said.

"How do," Josef said.

"What do you need, guy?" Frankie V said, looking at me like I was a stranger.

Confronted with the bartender, I felt compelled to explain my presence.

"Just thought we'd stop by," I said. "Thought we'd have one. He's back. I'm back. We saw the sign."

He laughed expansively.

"Nice move," said the bartender. "Pilsner?"

"One for my brother and me."

I shoved four dollars forward along the bar for the two of us.

Frankie V pushed two bills back to me.

"No charge for the legend. Back for good, Josef?"

Frankie V and Josef shook hands.

"No, I'm on to play in Australia next," Josef said.

"Australia? Way down there? You and Ziggy are the only ones. Not like the rest of these bums," Frankie V said, glancing at me and the rest of us in the bar.

Zbigniew "Ziggy" Storanovski lived on California Avenue. His parents owned a drug store on the first floor and they lived on the second floor overlooking the intersection of California and Cermak. He was a tenacious defender on the perimeter and a battler under the boards. After playing for the University of Illinois-Chicago Flames, Ziggy had enough to make a professional team in Greece three years ago. The complete package and great white hope at just 6'1".

"What was your name again?" the bartender said to me. The guy was serious. We were the dynamic duo. Three NCAA-Division III championships and all-area selections at Mendel H.S and he only remembered Josef.

"The same as yours," I said.

"What are you up to?" Frankie V said.

"I've been playing with the Česká California sokol and in that summer league over at Margate Park. Remember, you sponsored us?" I said. The bartender looked like he stopped listening.

We watched Frankie pour the pilsners off the tap.

"Decent beer here?" I said as the bartender slid them across the bar to us.

"I should think so. Any dumbkopf knows that. Where have you been? This is the *Bohemian* after all," the bartender said so everyone could hear.

I drove the ten minutes to my parent's house on Christina Street. As we pulled past the front of house, I passed it and proceeded around the corner.

"Where to, Ferenc?" Josef said.

"Mrs. Darovnik's. It's been years since you've seen the woman. You used to work for her. Didn't you?" I said.

Gertrude Darovnik lived across the alley from us. We both worked for her before we went to college. Inside work mostly, toilets, vacuuming, dusting, sweeping, organizing, and even dishes. Our replacements were neighborhood teen girls after we left.

"Okay, it will be good to visit old Gert," Josef said.

I pulled around the block and parked along the curb in front of her brown brick bungalow. We walked up the steps and I rang. She peered out through frosted glass front door. The silhouette of her 5'3" frame fit the intricate design in the glass perfectly. Her head had horns and the downward slits in the face made her look like a demon standing there. It always did, not just on Halloween.

This white-haired lady answered the door in her slippers and pajamas. Her face lit up. And no sooner was she hugging us with her big body. She took her time, me first then Josef.

"Come in, boys. It's great to see you. You know I turned 90 this year," she said in Czech.

A widow, she took in boarders. There always seemed to be two old men in the house. My special job related to them was to vacuum their toe nail clippings off the carpeted floors of their bedrooms. I started working on Saturday mornings, and then when I went off to college, Josef took my place for year.

"We just came by to say hello," Josef said in Czech. Speaking the home language showed me that he was respectful of her.

She ushered us into the living room.

"I'm glad you did. Have a seat so we can catch up," she said.

A soap opera was playing on the TV. We sat down on La-Z-Boys facing her on the sofa.

"Josef, your mother said you were coming back for good."

'No, not for good. I'm going to Hobart, Australia, to play basketball in a few weeks," said Josef.

"You both always loved basketball. Good for you, Josef," she said.

My mother resented Mrs. Darovnik because when we were working for her, we avoided the necessary work at home. She said not only does that woman across the alley, who had no children, take the time of my sons but she will also call me on the phone to gossip about things. The nerve of her.

"Ferenc, you know your name is of Hungarian origin, although you're as Czech as any of us."

She said that many times over the years. I didn't know why my parents named me Ferenc but I went by Frank anyway, so it didn't matter. Before I could say anything, Mrs. D was onto the next question.

"How are you? How's your girlfriend?"

Before I could answer she craned her neck toward the TV and held up her hand for me to wait. We watched a scene from a Czech soap opera for a minute. Josef and I looked at each other and laughed at the absurdity of the situation. In our teen years, that same playfulness and horsing around in the kitchen was the reason Mrs. D never let us work together. Only one at a time for chores because of that.

"Okay, as you were saying, Ferenc?" she said.

"It's over with her. No girlfriend for a month. The priesthood looks better lately," I said.

"Priesthood? Oh no Ferenc, you can't do that."

It wasn't because she was Protestant/Lutheran that she said this. Here was a living, breathing Protestant here in our mostly Catholic world, and because of her, I was more tolerant toward Protestants. She had a nephew named Ferenc who was gay. My not having a girlfriend made her anxious.

"Have you given up journalism? I hope not. Will you have a job soon?" she said.

"It's taken a good turn. I have some interviews next week with a few public relations firms downtown."

The lie was absurd, but I felt the need of it.

"That's good. I hope you get something soon," she said. In addition to having us clean the house, she had us organize her books and files. Mrs. D loved Eastern European royalty: Hungarian princes, Romanian kings and queens and great figures in Czech nationalist history. She kept a whole room of files on these aristocrats and when a newspaper article came out that Prince Stefan of Romania and his wife named their new baby Beatrix, she had me start a Beatrix file.

"You come by so rarely, Ferenc, these books and files we worked on will go to waste. By the way, I'd like you to have some of them," she said.

"Maybe not quite now," I said.

""He's trying to lighten his load. Not take anything else on. I'm here to help him do that," Josef said.

"Okay, well you've come to the right place. I've got some great books when you're ready," she said.

"Good," I said, standing. "We can't stay. The parents are waiting to see this guy right now."

"Here, come to the kuchyně. That way you are closer to home and then you can go out the back door," she said.

She led us along the well-worn vinyl floor into the kitchen. The cupboards seemed smaller than I remembered and the refrigerator and stove looked ancient now. There was a tiny table with a few chairs around it. The only thing that looked new was a bouquet of daisies in a vase on the table.

After I did my chores, Mrs. Darovnik would make me lunch—hot chocolate, a ham and cheese sandwich, and some fruit. We would have lunch together for a half hour and then she would pay me for my work and even included the time for lunch.

"Did you both want a hot chocolate and something to eat?" she said.

"No, we have to get going. My parents have dinner for us," I said.

I missed this old lady. She gave me so much. If it were just me, I would have stayed. But Josef raised his eyebrows and gestured toward the door that I took as his desire to go.

"It was great to see you," I said.

We hugged her and waited for her to unlock the intricate system of locks and deadbolts on her back door.

"Don't be strangers, Ferenc and Josef. Say hello to your parents, especially your mother. She's such a good person," Mrs. Darovnik said.

There we were on the wooden back landing. I wanted to run through the grass of her backyard through the bushes and into the alley like old times. From there, we would catapult over the back gate without even opening it. We would land standing upright and be on our property. But instead we turned and walked back to our car.

I drove past the four houses until we pulled into our driveway. We both got out slowly and looked at our house a moment and then walked up our sloping concrete sidewalk to reach our front concrete porch. My father, being a contractor, had the best designed and elaborate front sidewalk in the neighborhood: a jawbone pattern of inlaid bricks, on a curved path, to a wide set of steps.

Meeting my parents made me uneasy because they wanted life to be different than it was. Oftentimes I found myself being evasive to deflect their unnecessary angst. I wanted a relationship with them where I could be real.

I knocked on the old-fashioned red door on the top of the landing.

My mother opened the door. Her blonde hair was up in a bun. She was more handsome than ever in her 60s.

"I was wondering about you two," she said.

She gave a hug and a kiss to her long-lost son, Josef. Then to me. The one she saw at least once a month or so. That was nice of her.

"We just visited Mrs. Darovnik and stopped in at the Bohemian before that," I said.

"The Bohemian? You didn't have to drink. All you had to do was come home," she said.

"Mrs. Darovnik isn't going to be around forever," I said.

"Neither will we. How could you? We're waiting for you," she said.

Her earnest blue eyes were directed at me, the older brother, for not being on time. Her long elegant face was rigid and lipless when she got angry.

"Vitejle, you picked the last minute. Dinner's ready," said the voice of our father from around the corner.

This man with thinning short-cropped black hair sauntered into the center of the foyer with a seemingly effortless glide to his step. If my father hadn't had back problems over the years, he could have been a professional ballroom dancer.

He gave Josef a hug and then a hard slap on the back. Then he maneuvered around behind us, one arm on each of our backs, as he guided us into the dining room to the table with an oilcloth cover.

"Have a seat," he said.

We all sat down as the perfect family together again. Classical music was playing on the stereo. Even a fire was burning in the fireplace.

Our mother started bringing out the food. In the center, she placed a platter of Moravian sausage, then potatoes and shredded pickled beets.

Josef pulled out the *Sports Illustrated* and the half-brick of Belgian chocolate. The magazine had Michael Jordan and Scottie Pippen on the cover.

"For you, Dad, it's the current issue. And the chocolate for mom," Josef said.

"The Bulls? You two could have been on this cover. Do you understand?" he said, thumping the magazine cover and setting it on a side table.

"I understand fine," I said. "You wanted more for us and basketball. And we didn't deliver."

"This playing in England has been good for Josef," my father said. We all sat down.

"If only one of us could have made it to the continent like Ziggy. He's the only one from around here," I said.

"Ziggy—that little zip—he's not a real basketball player. Certainly not the athletes you two are. Don't even bring him up," my father said.

That is just like my father—to shut down conversation and force things to where he wanted it to go.

"How are you, Josef?" my father said.

"I'm well. Better now that I'm back home," he said, filling his plate with food.

My parents looked at him intently.

"You look thinner in the face. Like you haven't been eating well over there, Josef," my mother said.

"I've had a great season there," said Josef.

"To be playing at your age is a good achievement. But it's not going to be forever," said my father.

"I'm lucky. You're right."

"Josef, we don't see your brother much. And he lives here, so he has no excuse," my mother said.

It's true. I preferred talking with them on the phone more instead of coming home.

"You don't call them—your own parents?" Josef said.

He was being hypocritical because he had distanced himself from them for his overseas basketball and used that as his excuse.

"How is the job search? Any luck?" my father said.

"It's been harder than I expected," I said. "Nothing yet."

"You have to work harder at it, son. Maybe you just are going to have to take something to get going again. It won't be ideal. It's not good for you not to be working," my father said.

"Don't you think I want to find something? It's driving me nuts," I said.

"I came here with very little money but I made something of myself. You just have to be willing. Make an effort," my father said.

These people were too much with their prescriptive ways. No wonder why I avoided them because of stuff like this.

"There's more you can do, Josef. There's more you both can do," my mother said.

"We're doing it," I said.

"Maybe Josef but not you Ferenc, to be at this stage in your life, it's a shame," said my mother. She looked at my father.

"Josef's playing professionally so for him he's thriving," my father said.

Was this some kind of rehearsed line or unified front between them?

"That's not fair. I play," I said.

"Yes, yes but what kind of basketball?" said my father.

"Just two days ago, I played against Sam Hill, who played at Iowa State. He's about 6'8" or 6'9" and I slowed him. He didn't score or rebound as he normally does to teams in the Margate league," I said.

"We're not talking about playing; we're talking about your life. You have to move on with it," my mother said.

"Getting on with my life. What's that mean?" I said.

"Finding your way. You're lost," she said.

"What your mother means, Ferenc, is that you could do more. So much you both have and you're not doing it, especially you, Ferenc," my father said. "Could you answer your mother about what your plan is?"

"Wait, I forgot the beet soup," said my mother and she stood and bolted back into the kuchyně.

"It's not the right time for these questions," I said.

"When is it ever a good time?" my father said.

My mother came back in the room and said, "I just can't take it. I've had enough of the fighting."

I walked into the living room and turned off the Dvořák music on the CD player. Then I looked to one wall of the living room lined with bookshelves. There were volumes by John Gunther and Bohumil Hrabal, a video about John Havlicek, and *Disturbing the Peace*. Their present uselessness repelled me.

When I came back to the table, they were turning their attention to my brother.

"Maybe it's time to settle down and stay in one place. Are you back for good, Josef?" my mother said.

"I'm playing again. Basketball will continue. The question is, Will Ferenc go where I've got an opportunity for him? If he's smart, he'll follow my advice," Josef said.

"What does that mean? What advice? As you can see, he won't take it from anybody" said my father.

"He can play in the Czech Republic now. The team I signed on with in Svet needs a player—a scorer, a rebounder, and defender. They've given me an offer," Josef said.

"Both together again. Now you're on to something. You're great as a pair. You remember that last game against the Czechs? Ferenc worked into the package with you then. Is that it?" said my father.

Josef looked at me for a moment.

"No, not at all. I'm going to play in Australia next season," said Josef.

"Australia? How did that come about?" my father said.

"Some Brits I played with went down there and said it was a strong league."

"What? So the Czech team is off?"

"I'm going to play in Svet. Under his name," I said

"Is that true?" said my father.

"Yes. I'm going to give it a shot. Svet needs a player and I can help a team," I said.

"I don't want to hear your basketball fantasies," my father said, cutting me off.

My father shook his head.

"It's a bad idea. You say plan, it's no plan. You don't have shit. Do you want something that someone else gives you? Josef has made this for himself. Now you're honing in. It's simple as that," my father said.

"But it was okay if we played on the same team together? Then that would meet your approval?" I said

"Maybe that would be good. Both of you playing again. Brothers/family should help family," said my mother.

"Yes, but under these circumstances? A fake is what you'll be, Ferenc. Don't come to me when it doesn't work out. Don't you want to establish your own opportunities? Legitimate ones. You're better than this," my father said.

"What opportunities? The ones you say exist in Chicago but don't. It's more like you've always favored him. Sounds insincere to me," I said.

"Ferenc would be helping me out. He'll go in there and do well," said Josef.

"Really? Isn't it more like he's bailing you out of a jam? An over-promise?" my father said.

Josef got silent. "No, that's not it," Josef said.

"He's trying to do a good thing. You've hurt his feelings," my mother said.

"These are grown men; I've hurt nobody here. No reason to be sensitive," our father said.

“This is like a movie with you two out there,” said my mother. “It’s risky and dangerous. As a mother, it’s hard seeing you through these things. These are the scary parts, and when this comes, I have to close my eyes. But I trust in the end everything will turn all right.”

“We have to move toward the future, that’s the past. I left Czechoslovakia, and don’t expect anyone to go back there,” my father said. “Neither Brno, nor this dubious situation in Svet.”

Come on, it’s basketball in the Czech Republic. Taking the place of my brother was risky and uncertain, yes. But dangerous? No. At least, not the kind of danger that I couldn’t find my way out of.

CHAPTER THREE

JOURNEY ACROSS THE DIVIDE

Jiri Hasek, the coach of the Svet sports club, slammed on the brakes of the black Skoda. We stopped just in time behind another Czech-made car.

His driving had already set me on edge especially through the patchy fog of the Weinviertel. We'd survived a few near misses on the autobahn after leaving Schwechat Airport in Vienna. Jiri accelerated on a blue steel bridge across the Danube, then flanked left around slower traffic. Then swerved back to our original lane. The slot we were about to enter was taken. A straight truck barreled past. Later he chuckled when we passed the straight truck near Stockerau. While we wound through a mountainous region in the vicinity of Korneuburg, Jiri never seemed to use his brakes. We raced ahead and down the steep grades like a juggernaut. The speedometer needle showed we were going 160 kph at one point, careening to one side with all the centrifugal force the car could bear. We were lucky to stay on the road through the alpine forestland.

"We are at the Znojmo border point. Give him the work visa, Gustav," Jiri said.

We began to crawl toward an Austrian checkpoint. In the distance the blur of red lights could be seen for the next 100 yards.

From the passenger seat, Gustav, our assistant coach and team trainer, fished through a file he had next to him and handed me the visa paperwork. I scanned it—Josef Savek—my brother's name was listed throughout the document. My brother had sent his passport by express mail from Australia. I opened it. I noticed Gustav intently watching me. I looked in his direction.

"Are you, or have you been, married, Josef?" Jiri said.

"Not yet. Almost had a wife, but it didn't work out," I said.

"You're 30 and not married. That will help you," Jiri said. I was about to correct him that I was 31, but then remembered that my brother was 30.

"Basketball is a bachelor's game. You will spend hours at the gym training, playing in games. Plus, long trips on the road. We expect dedication. That's what it was like when I played, that's how it is now at our club," Jiri said.

"I had a girlfriend but it ended a few months ago," I said.

"It's better that way. You'll have basketball on your mind," Jiri said.

When I arrived earlier that afternoon, I went to a prearranged meeting area. When Jiri didn't show, the panic set in. 2:25. Is he coming? Have I got the right place, time and day? Austrian Airlines arrival area, 2:00, September 3rd. Could he be standing somewhere nearby, looking at me? Maybe he had already determined I was a fraud, and he was already on his way back to Svet. And I will have come all this way for nothing. I looked up seeing two men standing in front of me.

"Are you Josef Savek?"

"Yes."

Here we go. The first of what would have to be many lies.

"Dobry Den, I am Jiri Hasek. And this is Gustav Kezmarok."

I shook hands with both of them. Jiri had dark wavy hair and stood just over six feet tall. Gustav had very short cut brown hair and a shorter muscular build.

From there on, everything was in Czech.

"How was your trip from the United States?" Jiri said

"It went well. The flight arrived in good time."

"Let's get your bags. We're parked not far from here." Jiri said.

As we walked toward the parking area, Jiri spoke back and forth to Gustav, but I couldn't hear their conversation.

"You look shorter than they said. How tall are you?" Jiri said, looking at me.

"They exaggerated about my height. I'm 6'5". What's that, 1.98 meters?" I said, walking taller.

"Our scout in Britain told us you were well over two meters tall."

"Okay, what can I say?" I said.

Outside the window I could see the last farm in Austria. There were cows in fields and a farmhouse in the distance.

"This tryout period should be a good chance to see you play," Jiri said, making eye contact with me through the rearview mirror.

"Tryout? I thought this was training camp. At least that's what your offer sheet said."

"It's both, you could say, because we have to protect ourselves, too. We'll give you a good looking over, you can be sure of that," Jiri said.

I was shocked by the word "tryout." Josef scored 16 per game in the English league and I was no scorer at that level, but I could score when I needed to. There was no way I was going back to Chicago.

"When does this begin?" I said.

"Tomorrow morning for you. The rest of the team has been playing for a few days already. In fact, we practiced this morning."

A tall man in a tan suit and a visored hat asked Jiri a few casual questions in German. Then he waved us on with his clipboard.

"Since we are leaving Austria, they don't care to ask much. It's up here where you are scrutinized." Jiri said, rolling up the window as he pulled away.

He drove up farther, then gradually edged along behind a lineup of cars and trucks in front of us. The goal was to reach a huge gray rectangle that looked like a 60's style toll plaza along the Chicago

Skyway—all the lanes of traffic squeezing down to three open booths. Our black car rolled into one booth and an agent stepped forward. Two Czech soldiers with automatic rifles facing out sauntered past us.

Jiri and Gustav showed their Czech passports. The agent stamped and returned their passports to them in the car and then bent down to make eye contact with me. I handed him my passport and visa. He examined them and then swiped mine through a scanner.

"Josef, that's you, correct? United States, I see. What's the purpose of your travel—business or pleasure?" the guard said.

"Business. I'm here to play basketball for the Svet team. This is my coach and my assistant coach/trainer," I said.

"I see the visa. But what's this? An Australia stamp, Josef, what's this about?" he slowly held up to me when he came to that page.

"I visited my brother there a few weeks ago," I said.

"How come there is only an entry stamp into Australia but none for leaving? Where is the page stamped by Australia when you left there?" he said.

We had taken the page with the work visa for Australia out of my brother's passport. But we never took the Australia entry page out because he never left the country. I had my real passport in my pocket; it was stamped with my arrival in Vienna.

"I thought they stamped it," I said.

"You travel around, it seems. However, this is irregular," he said, looking at his screen. "Plus, the computer is not working and I can't bring up your record. Drive the car over to that bay and park it."

The agent pointing to an area where the two armed soldiers stood.

Jiri drove forward and we parked.

"Step out and follow me," one of the soldiers said. I exited the car and then Jiri and Gustav followed me. The soldier escorted us to a building off to the side.

This whole thing was backfiring. It wasn't good.

Inside the building, we were told to take seats at a table. An older man in a tie and maroon sport coat was holding my passport. The original agent joined us in the room.

"I phoned Prague for clarification," he said. "They said he already has a visa for Australia."

"No, they're mistaken. I only have a work visa here. There's only one me," I said.

"This is suspicious. You can't have two work visas," he said.

The supervisor got on the phone. As he waited on the phone, he studied me. He spoke a few minutes with someone and then he slowly hung up.

"What's the story here, Josef Savek?" the supervisor said.

"I'm coming to play with this team in Svet," I said. "It all came together at the last minute."

Then Jiri broke in. "I'm Jiri Hasek, the coach of the Svet Basketball Club. Josef's under our supervision during the whole time we will have him. All of our players are. They all live in a dormitory provided by our owner, Milos Koliar. Here's his business card," Jiri said. He handed him a business card with Milos Koliar's information on it.

The supervisor gave it to the other agent.

"Get this Mr. Koliar on the phone for me," he said, handing him the card.

"Do you have a contract that explains this arrangement?" the supervisor said to me.

"No, nothing signed by both parties yet," I said.

The supervisor and the other agent on the phone across the room shook their heads like it was bad news. There was an awkward moment of silence as if I had thrown the ball out of bounds at a key moment.

"We do have an offer document that Josef signed with our agent in England in March," Gustav said from the rear, pulling it from a file and offering it to the supervisor. I recognized my brother's concise signature on the line alongside another signature.

As the supervisor read it, Jiri said, "He's our only foreign player besides a Bulgari we just signed. It's necessary that we have this American for our team. It's a strong competitive league and he's a very talented player. The second part of the season starts soon."

"Is he your hope then, coach?" the supervisor said.

Jiri looked at me.

"We think he'll help us, it's important to us," Jiri said.

The second agent bounded over to us after hanging up the phone. He said, "Just talked to this Koliar. It checks out."

"Okay, then. Josef, do you have anything to declare?" the supervisor said.

Yes, I've abandoned my usual good sense for basketball, my brother and some unknown future. The whole thing's a crazy stunt. I'm not Josef. My real passport's in my sweaty pocket.

"Declare? Not sure what you mean," I said.

"With your bags! Are you carrying anything in that's on the prohibited list?" he said.

He pointed to a chalkboard with a list of banned items over his shoulder.

"No."

"Then welcome to our country," said the supervisor.

He handed me my passport. I flipped it open to see it stamped for entry into the Česká republika.

I stood up from the table and headed to the door.

"Besides, if anything further comes up we know where to find you," the supervisor said.

"Yes, at the address listed in Svet. Thank you," Jiri said. He shook the supervisor's hand.

A few minutes later we were rolling toward Znojmo.

"That was ridiculous. I've never had such a problem. What was all that about Australia and the other work visa?" Jiri said, looking back briefly over the seat.

"My brother received an offer to play basketball down there. They must have mixed up his work visa with mine," I said.

"And you went to Australia there with him. Why?" Jiri said.

"I'd never been there before. I wanted to help him get settled in. We're pretty close," I said.

Oh man, that was ugly.

"How long will it take us to get to Svet?" I said.

"We will be in late. Maybe eleven or twelve tonight."

"Back to your brother– are you sure it wasn't that you wanted play down there, too? But maybe it just didn't work out?"

"No, I knew I was coming here and had committed to you," I said.

"That makes me feel a little better. This brother–what's his name?"

"Ferenc," I said.

What a complete mess. Why did I have to get into any of this?

Jiri turned off the highway onto a two-lane road. He pointed out several steel plants along the side road. Gray smoke and steam rolled over the walls of one of them. Then we came upon a sign for a local ski resort. "Closed until 1 November," it said underneath.

"You like skiing, Josef?"

I had skied with my girlfriend Nancy, or should I say ex-girlfriend, in the Porcupine Mountains, known as the Porkies, in the Upper Peninsula of Michigan. Once. That was during the good times.

"Yes, but it's been a few years," I said.

"This border town has several resorts open only in the winter, but then you have both that and the heavy industry. The Communists thought that was a good combination in Žďár. Let me just say, we have better skiing near Svet," Jiri said.

When we reached the downtown, the facades of limestone buildings were blackened with soot.

"We are in Žďár nad Sázavou. That's its official name. You'll try your first authentic Czech meal here," Jiri said.

As I stepped out of the Skoda onto the curb, I could smell human sweat and plaster. We walked a half block down the street and then around the corner to a house with a large plate glass window in front. Instead of ringing a bell or knocking, Jiri led us right in. We went through a foyer and then right into a large kitchen. A woman was clearing plates and glasses off a long Formica top. She smiled at us.

"Dobry den, have a seat," she said.

We sat at this table in the middle of the kitchen. Some other patrons came in after us and sat at the other end of the table.

Jiri asked the woman if we could have zelná polévka to start. Another woman brought out the steaming bowls of sauerkraut soup while we were still reading a chalkboard of menu items. I wanted to take command, so I requested a kuře dish with vařené brambory on the side. That sounded safe. Jiri and Gustav agreed on vepřové covered in an omáčka.

Soon the woman brought out their orders: two steaming plates of pork covered in a mushroom sauce.

Mine took longer. I ate black Czech bread while my coaches ate. Then the woman brought out kuře all right–chicken liver. Somehow I missed the liver part. I hated chicken liver. But they got the boiled potatoes part of my order right at least.

"This brother Ferenc, what kind of player is he?" Jiri said.

"He's similar to me. A little shorter. But a good player," I said.

That was crazy, he's two inches taller but I didn't want them to figure things out.

"Sounds intriguing. Go ahead eat your kuře" Jiri said.

As I took a bite of it and then another bite, they watched intently as I swallowed the chicken liver.

"Josef, tell us more about yourself."

This guy was getting on my nerves.

"What would you like to know?" I said.

"You played for the Hemel Royals in England. What kind of league was that?"

"It was a good league. We played teams from all over England, and some teams from the Netherlands and France, too."

"I understand you posted some good scoring numbers there. But can you also stop another scoring threat like yourself on defense?"

"Yes, I can do both," I said.

"You averaged 16 points a game. You must been the main scorer."

"No, there were better scorers than I was."

"How can that be? 16 points is no small amount of points," Jiri said. I felt nervous that I wasn't getting it right.

"We had a 20 point per game guard as our high scorer. That guy was an accurate shooter from long range," I said.

"We want you to score. Be a strong presence on both ends of the floor."

I could score, but if everything depended on me being the main scorer I would soon be history.

"I'll do my best, coach."

"As an American, you might shy away from contact on the court. This league is very physical. What do you think about that?" Jiri said.

"I can handle it," I said.

I envisioned Eastern European players having brute strength. Massive forearms, strong backs and well-developed shoulders in the Czech players. Since my game was so much about initiating contact under the basket, I expected to take and deliver a pounding. I was lifting weights before I decided to go, but then I got on a plan to increase the amount of weight I pumped each week. I liked my chances of mixing it up physically with the opposition. My brother shied away from that contact, but I loved it. So maybe I was the right man for the job after all. I just hoped the team wasn't so overwhelmingly powerful right away and I could make a good showing.

"Tell us more about your family," Jiri said.

"My father is from Brno. My mother is from Prague. We're a basketball-crazed family."

"Do they like it that you've come to Svet?"

"They don't know much about the Svet area. But mostly they are excited by the adventure of it," I said.

"Svet is a hard-working city in the region of east Cechy. Our team is owned by Milos Koliar. He was a ranking member in the Communist party. When the new government came in power he turned his attention to business. He also owns a glass factory in Svet that he bought from the post-Communist government when they were selling off all their state-run industries," Jiri said.

"What kind of basketball team do you have in Svet, Jiri?"

"We have struggled to compete against the bigger city teams in this league. We've already played 14 games—we're 7-7 so far. That puts us in seventh place in the ten-team league. Our league is very competitive, with furious rivalries between towns."

"How many Americans are on the team?"

"There's a limit of two foreign players per team. The bigger cities like Prague and Brno are where the foreign players go. Typically, we have one American on our team. This year we are bringing in one that we hope has some talent. That's a man named Josef Savek from Chicago," Jiri said, laughing.

He paid the bill and we left the restaurant.

"We have always found it near impossible to beat the four `P' teams of the superliga: Praha A, Praha B, Plzeň and Pardubice. Especially Pardubice. They won the league championship last year. The winner of the Czech league plays the Slovak superliga champions for the Czech-Slovak title."

When we had entered the restaurant it was still light across the hills of Žd'ár. As we walked back to where we parked the Skoda, a streetlight switched on. Once in the car, Jiri continued on the northern highway that leads to Svet.

"What kind of player will we see tomorrow, Josef?" Gustav said.

"You'll see. Instead of talking about it, I'll show it. That's what I've done before," I said.

"Good, because our owner Milos Koliar will sit in on practice tomorrow morning," Gustav said.

"Great—off an airplane one day and onto the court the next. That's pressure," I said.

"Don't worry about Koliar. Play your game," Jiri said.

"If you have one," Gustav said, glancing at me.

That's funny deadpan humor if that's what it's supposed to be.

Jiri smiled at Gustav and then turned to me.

"Josef, within the first five minutes out on the court, we should have a good idea who you are. The real Josef. The rest will take care of itself," Jiri said.

So there's a problem with that already. The real authentic Josef is Down Under. I'm his replacement trying to act and play like he would. Take care of itself? That sounds ominous.

"What's your background, Jiri?" I said, trying to deflect the focus away from me.

"I was born in Olomouc but my parents moved to Svet when I was young. I've been coaching for years. In 1990 I was offered the head coaching position by Milos Koliar after he bought the team. My wife and family enjoy Svet. My background? I played guard on the Czechoslovakian National Basketball Team for nine years '65 to '74, including at the 1972 Olympics in Munich. Sixth man, mostly, until the 1973 Eurobasket Tournament, when I was elevated to starting point guard."

"How did you do in the Olympics?"

"We had a very good team in Munich. But we lost to the U.S. and Brazil and finished eighth out of 16 teams. Our center Petr Bialek felt the Americans should have won the gold medal. He was quoted to that effect in a West German newspaper and the *Stars and Stripes*. He never played another game of basketball with us again. The Soviet Union banished him from Czech basketball," Jiri said.

I remember watching that finals game with my father on the television in our living room. Doug Collins, who eventually coached the Chicago Bulls, was on that team. My father leaped up and celebrated when Collins hit the two free throws to put the United States ahead with a few seconds to go. The Americans lost because the Russians kept protesting the final clock. Three seconds were set back on the scoreboard. A long lob pass and layup won it for the Russians. Russia beat America, the king of basketball, for the gold medal.

"You played in the '72 Olympics?" I said.

I will be lucky to make this team with a coach with as impressive background as this. Maybe I'm over my head with this team. How good can I be? Wait, that's self-doubt. All I can do is my best.

"Yes, that '72 team was the high point in the annuals of Czech basketball. But after that, the Czechoslovakian Basketball organization was never the same because having Moscow excessively involved and having Petr banished from our team hurt us," Jiri said.

As we moved closer to Svet I could see the light of small farmhouses close to the road. For the trip from the border to the north, the fog or smoke had obscured much of the highway enroute to Svet.

"Our team quarters are coming up ahead on the left," Jiri said, as we passed a row of factories. When we approached a large factory the size of a football field, Jiri pulled onto a dirt service road that ran alongside its fence.

"This is it?" I said.

"No, it is the Oleg butter factory. They churn more butter there than anywhere else in the republic," Jiri said, as he accelerated past this diversion to our right. We stirred up orange dust that began to gather on the back window.

When we reached another factory complex, Jiri slowed down at a security gate. A massive red brick building that looked like it was built during the Communist era stood in front of us. Everything I saw was through the filter of the Communist legacy. From a long strand of glass block windows, white light reflected out into the Czech darkness. Behind this structure, rose hills were covered with dark trees. Jiri pulled into the parking lot that was filled with cars even at that hour of 10 p.m.

"We have arrived. Welcome to Svet, Josef!" Jiri said opening the car door. It didn't look like the place I imagined. But it was dark and I felt I wasn't seeing much of Svet's inner core. It felt as though we were on the outskirts and not really in the town.

"Is this the gym?"

"No, this is where you will be staying," Jiri said.

"This looks like a factory," I said, feeling the cool night air all around me.

"It is. This is Mister Koliar's glass works plant. The gymnasium is down the road. You'll see that in the morning."

"I'll be living inside the factory?" I said, feeling something was amiss.

"Yes, of course. This is where the whole team stays."

As I got out of the car, I tried not to panic. Living in a factory. This is the dormitory style living? My brother has set me up. He must have known. He's probably laughing with his Aussie buddies right now over a tall can of Foster's about what he's got me into.

Jiri and Gustav each grabbed one of my bags from the trunk. They led me through a dimly lit, unoccupied main reception area, and then up a flight of stairs. A narrow walkway with a metal handrail extended around all four sides of the factory floor. Orange fluorescent light burned down on them from fixtures just above where we were standing. People scurried around conveyer belts and heavy machinery. A young-looking, black-haired man on a forklift looked over to me as he wheeled a pallet of wooden crates toward a loading area. I felt the heat from furnaces on its way up toward the ceiling.

"Josef, is there something wrong?" Gustav said.

"It's different than I expected. That's all. What kind of glass is manufactured here?"

"Glass items for chandeliers, wine goblets, and tableware. We produce it for export across the world. You may have seen it already. The United States and Germany are our biggest markets. We affix `Made in the Czech Republic' labels to everything we make, as a certification to our craftsmanship."

We walked farther along toward a large wooden door.

"This is it. The place where the team stays," Jiri said.

He ushered me into a large room with a high ceiling and large windows positioned at least ten feet above the concrete floor. Small cubicle-like partitions divided up the space into "rooms."

"I will have you meet the team," Jiri said.

Within a few moments, eleven players gathered in the common area of the living quarters. They were waiting for my arrival, it seemed.

The first one I met was a muscular player of about 6'4" who emerged from the cubicle closest to the door.

"This is Anton Cermak, the captain of our team," Jiri said.

"Any relation to the first Czech mayor of Chicago, Antonin Cermak? Same name as yours," I said.

I looked him directly in the eyes and we shook hands awkwardly.

"None whatsoever. Sorry can't help you there," Anton said.

That's wild. This guy may well be my very good friend by the end of this. It's fateful that that's his name.

Next I met a longhaired guy with a mustache who stood about 6'7". He had a cynical look as he extended his hand. We shook. Then he threw my hand downward. What's his problem?

As the introductions continued, several other players looked at me with suspicion and hesitantly shook my hand. A tough and judgmental crowd. What had I gotten into? But Anton and another guy whose name I couldn't remember were welcoming and genuinely curious. They smiled when we shook hands. That gave me some hope that everyone might not be like the mustache man with attitude, who was the tallest player on the team. I would probably match up against them on the block on the court in the morning. Maybe even compete for their positions.

When I had met them all, everyone looked toward me, waiting for me to say something. It was if I'd completely forgotten Czech. None of the names I had heard registered except Anton, the first one I had met, who looked to be the best athlete among them.

"I look forward playing for the team. And getting to know you better," I said.

"Josef knows tomorrow is a tryout. And he hasn't met Mr. Koliar yet. Thanks Josef, we hope it works out, too," Jiri said.

All of them retired to their cubicles for the evening. As their voices sang undecipherable words, Jiri showed me my living area. A small single bed, wooden round back chair and a lamp on a small brown desk were all the furniture in a cubicle before me. A dark brown partition, six feet in height, gave little security or privacy.

"Here is your room. As far as the noise from the plant, the glassworks is being retrofitted with newer, quieter machinery. We will see you tomorrow morning at practice at 9:30," Jiri said.

Yes, I did hear mechanical sounds reverberating through the floor. It was noticeable because he called attention to it. I figured it was something I would get used to.

Later, I was startled by a voice from over the adjoining partition.

"So he gave you 'the plant is being retrofitted with new machinery' story, I see. He says that to everybody. It's a dying Marxist economy. Koliar won't improve this place if he can help it. You should see how he treats the people working in this factory," Anton said.

"The coach put me next to you because I am the only one on the team who speaks English. But as I can hear, you're not half bad with the Czech."

"Where else have you played before this?" I said, realizing we were still speaking Czech.

Anton said, "Come to think of it, your Czech is not so good either. I played in Bordeaux last year. We had a few guys from New York on that team that I became good friends with. I'm from Prague. What about you, where have you played?"

"England for a team north of London last year. But I'm from Chicago." I said in English.

"It seems every American visitor walking around Prague is from Chicago," Anton said.

"What made you decide to come to Svet?" Anton said.

"I wanted to try something different. This area is something I wanted to experience," I said.

"It will be different; you'll see that right away."

"How so?" I said.

"Besides the fact you live in a factory, there will be plenty of time to see for yourself."

Anton ducked back down in his cubicle. I was alone for the first time. The pure exhaustion of jet lag poured over my body. I was too tired to unpack my gear. I made up my bed and tried to sleep over the Czech voices and laughter still stirring around me. The partitions did a poor job of filtering out the sounds coming from the other cubicles.

Later I heard Anton said this or I imagined him saying this:

"One more thing, the rats bite and mice nibble, but other than that, you'll survive the night."

CHAPTER FOUR

SVET DREAMS

I awoke in a strange dark place. The bed was shaking. After a few seconds I realized I was in Svet, in a factory, and with a basketball team sleeping all around me. I leaned my head out to see that the floor underneath me was shaking. Shock waves were reverberating through the floorboards into my metal-framed bed. I wondered what part of the building the turbulence came from. I wanted to believe that the factory machinery below, running round-the-clock, was the cause. But I wasn't sure.

I looked at my watch and saw it was just after two a.m. For the next hour I was completely awake, staring up at the exposed timbers running across the ceiling.

The floor shook. That was too much to take. It finally hit me why Jiri made the new quieter machinery remark to me. It was to gloss over the fact that the floor shook while you were trying to sleep.

I calculated it was six o'clock in the evening in Chicago, and if I was there I would be running up and down the court at Margate Park. My Bohemia team had a playoff game against the team with Sam Hill on it. Right at that moment. Maybe that's why I felt like a racehorse, ready to jump up out of the bed and then drive hard with the ball around Sam Hill for a power layup to the bucket.

Then I was reminded of Nancy, the Irish-American one I hoped would work out. Even at the end, I kissed her more often than she ever spontaneously kissed me. In my next relationship I wasn't going to try too hard and have that imbalance. Shouldn't the attraction and love be mutual? I wouldn't make that mistake again, that's for sure. Forget my ex-girlfriend, I've got to make this team.

Next my parents, what was with them? They didn't think the Czech Republic opportunity was worth it. They were upset with both Josef for encouraging it and me for undertaking this fraudulent situation. They said they hoped I wouldn't get caught. If I did it would be a poor reflection on them in the community and would make them look bad. Then my father said he hoped I got caught; it would be a good lesson for me. With that kind of harshness, I had to back away from them. There was pain in all these situations that I hadn't yet dealt with. After ruminating about Nancy and my parents for another hour, I fell back to sleep.

In the morning I opened my eyes for a moment to see light streaming through the large windows high over the player stockades. Motes of dust were dancing in the sunlight. I went back to a deep jet-lagged sleep.

The stirring of activity and unfamiliar voices jarred me awake sometime later. My head was pounding with heaviness. I protected my tired eyes from the light by keeping them closed. As the noise around me increased, I wondered from under my eyelids whether I should get up. Maybe I should be awake and out of bed. I felt like I only had a few hours sleep. My head felt too heavy to lift off the pillow and my eyelids stung in the corners. In a few minutes I'll get up, I told myself. Just a few more minutes of sleep, after all, I'm a visitor and this is my first day.

Water hit me in the face. I pried my eyes open to see Anton standing there with a bucket in his hands.

"Wake up, you long streak of pelican shit," Anton said.

Behind him was the tall guy who had pulled my hand down the night before. Nick, nick, nick. It was the strangest laugh I ever heard that came from this creep with the long hair. They stood there watching me struggling to get the lake out of my bed. The water was brown. I sprung up on to my feet.

"What's your problem, Anton?" I said.

"Did you know that you slept with your mouth open?"

I grabbed the plastic bucket from him and scooped up some water off the bed. Then I threw water back at them, landing a direct hit on Anton. They shied away. Then they backed off even further and fled like middle-school boys.

I discovered communal washroom facilities through a door next to the living area. "Where are the showers?" I asked one player.

"There are none in the factory. The showers are in the gymnasium," he said.

I went to my cubicle to get my basketball shoes and clothes together. When I saw the time on my watch read 8:15, I hurried to find out where the other players had gone. I caught up with Anton in the hallway talking to a group of the other players.

"Where do you usually eat breakfast?" I said.

"The rest have already had breakfast. I'll show you, come with me," Anton said.

I followed him out of the factory and through the parking lot. Then we slipped through a hole in a wire fence.

"The restaurants are along this corridor. This is where we eat breakfast every day," Anton said.

There were several restaurants along the road outside the factory. I hadn't noticed them the night before. I walked under the two large linden trees and entered the white stone building where I would have breakfast every day. My eyes adjusted as we went into one darkly lit restaurant.

The second floor restaurant had a bitter odor of Absinthe liquor mixed with cigarette smoke in the air. The soundtrack from "Grease" was playing on the phonograph. Everyone in the room, five men sitting at tables and several people in the thickly upholstered booths, seemed to be watching me. I took a seat in the booth and read a whole article in the *Svet Monitor* newspaper about the last detachment of Russian soldiers leaving Prague and Brno.

"What kind of breakfast do they serve here?"

"The Czech breakfast of champions. Black bread with berry jelly and coffee. That's what I advise."

We ordered it up.

The only light the restaurant paid to provide came whenever the waitress backed through the swinging kitchen door with trays of rolls in one hand and an urn of coffee in the other.

As Anton exchanged in a verbose banter with the heavy-set, big-breasted woman taking the order, I looked out at the tables of working men drinking coffee, with steam rising from Styrofoam cups.

"How do you like being here?" I said.

"I hate the living conditions. But it may be worth it because this team will be very good. Koliar has brought in many good players from across the Republic. I'd like to think we have most of best Czech players available. The Americans in this league have made it better, too."

I scanned his brown eyes to see if he was being genuine. He was.

"How was he able to bring in so many good players?"

"He searched out the best Czech players. It's a big thing to him—recruiting Czech players. Other teams have more foreign mercenaries: German, American, Lithuanian, Croatian, even Serbian players on their rosters. But the problem is we pay less than the other teams, plus the fact that we are out in the middle of nowhere."

"Why'd you come here?" I said.

"Not for the money. I could play in Prague for more. The team pays five thousand crowns per month across the board to every player. Crap really. Not many francs, that's what I was paid in the French league."

I remembered the pay was equivalent to $700 U.S. dollars.

"You're right about the money. So how does he do it?"

"They come because Jiri is one of the best coaches in the Czech Republic."

Again, I scanned his eyes. I didn't quite trust this guy after the bucket of water prank. He seemed to be speaking the truth

"What's this owner Koliar like? What kind of person is he?" I said.

"The boss is decent guy once he gets to know you. As a matter of fact, you'll get a chance to meet him very soon. I hear Jiri wants you to meet Koliar this morning," Anton said. He looked at his watch and we left.

Jiri led me down a narrow corridor to a large second floor office. It had a long glass window that looked out over the factory floor. We pushed our way through the door into a cluttered work area. It was like stepping into a men's lounge rather than the office of the head of the glass factory and sports club. The man sat in front of a whole wall of books with Czech titles of all kinds, plus some wooden carved eagles and beer mugs. Sitting behind an ornately carved black wooden desk was the boss in a tie and white shirt talking on the phone while smoking Tiperello cigarettes that aggravated my nervousness as I stood there.

"This is Milos Koliar," Jiri said.

Koliar motioned toward us with his hand to have a seat while he talked on the phone. He was built like a wedge with broad shoulders, flaring nostrils, wide ears, and a gap between his front teeth.

There were dusty piles of paper all over his desk and behind him was the shine of clear wineglasses lying next to packing paper on a table. *Svet Glass Works* wineglasses looked like the kind of stuff you see at a *Crate & Barrel* store. Meaning, from what I could see, good quality and beyond my means in the States. I remembered Jiri had said Koliar spoke Czech, German, but no English. He was a darker, tougher looking type like Gustav, the team assistant coach and trainer, only older. Up in his fifties somewhere, Koliar had jet-black hair that was thinning on the top. While Koliar was busy making a point on the telephone, he took a drag on his cigarette looking squarely at me. The critical squint of Koliar's eyes made me feel uneasy. He's never seen me play on the basketball court, and it looked like he has already written me off. Josef said he had never met Koliar so I don't think he could be on to the fact that I am not my brother. Hanging up the phone, Koliar gave me his full attention.

"Milos, this is our newest player. Josef's fluent in Czech," Jiri said.

"Dobry den, Mister Savek. It's going to be very competitive for a spot on this team. We have twelve with you and the plan is to pare down to ten to start the season. We overcommitted so we'll see if you offer what we want. Are up to the challenge, knowing these odds?"

"Yes, I am," I said.

Not really. This situation is worse than expected. No guaranteed spot and have to fight for it in my jet-lagged condition.

"I hear you'll practice with us this morning. I'd like a chance to see this," Koliar said, putting on black-rimmed eye glasses to look at a document on his desk.

"You have some impressive scoring totals. We can always use a talented player such as they say you are. A contract for the upcoming season could be in the works but let's see how you do," Koliar said.

Jiri stood up to signal it was time to go. I wondered how tall this man sitting in front of me was. I rose from the chair extending my hand only so far. Koliar stood. He was short, no taller than 5'11", and wore black wing tip shoes. Koliar nearly cracked my knuckles as we shook for a few seconds longer than I wanted.

CHAPTER FIVE

FROM EVERY DIRECTION

I hoofed over white lines of a running track that ringed the perimeter of the basketball court. My stomach churned from nervousness and lack of sleep. As a result, I stepped out on the slippery wood floor feeling not prepared and not quite myself.

The Svet Gymnasium looked more expansive than I imagined especially as I approached the midcourt. Fluorescent lights glowed in round canisters on the high ceiling. The only natural light was the sun streaming through slits just above the rafter seats.

The gym's bleachers were pushed into the walls. It looked like it could fit about 3,000 rabid fans. And I wondered if this team ever attracted that many to its games.

Anton threw a hard welcoming spiral to me. I reined in the dark leather basketball and launched a jumper at the basket I found myself standing near. Getting warmed up was the most important thing on my mind. The players shooting baskets in small groups around the gym sent sly looks toward me as I launched shot on these foreign baskets.

"Don't worry about shooting much today," Anton said, approaching me.

"Why's that?"

"His practices haven't had much offense so far. Jiri's a defensive coach."

Practice began with a whistle from the other side of the gym. I felt like I had barely got a few shots in.

Jiri called the team to gather in the corner. We sat on the floor as Jiri stood in front of us. I could feel the coolness of the varnished wood floor and someone near me reeked of menthol odor that was the equivalent of Ben-Gay.

"Willingness and motivation are everything. That's what I want to see. It's time we start coming together and build up team cohesiveness. Pardubice plans to come in here to crush us to start the second half. Is that what you expect, too?" Jiri said.

"We're going to send Pardubice out of here with a loss, coach. No one here doubts that right, team?" Anton said.

The players jumped up and yelled. This wasn't a spontaneous outburst of team spirit so much as something practiced, as if they did this each day. But I could see the fire in a few of their eyes. So there was some agreement that they could beat Pardubice.

"Today we are working Josef Savek into things here. He's an American Czech and speaks our language. He played professionally in Britain for four years, two in Scotland and two outside London. Have I got that right Josef?" Jiri said.

I nodded yes.

"Josef's the offensive threat to match you, Anton, so at the end of the practice, his team will scrimmage against yours," Jiri said.

Offensive threat? That's pressure because it's not true. There's no way I can I live up to that billing.

We threw the balls toward Gustav who gathered them all up in metal ball holders. Plié squats, Jiri called out.

We crouched down into a defensive position. He blew the whistle and we were off. We took off across the gym. Sliding without crossing the feet. We moved back and forth from one side of the gym to the other.

"Make your movement smooth and continuous. Bend the knees and keep the rear down, Josef," Jiri said.

I stayed up with the row of players shuffling, their feet moving in synchronicity. I did it. Not a bad warm-up.

After five minutes, Jiri shifted the action to more conditioning. We began running suicides from the free throw line to the base line, then the baseline to half court, and into full court sprints. The shorter quicker players led the group. I was determined to use my long stride to break into the group of frontrunners. At least my coach at North Park College called me fleet-footed. He said I had breakout speed; a rare element of surprise for a player with my height.

He'd say, "Use it to your advantage, Savek."

I caught Vojtech, the player who had given me the menacing look the night before, and I blew by him. In the beginning, I did well. But as we continued the sprinting, I was laboring like an NBA 7-footer and uncharacteristically bringing up the rear. But as hard as I pushed, my body was reaching its limit. And we had just started. Vojtech and I finished last together. Breathing heavily, I had no time to rest.

Jiri called for a drill that involved passing the ball, then cutting behind a group of players, whereupon I received another pass by more weaving players. The balls seemed to fly in my direction in a relentless blitz. Now it was not just matter of staying up physically: my quick decisions were needed. The whole drill stopped when I passed to the wrong player once. A few minutes later I misfired again. And then again. Jiri did not come over to work it out. He let it keep breaking down until I got it.

Then Jiri blew his whistle. We stood in two lines near center court. The new drill had one line of defenders and second line of penetrators. I was handed the ball first. The guy defending me was a guard who stood about 6'1" and I drove to the basket against him. He thwarted my effort to outflank him. I tried to blast through him to the basket. His smaller body absorbed the contact. My forward thrust was checked by his good chest-to-chest defense. The closest I could get was eight feet from the basket. I faked one way but he didn't fall for it. Then I took a jump shot with his hand in my face. It bounced off the rim and he snatched the rebound.

"Now you cover Rudenic," Jiri said. Okay, got his name. Rudenic was the guy that just covered me. His first step toward the basket helped him glide past me. This guy was smooth and had Division I quickness. He was able to seal me off with his body when I did catch him. I tried to block his shot from behind but he tossed up a scoop shot for an easy basket.

When that drill ended, I looked up and saw Milos Koliar in the bleachers watching. I wondered how long he had been there. We shifted to a new drill. Gustav heaved a shovel pass that I caught. Anton stood ready to defend me. I dribbled toward the basket, then turned using my body to shield the ball. He pushed against my spine. When Anton reached for the ball to steal, I sped past him along the baseline for a reverse lay-up. My first basket of the entire session. One I needed badly. When my turn came again I tried the similar move against a six foot guard named Jaroslav. He stole the ball from me mid-dribble.

Jiri whistled for a change in the action. A rebounding drill. Players lined up on both sides of the floor near the top of the key. When Jiri threw up an underhanded shot toward the rim, I raced to the basket and beat Vojtech, the team's tallest player at 6'7", to a spot five feet in front of the basket. The ball caromed off, just over my finger tips and into Vojtech's hands.

I came this far to rebound and refused to be defeated. One player from the left and me on the right, blasting off from positions near the free throw line to rebound. I raced to the spot in front of the basket, right where I needed to be. Several times it was taken out of my hands. I didn't get the rebound, the other player did. The rebounds eluded me. The harder I tried, the worse it seemed.

When the drill finished I wanted the practice to end. We had already been in action for two hours. Jiri divided up the team into two groups, the first unit and my team. Gustav turned on the power to the scoreboard over the main court.

The smell of sweat was in the air. The scoreboard clock read 12:00. My "tryout" was going miserably.

I felt drained but I had to push ahead. I didn't come to the Czech Republic to fail. Just 48 hours before I was living another life in Chicago. Now I was running up and down the court attempting to play this strange game in some far away land.

Jiri came over to me and said, "You will be playing with this group. With Charles, Milan, Staroslav, and Jaroslav."

Gustav sounded the buzzer for the players to take the court. I could see I would be playing first against a unit that was stacked with the team's best players. Gustav threw yellow pullover practice shirts on the floor. I grabbed one and pulled it over my sweaty gray shirt. Our yellow squad gathered as a group in the corner. I looked into their wary faces. As we moved out to the court, I wanted to know what kind of defense they would play.

"Are we in man-to-man-defense?" No one understood what I was asking. I turned my palms up in the air. "Who's your man?" I said to Jaroslav. He didn't answer.

"We play in a 2-3 zone defense." Anton said, who was on the opposing red team.

Jaroslav, a dark-haired point guard on my yellow team, took the ball out of bounds along the sideline. He dribbled out into open court. I felt light-headed but my main objective was to play defense and rebound. After a missed shot from the outside by Jaroslav, our team went back down court to play defense. I moved back to fall into the middle on a 2-3 zone. I realized everyone was covering a man. After one pass from their point guard, I saw who my man was. It was Vojtech, the guy with the weird laugh standing outside the paint. The "paint" is the area inside the lane lines from the baseline to the free-throw line. He received the pass there on the perimeter with no one on him and then took an easy three-pointer that rippled through the net. I was ten feet away and could do nothing. Anton laughed. I could see that my strategy of playing solid defense and rebounding would not work, as our team fell behind early and lost by a score of 24-14. Given a second chance we lost again even worse: 24-10. One more game to redeem ourselves.

Our yellow team huddled together as a unit before our last game.

"These guys on the first team expect to win every time and we play like we are giving it to them," I said.

When I said that, our point guard Jaroslav smiled and said, "We can beat them."

In the last game I got on a roll. I hit three baskets from the outside early and began yanking down offensive rebounds. When Jaroslav drove to the basket in traffic, he missed and I spun inside for the rebound. I powered it back up over the rim and in to give us 14-8 lead. As I ran back on defense, I saw that Koliar was no longer in the bleachers. He was nowhere where I could see. The first team ran a sophisticated pick and roll system and utilized good passing to find openings. Then they rallied with a furious streak of points to tie the game at 22. We raced back down to our basket and our guard Charles took a hurried jumper. He missed. Anton came down with the rebound and passed the ball to their point guard. They patiently set up their offense and then Anton hit a bank shot from the side. It went in. We lost 24-22. Beat three times in a row. It was a very solid first unit that dealt us defeats and it seemed that I was never beat so quickly.

Jiri had us run wind sprints for 15 minutes. I felt like I was going to pass out after I finished my last sprint.

"We are done, Svet. Until tomorrow morning," he said.

Jiri walked over to me.

"Come into my office."

His office was through a door off to the side of the court. I sat down in a comfortable chair across from his desk. He had photos of teams on the wall that went back to when he was a player. On his desk, was a photo of his pretty brunette wife and three kids.

"What did you think about our practice?"

"It's a good team you have here. I don't think I did too well," I said.

"At least you recognize it."

"I just want to find a way to fit in."

"I talked to Milos in the hallway before he left. He said we can't use you."

"I'm better than the player you saw today."

"Then bring the real Josef Savek out. Milos doesn't want to move forward with you."

"That's it? I just arrived and that's all. How can that be?" I said.

"You'll need to show us much more," Jiri said. "Let me add that I asked him to give you until the end of the week. He agreed to that at least."

"Does he make the decisions? You mean he decided on all these players who are here now?" I said

"We both did. The only reason he let you stay until the end of the week is because you came from so far away. We want more scoring from a player like you. Today that didn't show through."

"I know I can do better," I said, hoping my promise would be kept.

"Josef, come with me let me show you the other parts of the facility."

We walked through a door into a room with a chalkboard and examination table in the middle.

"Gustav wraps a few of the player's ankles here. Jaroslav, Milan and Staroslav each get wrapped before practice and games. Gustav has medical training from Charles University in Prague. It helps out when it comes to injuries and keeping players healthy."

We walked down stairs and along a corridor into a basement wing of the building. Jiri took out his key and unlocked the weight training room. He flicked on the lights to a spacious room with archaic looking weight machines in the middle. Lined up on the faded blue floor were battleship gray barbells with the paint chipping off them.

"This is the weight room? Do the players use it?" I said. It smelled musty down there.

"Yes, all of them do. Some of them do right after practice. Others lift weights at night."

"I am planning on getting going right away."

"That's very good, but I suggest you take it easy today. This morning's practice and the time zone switch may get the best of you."

"You're right. Later today."

"No. Tomorrow. Start up on that tomorrow. Besides you haven't seen Svet. I'll give you a tour this afternoon."

As I walked to the locker room, I felt like sleeping on the bench right there, but it was only 1:15 in the afternoon. The locker room ceiling was just a few inches higher than the top of my head. A damp musty smell filled the air and drops of water were gathered on the low ceiling from the condensation. As I looked up, a big drop hit me in the eye. Even though there were twenty lockers it seemed that no more than six players could be in here at once. Most of the players were showered and dressed. I found an available locker next to Jaroslav, the point guard on our losing team. Jaroslav and Anton were talking before I came in. It was something about me because I heard Jaroslav say my name or rather my brother's name, Josef.

I twisted a handle in the shower room and frigid water burst out of the showerhead. I let the water from the shower pour over me. Even though it was a warm summer day, I wanted to take a hot shower to get some comfort from this cold place. I quickly turned it off and reached for the shower knob on the right. Rotating it on, I found the water to be heated to a temperature I could tolerate. I continued to run the water to get something even warmer.

All I got was lukewarm.

CHAPTER SIX

KLAS KUCHYNĚ

The two-lane road was slowed in sections because the worn pavement was being replaced with a new super slab highway. I had a full view of the scene in front of us, looking out the car window as a traffic control officer halted all movement ahead because of the construction.

An earthmover roared as it broke through the layers of asphalt and concrete to reach a sub-stratum of soil, the very foundation of this antiquated track. Sweaty men in orange vests used shovels and their gloved hands to load broken sections of the road into massive crane buckets. Then the debris was hoisted and dropped into waiting dump trucks.

The debris hit the bed of one truck with a boom and then a cloud of white dust rose in the air. As I was looking out, my mind's eye was looking in, to a remembrance the dust stirred up in me: a flock of startled pigeons taking flight all at once in the central plaza where I had cashed out my bank account in Chicago. It was hard to believe that was just three days ago.

Jiri explained the situation as we drove toward Svet: "If you lived in one of these houses along the side of the road, you would welcome this noise. This public works project is a sign of progress. It was not that long ago that you would be hearing other sounds: Russian tanks and trucks rolling through here night and day. Over the years the Russian army's transport trucks tore up the Svet road."

"Traffic could be blocked for hours when they were here, which was often. Thankfully our days of occupation will become just a bad story in the glimmering past. The Czech lion has begun to rise," he said, as the man holding up traffic flagged us to proceed ahead.

Jiri maneuvered the Skoda onto a smooth stretch of newly laid asphalt as black as the car itself. Soon farmhouses along side of the road gave way to masonry brick apartment buildings. While these three-story buildings were all painted the same pale yellow, each clearly had its own character. One had children playing beneath colorful sheets and pillow cases hanging from clotheslines strung from window to window. Another had a few boarded-up windows and nothing on its clotheslines. Still another had no line to hang clothes at all; but instead, planter boxes sprouting tomato and green pepper plants.

I looked out to forestlands that stretched out densely into the mountains. Jiri pointed out the window to where I was looking.

"See the brown up there on the trees. That's from acid rain from industries from the west on the Rhine," Jiri said.

Amongst the shades of green were bands of oaks with brown leaves and some trees with no leaves. Their dark barren forms brushed the afternoon horizon as we moved past.

Jiri pointed out the Krkonoše Mountains on the eastern edge of Svet. Even though it was still summer, September 4, the upper peaks were dusted with snow. He said that somewhere on the top of the range was the border with Poland.

The road ran along a ridge from which I could see slate rooftops of houses, and several church towers of the town stretched out below us. The buildings fanned out across the bottom of a football-shaped canyon.

The thoroughfare began to taper off as we entered the old town center of Svet. It looked like the most handsome village in the Czech north with narrow brown cobblestone streets, small courtyard gardens, and three stone bridges that spanned a churning blue-green river. The restaurants and bakeries were packed close together in the old town quarter.

I felt lucky to be there. Maybe this whole thing might work out and I could love this town and the situation. It could be the very thing I needed.

But then again, I was a guy from a bustling city of three million. Sure, I'm Czech, but maybe this place was a forgotten relic, so completely backwater and unsuited to me. I might be miserable in Svet.

"What do you think?" Jiri said.

"Svet's a good place. It looks to have survived World War II pretty well," I said.

"It has. Some houses date back to Central Europe's Golden Age in the 15th century. Like that one there," he said, slowing the car in front of a gray two-story house. It was well maintained for its age, with a pitched roof and leaded windows.

"By the way, Svet was spared because the major fighting in the war occurred fifty kilometers to the east, on the road over the mountain pass. A dozen tanks are still there at the battle site. Mostly Panzers with holes in them that the Soviets left in place as a memorial," Jiti said.

Jiri chose a place with the sign *Klas Kuchyně* over the doorway. Everyone called it Klas. It was decorated in a German alpine style with dark wood tables and lattice windows that looked out to Predni' Street, or Front Street in English. The restaurant was crowded on that Sunday afternoon. There were twenty tables across an open space surrounded by dark wood paneling. A waiter with shortly cropped gray hair shook Jiri's hand. "What will you have Jiri?"

"Two salads and potato dumplings. This is our new American on the team. Today was his first practice," Jiri said to the waiter.

I shook hands with the waiter.

"How did you do, Josef?"

"This coach runs a good hard practice. This is a solid team but today for me it wasn't pretty," I said, feeling like I was performing as I said it.

"Josef, nice to meet. We'll be following you."

The food arrived at our table. The dumplings called "sinkers" tasted like a combination of pasta and mashed potatoes and were covered with bacon, onions and melted butter.

"Life will be different for you here in Svet. Things move at a slower pace than in Prague or Brno. This town was disappointed with our showing in our first 14 games. We have to do better," Jiri said.

"How many players are back from last year's team?"

"Five players: Anton, Zedenik, Kolin, Jarsoslav and Manioli. Six new players with you. I can provide guidance but it means nothing if we don't have leadership on the floor. We're struggling to find that."

I'd rise up to lead them. And I had to break into the starting five to do it.

Jiri excused himself. I sat there watching him saunter across to the room to the restroom door. He talked to the people at the tables. I looked away to the tables of four and six. Jiri spoke to them, pointing me out. For a few minutes people zeroed in on my face as Jiri spoke with them. Another group of older men and women listened curiously to Jiri's conversation with this other table. Their faces were tanned and windburned. The men wore boots and coveralls.

When Jiri arrived back, he slapped me on the back.

"They are interested in what kind of player you are."

"What did you tell them?" I said.

"I said, `He has no jump shot, cannot drive left, speaks tourist Czech, but may be the spark we need on this team.' They asked why we had to go so far away to get a spark. I told them we have to get it where we can find it. There are some people over here that I have to introduce you to."

Jiri and I stood up and went over to a table along the wall.

"Josef, I would like you to meet John, Monika and Nitra. They work at the glass factory where you stayed last night."

I shook hands with each of them. They looked to be in their early thirties. John and Monika stood very close to each other and held hands like they were lovers. The group appeared as if they had just gotten off their shift at the factory. Each wore the blue jeans and dull green t-shirts that seemed to be the uniform of every worker at the Svet Glass Works.

Jiri moved me along but not before I shook hands with them all again.

"We should leave. Here, let's take care of this," Jiri said when we turned back to get the bill on the table. He reached into his pants pocket for his wallet.

From a table across the way came a tall man with shaggy brown hair.

"This is Vladimir Novak. Vlad owns the restaurant."

We shook hands and he smiled as if he knew me. As he talked animatedly with Jiri, he looked at me in a friendly way.

As Vlad left, his meaty hands grabbed the bill for lunch and he winked at us. He sat down at a table in the corner with a group of four older men drinking steins of Pilsner Urquell beer.

We left the restaurant to go back to the factory. Since it was Sunday, no bank in Svet was open to exchange money. Jiri drove past where I could go the next day after practice to exchange U.S. dollars for Czech currency.

"Here, take this," Jiri said. He handed me 100 Krona.

After a long moment of silence, Jiri said, "Those people are excited about your coming here. They actually think you are a very good player. Little do they know how you played today. Don't disappoint them, and most of all don't disappoint me."

CHAPTER SEVEN

THE TUMBLE

Fog crept around the base of the trees in front of me. Sweat rolled between my shoulder blades down my spine and to my tailbone, soaking my shirt. As I ran, I strained my eyes to see the serpentine footpath as it wound past rocks and pine trees. Small quick steps helped me get enough traction to climb what seemed be a 45-degree incline.

I let out a yell. The same kind of yell I unleashed when I was open and wanted the point guard to pass me the ball. My yelp didn't echo back to me the way it would reverberate off the walls in an enclosed gym. Instead, it escaped into the forest.

"You won't make it, Josef. Give my regards to Chicago," Anton said from up ahead on the route.

"You don't even know me, Antonin Cermak. You'll be the guy with the trouble finishing," I said to Anton through the mist.

"Anton, that's my name. Don't call me by anything else."

He had a great name. There were other variations, too. He could be Cermak Road or AC.

I saw Jaroslav, the point guard from Plzeň, walk in, striding in front of me. He held both his fists tightly in front of himself at chest level as he ran. At the front of the pack, Charles and Zedenik jogged alongside each other with tight lips and squinty eyes that focused on the trail.

My energy went into my avoiding patches of wet mud on the trail. I stepped in a puddle with leaves at the bottom. My shoes were laden with mud so I dragged my feet in some exposed slate in attempt to remove the debris. It didn't work. I stepped into more puddles and my shoes got heavier with leaves and mud. I began to hobble and my legs burned as I pumped upward. I'd run plenty of kilometers along Lake Michigan in Flat City, but never anything like this. I continued to run at a steady pace but fell back further.

It began with this earlier that morning.

"Conditioning is going make us the supreme team in the league this year. You have seventy minutes to make it up Svet Mountain and back," Jiri said at the start of practice.

"This is going to ruin my shoes," Anton said. He wore black Adias, the most expensive basketball shoes of anyone on the team.

"No changes. Anton, you'll thank me when you stay in Muller's jock strap for 40 minutes against Pardubice," Jiri said. He flicked the stopwatch on. After five seconds ticked off, Anton heaved the basketball he was holding across the gym in the direction of the blue "Svet Pride" banner on the opposite white tile wall. Anton ran out the door and the rest of the players followed.

"What's the distance coach?" I asked as the stopwatch continued to tick.

"Twelve kilometers. Stay on the path. Get moving," Jiri said.

I laughed at the ridiculousness of the whole situation. I could no longer see anyone except Anton twenty yards in front of me and Jaroslav in front of him. They seemed to emerge from this first part of the way unscathed. On top of a steep rise, I saw the pack running on a narrow track through a mountain meadow. I shuffled ahead and saw my salvation in waist high grass that smelled like wet hay. I ran through the grass and wildly kicked my feet in the air. Pieces of mud and then slabs cracked away from my shoes and went flying. Most of it came off including a wet one that landed directly between my eyes.

I tried to remove it but made it worse because mud slathered down my nose like an upside-down exclamation mark in the center of my face.

I veered back on the trail. Strong gusts of wind blew past me and drops of rain hit my forehead. I felt a renewed burst of energy. I caught up to Charles and Jaroslav and then passed them on a flat section of the trail. Then the narrow ribbon began to rise again through the dense spruce. A group of a dozen black cows looked down on me from the hill above. The track doubled back and then I was headed straight toward the cows. Two small calves blocked my way. Stopping, I reached to pet one of them. A huge cow stepped up and unleashed a fog horn blast. As the two cows hurriedly attempted to run behind her, I turned sharply off the byway and lurched through the underbrush, never taking my eye off the big cow. Her intense black eyes transmitted hostility and contempt toward me as she breathed columns of steam from her nostrils.

Once past that roadblock, I was moving again on the trail. A misty rain began to fall. I could see through the trees that Svet Mountain was not the largest peak in the Krkonoše range. Several other plateaus were taller. But Svet Mountain had the flattest top.

I wiped sweat and rain off my face as I ran. I wasn't trying to win this race or beat anyone. I just wanted to finish under 70 minutes and make the team.

There was a rock field of jagged stone that led to an abandoned castle. I promised myself that I would return to this mountain top and explore the castle ruins. Through an opening, I was disappointed there was no panoramic view of the town below. Just clouds and trees. There had to be a great view on a less cloudy day from that summit. And I'd see if I could get back up there another day.

Gustav stood there in a yellow rain coat standing on a huge boulder. It was a strange thing to see our assistant coach and trainer out there waving a clipboard in the air. Gustav's long black hair and long angular nose made him look like a Mongol rider from the east. I could picture him on a powerful horse sweeping across the plains in a pack of helmeted warriors with Genghis Khan. The only thing that ruined this impression was his mustache. He wore it small and tight under his nose like a Czech.

When Charles and Zedenik reached Gustav, they exchanged high-fives with him. These two front-runners circled around the boulder, then followed a trail downward. When Vojtech passed, Gustav not only gave him a pat on the back, but shouted encouragement to him. When I reached him, Gustav wrote down something.

"You have 35 minutes left and the hardest part has yet to come," Gustav said.

"The toughest part was getting here. How could it be harder? It's all downhill," I said.

He only smiled and said nothing else.

I charged down the trail. My feet barreled down the center of a mostly dry riverbed with dark brown earth and sandstone on both sides. I could see some of the others splashing through water up ahead before the wash dropped off steeply. My momentum propelled me. I lost my footing. I extended my arms to brace for a landing. Then I hit the rocks and slid chest down into a mud puddle.

I lay on the ground face down.

"Ahhhhhh!" I yelled a few moments later. My delayed reaction struck me as odd. I glanced around. No one was nearby. Besides me sprawled out with my palms embedded in the mud, the forest was empty. My palms and my knuckles stung. I lifted my arm out of the thick black muck. But I couldn't tell how badly I was hurt because both were coated in wet earth. I could smell it on me. I felt like lying down there and resting, but instead, I rose up and began to run again.

The front of my body was covered with clay and leaves. I was stiff from stopping and it was hard to resume my pace from a few minutes earlier. As I ran, I tried to shake off the mud. With a tumble like that, I was lucky not to be hurt worse. I ran my hands over my bare arms and legs to peel off the sludge. It was futile. I was just smearing it. I extended my arms in front of me in hopes rain falling would wash it off.

Even that didn't work because it wasn't raining hard enough. Mud was stuck between all my fingers. Underneath the caked mud, I was bleeding. Red and black oozed out from my knuckles and palms.

I looked down and saw that my blue t-shirt and gray shorts were black.

As I ran down the mountain I continued at a good pace. I slowed down for a moment, unsure which way to go, when I reached a fork in the trail. There were several fresh shoe prints in the mud going to the left, so I went left. Then heavy rain began spotting my mud-soaked clothes. We were all experiencing the same thing, which comforted me somewhat. I began to recognize places that I'd run through earlier. The trail must have looped back onto the trail we started on. This helped me because I remembered a few of the locations of the obstacles and mud patches. The rain washed more of the blood and mud off. But I was still bleeding and some of the blood was running up my arms as I ran. The rain drenched me and soon my clothes stuck to my body. It felt utterly ridiculous to be out there in such conditions. In spite of feeling like a heavy truck, I began to pick up speed in the final stretch. The rain was not going to stop me. I could see Jiri standing under an eave at the door of the gymnasium. He had a stopwatch in his hand. I raced to the finish and stopped immediately after I passed him.

"Sixty eight minutes, twenty two seconds. Josef, you'll have to be better next time," he said.

"Great, I made it. When's next time? Tomorrow?" I said, pinching the cramp on the side of my ribs.

"It's when I choose. Once you are in shape, you could be a good player. I want to see if the scouting report on you as 'A top scorer in the post and on the perimeter' is true. Hopefully we'll see that today," he said as he looked at the dirt all over me.

"Wow, you look like the monster from the black lagoon. Go downstairs, clean up, and then be back up to the floor in an hour for practice. Give me your best today," he said.

I showed him my hands. He grabbed my forearms, "What happened?"

"I fell and scrapped them pretty bad," I said.

"Gustav will meet you downstairs and wrap them with battle ribbons and tape. First get this stuff washed off," Jiri said.

One hour later, we lined up on the out-of bounds line under the basket. I had white tape on my hands and wrists. They throbbed. At least the bleeding had stopped.

Jiri blew his whistle and I sprinted down the full length of the court. I touched the thick white line with my taped palm and began to run back to where I started with everyone else. As I crossed the line, Jiri blew his whistle again. I turned and began my chase of the rest of the team thundering down the wood court. On the seventh lap, Jiri blew his whistle twice signaling for us to move on to another drill.

As I tried to catch my breath, I looked up and saw Koliar watching from the sidelines. I wondered how often he came to practice. We formed two lines at the top of the key for the rebounding drill. Gustav stood at the free-throw line with a fishnet bag filled with orange basketballs. Jiri blew his whistle while standing in the midcourt. A player on each side ran to the basket to jostle for position and Gustav launched a one-handed shot that caromed off the back of the rim. Anton and I raced to the area in front of the basket. The ball rolled off the lip of the rim. I maneuvered to get in front of him, a perfect position to get the rebound. Anton leaped when I did, but then somehow pulled the rebound away from me.

During a one-on-one drill, Vojtech and I faced off. He was the starting forward that I needed to knock out if I was to crack the starting lineup. He dribbled toward me, slanting his upper body toward me. I checked his body with my hips to slow his forward momentum and waved my right arm to block his vision of the basket. I stretched my left arm outward to slow him further when he crossed over to his strong hand. I kept my center of gravity lower than his. I bounced back-and-forth. This was a good feeling because I felt like my agility was coming alive. There would be no burst outs by him to the basket; I wasn't going to let that happen. He drove to the side and pulled up his dribble about six feet from the basket. I felt good because I had ground him to a halt. He could do nothing else but shoot. As Vojtech shot, he flared his pointy elbows toward me. I leaped up and blocked the ball out of bounds.

Jiri passed Vojtech another ball. He drove down to the baseline. He threw his shoulders toward me to feign that he was driving toward the basket. I was starting to figure out that Vojtech was a master of the fake. His fakes had embarrassed me the day before when he scored several times off me in the scrimmage. I vowed I wouldn't fall for it again. He went up again with another fake pretending that he was about to release the ball but didn't. I held still. He went back up again with a one handed hook. I blocked it, and we both raced toward the errant ball. He was closer to it. He scooped it up with an ease that shocked me and went up for an easy score. I stood there as the ball swished through then the net into my hands.

After passing drills, free-throw-shooting and more running from one side of the court to the other, Jiri blew his whistle to change to the final part of practice. He said we would scrimmage in the same groups as the day before. Up to this point, I had a few blocks but not much to show for all this sweat and tiredness in my bones. Nevertheless, these scrimmage games were the way I could show them I deserved to be on the team.

I pulled on my yellow jersey over my wet shirt and walked out onto the floor.

"Play the three again," Jiri said to me.

"I want to play the four," I said.

"Okay, we'll try you out at the four," he said.

He called over to Jaroslav, our point guard, to have me run at the low post position. This was my chance to break out of the mold since I wasn't a swingman or my brother. And if I stayed in both these roles much longer I would be heading back to Chicago sooner than I had planned. As our unit inbounded the ball to begin the first game, I glanced over for a moment to see Jiri and Koliar standing next to each other to watching the scrimmage.

I switched my focus to see our point guard Jaroslav peering at me as he took his first dribbles across the half court mark. Vojtech was overplaying me on defense. As I moved closer to the basket, he shadowed me with all his attention. Jaroslav launched a pass in my direction. Why would he throw me the ball from that far out with someone covering me this tight? I didn't know if this was audacity or stupidity on Jaroslav's part. Vojtech didn't even notice the ball heading in our direction. Both of his big Bulgarian hands were up above his shoulders in a true defensive posture. His intense eyes centered on my yellow practice jersey. When he switched his gaze to my face a microsecond later, I hid the surprise I felt and tried not to let my eyes follow the path of ball sailing in. I didn't want to tip him off. I turned to my right and the ball was in my hands. I shot the ball with some spin on it, what my father called "putting English" on the basketball. The ball spun of the board and rippled through the net and into my hands for our first points and an early advantage. "Shit" was all Vojtech said as he ripped the ball from me to inbound it back to go in the other direction.

As I ran back up the court I looked over to the side see the owner Koliar smile to Jiri. I was struck by the cleverness of Jaroslav and they must have been, too. This guy knew what he was doing. When I ran past our sneaky point guard, we slapped hands.

"Great pass," I said.

"You have good hands so we can do that often," he said with a controlled smile. I stumbled past him, almost giddy with amazement, to get into defensive position.

A few minutes later, Jaroslav launched another pass in my direction from off the dribble during the transition. The ball came in with the same speed and accuracy from the half court line. I took two steps over to get it but it flew through my hands out of bounds. As I ran back on defense, he dashed over to me.

"Never take your eyes off me when I have the ball. Never," he said.

From that moment on, I did what he said. Jaroslav was the primary ball handler for our team, and that meant that nearly every time the ball changed hands off a rebound, a basket by the other team, or a steal, I threw the outlet pass to him. No one was better than Jaroslav to quickly exploit opportunities when the ball changed hands. And he responded by looking toward me. He didn't throw his lightning bolt passes from far out every time. He picked his moments.

Zedenik, who was covering Jaroslav at the point, had a crew cut and a muscular physique. He did everything he could to harass the quicker Jaroslav on defense. Zedenik tried to oppose Jaroslav every step of the way in the backcourt when Jaroslav drove up the floor. He was surprisingly effective at slowing Jaroslav down and blocking his drives toward the basket as the scrimmage wore on. The duel between those two never seemed to end, no matter what the score. Zedenik stole the ball from Jaroslav and went down the court for an easy basket, bringing their team to their first lead, 10-8. I could see that Jaroslav was furious. The next procession, Jaroslav sprinted up the floor. I passed to him at half court. He was all alone in the lead near our basket. Instead of taking the easy layup, he pulled up behind the three-point-line and with no one covering him, launched an arcing rainbow with perfect spin on it. It rippled through the net for three points and brought us back into the lead.

There were a lot of good players on the floor, but Jaroslav was the only one who consciously made an effort to make me play better. I couldn't tell yet if he made everyone around him better or just me. The important thing was he passed to me. In spite of the connection we established in the early part of the game, the tables turned against us. The first team came down the court and slowed the game down.

But that was the start of my directing my full attention to Jaroslav every time he had the ball.

Anton's team patiently worked the ball around with passes around the perimeter against us. I counted at least twelve passes that went back and forth between them on one possession. Then Anton passed the ball into the Bulgari Vojtech in front of me. Vojtech swung around me and went up with a shot from a few feet out. I tried to block it from behind but missed. Apparently I was able to harass him enough because his shot rolled off the rim. Anton came around from the backside, rebounded the miss and went back up for an easy score. After that, the first team put up a stifling defense that shut us down. They came back on offense with a drive by Anton and then a bank shot by him that went in. Their lead opened to 14-11. A minute later, Anton scored on a breakaway dunk. He ran back down the court with his hands in the air like a triumphant conqueror returning to his home village on horseback.

I couldn't find a way to stop their momentum as they continued to score and we didn't. Late in the game with us nine points down, Zedenik fired a quick pass to Anton running toward our basket. It looked like it was going to be a repeat of his humiliating slam dunk earlier. This time I was a few steps behind him as he drove toward the open basket. I caught up with him as he passed the free throw line. He gathered the ball up and began his flight toward the basket. I hit his arm and then his torso with my hip. We came crashing down to the floor together in front of our basket. The ball flew out of bounds and up onto the stage behind the basket on that side of the gym. I was tangled in a pile with Anton, and didn't feel anything for a moment. Anton tried to push me away in anger, but he couldn't because we were so tangled up. I tried to assess if he was hurt. I didn't want to hurt the guy, just stop him from scoring. His basket would have ended the game.

I rolled over and stood up on my own. Anton's teammates gathered around him. He continued to lie on the floor. I walked away gingerly from the collision zone to collect myself. My hip was sore because that was where I had fallen after the impact, so I massaged it. I took a few deliberate long strides to test it. Vojtech gave me a menacing look. Then he ran up to me.

"Why didn't you let him have it?" he said.

"I'm not *letting* him have anything," I said.

He pushed me back on the shoulder and Jaroslav stepped in to intervene. Vojtech tried to move past Jaroslav to confront me. Jaroslav moved in front of him with his hands up near his shoulders. Our point guard kept sealing him off. Jaroslav kept his voice lower than Vojtech's and it seemed to settle the Bulgari down. I could feel the adrenaline race through me. I resisted the urge to step forward and held my ground for a moment. Then I backpedaled to cool things off.

Jiri came over with a concerned look on his face to see if Anton was all right. Koliar hadn't moved from the place he and Jiri were sitting. He was standing and scowled at me. What did I expect? I had just knocked over their star player, his Czech all star. Zedenik extended a hand to his fallen teammate and pulled him to his feet. He gingerly straightened up and began to walk stiffly. As Anton continued to walk, his stride started to look normal. It looked like he was okay, too.

After a few moments by myself, Jaroslav walked over to me.

"Are you okay? he said, quietly.

"Besides my sore hip, I'm fine."

"It's going to be all right. It was in the heat of the moment. You were trying to stop him and there's nothing wrong with that," Jaroslav said.

I was happy to see Jaroslav jump in to protect me. This guy that I met three days before in this small mountain town on edge of nowhere was acting like Josef, my brother. I had no illusions that Jaroslav was my instant best friend. One rule of life that I felt certain of was this: it takes years to build and deepen a friendship. But you have to start somewhere.

I committed a foul. But before I knew it, the other team was ready to inbound the ball. My guard was up against everyone from their team. I had to cover Vojtech so as I moved closer to him, I was wary he might try to attack me now that he could deliver an easy blow. He seemed to show no outward animosity so I cautiously continued to move closer. I had to since he was my man on defense.

Jaroslav was up on the point covering Zedenik. He looked back at me to see if any other "excitement" was going to ensue. I warily looked over to Anton who was out in front of me on the wing. He seemed like he wasn't going to take anything out on me either. I was surprised because these guys seemed like the kind who would retaliate at any moment.

Zedenik drove toward the basket and launched a 15-footer. It went in. We lost our first game by a score of 24-13. I calculated they that outscored us 14-2 at the end. After such a promising start and early leads, I was disappointed that things changed so dramatically. Before our second scrimmage game, Jaroslav put his hand on my back.

"We can beat them. I know you have it in you," Jaroslav said, quietly. His eyes conveyed an intensity of a man more determined to win than ever.

I continued to play hard in the second and third games. There was no team collapse or collisions like the first game, but they both ended in losses, 24-16 and 24-20. We had not figured out a way to beat them. I felt that I showed more of the kind of player I was during that practice. It would take a while to get into better shape. The last game I did run out of gas and could not play the kind of game that I wanted on defense. But I knew Jaroslav and I could make things happen. What we did in that first game had given me a glimmer of hope.

I was the last one out of the showers because I was tired. My body was moving slowly after the morning run and practice. My knees cracked a few times as I walked from the locker room. I watched as some of the last players exited out the side door of the gym to the parking lot. Jiri locked his gray office door along the opposite wall.

North Park's Gymnasium had the simple metal door next to the seats, too. Behind that door was Charlie White's office. I sat talking to this NCAA Division III award-winning coach many times during the four years I played for him. Coach White was a tremendous teacher of the fundamentals of basketball, but I felt Coach Jiri Hasek could be an even better example to learn from. As an Olympic competitor for Czechoslovakia's 1972 team, he had a unique perspective. He seemed to have fewer fixed notions about how to play the game. What I didn't recognize, was how hampered he was by the owner of the sports club, Milos Koliar.

"Maybe you can show me more of the Svet tomorrow," I said as I walked over to him. He turned to face me.

"There isn't going to be a tomorrow, Josef," he said.

"What do you mean?"

"I have to release you. I talked to Koliar and that's what he wants," he said.

"Does this have anything to my foul of Anton in the first game?" I said.

"No. We need someone who can come in here and make an impact right away as a first team player. That's what we hoped," Jiri said.

"Coach, what about all that stuff you said to me yesterday, about me being a spark?"

"If it was up to me, I would keep you. I saw what you did in the first game, that working with Jaroslav on the fast breaks. That nice drop step and spin you did to score against Vojtech in that last game. I stated my case to Koliar about what you can offer this team. He said no on you," Jiri said.

CHAPTER EIGHT

DEPARTURE

Koliar was the most unreasonable person I'd ever met. The guy initially said I had a week to show myself and now I was released after two days. He didn't even give me a real chance. When I reached landing on the mezzanine level of the glass factory, I came face-to face with Jelina, the executive assistant of Milos Koliar. We paused for a moment, speechless, in a kind of instant attraction. She brushed her long brown hair from her face with her slender ringless hands. I smiled at her self-consciousness.

"Hello. How are feeling after your second practice?" she said.

"I'm tired, hungry and thirsty. I didn't make the team. This is it."

"You just arrived. How can that be? We haven't done well in the first fourteen games so far, they need you. That doesn't sound like Jiri."

"Ask your boss, he's the one that decided. I'm not what he expected. I was just starting to bring my best parts out, too, especially during the scrimmages."

She thought for moment and then said, "Follow me."

We walked together back up the stairs. Jelina wore a silk red blouse with thin gold lines running down it, a black skirt, dark nylon stockings across her long legs and high heel shoes that clicked on each stair. Her brunette hair curled down past her shoulders. I liked the subtle highlights running through her smooth hair.

"Where are we going?'

"You'll see," Jelina said.

Seeing her move was an added dimension that heightened my interest. When we reached the mezzanine, she looked both ways to make sure no one saw us. We walked down the hall to an empty conference room; she motioned for me to have a seat. This Bohemian beauty moved over to a small kitchen that was hidden in a cove off to the side and soon I could hear the sound of a microwave. The room had the smell of new carpets and the cherry-paneled walls were immaculate. There was even a fireplace faced with white quarry tiles. This room was wildly out of character with the rest of the room spaces of the glass factory. Even Koliar's office was not so elegant.

While she was in the kitchen, I stood to look out the window that ran like a ribbon along the wall. A group of workmen were smoking cigarettes and laughing on a dock loaded with palates of crates and boxes. Life was continuing, seemingly indifferent to the fact that I had to leave and wouldn't be a part of the place. A truck hit a rut filled with muddy slop. I could hear the splash from that far away. The driver continued out, through a gate in the the razor wire fence that surrounded the spacious rear yard, to a dirt service road. Beyond that was a slope with rock and trees very similar to the ones I ran past that morning.

Upon that sheet of glass between conference room and the rear yard was my reflection. I checked my face, its degree of sadness, and the state of my hair.

From the kitchen, Jelina brought out steaming roast pork loin, potatoes with dark gravy, and pickled red beets. Next she brought out a pitcher of water and even a cold lager in a bottle with a Czech label. The first thing she did was pour the beer into a tall glass. As I took a seat back at the table, the electricity went off. I could hear the machines on the floor beneath whirl to a halt.

"What's this?" I said.

"This happens every now and then. It's our inheritance from the Soviet Union."

The room was filled with an enchanted darkness. Through the window, I could see gray clouds inching along. Jelina pulled out matches. Lighting a taper candle, she put the stick in a glass holder. She gently slid the candle closer so I could see all that was laid out before me. She sat down across from me on this end of the conference room table and watched me eat.

The tart of the beets brought out the best in the pork and potatoes. I savored each sip of the beer from its smooth start to a spiky final hook. This brew was more satisfying than any I'd ever tasted. It made the American beer I was accustomed to seem one dimensional, all wicked aftertaste. As I ate and drank, I realized how foolish I'd been to think that any of this would work out. Probably my parents were right when they said that the whole thing was a mistake that I'd regret.

Meanwhile, I gazed at Jelina's remarkable beauty. The dim light of the room lent a mysterious cast to her features. Her eyes were deep pools of blue. They had an aliveness in them. But I also detected wariness in those eyes, the sign of someone who lived a life that was harder than expected. Then I shifted my focus back to her perfectly symmetrical pink lips. With that, Jelina looked away. That helped break the intensity of the moment and made her more real.

Wherever I looked, there was beauty and goodness in the moment. Her kindness was something I didn't expect. I felt sad again, mostly because that the possibility of her us together would vanish. I wished I could sit with her the rest of the day and the power would never come back on.

Then the lights did flash on and all that was left to finish on the plate were pickled beets. As I finished the red vegetables, there was nothing to balance out the sharpness of the vinegar in them. I must have made a face because she smiled. Jelina blew out the candle. We picked up the glasses and dishes. We carried them to the kitchen area.

"Here let me wash these," I said

I washed them and she stood next to me with a towel in her hands. As I handed off the dishes for her to dry, our hands touched. She dried each dish and placed it back in a cherrywood cabinet.

"Are you better now?" Jelina said, after we finished.

"I'm not. It's over. What was I thinking about coming here? It's crazy that I'm leaving now," I said.

"I'm sorry this has happened, too. You will do well whatever direction you take," she said.

"One thing I appreciate is you. Thank you for this lunch."

"I'll miss you."

"Miss me? You don't know me," I said.

"There was a lot of expectation after you agreed to come."

Jelina smiled. Then she took a step closer to me. We looked into each other's eyes. My lips grazed her neck first then brushed her cheek. We kissed first hesitantly, then more passionately. She wanted to continue kissing, longer than I wanted. I decided to go with it. It was my first Czech kiss and my last all at once. I could feel heat from under my cheeks. It felt like I was going to cry, but I held back, sad that this whole damned thing had come to an end. Jelina turned her head away and smiled with amusement.

We both seemed to recognize the fleeting nature of going further but she was the first to say it.

"You have to go and I have to go back to work," she said, breaking the intensity.

She was right. Our assistant coach Gustav was probably looking for me. Jiri had arranged for him to drive me to Station Square in downtown Svet. Jelina had duties to attend to as the secretary to the guy that owned the place. There were important affairs of the glass factory she had to handle, I knew.

When we exited the door of the conference room, she went one way and I went the other. When I got to the door of the players quarters, I looked across the mezzanine. She was watching me from in front of the executive offices. I waved to her. She gave a quick smile and went into the cherry wood door leading to the office suite.

Falling in love is easy, staying in and building on that love is the hard part. I wouldn't have to do that and was actually relieved.

What a nice sendoff. At least I had those extremely good moments with Jelina and could think about her as I travelled away from Svet. That might even be the thing I needed to get over my ex-girlfriend Nancy back in Chicago. It still stung pretty badly that she'd left me for another guy when the going got a little rough. Maybe I should head right to Prague. I did come this far to see it, but then maybe I should head out back to Vienna and home. A practical solution but a real defeat. A risky adventurer would never do that.

When I walked to my cubicle where all my gear was, I saw Anton, who was standing in his living area next to mine.

"Thanks for decking me, you son of a bitch," he said.

I looked at his face to detect his intent. I couldn't tell if he was simply being sarcastic or really meant it.

"Anton, again, I told you sorry before," I said; weary that he may try to start something right there.

"Where are you off to from here? Back to Chicago?" Anton said.

"I haven't decided yet. I didn't expect this," I said.

"Why don't you go over to play with Pardubice? We play them next week. They may have a need for a scrappy rebounder and defensive player like you. And a guy missing a chromosome," he said, laughing.

I was in no mood to play the straight man to Anton's tomfoolery. I walked over to my living area. As I was packing all my clothes into a green army bag, Gustav walked in.

"There you are, I was looking for you. Did the coach tell you I was driving you?" Gustav said.

"He did. I'll be ready soon," I said.

While I was busy trying to fit everything into my bag, Gustav took an intense interest in my reading material. He paged through a few of books on my bed, noticing that they were all in English even though a few were about the Czech Republic. I was a Czech that knew the Slavic language well, but it was still my second language. I didn't realize what a strain it was to speak and think in Czech all day. It was going to be good to return to English again.

"Are you ready to go?" Gustav said, looking up from the books.

I was unprepared with no Plan B in place. I'd gone down in bitter defeat, and returning to Chicago with no accomplishment or adventure was the scenario I had to avoid at all costs. This wasn't going to happen.

I grabbed the rest of my gear and jammed it in my bag. I was able to get everything in except my high-top basketball shoes. I looked around one last time. I had everything, so we exited the players' quarters. The only people around were Anton and a few of the players from the first team. They watched me as I carried the big green bag and Gustav carried my shoes. We went down the same stairs where I'd run into Jelina earlier, and walked out into the front parking lot. We put my gear into the trunk of the black Skoda sedan in which Jiri and he had driven me in from Vienna. We rolled through the lot and approached the main gate. I heard someone calling us. I looked back, and there was Jaroslav running toward us.

"I must have forgotten something. Let's see what Jaroslav wants," I said.

Gustav didn't respond so Jaroslav continued to run and knocked the glass on the driver's side. Gustav braked on the gravel surface. He rolled down the window.

"You need to turn around. We'll talk with Koliar," Jaroslav said.

Gustav looked doubtful, but agreed. We walked up the stairs. Gustav chose to wait near the entrance to the office suite. He leaned with his back against the mezzanine railing that overlooked the glass factory production line. Jaroslav and I entered in and went directly to Jelina, who was on the phone. Jelina was shocked to see us but then gained her composure. She told the caller to hold on.

"Good afternoon, Jelina. We want to see Koliar. Is he in?" Jaroslav said, in a clear calm voice.

"He is but he is preparing for a meeting he's got in twenty minutes," she said.

"We need to speak to him right now," Jaroslav said. Jelina called him on the phone and persuaded Koliar to take a few minutes to meet with us.

Jaroslav and I went in. Koliar stood up and when he saw me, he waved me away saying he would only meet with Jaroslav. Jaroslav ushered me out and closed the door.

While holding the phone to one ear and writing things down on a notepad, Jelina gracefully motioned for me to have a seat adjacent to her. I felt awkward sitting there. She smiled at me a few times as she continued with her phone conversation.

After a few minutes the door to the office opened, Jaroslav came out. He had a smile on his face and a bounce in his step. He shook my hand.

"He gave you the week. You have five more days to prove yourself," said Jaroslav. We slapped each other on the back and then he gave me a playful push on the shoulder. Jelina was ready to give me a high five too before she restrained herself. She looked around her and got back to work but I couldn't help notice the smile on her face.

After practice the next day, I went with Jaroslav and Milan to lift weights in the weight training room. The weight room and the locker room were down a series of stairs in a basement area underneath the gym. A dark corridor with empty whitewashed walls connected the two.

As I walked by the locker room I saw the rest of the team was showering. I heard Vojtech's laughter.

I didn't want to use the ancient-looking weight machines, but I did think the free weight barbells could be of value. Even though practice tired me out, I had a high motivation level to continue what I started in Chicago.

Jaroslav and Milan had a routine down that they had been doing since I'd arrived. This pair weren't talking much to each other, even though I could feel that they usually did. There is something to be said for spending time in someone's presence in near silence. It brought the bonds between the three of us closer.

With thirty pounds of iron in each fist, I pictured having the ball in my hands with Vojtech guarding me. As I brought the weights over my shoulders I powered the ball to the basket. In one repetition, Vojtech was grabbing my arm. In another, he was hitting my elbow. There was no way that guy was going to stop me.

As I walked out of the locker room, a man in a trench coat stepped out of the shadows of the hallway.

"Josef Savek? I'm Tades Pavelosek, a reporter for the *Svet Monitor*," he said.

The *Svet Monitor* was something everyone read at the restaurant where I had breakfast. I was a reporter myself until I went into public relations. I got pretty good at steering print journalists like this guy but I knew that might not save me. I wasn't my brother and this guy could blow my cover even before I got started.

"What can I do for you?" I said, wondering how that came out in Czech.

"I'm on deadline and need to ask you some things. What brought you to play here in Svet?" he said, taking out his notebook and pen.

"I haven't made the team yet. But to answer your question, I wanted to try something different," I said. He scribbled something. I decided to hold back and learn what he knew.

"What do you mean by that, how's Svet different?

"I like the small town feel. It's certainly not Prague or Brno but I've never been to those places. Why Svet? It seemed to have friendly people," I said. He wasn't buying it.

"What's this really about? To explore your Czech roots?"

“I’m Czech. So you won’t be wrong saying that,” I said.

“I’ll write the story, okay,” he said, squinting his eyes into a skeptical look. “You played in England and I understand you were one of their top scorers. Do you see yourself doing that here?”

A loaded question. “I see myself being a different player than I was before. My defensive and rebounding skills are what I plan to emphasize,” I said.

“Why is that?”

“That’s where the greatest need seems to be. This team already has plenty of scorers,” I said.

“That’s not what I hear. Besides Anton who else do you have? Koliar said you’re the second scorer they need. But it turns out you’re not the scorer they think.”

This guy’s an astute observer and a threat. “What can I do about what anybody expects? I’m just here to play my game and see where things fall,” I said.

“As an American, what do you offer that we don’t already have?”

“My basketball experiences are different. So I offer some energy and perspective. I’m here to learn, too because Jiri Hasek is a good coach. I’ve been impressed with him,” I said.

“That’s not what I asked, why would you come here?”

“This opportunity looked best. Let’s see if it all works out. One question for you: do you like being a reporter?”

“Most people only give you about three percent of who they are. The rest, the ninety-seven percent, is what you have to fill in. I’ll find the full story,” he said.

“If you had to pick one over the other, do you like the human interest piece or the investigative story?” I said.

He filled up two pages of his notebook.

"Both. I have what I need," he said.

CHAPTER NINE

THE NOTE

I walked to the glass factory, happy to get into the light of day. On a shortcut between the gym and the factory I saw some small flowers growing amidst the longer grass on the side of a hill. They made me think of Koliar's secretary. I went over and picked a yellow flower with purple in the center.

In my pocket was a note for Jelina. I pulled it out to read it one last time.

Dear Beautiful Woman,

Your beauty is like this flower from the upper meadows of Svet Mountain. I have come across the moving sea to be with a person like you and think about you often. Can we meet to get to know each other over dinner? How about something scenic and fun or something characteristic of this place? We can walk in the beauty of the night so I can see your eyes in the starlight. I'll wait for word from you.

Yours truly,

JOSEF, THE AMERICAN CZECH

I wondered whether I should address her by name. I decided to keep it the way I wrote it. Mysterious is better. The outside of the card was an ink drawing of the Chicago shoreline that showed Monroe

Harbor, Buckingham Fountain and the Planetarium. I bought a pack of twelve of them at an expensive shop across Michigan Avenue from the Art Institute before I left. I pressed the small yellow and purple flower in the white area between the heavy card stock cover and the note. The flower wasn't really from the upper meadow but it was the best I could do. I hoped it wasn't a weed.

I knew my moment had come when I saw two of her co-workers walking in the parking lot. The third woman was sitting at a table eating an apple while reading a book. She didn't even look up as I passed.

Up the stairs, I went into the outer office. Jelina had two desks, a small one outside Koliar's office and another in the area with the other secretaries. I heard Jelina on the phone outside Koliar's office. In the United States, you could never get this close to a CEO, but in Svet, in the Czech Republic four years after the Velvet Revolution, security was more lax. I scanned the space. Four similar desks there sat in a different configuration than I remembered. I smelled rubber and whatever else is released when new carpet is installed.

Koliar came out of his office and I could hear him talking with Jelina. I had to decide quickly, so I walked over to Jelina's desk in that outer area. It was neat and clutter-free unlike several of the others, so I slid the note under the black day-planner on it. I wanted it be found but not at first glance. And then I slipped out the door. In spite of my confusion, I thought I got it right. Jelina would get my message.

CHAPTER TEN

WATCHING THE EYES

I awoke in the darkness, feeling as if a medicine ball was rolling around the bottom of my stomach. I wasn't feeling good about my prospects with the team. I was running out of time to show myself. In the three practices to that point, my team hadn't won a game. Nine losses in the scrimmages. We'd made progress but not enough to knock off the first team. For example, the day before we were competitive in all three games but the first team controlled the momentum and rolled to wins.

Vojtech, Anton and Zedenik were confident and cocky beyond their abilities. They were still out-rebounding me and sealing me off from offensive rebounds. I broke through every so often with an unexpected rebound and putback under our basket. But I couldn't get them in droves because Vojtech and Anton employed coordinated coverage against me. They rotated with one of them in front of me and one in back. One pushing their back and the other his hands into me.

I hated that.

Zedenik and Anton hit their shots from the perimeter. Jaroslav hadn't quite solved Zedenik. On defense, Jaroslav made some key stops on Zedenik but not enough to slow that their offense.

I decided the restaurant across the road from the glass factory was the best. It had better breakfasts and the thin waitress was nice, too. That morning she wore a triangular scarf of rough but colorful linen over her shoulders, tied in a loose knot at the breast.

I had a long day ahead of me and wouldn't make it to the end of practice the scrimmage if I didn't eat well. I had to gulp down breakfast, hungry or not, so I ate oatmeal with milk, white cheese, and an orange at the restaurant with the thin waitress. I felt as uneasy as the day before. Even with our tremendous breakthroughs at the last two practices, Jiri's noncommittal response after practice gnawed at me during the night. I teetered on the edge of the cliff again. I told myself if I didn't make the team I wasn't sticking around to watch the game against Pardubice. I had more pride than that. I would be gone to see the rest of the country and then home to United States.

I walked down the dark road to the gymnasium to prepare for practice. The Svet field house was a rectangular building with a façade of smooth sandstone blocks and a pair of cold bronze doors. With my bag of basketball gear over my shoulder, I walked along the path to the front door of the building. It was locked. Not knowing if I could even get into the gym an hour and a half before practice was to begin, I walked around to the side of the building and found a single gray metal door. It clicked open.

The building lights were on. They burned with brightness and intensity. It was light inside and dark outside, simulating the big show I was working for—game time for Svet against the real villains of the Czech club sport scene—the other nine teams. But that felt like a distant dream. A man in dark blue work clothes pushed a dust mop across the shiny plank floor. He looked at me from across the gym. I waved back. I continued ahead along the side in the direction of the locker room.

"Hey," he yelled. I didn't pay attention and pushed ahead toward the locker room. He whistled to get my attention. I ignored him. Then he blasted a whistle with a finger from each hand.

I changed directions to make a bee-line toward him. When I stepped on the court, he violently waved off me the court and motioned for me to come to him by way of the side.

"Hey, I'm here to shoot around early," I said from far out.

"What are doing here? You are not allowed," he said.

When I reached him, we stood there a moment and took each other in.

"You're the American. What is it?"

"I need to warm up and do some shooting," I said.

"Stay off the court with the street shoes. Got it?" he said.

I nodded yes, turned, and walked back toward the door on the other side of the gym.

Then, after a moment of watching me, he resumed pushing the mop in front of him toward center court while shaking his head.

I pushed through doors that led to a hallway and then to a set of stairs that descended to a basement area. At the bottom of the stairwell, I staggered through the darkness. I ran my hand along a gritty wall in search of a light switch but couldn't find one. I forged ahead in the direction of a shower dripping in the locker room.

The dripping guided me through a doorway. Then I reached out to feel the cool metal of lockers on the wall. Where the lockers ended, I felt the damp cool wall and the light switch. I flipped on the switch, ending my blindness.

I changed into my workout clothes and laced up my Air Jordans. I didn't see the low ceilings as confining. It was in this locker room that I put a plan together. I prepared myself mentally by closing my eyes. I visualized the scrimmage a few hours in the future. I saw myself scoring over Vojtech from positions all over the low post. Jaroslav rifling passes to me and my scoring on the fast break at every opportunity. Rebounding like crazy, blocking shots and working well with my teammates.

Three hours later in the intra-squad scrimmage, I was running down the floor. I looked over at the scoreboard and we were leading 18 to 8. My team had never achieved this before. It was as if everything I visualized that morning was playing out a second time.

When Vojtech moved across the lane to position his body on the low post, I was there in front of him with my hands in the air to prevent an entry pass into him. When he moved across the free-throw lane to try to get the pass from another angle, I forced him to take an indirect route.

Zedenik, their point guard with the blond crew cut, tried to pass into Vojtech on the low post, and I intercepted it. I passed the ball to Jaroslav off to the side. I took off like a rocket and filled in the lane to the right of him. Soon I was in front of him and glanced into Jaroslav's eyes as I raced up the floor. Then he looked away and then back at me. He unleashed a lead pass over everyone's head toward the basket. Anton knew it was coming. "Hey," he yelled to harass me to throw me off. He stayed with me the whole way. I saw the orange ball flying toward me. I burst two steps ahead to claim it. I caught the ball with my fingertips, and in what seemed to be same motion, jumped and dunked it. As I returned to earth, I collided with Anton, stepping on his foot. He was knocked back and down from the impact. I landed on my feet and darted away. As I ran back on defense, I realized the excellent defender Anton didn't foul me or slam me across the head. And he certainly could have because he was on my back most of the time on that play.

On the very next possession Anton dribbled hard off the break and powered it up for an uncontested basket. Then my inbound pass to Jaroslav was picked off by Zedenik. My first reaction was we were seeing the beginning our collapse again. But when Jaroslav stole it right back and wheeled around to look for me off the break, I knew nothing would stop our win. He found me with a bullet, but I had two on me, Anton and Vojtech. Both were bracing like caged tigers ready to throw my shot into the bleachers and me to the floor. I shoveled it back to Jaroslav, who launched a perfect ten-footer that dropped through the net. A minute later, Jaroslav took another shot from the perimeter that bounced off the rim. I reached up and tipped it back up.

The ball bounced around the rim and came back off. I tipped it back up again and in. We won. My first victory in the Czech Republic.

A smiling Jaroslav ran over and slapped the center of my sweat-soaked shirt above my heart, then slapped my back.

"Your best game yet, Josef. That's more like it," he said.

I savored looking at the scoreboard, which read 24-12, and wished I could have taken a photo. My brother, Josef, wherever he was, would have been proud but not surprised.

Jaroslav and I could not be stopped. The next game we were losing by 6 points at one point, until the end. We calmly came back and hit basket after basket. And forced their misses. Final score: 24-20. Jaroslav and I won a game we were not supposed to win.

We lost the last game 24-16, but they couldn't deny the fact that we had beaten them. *Twice*. A great practice, my first one like this since I'd arrived in the republic.

As we walked off the court, Jiri pulled the two of us aside.

He said, "Good practice, Josef. You arrived here like a piece of raw steak. Jaroslav added the onions and now you're starting to sizzle." The other players moved slower to the locker room than they usually did at the end of practice. They hung around to eavesdrop.

"Jaroslav, marvelous ball control and leadership out there. Keep it up and you'll be seeing a lot of time the first game against Pardubice," he said. He turned to me.

"Have I made the team, coach?" I said.

"I can't say yet. Let's see more of your best tomorrow," he said with a smile.

That's not the answer I wanted to hear. That tomorrow he was referring to was the last one I was promised by Koliar.

I walked down the stairs to the basement of the Svet gymnasium. A cool draft poured from slits in the chiseled limestone walls. I came to an old wooden door that looked as ancient as the walls and heavy enough for a church. It creaked open and I went inside. The whole team was there. The guys were using all the weight machines and benches. It reeked of Ben Gay. I stood in the middle of the well-lit weight room trying to fit in. The guy I was trying to beat at practice,- Vojtech, bench-pressed with four plates of steel on each end of the bar. After that he shifted over to a leg press where he climbed in a seat low to the floor. From a squat position he pushed pedals with the bottom of his feet and extended his legs for three sets and jumped off when he was done. I could see how Vojtech built up his muscular thighs that were as sturdy as the legs of a shot putter. The effect was accentuated by the bulky knee pads he wore.

I benched with two plates and even that wasn't easy. All the gains I made at home to get stronger seemed lost. But I continued. At the end of an hour, I was sore and knew I was going to be even more so the next day.

The next morning I woke up to the sound of water funneling through a downspout pipe outside and rain that sluiced down the window above my bed. When the dim light of dawn came through the windows, I wanted to stay under my warm covers. After a few minutes, I crept out of bed. It was the first day I wasn't jetlagged and when I felt like I belonged.

I learned to run the water in the faucet until the brown color went away. I knew better than to drink that water, but I could trust it for washing my face and shaving. Unlike my first day when I ate with Anton, I decided to eat breakfast alone at the smoky restaurant across from the factory. I ordered dark bread rolls, thin sliced cheese, yogurt, applesauce, and bottled mineral water. As I ate, I thought the only way I could survive was to play my game of rebounding and defense. I also needed to score baskets with some outside shots from the perimeter.

After I paid my bill, I went to the gym to get some shooting in. I loosened up and took as many shots as I could for forty-five minutes before practice began. I had done a lot of shooting in the weeks before I left Chicago. As more of my teammates entered the gym, I pressed to hit more baskets. A few of them watched me shoot as they stretched on the side of the court. Each time I released the ball I worked to maintain good form on my jump shots. I let the ball go at the top of my jump, with elbows and slight rotation on the ball with follow-through upon the release. My shot had a nice arch and trajectory as it left my fingertips and traveled toward the basket. But nearly everything I fired caromed off the rim. As I ran around rebounding miss after miss, I felt embarrassed that my secret was exposed. I was showing them that I couldn't consistently hit the baskets from the perimeter when no one was covering me.

"That's not going to work, you're not a scorer," Anton said.

"Everyone has different skills; I'm not the same player as you."

"Another scoring threat would have been nice. I don't know how our scouting could be so wrong," he said.

Thankfully, Jiri came into the gym, blew the whistle.

Later, the scrimmage game began with a running hook shot by Anton over my outstretched hand. Milan inbounded the ball from under the basket to Jaroslav. As Jaroslav dribbled the ball across half court, he shielded it from Zedenik playing tight defense on him. Through the bodies moving past, I looked into Jaroslav's eyes. Anton was a step away and alertly splitting his vision between Jaroslav on the point and me. Jaroslav threw a long looping pass over my head. I tracked it down and with Anton on my back, I went right up with a layup to tie the score.

Back and forth the game went with a tie score until Anton scored on a reverse layup to make the score 16-14. Anton's team scored during two more possessions and held us to missed shots, opening their lead to 20-14. In a burst, my team raced back down court to score on a fast break lay-up by Jaroslav. In the transition, I stole the ball near half court and rifled the ball to Jaroslav. As they ran toward their basket, Jaroslav drew the defense presence of Anton and he flipped it to me for a seven-foot jumper that narrowed their lead to 20-18. We had a chance.

Anton's team was in the solid hands of Zedenik. He controlled the ball across the half court mark and then patiently passed the ball around until an opening was exposed. After five passes, Zedenik found my man Vojtech open on the hashmark three feet from the basket. Vojtech went up with the ball, and I fouled him by coming over from the backside to hit him hard across the arms. Vojtech's shot missed the basket. Play stopped. Vojtech lunged to attack me but Jaroslav jumped between in his way to prevent a fight. I looked over to Jiri to see him looking intently but with no emotion at the situation on the court. Anton's team got possession of the ball out of bounds. Zedenik found an opening in the defense and drove to the basket past Jaroslav. I converged on him and he threw toward Anton but Charles stepped in the way for a steal.

Jaroslav drove up court and found Milan for a ten-foot shot to tie the score. Again Anton's team missed and I snatched the ball through the struggle of bodies. I passed up court to Milan for a running lay-up. The scoreboard read 22-20. Eight points in a row were scored by our yellow team. Anton got the ball in the corner and drove out to the side. He threw up a twelve-foot bank shot with me in his face to tie the score at 22. Jaroslav drove hard off the dribble, then pulled back to launch and hit a three-point shot for a 25-22 come-from-way-behind victory. Three wins in two days. Not bad. Jiri had a smile on his face that told me enough for the moment.

The scrimmage ended with two wins by Anton's team. But the furious play in that last game raised the intensity level to a new high for both sides. Vojtech scored on a dunk on the last shot for the win. He yelped as loud as he could and ran by me pointing in my face. Practice was over. Our coach Jiri was smiling after practice.

"Any decision, Coach? Have I made the team?" I said.

"Today improved. That's all I can say," he said.

CHAPTER ELEVEN

DON GIOVANNI

The next morning I paged through the *Svet Monitor* in my normal smoke-filled café. The thin waitress set down my glass of orange juice with special care.

"Congratulations on making the team," she said.

"I haven't made it," I said.

"That's not what the paper says. Here, it's here," she said as she grabbed the paper from me, paged through it to a section I hadn't read yet. Then she folded the section open in front of me.

"I don't believe it. Where?"

I reached for it and she snatched the paper away.

"*Svet signs American player.* That's some headline. That's you, the same guy that comes here in the mornings," she said. She hit me in the shoulder with a menu in her hand.

"Let me have it. I can read Czech," I said.

"No, I'll read it to you."

And she did.

The Svet basketball sportsclub has brought in Josef Savek from Czech Chicago. Nearly two meters tall, Savek played for Hemel Hemsford in England for the last two seasons. The American forward has Czech roots as his father came from Brno and his mother is Bohemian. With this mid-season signing, Svet is hoping to turn around its fortunes in the Czech Superliga after a 7-

7 record so far. League rules permit two foreign players per team. Vojetch Hadjipetric, the center from Sofia, Bulgaria, and Savek from Chicago, Illinois, USA are Svet's foreign recruits. The second half of the season starts tomorrow against Pardubice, last year's superliga champion.

"What do you think?" she said.

"They announced it before telling me. Is that how they do things around here?"

I was also happy the article was harmless and really said nothing.

"They'll do that especially in something as important as basketball," she said.

I looked into her eyes to see if she was being sarcastic. She wasn't. That is what I loved about this small town in the football-shaped canyon near the Polish border. They loved their basketball.

Was it true or some kind of mistake? Was all this a set up before everything would come crashing down later that day or at some inopportune time when they found out that I wasn't Josef? Could there ever be a way that the real me could come out or would I be locked into being the imposter forever? This playing my younger brother was creating more problems that it was solving.

The waitress brought my breakfast and left me alone. I didn't like being the last to know.

Within a few minutes, a nicely dressed woman came into the diner. She stood out because no one in the restaurant dressed this carefully. I recognized this chestnut-haired woman as one of the three that worked with Jelina in the main office. Seeing her made me think of Jelina. It also reminded me that she hadn't responded to my note. I did want to see her and hear her response to my letter. Jelina's officemate scanned the restaurant and walked directly to me. She came up alongside me with a nervous smile.

"I heard the news about you making team on radio," she said in English.

Besides a few words with Anton, this was the first person that I'd spoken to in English in the whole time I'd been there.

"When was it on the radio?" I said.

"They announced it this morning. Congratulations, player American." She paused as if presenting herself to me. She wore a fancy light green blouse and a white skirt that revealed her knees. She had attractive legs.

"Yes, it's good news. I just wished they'd bothered to tell me first," I said.

"Also, I got your poetry. I really liked what you said," she said.

"My poetry?"

"The flowery note you wrote. You must have pulled that stuff out of the dictionary. It was very well to send me that," she said.

Oh crap, I didn't get the right desk. She was friendly so I decided to go along with it.

"I realize I don't even know your name," I said.

"I'm Shantel. You can call me Shantelina," she said.

"I'm Josef."

"I know, Savek's your surname," she said. I felt like a fool for saying it.

We shook hands.

"Have a seat, join me for breakfast," I said, motioning with my hand to a chair beside me.

"I'm late for work. You mentioned in letter to take me to dinner. I've the perfect place, *Ceska Moravu,* to show you what Moravia is like. The food is good but the parlandos even better," she said

"What are parlandos?"

"It's folk music. Have you ever heard of Moravian yodelers?"

"No never. I'd like to go to this place. With you."

"You are an answer to prayer, Josef," she said.

"You don't even really know me," I said.

"It's true, player American. But mystery is good, no? We'll have a lot to talk about," Shantelina said, as she fumbled with her purse.

We set a time to meet for three days from then. That would be the day the team would arrive back from the team's first road game against Hradec Králové. If I really did make the team, that would work. If not, I was gone anyway. It wouldn't matter. But I hoped Jelina would come around. She was the one I wanted most.

When I arrived at the gym, Jaroslav told me to see Coach Jiri in his office. His face was neutral and didn't reveal anything one way or the other. When I got to Jiri's office, Coach kicked out the chuck that held the door open. After the door shut with a boom, he sat down behind his desk.

"Have a seat," he said motioning with his hand to a chair alongside his desk. "I have something important for you. You've done some good, stirring things up the last few days," he said.

"What is it, Coach?

"You have made the team, Josef. Congratulations," he said. We both stood and shook hands. Then both sat back down.

"This is exciting, I said. "But you released it to the media and I didn't even know. Why?"

"That's what Koliar wanted. As the owner of this team, he felt that last night was a good time to let the word out," said Jiri.

He took out a document and a pen and placed them in front of me.

"It's the contract. Read it through and then sign it."

Everything in the document was what they promised. The wording confirmed our earlier conversations, including the pathetic salary. I signed it. He reached into a box and pulled out a blue and white jersey and shorts. I ripped the uniform out of its plastic packaging. It had a 33 on it.

"Two things that are most important to me are honesty and the ability to listen. If you uphold these for me, there will be no problems. Are we clear about that?" he said, looking me in the eyes for a few seconds.

"Yes. That's what I'll do," I said.

I hated to say it, but I felt I had to do if I was to play there. I had just passed through another gate that shut behind me. There was no turning back. It was like the run up Svet Mountain we took every week, I wanted to continue to see the flowery meadows, but also knew the trail could leave me slammed against the rocks, lying in a puddle of muddy water. The longer I got away with my switch with my brother, the more likely they might catch me and have my ass thrown out in humiliation, which would be worse than getting cut.

"You won't be a starter tomorrow night against Pardubice. Maybe that's better because we'll ease into things by having you spell Vojtech. You can help us, so keep it up. We are going to need your best," he said.

A few minutes later I was down in the locker room changing into my uniform. The blue and white jersey looked vibrant and felt rubbery in my hands. As I pulled the mesh jersey over my head, it smelled like the plastic packaging.

The shorts were a different story. They were baggy, a retread from several seasons past. As I put them on, they had a faint mildew odor. Before I went upstairs, I stood in front of the bathroom mirror. The tank top jersey top looked great with the big white letters *SVET* across the front. I stood there and looked at the imposter in the mirror. The person I saw could only go out there and be himself. I turned and saw my number on the back. It was the same number as Larry Bird. A very good thing.

I tried to pull the white shorts down as far as they could go. The gold-trimmed bottoms squeezed against my mid-thighs and the waist was super tight. I looked like I was all legs and was about to go back and get another pair from Jiri. Then I saw the other players walking past the locker room door to go upstairs. Everyone had these unshapely tents on. I pulled my white socks up to just below my knee like the others.

Before practice we gathered at the S logo in the center court to take the team picture. The photographer had me stand in the back row between our two other tallest players, Vojtech and Anton. Anton kept joking around before the photographer snapped off a number of shots of us eleven players, with coach Jiri on one side and our trainer Gustav on the other.

On a break during the middle of practice, I placed a call from the only pay phone in the corridor that rimmed the Svet gymnasium. I got the direct number to the desk outside Koliar's office. As the phone rang on the other end, I hoped there would be no mistakes this time.

"Good morning. Svet Glass Works. This is Jelina speaking."

"Hi, this is Josef. Jelina, how are you doing?"

"I've been waiting for you to call. You're inconsiderate; maybe you've always been inconsiderate. You never, ever thought of what I wanted in the last five days. I have to get back to work," she said.

I didn't like to hear this. I had never thought of myself as inconsiderate.

"I will make it up to you. Can I take you out tonight?" I said.

"No. You don't know where anything is here," she said.

"I'll follow your lead. You choose the place," I said.

"Ha! Meet me downstairs after I get off work at six."

"So it's a date, then?" I said.

"Yes. I heard you made the team. Don't come in a nightshirt or in athletic wear."

She was ten minutes late. She was wearing a thin white coat that went down to her knees, a red silk top with a black leather collar, black skirt, and black pumps that clacked the concrete as she walked. Even though her movements were more confined because of her shoes, I was drawn to the unusually quick glide of her hips and legs with each stride she took. She looked beautiful with the ruby lipstick on lips. Her hand brushed back the flowing dark brown hair that seemed to want to fall back into her face every minute or so.

Jelina's blue eyes swept over me from head to foot. I was wearing a dark sport coat with matching pants, an open-collared black and a gold striped velour shirt, and black shoes for dancing.

"Wow! You're all dressed up to go out to a discothèque. That's *not* what we are doing," she said.

"Where are we going?" I said.

"It's a surprise," she said. When we reached her light blue Skoda in the lot, she took a red flowered scarf from her purse.

"Put this across your eyes."

"You're kidding, I'm not wearing that. I don't know where anything's at anyway, so why?" I said.

"You said you would follow my lead, no? If you don't, our date is off," she said.

"I'll wear it," I said.

As I got in on the passenger side of the car, I put the scarf up to my face. It was silk and smelled of the same perfume that she wore. She tied it from behind and then pulled it down over my eyes. She fixed it a few times here and there so I couldn't see out.

"Where are we going?" I said as she put the car in gear and we rocketed out of the parking lot.

"You'll see," she said. She laughed as she drove, amused by the scene.

"How do you like Svet?" I said.

"I don't know what you are looking for but it's no Prague, that's for sure. There are too many conformists and Nazis here," she said.

"Are you from Prague?"

"I'm from here but spent four years in Prague when I went to Charles University. I went in when the secret police were still doing their business. In my third year, there was the Velvet Revolution. When I graduated we were one big happy free country," she said.

We came to halt and she turned off the car. She took off my blindfold. I looked around to see we were parked under a railway bridge over a river.

"What's this?

"We're almost there," she said. We walked out to a landing that looked over the river. In a few minutes, I could see we were walking on the brick streets of Svet's old town sector.

"Have you ever been to a marionette theatre before?' Jelina asked as we waited in a line outside an aged limestone block building. There was a smoked eel shop next door.

"What's a marionette?"

"Are you serious? You don't know? They're string puppets. We are seeing *Don Giovanni,* an opera that Mozart wrote. I have seen marionette shows when I was in Prague. But not *Don Giovanni,*" she said.

I scanned out to the church tower that stood higher than every other building in this town, and beyond that the green carpet of spruce running to the rock peaks of Svet Mountain. Everything seemed to glow in the half light of dusk.

"Not bad for our first date," I said.

"This isn't our first date exactly. We could call it our first date and a half since we had that lunch in the conference room," she said.

Once inside the building, we hung our coats in a massive cloak room off to the side near windows. There were coats neatly on hangers. I pictured people taking off their wet boots and putting them on top of the radiators that ran along the wall. Maybe she's was right about the conformity. I decided to shed my sport coat and hung it up. I helped her take off her light long coat and a scarf she had on over her smooth blouse that slid across her skin. We got seats in the middle of the theatre and sat in the dim light. Across the stage was a richly textured red velvet curtain that looked like something I might see if I ever visited Moscow. Discordant notes of practicing violins and horns came from a small orchestra pit below the lip of the stage.

When the tuning from the pit ended, the animated voices of those around us stopped too. People settled in their seats and craned their necks toward the front. All the house lights were shut off and the only light in the whole theatre was a radiant glow that rose from the orchestra pit. As everyone waited in anticipation for the show to begin, I noticed Jelina's flowing dark hair. I suppressed my urge to run my fingers through her mane.

The velvet curtain opened to a four-foot high string puppet, Don Giovanni, sneaking through a 17th century garden in Seville. A masked Don Giovanni crept into the house to seduce a beautiful young woman. I was amazed to see their intricate costumes, especially the fancy hoop dress on her and the detail of building and furniture of the set.

"Where are you from in the United States?" she whispered.

"Chicago."

On stage, the woman's father appeared and challenged Giovanni to a duel. The two puppets battled with swords on the stage while classical music played from the pit. Finally, Giovanni stabbed the father. The woman's father fell to the floor, as did the wooden board from above that controlled the strings. Dead. The puppeteer's two arms hung down over the stage for all to see. He held that position for about a half minute. The longer the puppeteer remained suspended in that position, the louder the cascade of laughter across the auditorium.

I reached for Jelina's hand. She hesitated, then moved it away from my reach. The theatre went dark during the first change of scenes. In the next scene, the nobleman Don Giovanni was attracted to a new woman and tried to seduce her when he got her alone at her wedding celebration. She thwarted him. In an aside, Don Giovanni's assistant announced that the nobleman Don Giovanni had many women across Europe, including 1,003 in Spain alone.

The slit in Jelina's black skirt revealed her thigh for a moment but then she closed it up when she shifted herself in the seat. As the story on the stage went on, I began to feel more uncomfortable. The ghost of the man Giovanni had murdered in the first scene showed up at his door. He asked him to repent from his lustful and womanizing ways.

Don Giovanni refused. The ghost grabbed him by the arm and pulled him down into the ground to a hellish underworld.

After the show, we walked to her car.

"How did you like *Don Giovanni*? Something you'd see in Boston?"

"Chicago, I'm from Chicago. I've never seen anything like it. Those puppets were great and so was the music," I said.

"What about the story? I find it interesting that you say nothing about that," she said.

"The story? Don Giovanni gives guys a bad name. What else needs to be said? I don't even want to talk about this," I said.

"Why are you uncomfortable? What did you expect?"

"It's not exactly the warm American romance I'm used to. This isn't the kind of stuff a couple sees on date night where I come from."

"Is that what we are, a couple? Yes, Don Giovanni was a real creep. Bad name? Maybe they deserve it, yes," she said.

"I don't think so. Each one is different," I said.

"How are you different? Given the chance, you'd act the same as Don Giovanni," she said.

"Not really. You'll see," I said.

"Will I?"

Jelina stood there in front of her car with her arms crossed that I took to be saying "keep away." I figured the date was over and she was going to drive me back to the glass factory.

"You want to go back to my place? I can make you dinner there," she said. I was shocked to hear her say this.

"What are you kidding me? After all you just said."

"Yes, I mean it. You have anywhere else you're going tonight?

This reversal made no sense. I was thrown off balance.

We walked up the stairs to her third story apartment in an old building on the edge of the town.

"I have to tell you, the place is a mess," she said when we reached to the heavy wooden door to her apartment. We entered and it was pretty clear her place wasn't a mess. She grabbed a small afghan from her couch, folded it, and placed it back on to the back of the couch.

She said I must be getting tired of all the meat, dumplings and sauerkraut. She made Thai food. When dinner was over, she looked into my eyes signaling that she was dessert. I had the urge to sweep the tablecloth, dishes and silverware to the floor with my arm.

"Slow down. You act as if the mood is going to leave the room. That it's going out the window," she said. We started to clear off the table.

"Let's move this to the kitchen," I said, as I tried to grab most of the plates and silverware.

"You make mistakes in what you say. You said we should move these over to the curling iron. You mean kuchyne, kitchen," she said.

She took the scarf back out from her purse and handed it to me. As she did, I grabbed her hand and kissed it. She reached up and cupped her hands behind my head. She pulled me toward her. We kissed. I wrapped my arms around her. She jumped up and wrapped her legs around my back as we continued to kiss.

"Put the scarf back on," she said. So I did. She helped me tighten it so I couldn't see out.

"Don't we want to reveal more about who we are?" I said. Why in the hell did I say that? She didn't know my real name.

"Yes, my dear. We have plenty of time to reveal," she said. She took me by her hand and led me to her bed. She reached into my pants. I was ready. She helped me take off all my clothes and I helped her take off hers at a furious pace. As she stretched over to light a candle on a side table, I grabbed her from behind and ran my hands across her back. I kissed her up and down her back. I tasted the subtle sweetness of her smooth skin.

"You're driving me crazy," she said.

"What do you mean?"

"Crazy in a good way," she said. She spun back around so we were face to face.

I tried to reach up to rip off my blindfold. She grabbed my hand.

"No, don't. Keep it on, it'll be more fun this way," she said

I touched the side of her breasts with hands and kissed them. They were just the right size. She kissed my chest and then along my neck. After that she reached down between my legs.

"Wow. Your friend down there is ready to go," she said.

Without saying anything else she went on top and we began. We held onto to each other and kissed, unable to take our mouths off each other's lips. I was as ecstatic as I had ever been and told her repeatedly. She teased me that all my Czech expressions were off. But I could tell she was satisfied too.

We lay next to each other. I took my blindfold off and we gazed into each other's eyes for a moment. I was exhausted but feeling pretty good. Everything was coming together for me; I made the team and had a great night with Jelina. I was really starting to move past just liking her but didn't want to say "love" at a moment like that. What kind of guy will admit that he loves someone after his first date?

"Your spark is gone," she said. "My roman candle from Boston fades and then you begin. It's about what we create together."

"It's Chicago, that's where I'm from," I said in my weakened state.

As the first light of morning illuminated the sky, we kissed each other goodbye and agreed to meet again. I went out the door of her apartment to go back to the glass factory. I didn't want the night with her to end so I was a little sad that I had to get back. I was also troubled because I hadn't revealed the whole story to her: that I was playing my brother to make the team and that my real name was Frank.

CHAPTER TWELVE

THE OPENER

Jiri strode back and forth between us in the tunnel that led to the gym. We were lined up from shortest to tallest, only Vojtech behind me. The song "What a Feeling" from the movie *Flashdance* was drifting under the doors at the top of the ramp. After Jiri gave last-minute instructions to Zedenik and Anton, he continued to pace. He stopped alongside me.

"You better give us something out there, Savek," he said, as he looked intently at me.

I liked being identified by my last name. There was accuracy and truthfulness to it that made me feel he was getting me right. I wondered why fate and the schedule makers had us playing the prior year's Czech Republic champions, Pardubice, that night. It raised the pressure and nervousness within me.

Earlier in the locker room, Milos Koliar had paid us a visit, in which he told us we were the pride of the Czech Republic and that he expected only the best from us. Pardubice played in the newly created Euro East select tournament last year against league champions from across Eastern Europe that included teams from Vilnius and Belgrade.

"Here's your chance Svet," Jiri said. He slapped Zedenik, the first one in the line, in the rump.

Gustav pushed open the double doors at the front of the line. Like bulls entering into an arena, we ran toward the light at the end of the tunnel. Jiri was standing there, making eye contact with each of as we moved past him. When I stepped outside the door, Gustav and some other young guys I'd never seen before were lining our path out. They held out their palms at around knee level. Each of us stretched out our hands and gave them low fives as we moved past.

Cheers and whistling rose up from around the court when we entered. As I ran, I felt like I was floating on air as the *Flashdance* song blasted out from black speakers in the corners. *I'm going to live forever; I'm going to reach for the stars.* The Svet gym was filled with more people than I could have believed. In fact, we had to move through an opening in the crowd to get to the court. It was a party atmosphere as men and women were standing in front of their seats and others were around the court. I could smell popcorn and beer. Many lifted blue plastic mugs in our direction, and I noticed that a good deal of golden lager spilled out as they did so. Others just coming into the Svet complex were filing into the seats higher up. Cheers came floating down from the rafters. I looked up to a group of boys whistling. I followed behind Kolin as we circled around the court. It felt as if all their eyes were on us. We ran around the periphery of the court once and then broke into two lines at the main court: one for lay-ups and the other for rebounding.

Anton received a pass on the right side. He drove down and threw down a two-handed reverse dunk that seemed to delight the crowd. More of my teammates drove to the basket but none could match what Anton had just done. My turn came. Vojtech threw a line drive a pass with a lot of velocity toward my chest. I caught his bullet.

Boos and jeers arose from the crowd. Wow, what a strange reaction from a tough crowd. I drove hard to the basket through the sea of discouraging noise and lofted the ball smoothly up and over the rim for a layup. But then I saw the real object for the jeers: the opposing team had emerged from the visitors' locker room. Dressed in fashionable gold uniforms, the Padubice twelve circled the rim of the court in a single line formation. They roared past us like a squadron of low-flying fighter planes. When they got closer, several of them did cast menacing glares in our direction. Like us, they broke up into two groups at center court for lay-ups toward the far basket.

Then the Pardubice players began their lay-up drill without acknowledging the crowd or even us watching them. They continued on looking straight ahead. Unfazed and confident. I sized up how good they were and noticed they did have a lot of height. I saw three players 6'6" or taller that could pose some problems. Their guards looked very athletic. They could give us trouble on both ends of the court.

Gustav unleashed 10 balls for a period of shooting around. It was good to have a ball in my hands to lessen my nervousness. I shot some, sinking each one, and dribbled the perimeter to loosen up. When the horn blew, we went to the bench. We were to play in just a few minutes. The starters took seats on a flat blue wooden bench. I stood behind them in a circle with the other second unit players. Jiri stood in the middle, speaking in a raised voice over the pounding of a song by London Beat in English. Jiri had spittle on his bottom lip as he talked. Gustav must have noticed it, too because he interrupted Jiri's flow and handed him a cup of water. Jiri immediately set the cup down and continued talking in this moment of excitement and nervousness.

I was right behind Vojtech and watching intently as Jiri drew out a few plays on the clipboard. Vojtech turned around quickly toward me.

"I can feel your breath on my neck. Give me some space, loser," Vojtech said.

I took a step back. Okay, I was crowding in too much in order to hear and see it all—but still, what a jerk. Vojtech would be the guy I would likely replace during the game. I hoped replacing him would happen sooner now because of his attitude. I didn't like Vojtech much since I arrived and this made me not like him even more.

In one way, I was glad that the weight of being a starter was on him, not me. I liked the freedom of coming off the bench. In a big win or defeat I saw myself as a bright spot, a spark of energy coming off the bench. But that had its own kind of pressure. I had less time to get into the flow. And I had to play well and make an impact from the moment I got into the game.

We lined up for the Czech national anthem. The starters stripped off their warm-up pants and shirts. I put my hands in a sea of hands near the bench. "One, two, three, Svet", we all said together. Anton, Zedenik, Vojtech, Rudenic and Kolin took the floor.

"Josef, you sit here next to me," said Jiri. Sitting down on the bench on the other side of Jiri was Gustav.

"This Pardubice is a great test. We have to establish the tempo early," said Jiri over the noise from music and the crowd.

Anton was on Johann Muller, who had won the league's *Best Player* award the season before. Muller had the ball tipped to him. The big German looked to be 6'5" as he brought the ball up on the point. Muller moved awkwardly with the ball, and his youthful reddish face certainty didn't convey that he was the best of anything. Pardubice passed the ball around until Muller found an opening inside for an easy lay-up. Zedenik had the ball in-bounded into his hands. He dribbled the ball up the floor with Muller covering him chest to chest. Anton freed Kolin by setting a screen. Kolin used it well and moved across the middle when a bounce pass came in his direction. It reached his fingertips and was swiped away into the hands of a player with a gold Pardubice shirt. The action moved back and forth and was filled with missed shots on both baskets.

A missed shot by Muller went through Kolin's hands to the Pardubice off guard, the shortest guy on the floor. He went up with the offensive rebound for two points. "That's terrible," said Jiri.

Before I really registered how badly this game was beginning, the scoreboard, *our* scoreboard showed us behind, 18-6.

"Get in for Kolin," said Jiri, as he hit my side with his hands. He never looked away from the action on the court as he spoke.

"Give us something," he said as I stripped off my warm-ups and ran over to the scorer's table. I kneeled near the table and waited.

Kolin was covering a 6'8" guy who was their tallest player and that Sasquatch looked pretty good. I resolved to keep my body on his to slow him down. The referee signaled a stop long enough to allow me to run out to Kolin and replace him. "Savek in for Vladar," said the announcer. I could hear cheers from the crowd.

"Kolin, I'm in for you," I said.

I reached out to slap his hand but Kolin didn't co-offer his. He shook his head in disbelief.

"Kolin, I'm in." I said, as I motioned with my thumb over my shoulder toward the bench.

"Why?" he said looking beyond me as if to Jiri and everyone in the stands. Then his shoulder collided with mine.

"What's your problem?" I said. He ran back to the bench with a look of disgust on his face. What a moody teammate.

I positioned myself between my man and the basket. The referee handed the ball to Muller underneath the basket. Sasquatch pushed at my back to get in position but I pushed back harder, which successfully sealed him off. Muller faked a pass inside and threw a long curving pass beyond the three-point circle. His teammate in the backcourt caught it. He drove three strides and launched a shot from way out. The ball had a perfect arch on it and when it reached the target, it rippled through the net into my hands. That was too easy for them. I inbounded it to Zedenik and ran past him to set up the offense.

"You better do something in here Savek," said Anton, in a tone that mimicked Jiri's voice and mocked me.

Anton had to get serious—we had a game to play.

"Use my screen here," I said. I went down and crossed my arms in front of my body and planted my feet in front of Anton's man. It didn't free Anton, as his man stayed close on defense.

For the next stretch of action, Rudenic missed a ten-footer. Anton rebounded it and slam-dunked it for two points. I could feel the momentum shift in the gym as I ran up the floor. We were down 29-20. I found the Sasquatsch man I was assigned to cover and battled to push him out from the block where he wanted to set up. We kept battling for position so fiercely it was just a matter of time before the referees signaled a foul on one of us. Muller passed into him but because I was covering him so closely, I forced him to pass it back out. The ball moved around the perimeter until a shot went up from 12 feet out. I moved into rebound position where I guessed it was coming off. The shot missed and just before I before I could grab it, a hand came over mine sending the ball down through the rim for a tip dunk. I looked around and saw Muller.

"Welcome to the Czech Republic, rookie," said Muller from behind as I ran back down the court. I looked over to the sideline for a second and saw Jiri looking out to me with a poker face. On our next possession, I got an offensive rebound and went up for a shot from four feet out and Sasquatch rejected the ball into Muller's hands for a fast break layup. I looked again to see Jiri shaking his head and heard him cursing. I felt discouraged about getting my shot blocked but I pushed my legs harder, running back on offense.

Zedenik dribbled the ball up the floor against Pardubice's yellow-shirted defender, who was about his same height of 6'1". He had a determined look on his face as he raised his three fingers to start the offensive set in action. Number three. It was what Jiri called the "Stonewall play" because it isolated Anton for a shot behind a double screen. Vojtech and I moved together to set up a shoulder to shoulder barrier on the side. Anton received a pass behind it and hit a smooth bank shot off the board as Muller tried to crash through our shoulders. I wondered why I felt so good after this basket and as I ran down the court I knew the reason: it was the first time I ever worked together with these two guys on the first team. They allowed me to contribute and it was successful.

As we ran the offense in the minutes before halftime, I burst out to the wing where I was wide open and a dribbling Zedenik looked at me and passed the other way. A moment later, I was wide open underneath the basket but Anton held the basketball on the wing.

Jaroslav would have passed it in each case. I was open again as I came to the free throw line. Three times in a row I was open and nothing. No passes to me. Instead Zedenik tried an impossible pass as he bounced the ball into a closely covered Rudenic on the block. He couldn't do anything with the ball, then he got it stolen. I was frustrated by the selfishness of Zedenik and Anton.

It must have been their planned strategy not to pass to me. They were trying to make me a non-factor so that Jiri wouldn't put me in the game. Or maybe they didn't have confidence in me. I had never played with the *first* unit before. When the buzzer sounded that half was over, we were behind 52-38. I had no points, seven rebounds, and my man had only one basket on me.

As Jiri addressed the team in the locker room, he scanned back and forth to the whole team.

"We have to do a better job on defense. Muller is killing us," said Jiri looking at the scorebook. "He has 17 points already. We've done all this work on defense for the few weeks. 52 points is ridiculous. We're better than this," said Jiri.

As we walked back upstairs, I could hear Anton talking to Jiri.

"Why did you take Kolin out for so long?" said Anton.

"He was dragging out there. Josef is a better match up on that guy," said Jiri.

"He hasn't done much of anything," said Anton.

"We need his defense. Maybe it will give Kolin a push," said Jiri.

"Kolin needs to be in there, not the American," said Anton.

When we came out of the tunnel, the crowd gave the team an ovation but it felt like sympathy more than anything else. Jiri reinserted the starting lineup with Kolin back in.

I took a seat on the bench next to Jiri to watch the second half. After Pardubice won the tip and advanced it up the floor, Anton stole the ball. As he drove to the basket for a break away a Pardubice player upended him from behind near the free throw line. A hush and then boos directed to the Pardubice culprit came over the gym. After a few moments Anton got up from the floor and hit two free throws on the foul. Anton limped back on defense. Jiri signaled to get his attention and asked if he wanted to come out. Anton shook him off with an angry determination on his face.

Muller dribbled up against the full court press that Jiri devised at the break: Zedenik and Rudenic up front, Anton and Vojtech at half court, and Kolin defending the long pass to the Pardubice basket. The press slowed down the quick push that Pardubice used to attack the basket in the first half. With furious harassing energy from Svet, Muller and his ball-handling partner began to hesitate for a split second before passing up the floor. It was starting to work. Once we fell back on defense, the Pardubice five began to take shots with a Svet hand in their face and from farther out than they wanted. With ten minutes to go in the game, Jiri called a time out. I slapped Zedenik's back as he came to the bench. Zedenik shook his head like he didn't want to be touched. What's with this guy? We had cut Pardubice's lead down to 5 points, 64-59. We were very much in the game despite our mistakes and tentative movement. Jiri signaled for me to check into the game for Kolin, who had sweat pouring off his red face. Milos, who stood behind the bench, called to Jiri. He said Kolin should stay in.

"Josef, sit down. Kolin will be staying in," said Jiri. I hoped this backfired because Kolin was tired, anyone could see that. I decided to focus on Kolin as the team retook the floor. Zedenik inbounded the ball into Anton. I felt tension in the air as Anton advanced the ball up the floor with a rhythmic bounce that stood out from all the background noise. Anton passed it back to Zedenik who pushed his body hard to the basket. Pardubice collapsed on him and he passed it out to Anton. He threw it to Rudenic, who launched a ten-footer off the wing. It went in and out. Pardubice quickly rebounded the ball and drove back on the fast break. I watched Kolin playing decently out there. Amid a sea of players Kolin came up with a rebound on very next play. On offense, he set a pick for Zedenik that led to an open three-point basket. On another he got a pass inside from Anton that he missed but got the rebound to put in back in for a score. Kolin still had something left after all. With six minutes to go we were still in the game trailing Pardubice 77-73. Jiri signaled me into the game for Kolin. I raced by the scorer's table and on to the floor. Again, Kolin didn't want to come out when I got to him. He ran to the bench looking right at Jiri shaking his head at him to show his displeasure. I was tired of the drama.

Muller drove up the floor to the wing and looked inside to Sasquatch. But I was fronting their big man. Muller held the ball high up and lobbed it just over my outstretched hands. It reached its target as Sasquatch went up for a shot and was hammered from the side by Charles. After his two successful free throws, Zedenik passed up to Anton who shot from 20 feet out. The ball came off to me. Sasquatch hit my hip as I powered the ball over the rim and in. My first basket and I was fouled. A cacophony of cheering burst out from across the gym. As I walked up to the free throw line, I knew I was battling not only the other team, but many of the doubters on my own team. I shot from the line; it bounced once on the front of the rim and in to complete the three point play. It felt good to do that.

Pardubice's Muller cracked open an eight-point lead with a long three point shot with Anton in his face. After a missed shot from Anton, Muller hit another three that quieted the gym to near silence with the clock reading 1:52 to go in the game. Zedenik's face was drained of color. As Jaroslav came in the game for Zedenik, I thought Jiri should have made this substitution earlier. Jaroslav was as good a guard as Zedenik if not better. As Jaroslav dribbled the ball up the floor, we looked at each other. There was a glimmer of hope to make it close. I got into position on the offense. The ball moved around the perimeter and Rudenic drove the baseline for a short jumper that went in. New Pardubice faces came into the game, but it was Muller who single-handedly held open the double-digit lead. The clock stopped with 19 seconds left as Muller went to the free throw line. I knew it was over. Fans were filing out of the gym. We had disappointed them and wondered if they would ever come back. Muller hit both free throws and Jaroslav drove the court against intense pressure from a gold-shirted player. He looked to me and fired a pass that I took and drove to the basket for an easy score.

The final horn signaled and I looked up at the scoreboard read Pardubice 78, Svet, 69.

"That's discouraging," I said to Anton.

"Yes, Jiri caused it. He put you bastards in," said Anton.

"No, that's not it," I said.

We could have won it if we had more time in there, not less. We lost with the first team and doing it their way.

I went to the sea of players that were on the floor to shake their hands. Muller had a smile on his face as he shook my hand. He and I both noticed Anton and Vojtech leaving to the locker room shaking no one's hand. I shrugged my shoulders.

"Poor sports?" said Muller.

"Yes, you're right with that," I said.

"Too bad. Your team could be very good," said Muller.

Muller's word's encouraged me. I also suspected Muller wanted to soften me up. We would play at Pardubice on the road trip in a few weeks. When I got to the bottom of the stairs and walked down the corridor to the locker room, Rudenic was leaning against the wall in silence looking up at the cobwebbed copper pipes along the ceiling. Kolin, who leaned sweating against the wall, gave me a dirty look as he neared the locker room. Anton slammed his foot against the door of my locker.

"That's mine," I said.

"Sorry," said Anton, half-heartedly. Then he said something to me that I couldn't hear.

Standing in the locker room door I felt like stepping out into the hallway. But a hand on my back pushed me back in. Looking back with a flash of anger, I saw it was Jiri. Gustav and the crush of the rest of the players were behind him.

"Josef, come on let's try to get everyone one in here for a team talk," said Jiri.

I had no choice but to step in toward Anton and the rest of the players in the place that looked and smelled more like a tomb than a locker room. I saw an opening on the wood bench between Anton and Jaroslav. As I moved toward it, Anton removed the gym shoes between them and filled in the space with his body. I didn't want to get into it with Anton so I found standing space in the doorway leading to the dripping showers.

"39 points. We gave 39 points to Muller tonight. We're better than that," Jiri said. "But that's just the half of it. We didn't execute like we have in practice. They come in here and pressure us and have us play a different game. You better be ready for practice tomorrow morning at 9:30 because we are going to improve."

"Especially you, Savek. No one on this team can afford to rest unless his name happens to be Muller. Be ready to run like you've never seen," said Jiri.

After a shower, I walked through the near-empty gym. A few people were still lingering in groups around the gym. There were some crushed paper cups in a section of the bleachers that the janitorial people hadn't got to yet. I walked over to pick up a blue ball of paper in the stands. Unfolding it, I scanned the program and a list of Svet names to see at the bottom Josef Savek Forward, Chicago, U.S.A. Under Pardubice I saw the name Johann Muller, Guard, Hahndorf, Germany. I crumbled it back up and hurled it in the stands. I walked out to the court and stood underneath the orange rim that looked so much higher than 10 feet. Was all this beyond me? It seemed so easy for Muller to throw down that dunk over me up there. Was this the same basket where the Satchquatch rejected my shot to Muller? Yes. Isn't this the same place where I scored that three-point play? Yeah. What a day it was.

After practice the next day, I went into Svet for lunch at Klaus restaurant where they seated me in the smoke-free area. While cigarette smoke from the adjacent smoking section drifted over, I ordered up a steak covered with a mushroom cream sauce along with a side of potatoes and pickled red beets. After lunch I phoned my parents from the darkened hallway that led in and out of the restaurant. My mother was happy I made the team and that I was doing well. I switched between speaking English and Czech throughout my conversation. When people coming into the restaurant heard me speaking English, they noticed. If anyone had a second language in Svet, it was German or Russian. No one there could speak English it seemed. An older couple coming in stopped in their tracks in the narrow hallway to listen to me talking in English as I talked with my father. The man gave me a nudge in the ribs and enthusiastically shook my hand.

As I stood with the phone to my ear, I wanted acceptance from my father. His oldest son was a professional basketball player and in his homeland, no less. I expected his concerns would evaporate, that I wasn't as good as my brother and that I would likely be caught for switching. My father was still hung up on the fact that any success I had was illegitimate and that the whole venture was silliness. He asked to hear about the first game so I gave a synopsis of what happened the night before. The guy was judgmental of my role in the game and said I needed to play better the next game. With that kind of response, I decided to let some time pass before I called him again.

Later that day Coach Jiri picked me up in his black Skoda outside the glass works. We stopped and parked on the side of the street near the main church. He and I got out and entered a cemetery. A man was raking red and orange leaves near a wrought iron gate.

"Coach, tough loss last night but considering who you faced that wasn't so bad," said the man, who leaned the rake.

"It was plenty bad, we should have beaten them," Jiri said. "Viktor, I'd like to introduce you to Josef, our newest player."

We shook hands. The man wasn't very tall, maybe 5'9", but he had the presence of a man much taller, with wide shoulders and burly hands.

"He's been working as caretaker of this place for—what has it been Viktor— twenty years?" said Jiri.

"Something like that," he said. "I was there last night, came late but wanted to see the two new foreign ones, the Bulgari and our American. Josef, nice job out there but I have to say you're not the scorer they say you are."

"Maybe not, but we have plenty of scorers. There's a guy on the bench, Jaroslav Matura, to watch, too. He didn't play much last night, but he's one that'll help us light up the scoreboard. We were outrebounded last night; I think that's why we lost but I think I can change that," I said, which was the same thing I said to Jiri on the car ride over.

"What do you think about that, coach?" the man said.

"I think Josef's on to something there. Both he and Jaroslav can give us something special that even the first team doesn't, I've seen it," Jiri said.

I was relieved to hear Jiri acknowledge that. Jiri lightened up when he was away from the basketball court and the glass factory.

"I sure hope so. We don't want a repeat of last season or it could mean the end to all of you," Viktor said.

"Typical coming from a man that stencils gold leaf lettering on headstones and digs graves for the dead part-time," Jiri said.

They laughed and we left him to his work. We walked on a gravel path past the plots. Birds chirped in linden trees that cast darkness on certain headstones. Jiri motioned for me to stay with him and I have to admit, I wasn't going anywhere else. Jiri explained how each family had its own plot. The cemetery was very well kept up, so Viktor was doing his job. We walked past a couple on the path. They had three kids with them holding hands: a little girl dressed up in a colorful dress and carrying a basket of flowers, and the two boys in identical red corduroy coats, all talking with their parents. They walked like they were comfortable with the place. We came upon a plot with a large granite marker marked Rodina Hasek. Rodina means family.

Red votive candles burned on the ledge as if they had been visited earlier by someone. There were six gravestones in the area behind that. There was a golden glow of light in this place at that dusk hour and even warmth to it.

"Here's my first coach. Hello, Dad. How are you?" Jiri said.

"When did your father die?" I said.

"Too early. I came back home to coach this team a few years ago and then he died six months after that. We can talk, Dad?" he said.

"What does your father say?"

"You just said "ocet," which is "vinegar," when I think you mean "otec," which is "father." You mixed them up. My father had no vinegar in him. He wanted more for his life and could've been bitter. Instead he was grateful and taught me to appreciate all this."

Jiri's father could have taught mine a thing or two. My dad was *Mr. Vinegar.*

After a few minutes Jiri and I exited the cemetery through another gate that led to the church. We passed through a courtyard and entered the place of worship. There was the yellow and white papal flag to the side of the altar. Another caretaker let us enter a set of stairs to the tower. When we got near the top we passed a bell tower that chimed every hour. Jiri explained that it has always been in operation since the church was built in the time of the Hapsburg's Austro-Hungarian Empire. It even rang during the Soviet era when they secularized the church and made it into a storehouse. When we reached the top of the square tower, we stood and looked out from the highest spot in the town. We had four windows that faced out in each direction from up there. We weren't the only ones.

A woman and man leaned against the guardrail. They didn't even pay attention to us. He had his arm around her shoulders as they looked out from one of the vantage points. Jiri and I went to the opposite side of where he said was the best view. I could see a lot from up there: Central Square, three bridges over the river, reddish brown rooftops with dirty gutters, and Svet Mountain in the distance, which I was coming to know well.

"It's not easy coaching this team. There's pressure from all fronts. Our owner Koliar, fans, and even those townsfolk that don't come to the games. Plus, I've got to keep all the egos in check, especially the starters," Jiri said, leaning over the guard rail.

"That's for sure," I said, wondering where Jiri was going with this.

"I have trouble fielding the best team against these bigger powers that can offer more. Pardubice's Muller is great, but what makes them win is their strong bench. We have a solid first team and even stronger bench. With that combination, who can stop us?"

"How come you didn't play more of that bench last night then?" I said.

"You're no superstar like Muller or Anton, but you can do good things. Show us more of what you can do and you'll get your time," he said.

"Do I have a chance to break into the first team and start?"

"I don't see that happening," he said, and he recognized that wasn't the answer I wanted to hear. He continued, "Milos wants this current group to represent us as the team's starters. Plus, in my opinion, the battle between the first and second squads has been a good thing. It makes us better."

"How can that be? You mean I don't have a chance at all to start on the first team? That's disappointing," I said.

"That's the way it is and will be. Koliar wants that. But we need you, Josef. Keep playing your way and you can make an impact. You already have," Jiri said.

When we turned to leave, I saw Shantelina with a guy up there.

"Dobry den, how are you, Coach?" Shantelina said. She strode over to Jiri and me.

"Shantelina, good to see you. Hello, Wencel," Jiri said.

They shook hands in a friendly manner. This man was handsome and well dressed. He was about 6 feet tall. I shook the hand of this guy with a helmet of curly brown hair.

"Josef, this is Wenceslas," she said. Shantelina and I smiled at each other. What an awkward moment. She peered deeply into my eyes.

"Is this your boyfriend?"

"Yes, he is." She said, casting her smile toward him.

I was shocked that she had a boyfriend, especially after our interaction in the restaurant. And that fact that she and I had set a date to have dinner. Wenceslas looked like a nice enough guy.

Shantelina and I looked into each other's eyes. I broke my gaze to feign that I wasn't interested. Then I was afraid avoiding looking at her would noticeable, too. So I tried to divide my attention among the three of them as naturally as possible.

"Do you two know each other?" said Wenceslas.

"We met for the first time a few days ago. I offered him my congratulations on making the team. Josef is the exciting new American player on the team. He's brought good things already—right, Coach?"

Jiri nodded yes. He and Wenceslas stood there observing for a moment like spectators.

As we walked down the stairs, I was intrigued by Shantelina.

"I've seen them together the last few years. He's a Czech success story. He works for an Austrian wine conglomerate and they have him travelling. Although I'd say he's not moving very fast with her. He's not stayed around Svet long enough to make it work. That's my opinion," said Jiri.

"I have to tell you something. She's taking me to hear parlandos in a few days. I thought it was a date," I said

"This interest from women, it's expected. You're American. Shantelina is a fine girl. She's being nice, that's all. Besides Josef, we want you to focus on the game, not women."

"Is that the team policy?"

"No woman is worth breaking curfew for and getting suspended. I believe in you."

"I know. You want me to give my best and care about what we are trying to create here."

"If you listen to me, your time will come."

CHAPTER THIRTEEN

JELINA

We were to meet at a restaurant that she suggested for its good German breakfasts. I scanned the dining room but didn't see her, so I took a seat at a table for two in the corner. After several minutes of pretending interest in a collection of tarnished wooden ski poles and snow shoes on the wall, I went out through some French doors to the patio. She wasn't there, either. No one was and I saw why: it was too cold that early.

I walked past empty groupings of square tables to a thin-gauge metal railing that rimmed the edge of the brick deck. Down at the bottom of a steep embankment was the river in its late summer glory. Mallards swam in a side pool, seemingly unconcerned with the main force of the current that roared past. Blue-green water queued upstream at a level that was a few yards from the top of the bank. It was moving in such force that it seemed as if the all the snowmelt in the entire southern flank of the Krkonoše Mountains had been released.

Someone tapped my shoulder. I turned and there was Jelina with a smile. She kissed my cheek. She had those sexy curves that her enveloping coat couldn't hide and smelled of that distinctive perfume she wore the last time we saw each other.

"Hello, Josef. Come, let's go inside," Jelina said.

She stood about 5'10" and carried herself well. She was a good four inches taller than Shantelina. So she won in the height department. And in the availability category, she didn't appear to have a boyfriend.

Our waiter placed a bread basket on the table. It had six or seven kinds of bread that were mostly dark, grainy and fresh baked. He gave us our menus.

"These aren't necessary," she said giving the menus back. "I'll have the Münicher Breakfast and so will my friend. Are you okay with that, Josef?"

I nodded yes to the waiter.

When the waiter left, I said, "Tell me about some of your past boyfriends."

"None of them have been right. This could be good. I saw that the other night."

When she left to the restroom, I noticed a piece of paper on the floor under her chair.

It had all these categories on it: Funny, Handsome, Healthy, Athletic, No Alcoholics, Neat, Smart, Exciting, Czech. It had several of the words circled. All the things she was looking for, I assumed. Including the things I had and didn't have.

She came back to the table looking great.

"I think you dropped this list."

"You weren't supposed to find that." Based on her reaction, this was her dating criteria list.

"Consider it captured," I said, handing it back to her.

"You must think I'm heartless."

"It's great. It's what makes you interesting. How do I measure up?" I said.

"What do you mean? On the list items?"

"On your check list," I said.

"You are nearly everything I wanted. Higher than anyone else I've met. Except you're not Czech."

"I am Czech. What do you mean?" I said.

"You're American. That's how I see you."

"What's the difference?" I said.

"It doesn't matter. It's not important," she said.

"Have you used this list with others?"

She shook her head no.

I wasn't sure I liked this.

A waiter barged in with several different kinds of cheeses including brie, Swiss, cream cheese, ham and a small plate of sausages. Then a dish of boiled eggs. She seemed happy for the interruption.

Finally cherries, peaches and apples were brought. I didn't go overboard like I normally would.

"This restaurant brings in the German tourists. They come here to ski. Now that East and West Germany are reunited, there are opportunities to capitalize on that. Dresden is only 90 kilometers from here," she said.

"Sounds like you have a stake in this place," I said.

"I like it. The Germans haven't really come in big enough numbers yet but they will. There's potential here, just like with you, Mr. American Tourist. I'm just starting to get to know you," Jelina said.

"Only I'm not a tourist," I said, knowing I butchered cestovni, the Czech word for tourist.

She laughed at my pronunciation.

"You can't even speak this language. You're a not a Czech, you're a tourist who will be on to some other place when someone or something else strikes your interest," she said.

Jelina was right about one thing: my Czech was broken. Most of the time my efforts to speak Czech were good. But when I had to communicate quickly I felt my Czech failing.

"No, I'm here to stay," I said in English, then repeated it in Czech.

"It's you who needs to decide. On me, on this place, everything," she said.

"This place? I'm here and on the team so that settles that. But as for us, I just got here. We have to continue to get to know each other," I said.

"I know it's early for that. Finished, Josef?"

"Yes. Thanks for the breakfast," I said.

I stood and put on my coat. She stood as I zipped up.

"Remember that day when you were cut from the team? I was there with you the whole time through all of it."

"I do. You helped me." I said.

"I got you on this team, spoke to Milos about this."

"Jaroslav did. He's the one that helped make it happen, Jelina," I said.

"Is that what you think? That it was only him?"

"Jelina, you helped me. I know it. And I'm grateful, but what do you want from me?" I said.

"I'm interested in you. You are an intriguing man."

"Here is some money for the bill," I said, "I insist."

She waved it off like I'd insulted her. She turned her face toward me. We held each other for a few moments and kissed.

"See you soon," she said.

"Yes, that would be great," I said. But I didn't really feel it. My leaving this date felt awkward, that's for sure.

Then I left out the door of the restaurant. I angled down to a ribbon of gray gravel that traversed under the river bridge. A light misty rain fell as I forged ahead through it.

I had a Czech girlfriend and advocate. I needed that in Svet, but if my relationship with her ended; she could become my worst enemy.

I saw that the path ended and there was no way to continue on it. So I turned back and realized it was leading back to the restaurant. There was no way I wanted go back there. So I jumped over a metal fence and through a patch of briar. I forged ahead but found myself ensnarled in the full wrath of the thorny shrubs. One grabbed hold of my ankle. I pulled away the woody stalk but the damage was done. It ripped through my beige sock. That hurt. Eventually I stomped my way out to the edge. And out to the main road that led me away from the restaurant.

CHAPTER FOURTEEN

DIVINITY AT HRADEC KRÁLOVÉ

Later that day, we were on our way to Hradec Králové for an evening game against the Hradec Králové sportsclub. Gustav was behind the wheel of the team bus. Our black-haired driver with the short mustache did many things as our assistant coach and trainer, but it was his role as the team's official driver that he seemed to relish more than any other. I couldn't forget how eager he was to sprint me to the Svet station when I missed the cut the week before.

I felt foolish that I spent the last week thinking about Jelina. Even the other part of my life, playing basketball for the Svet team, was in question. I had made the team but needed to play well that night; much better than my first game.

Hradec Králové was geographically the closest team to us, only 110 kilometers away. Gustav took us on backroads that were mud in spots and gravel in others. We passed a small castle with a round tower on the top of the hill. Farther up the road, there was another castle with square abutments on another hill. I wished I could slow down time to visit them that very afternoon but I would think too much about the Jelina situation. Did I want her as a girlfriend? Maybe not. I had to get it out of my mind. After all, I had a basketball career to attend to. We forged ahead toward Hradec Králové, which in English literally means Queen's Castle.

We entered the small city and breezed through residential neighborhoods. Then Gustav maneuvered the bus down a street that ran along the outside perimeter of an ancient wall. We continued on that ring road along the buttress. When we pulled up to a stop sign, Gustav gunned the engine ahead. Jiri stood up and directed Gustav to turn right.

"But coach, the gym is straight ahead," Gustav said.

"I know. I know. I want Josef—our newcomer—to see the old town section. This is all a first for him," Jiri said.

"It's a wasteful diversion," said Gustav. "An hour from now, I'll let Milos pummel you with questions on why we are late."

"I insist. There is time in life. Just drive down the center like a point guard," Jiri said.

Gustav jerked the steering wheel hard to one side. Immediately our enormous diesel machine whined as it performed a right hook pattern. We surged up a steep abutment. There were only a few feet of clearance on both sides as we threaded the narrow opening.

"This was one of the two gates into the castle complex. It was originally a hill fort that Celtic tribes and Slavs built here. That was thousands of years ago but it's still there in good shape, only fortified in the Middle Ages and enlarged," said Jiri to me.

"Thousands of years ago? Professor Coach, can we get out for a pilsner at one of these hotels?" said Anton.

"No stopping. We have a game to get to," Jiri said.

The old town section of Hradec Králové looked inviting. Bars, restaurants and hotels were on both sides of us as we motored through the neighborhood. We crossed through a gate on the other side and proceeded along the wall. Then our team bus reached an oval-shaped arena and we pulled off into a special roped-off parking area.

As I stepped off the bus, my feet sunk into gravel. Millions of black and white stones the size of peas. Each of us had the burden of carrying team gear besides our sports bags. Jiri handed me an enormous fishnet bag stuffed with 11 basketballs. I tossed it over my shoulders onto my back. We moved together like a platoon of soldiers on patrol. As we trudged along, our feet crunched. The noise that we generated sounded as if we were marching across snow. My mind associated that with walking across the snow on the path to my parents' home on California Avenue. Our trek seemed endless as the ground was laden with this deep base of gravel that extended all the way to the front door of the gym.

Once inside, the complex was chilly both in the hallways and also entered the main arena. Monster-size banners hung down over the court advertising Hradec Králové's professional ice hockey team. The roped-off path that led to the basketball court was like a bridge over ice. I looked down at a frozen ground on both sides of us. The basketball court was situated on top of the ice rink.

We turned away from the court in front of us and climbed some stairs up into the seating around the court. Some kind of junior league game was being played immediately before our game. So our Svet team sat down to watch. It was amusing to see these teenage players who had the bodies but not the brains to play the game. Missed shots and overlooked opportunities abounded. I sat alongside Jaroslav, our flashy guard who helped our second unit produce such great things. But what did it matter if we didn't get a chance to play?

A man and woman sitting next to us smiled at me like they knew me. It was as if they had been watching me while I was watching the game.

"Are you fans of one of these teams?" I said.

"Yes, our son is on this junior league Hradec Králové team. He's number 54," said the woman, pointing out to the floor.

I scanned the court and found number 54. Just the way that kid of 16 or so ran the floor stood out. He was athletic and muscular, around 6'5".

"There he is, a forward out there," I said.

Jaroslav tapped my shoulder. He pointed to the scoreboard.

"Look at the clock, Josef. It's time to go," said Jaroslav.

"I know," I said.

"We hope he'll play on the next level someday. What about you? I detect a dialect. I know you play with Svet, but where are you from?" said the woman. She glanced at me and then looked back toward the action on the court.

Their son posted up, then received an inbound pass on the block, faked one way, and spun the other with the ball. He missed the power layup but snatched his own rebound and put it back off the glass for the score.

"The United States. This is my first season here."

His parents interrupted. The father jumped to his feet and the mother cheered their son.

"He's got an impressive little drop step there. And he's aggressive. That's a good sign," I said.

"He's going to be good," said the father.

"Don't tell me Chicago or Pittsburgh?" said the woman.

This couple reminded me of a younger version of my parents, only the father was tall and the mother was much smaller.

"Let's go," said Jaroslav, who was already in the aisle moving toward the locker room.

"Chicago. Pleasure to meet you! He's pretty good," I said. I stood up to leave. They both stood to shake my hand.

"We will follow you, next game and over the season," they said warmly.

When Jaroslav and I arrived down in the locker room, everyone was almost ready.

"You're late, you two. Hurry up and get ready," Jiri said.

While we were getting ready, Jiri began his pregame talk.

"I wouldn't trade one of you for Muller or anyone in this league. Pardubice has been playing together for three years and in that time has had five loses. HK has been playing together even longer, but they're a bunch of old men. We can beat them. They do have a new American player, Darryl Divinity, but he shouldn't hurt us. Don't worry about any of them. Just play your game tonight."

As we came out on the floor, Hradec Královė did look older. Several of their players were pushing 40. More important, they looked much less athletic than Pardubice. Their new guy Divinity was African-American and looked about 6'3" or 6'4". When the buzzer sounded and the referees walked over to our bench, Jiri looked up from our huddle. He tried to give the starters last minute instructions about our strategy to control the tempo from the beginning. Then our starters took the floor for the opening tip. I sat next to Jiri on the bench. Hradec Královė's off guard, a wiry guy with salt-and pepper hair, received the ball off the opening tip. He came down and scored on an arching shot over Anton to put HK in the lead.

"Divinity is only the third black player we've seen," Jiri said.

"Divinity is also a word in English," I said.

"What does it mean?"

"Divinity is God-like, something extremely good," I said.

"For our sakes, let's hope this guy is not like his name tonight," Jiri said, hitting me on the thigh, but looking at me for the first time as he said it.

Soon after that Divinity stole the ball from Zedenik. He dribbled back to our basket and scored on a lay-up. A smooth finger roll over the lip of the orange rim. HK's crowd let up a cacophony of cheers and whistles. I couldn't believe how quickly we were down. It was clear to see in these opening minutes that Divinity had first-rate skills on both ends of the floor. My brother and I were good at shutting down guys like this. I'd faced black scoring machines with awesome ability on nearly a nightly basis during my North Park College years, so I wasn't intimidated.

As the Hradec Královė team scored, we missed on our end of the floor. They were leading 16-6 before Jiri called a timeout. Hradec Královė widened their lead after several more minutes of play. Divinity was making the difference; he was scoring and passing them to a huge lead that would be hard to come back against. Then the action seemed to shift from a one-sided HK annihilation when Anton started scoring. He hit three shots in a row, the last one being a dunk. That brought us all to our feet on the bench. But it seemed to be a ripple that was not slowing Hradec Králové. My frustration was rising because I wasn't playing. While Divinity and Kolin were running alongside each other, I heard Kolin call Divinity something I couldn't believe.

The N Word.

This was plain wrong. And ignorant. Our team's biggest jerk had stooped to a new low in taunting Divinity. I had never heard Kolin speak English before. I wanted to apologize to Divinity.

Divinity ignored Kolin's insult. He focused on the game, and on the next play he received the ball and launched a shot that kissed off the backboard glass for another two for HK.

"Kolin is struggling. I can stop Divinity from scoring," I said to Jiri.

"Let's see what you can do, but go in for Vojtech instead and have Kolin switch to cover Vojtech's man. You cover Divinity on defense," Jiri said.

I checked in. It felt like I was given the assignment of covering my brother on defense. The American on the American. I didn't have anyone else to rely on and no one to help me if I made a mistake. Jaroslav was in the gym but on the bench, and my brother far away. I sidled up alongside Divinity. My goal was to shut him down, period.

"Are you a racist, too?" he said in English as he dribbled on the wing.

"What do you think?" I said, as I looked him in the eyes. I squared up to him on defense. My center of gravity was low and my hand waved in the air to prevent any passes up the middle.

"Yeah, you are. An American, at that. Doesn't matter, I'll beat y'all anyway."

He bolted to the basket and I was with him the whole way. He shot a ten-footer in the lane and it caromed off the rim. I sealed Divinity off and snatched the rebound.

Divinity missed several more attempts during later HK possessions. Amid all this, I envied the confidence Divinity's teammates had in him. I wasn't given that. No one passed me the ball. Instead, I scored on a few offensive rebounds, including one where I drove the baseline and looped in a reverse layup with Divinity on my back. I missed but grabbed it and put it back in for two. Whenever Divinity had the ball, I forced him to miss or pass off. He started to get agitated because his scoring had come to halt.

"Mr. Defense. Is that what they call you? Where are you from?" he said as we ran up the court.

I decided not to answer.

"Not talking? That's fine, too clever," Divinity said.

He wanted to get me talking, to let down my guard, and forget about what I was there to do. My game and the result could speak for itself. Plus, I was cautious of talking to anyone from the United States. They were a threat that could unravel my cover faster than anyone. When the halftime horn echoed across the arena, Hradec Králové's lead was only 34-31. We were back in the game.

"That's the fire we needed, Josef. Great work on Divinity," Jiri said as he slapped my back. We excitedly headed for the visitors' locker room. Jaroslav was keyed up for me too, but I knew he must be having a hard time seeing everything transpire from the bench.

Coach Jiri kept me in the game for the start of the second half and I went back to work to shut down their American star.

"You can't fool with Double D, I'll find another way to smoke your Czech-American ass," he said.

Double D—Darryl Divinity, I got it. But what he didn't know was that my nickname that evening was Double D Plus One. My defense was working. Since I got in the game, their shooting guard and main scorer had only three points, so my efforts were successful. The center of the Hradec Králové wheel was kaput.

Hradec Králové's coach adjusted their strategy in the second half. It was like they were a new team. Their balding blond coach, clad in a brown sport coat and red tie, had his team moving and passing. Divinity still could find no breathing room to score: I made sure of that. But he started to pass with increased accuracy to his teammates. Their baskets began to drop in and we fell behind, 50-41, Kolin used the N-word again. Divinity just smiled this time. Jiri called for a timeout. I looked up to see that 4:22 remained in the game. As we sauntered over the bench, I talked to Kolin.

"Don't call him that. I don't want to hear you say that again," I said.

"Don't tell me what to do, American," Kolin said. Kolin pushed back at me, two hands to the chest.

"That's enough," Jiri said as he stepped in between us.

Jiri looked around and grabbed Jaroslav by the jersey. "Report in for Kolin."

I was happy to hear that.

Back at the bench, Jiri tried to get us to return to the basics again by drawing the motion of the offense with X's and O's on the varnished floor. When he stood up, Coach rubbed out the symbols with his shoe as we retook the court.

As with the Pardubice game, I was battling for my basketball life, so I didn't pay much attention to the crowd, but for a moment I looked up to the family that said they would be watching me. I connected with their eyes for a second. As a result they yelled out to me and put their thumbs in the air as a sign that they liked what I was doing. Someone pulling for me in this crowd! Here I was a visitor in more ways than one and they cheered me on like I was in their family.

With Jaroslav in the game, I had someone backing me up on defense. Jaroslav stole a few of Divinity's passes. He started passing the ball to me on fast breaks, and I scored on a layup and with a five-foot jumper. He had a way of involving everybody, but nobody more than me.

Within two minutes, we narrowed the score to 53-49. Jaroslav's determination on top of what I was doing to Divinity was the difference. Whenever HK missed I was there for the rebound and passed the ball out to Jaroslav. Anton came alive, too. He scored eight out of the next ten points during a run we mounted. We were able to stop HK's frantic attempts to score; all they scored during their possessions was from the free throw line. We took our first lead 59-57 with 40 seconds remaining in the game. If you compared us to boxers in the 15th round of a fight, we were scoring most of the direct hits on our opponent. They were getting a few hits on us but we had captured the momentum. I expected that we were going to win the game but that was interrupted when HK's old man off-guard with the salt-and-pepper hair tossed up an impossible long range shot from behind the three point line. It went in and the HK crowd went crazy. They had the lead back, 60-59.

Jiri quickly called a timeout with seven seconds to go. He devised the stonewall play where Anton would get the last shot. We went back out on the floor and made it happen exactly the way we planned. Jaroslav and I set the wall up 15 feet from the basket. Anton launched a shot from behind our phlanx. The ball was on target and circled inside the rim, but spun out. I battled to get my hands on the ball. But I couldn't. Divinity came down with the rebound and burst out of the pack. He dribbled with a fury toward the corner, eluding everyone. Three of us chased after him to foul him and stop the clock. I reached him first to whack him with my hand but stopped when the final horn sounded.

We lost again. 60-59 was an improvement but a loss nonetheless. Anton shook his head in disgust as he walked off the floor. I was upset with myself for believing our strong play and steady comeback had produced a win before we actually won. Divinity and I shook hands like gentlemen.

"Where did you play in the United States?" he said in English.

"North Park College."

So did my brother.That was the truth.

"North what?"

It's a small Division III school in Chicago. Where did you play?" I said

"I played a couple of years at Niagara University but after that mostly street stuff in Philly until I landed here."

I shook hands with all of HK's players and so did Jaroslav. HK's jubilant head coach made a point to find me as I moved toward the locker room. We shook hands then he placed his hand on my back as we walked.

"Savek, you made it hard on us. Surprised us really. You got to be the best team with a losing record in the league. I wish you well the rest of the season except when we play you next time," their coach said with a laugh.

Jiri had intensity in his eyes as he opened his post game debrief in the locker room.

"We don't like to lose, but there were positives. We can build on them. Josef played well and was very successful against Divinity. Our American showed us all how to rebound and play defense tonight."

I liked hearing what our coach was saying. It was the first time he'd held me up as an example to the rest of the team. It was a sure sign of desperation for a coach to do this. Anton flashed me a glance. Kolin shook his head in disgust. Jiri had just made my job harder and it didn't help build team unity.

"Vojtech, you better watch out because Josef is playing for your job. If he continues to play like he did, he'll have it," Jiri said.

Jiri had crossed the line. It put me on thin ice with my own team, especially because the first team resented me as it was. Plus, it wasn't true; he wasn't going to make me a starter because the team owner didn't want it. He had his starting lineup set.

After showering, we boarded the bus outside the arena. Instead of going back the 110 kilometers to Svet, we were to stay for the night in HK. Jiri held a clipboard and a pen as we rambled along a road into a nearby neighborhood. He looked down at a list of names and addresses.

Jiri had said on the first day that we would stay in homes of friends of Milos and him. But I forgot.

Jaroslav and I were dropped off in front of a house in a residential neighborhood. An older woman around 60 answered the door.

"The room's not available. Stay somewhere else."

"Sorry, do we have the wrong house?"

"Yes, it is correct," said the lady. "We usually have players stay here but not tonight, we're full."

"Could you suggest somewhere else?"

"Maybe the hotels down the street. Sorry."

We went back outside to see if the bus was still there. It was gone. We walked around the city in the night looking for a hotel. We headed to the train station and asked around. We were tired, and eventually we found one place that would take us in.

We dropped our bags at a hotel, Nove Adalbertinum. A flyer at the front desk said the building was built in 1742 as a Jesuit residence until it was converted into a hotel in 1948 for the Communist party guests to the town. High ceilings and drafty rooms. But it was better than nothing.

The next morning we hurried back to the pickup point in front of the house where we were supposed to stay. We made it just when the bus arrived. There was no time to see Hradec Králové. Later that day, we were back in Svet.

CHAPTER FIFTEEN

PARLANDO IN THE CELLAR

"Josef, you surprised me. What can I do for you?" said Jelina seated at her large maple desk in the inner office.

"I received the note. What additional documents would you like me to sign?" I said in Czech. Her insults about my inability to speak Czech came to mind.

"No. I didn't write you a note," she said.

"Coach Hasek passed this me message. You wanted to see me about my contract?" I said, I handed her the note.

"This is not my handwriting. Your contract is all set," she said. But it was in a woman's handwriting. It had to be Jelina.

I sat down in a chair adjacent to her desk. She swiveled and slid toward me so that her knees discreetly touched my thigh.

"Those three flirts in the outer area were talking about you this morning, about your solid performance last night. It's a shame you lost. I could have told them a thing or two about your strong performance," she said touching the top of my hand for a moment.

"There's nothing you wanted me to sign, then?" I said in my labored Czech. She shook her head slowly to indicate no. I stood and exited.

Shantelina, who wasn't there when I passed the outer office area earlier, greeted me with a smile.

"Player American, may I talk to you?" she said in English, motioning with her dark eyes out the door. We stepped out into the low-wattage orange world of the mezzanine walkway that rimmed the main floor of the factory.

"Do we meet tonight?" Shantel said.

She noticed me hesitate.

"I want to show you around Svet. I've made a reservation at the place I mentioned. You asked me, remember?" she said.

"Yes, you mentioned that Moravian-style restaurant. But what about your boyfriend?" I said.

"You are new, I help you. I think it be good to talk. You understand?" she said.

She only spoke to me in English and I liked that. Our secret language.

"Yes, I'd like that," I said.

Milos Koliar appeared from the stairwell and, upon seeing us, sauntered over to make our conference a threesome.

He instructed us to look down to the factory floor. As we did, a few workers opened the door to a massive furnace. From the fires within, two of them slid out a glowing orange block.

"That's molten glass. From that we can fashion at least a thousand goblets," Koliar said in Czech. Then he turned to consider the two of us for the first time.

"Josef, you won't go wrong with her. She's a nice girl," he said in Czech. I wondered if he knew that Jelina and I had possibilities.

"I'm not a girl, I'm a woman, sir," Shantel said.

"You were a girl once," Koliar said.

"Yes, but I would appreciate if you refer to me in the right way. I'm 28," she said.

Koliar was going to say something else but held back. He turned and went into the office.

Shantelina stood in the doorway of the restaurant waiting for me. She was dressed in a long white coat with sleeves that ran halfway down her arms and it was tight at her shoulders.

"This weather is unusual. It's cold and windy and we're only in September," I said in Czech. She unbuttoned her coat slowly, revealing her basic black dress with the puffy sleeves.

"What did you expect? We're in mountains," she said in English, struggling to slide her outer wear off.

"Let me help you with that," I said. I seized the collar of her coat.

"We're on the same parallel as Winnipeg," she said as our extraction efforts worsened.

"Winnipeg, Canada? That's cold."

She jimmied and contorted. I pulled and tugged. We laughed and grimaced. Her snow-white coat from hell didn't want to come off. After a collective pause to catch our breath, we redoubled our efforts. Finally, she slid out. I whisked it away and onto a hanger in the cloak room.

As we walked down a hallway, I could see diners sitting at yellow-linen-covered tables with flickering brown candles through a window. Shantelina took the lead, bounding a step ahead of me. I liked a forward woman that took charge. She didn't have the same sexy curves and strut as Jelina. For that, I was grateful. I didn't want to get drawn in, especially since she had a boyfriend.

A moment later, we were ushered to a table whereupon I pulled out her chair and motioned for her to have a seat. She did, and I pushed it in. I even surprised myself with my manners.

"Condolences for the slip-up today," she said as she settled in her seat across from me. Then she tucked in her white napkin on her lap.

"Slip-up? What do you mean?"

"I sent Coach Hasek the note that asked you to the office. I missed reaching you and you got to Jelina first," she said.

"So that was you? I thought Jelina did it as an excuse to talk," I said.

"Excuse? I don't understand, is there something between you?" Shantelina said.

I paused to consider how I should answer.

"I'm interested in her. We've gone out a few times. She is a nice woman but has very definite standards for the perfect man," I said.

Why did I tell her this? This was supposed to come later over coffee at the end of the main course or maybe never.

"Tell me, do you have girlfriend back in States?" she said.

"Not anymore. Nancy was her name. It didn't work out. I guess I was meant to be here. I wouldn't be surprised if my mother will tell me the family has received an invitation to her wedding."

"You'll find girlfriend soon, I am sure of it. You know those two I work with in the front office, Jitka and Svetlana? The three of us live together in same apartment. We're friends. We've all had bad experiences with players—your teammates, who shall remain nameless. Each developed *stridavy hvala*," she said.

"You three have had a thing for basketball players?" I said.

"No more than you have for secretaries who work in a glass factory's front office," she said.

I laughed at her sharp reply. She had a point.

"You have an unusual way of speaking. Your word for thank you in Czech dekuji is dakujem and your expressions like *stridavy hvala*. Are you Moravian?" I said.

"I'm not Czech or Moravian. I've always been different here because of it," she said.

"Then what are you? You speak Czech and you're respectable with English, too," I said.

"Dakujem. I'm a woman of East. Slovakian. I've lived here five years but foreigner now, thanks to the Velvet Divorce," she said.

I noticed that her eyes were hazelnut brown. It was the second physical thing I liked about her besides her beautiful legs. I remembered that detail from our first meeting.

Two formally dressed violinists playing the music of Smetana and Mozart strolled near us to interrupt the flow of our conversation.

"Have you studied this gigantic menu and know what you want, Shantelina?"

"Yes, I know."

"I'm not familiar with Svet restaurants," I said, "so tell me what you are going to have and then I can just say, `The same for me, please.'"

"Certainly. I will order sautéed liver with raw tuna to begin," Shantelina said.

"Maybe I *should* take a peek at that menu," I said.

The violinists moved away to other tables.

"I'm sorry, Player American, that was joke. Slovak's humor. Now to tell you the truth: I'm having Moravian-style pork with roasted potatoes if our waiter should come."

I found myself laughing. Shantelina started to laugh out loud.

"You make the strangest sounds when you laugh," she said. The crowd sitting nearby was giggling, which made Shantelina laugh louder. Pretty soon the whole café was laughing. I looked at the crowd laughing at me and suddenly burst out laughing so hard that tears began to pour out of my eyes.

"Thank you, Shantelina," I said wiping my eyes. "I haven't laughed, or cried like this in a long time."

"It's good to laugh. Good for your liver, good for your heart. So now, Player American, what should we do about ordering? We can't wait any longer."

"Yes, you're right, we're both starving," I said as I got up and walked through the crowd and straight into the kitchen area where least five or six people were cooking food. Others were washing dishes.

"My name is Josef Savek and I've just come here from America," I said in Czech. The violinists in the restaurant stopped playing. It seemed that everyone in the restaurant could hear me. "I'm on the

Svet basketball team this season that will be battling the rest of the towns of the Czech Republic with my Czech teammates. My lovely date and I are really needing to eat, so could we have Moravian-style pork with roasted potatoes and a little white wine?"

Silence for a moment, then one of the kitchen staff started singing, the Czech version of "For He's a Jolly Good Fellow." Then the rest of the staff joined in. By the second round, the violinists and the whole café joined in the song. When it was done, they applauded me.

Embarrassed, I lowered my head and drifted back toward my table. Most of the men in the crowd rose up from their tables shook my hands, saying dobry den and welcome. And I got hugs from several of the women. I finally arrived back at my table and Shantelina.

"I don't know what got into me," I said.

Shantelina got up and gave me a hug. "You are amazing, Josef," she said, calling me by first name for the first time and giving me a kiss on the cheek.

"Oh thank you. Was the kiss in sympathy for making a fool out of myself or because I called you lovely?" I said.

"No, you silly one, it was getting us our dinner," she said.

The musicians were competent, but there was no soul in the way they droned on until closing time. When dinner was over, the restaurant cleared out quickly. Even the waiters seemed in a hurry to leave.

When the bill came, I picked it up and scanned it. I agreed to pay the bill and she let me. By doing so, it felt like a date.

Shantelina and I went down a staircase into the basement. There in a darkened room we sat at a table with groups of others to listen to Moravian folk singers.

"Tell me about your boyfriend, Wenceslas," I said.

"We've been together two years. He's well liked by everyone. What did you think?"

"He's a nice guy. That's how it seems," I said.

"Yes, I'd say so. We've seen each other long enough. He treats me well," she said.

"That's good, Shantelina," I said, focusing on the singers. This wasn't music of the nobility like I'd heard upstairs. There were no instruments but only a few troubadours belting out Moravian songs *a capella* for the next hour. Their rhythm was imprecise and wrong. Their yodels were drawn out but there was something magical about this after-hours set of peasant music. Shantelina could see that I liked it.

Her eyes shone, and despite her tired appearance, I found her strongly appealing.

I must have been looking intently at her because she frowned and said, "What?"

"Nothing," I said. I looked away at the parlando performers but later back at her.

"You're staring at me," she said.

"I know."

"Why?"

I want to remember what you look like later," I said.

She agreed that I could walk her to her apartment, which was in the same neighborhood as the restaurant. As we strode along, I realized there was a kind of harmony to our steps. Time had passed quickly, and I felt it was a great night. We paused when I got to the front gate of her apartment.

"Koliar was right, you are a *nice* woman. Shantelina, I'd like to stay in touch with you," I said in my best Czech.

"I'd like that, too," she said in English. She turned toward me. It wasn't a kiss she was after. We hugged and hit heads. Rather than feeling awkward, the collision showed some alignment between us. Then we headed back to our separate worlds.

CHAPTER SIXTEEN

WHAT HAPPENED IN THE STAIRWELL

I got to the gym later than I wanted the next morning. Even after my solid performance in Hradec Králové, I was back playing with the second team squad. As I stretched and tied my shoes, I looked around at some of my teammates from that team. We were not just second stringers, we were second chancers. Troubled guys like me that were given another, or some might say, last chance.

Milan, the guy with a "CCCP" tattoo on his right shoulder from his days serving in the Soviet army, was shooting jumpers on a side basket and missing. He and Charles had been on the team when it was controlled by the Party. He had left the team for awhile and then came back this season. Even though the era of basketball colonialism was over and Moscow no longer controlled his destiny, he didn't demonstrate that independent streak or initiative to become a better player.

I looked over to Charles with his big teeth that were spaced out like pieces of white corn. He was a talented post player, a good passer and could score off of slashing drives around the basket, but he would be even better if he didn't have wicked bouts of self-doubt. That was the trouble: our second team didn't have enough belief. Yes, we were never going to be Czech superstars like Anton, who was going to play with the Czech national team after the season. But we had to believe our unit was better. We had to start in practice by consistently beating the first team in the scrimmages at the end of our daily practice.

The day before, we had won one of the three at the end. Jaroslav and I knew we could beat the first team, but, as a whole, our team didn't play like it. I was disappointed because it felt like it was only Jaroslav and I who wanted more.

I took longer than the rest to shower after practice and when I couldn't find my basketball shoes, I found them on the floor of the shower. They were waterlogged and looked ruined. Even if they could be worn again, they were out of commission for several days until they could dry out. I would find the pranksters who did this and I decided to find them immediately.

As I entered the dark stairwell to the main court, I heard footsteps of several people coming down. I approached the central landing, where Anton stood in the dim light. Kolin and Vojtech were behind him on the steps. I knew something was up when Anton blocked my path. His eyes were dilated like steel ball bearings. I always felt there was something good, maybe even salvageable, behind Anton's facade of a being a tough guy and joker. But at that moment I saw differently.

"Did you toss my shoes in the shower?" I said.

"Yes, I did," Anton said.

"What's your problem?" I said.

"My problem is you. You're not needed here. You're an intruder who's come in here in the middle of the season," he said.

I couldn't understand his antagonism toward me. I never did.

"You're angry because you don't know how the future is going to turn out," I said, stepping up to solid ground of the landing.

Anton threw a punch that hit me in the cheek. I lunged forward with my forearm and connecting solidly with Anton's chest. That forced him back in the direction where Vojtech and Kolin stood on the stairs. Then Anton ran at me with both arms outstretched to tackle me. I stepped aside but he adjusted, plowing into me shoulder first, head down. His arms clamped around my core. I couldn't break free from his hold.

So I maneuvered my body around. Then, with Anton still holding onto me, I slammed him against the metal railing, effectively pinning him there.

"Anton Cermak. I know Cermak Road. It's about to be paved," I said. I soon regretted saying that because he let out an unintelligible yell. The last thing I needed was an Anton even more energized against me.

I looked over to see how this was all playing with his two friends. And I was grateful that they looked neutral. I figured they would jump in at any second to stop the fighting. I held Anton against the railing. I peered downward and saw that the bottom was about 20 feet away. I told myself that this was crazy. That's a long way down, and someone would be seriously hurt if this nonsense continued. I wanted to stop right there and end it. I figured Anton would come to his senses when he saw how far down that really was. We caught our breath for a few seconds, then I burst back into action. I pushed Anton back to get him off me. Right then Vojtech and Kolin jumped in and started throwing punches at me. One connected against my lower back. Anton surged ahead with rage and punched me in the shoulder. All three of them came at me from different sides—this was more than a chance meeting, it was a planned ambush. There was nowhere to escape.

Anton kicked me, his rubber core of gym shoe hitting my thigh. Vojtech and Kolin grabbed me, wrapping me up with their arms and lifted me. I struggled to regain my wits, and tried to break their hold of his arms. My objective was to rain multiple punches down on each of them as they shoved me to the railing. I instinctively feared they might try to throw me over. If they do fling me over, I told myself, I'm taking one of them with me. I grabbed Vojtech's sweatshirt and didn't let go. He moved away and it started to rip. I could see the concrete floor at the bottom of the stairs. I let go of the sweatshirt and they rammed me into the metal railing. My elbow and head hit the metal. I grasped for the barrier with what seemed to be mangled hands. Then I heard the door open upstairs. The three stopped, turning their focus away from me. They turned and ran down the stairs.

I pushed myself away from the railing and lay back on the cool metal landing. Blood poured down my face. There was a slickness and sharp pain across my brow. The footsteps moved closer to me on the stairs.

"What the hell is going on?" It was Jiri's voice.

I could hear Jiri's breathing as he lifted me up. I ran my palm along my forehead until I came to my slick eyebrow. I pulled it away to see that it was covered with blood. Then I dried my hand by running it through my hair.

I felt helpless. Embarrassed. Weak. I didn't want my coach to see me in this condition. I always wanted to show him my best face. Those three and I are the same team. What's wrong with them? Maybe it's time to go home.

"What happened? Josef, who did this?" said Jiri.

"Anton," I said. Jiri didn't look surprised to see my answer.

"Only him?" Jiri said.

"Vojtech, Kolin too," I said.

With Jiri at my side, I struggled to raise one leg, then the other, so my feet could clear each stair riser. One of my arms pressed down hard against Jiri's shoulder and my other arm shakily held onto the handrail as we went up the stairs. I was happy to see the light coming through the door at the top of the stairs. Gustav came running with a white towel that he put against the side of my head. As he worked on the source of the blood, he spoke to Jiri. A moment later, Gustav was in front of me with a bottle of liquid. I recoiled when Gustav poured from the bottle on my eyebrow and then on my elbow.

"What is that stuff?" I said.

"It's disinfectant," said Gustav, then he showed me the *Dezinfekcni prostredek* label on the bottle.

When we got to Jiri's Skoda in the parking lot, I ducked my bloody head through the door and felt pain in my lower back as I got in the back seat. I ran my hand through my hair. It had a slickness better than any oil shampoo I have used. I felt light headed and exhausted. Cars outside the window whizzed by. My eyebrow throbbed underneath the towel I held in place. There was another towel wrapped around my elbow. Jiri in the driver's seat and Gustav riding shotgun reminded me of the last time we rode together— the day I first arrived. The three of us in these very same seats cruising from Vienna across the Czech frontier. It seemed like months ago, not the eleven days that it was.

I could see Jiri's eyes looking back at me through the rectangular mirror above the dashboard—just like the day I arrived in the Czech Republic.

"How are you doing back there, Josef?" Jiri said with concern in his voice.

The way he said it reminded me of how my sokol coach spoke to me when I broke my collarbone falling from the balance rings at the Czech Hall on Cermak Road when I was 13.

"I'm doing better than I was a while ago," I said.

"I should hope so. You were hanging on the railing not long ago," said Jiri.

The throbbing continued, along with the bleeding. I saw the sign "Svet Nemocnice" through the front window of Jiri's car. Jiri maneuvered the car to the front door of a hospital. Gustav opened his car door and went through the emergency room entrance. He came back out with a gray wheelchair and opened the car door next to me. Jiri reached over from his front seat to help me get leverage. Gustav stood outside the open car door with the chair. I tried to get out on my own but the pain in my back stiffened up.

Gustav grasped my arms to help pull me from the car and into the wheelchair. Once I was seated in the wheelchair, Gustav pushed me through the hospital doors. We were met by a man in a white lab coat who led us down a dimly lit hall. An automatic door opened to a room with an unbearably bright light coming from the ceiling. We moved to the center of a large room and a few attendants laid me on a table.

A nurse in blue scrubs waiting for me said, "Let's find the degree of the damage here, Mister."

Her gloved index finger poked into my shoulder. Then she peeled back the white towel on my head covering my eyebrow.

"It looks like you have an angry wound there," she said, poking me with her nails in my chest. Nice way to make me feel comfortable, lady, with the nail stabs.

This nurse washed and scrubbed the area around my eyebrow.

"That really hurts and irritates it more," I said in English.

"Nemluvím anglicky. Může někdo přeložit?" she said, then raised her hands as if exasperated.

"He speaks Czech. Josef's saying, take it easy up there. That's all," Coach Jiri said.

She shaved my eyebrow where the blood had been coming from. It began to pulse even more. The pain was unbearable.

As I lay on the table in my sticky practice jersey, I could hear another woman nearby asking Jiri and Gustav questions. She recorded their responses about me on a typewriter in the corner.

Next I saw some familiar faces: Jaroslav, Charles, Milan, and Staroslav. Right there in the emergency room. The whole second team assembled around the table under the bright light.

A tall doctor sporting a ragged ash-colored beard strolled in and introduced himself as Dr. Urbanek.

Through his spectacles, he scanned the people gathered around me.

"Look at this following. You must be somebody. Besides the whole Svet team around us, let's see what we have here, Josef," said the doctor.

The doctor massaged my shoulder with his hand. He had a puffy face, maybe from overwork, but he produced a genuine smile.

"He's our best rebounder and defender inside. Savek helps us tremendously, doc. We want to keep it that way," Jaroslav said.

"I can see that. Now it's the others he has trouble with then? Is that it?" the doctor said. I imagined him to be bald underneath his white skull cap.

"He got in a fight with three players in the stairwell," said Jaroslav.

"Ambushed is more like it," I said.

"That's not good. This shouldn't have happened, coach," said the doctor.

Jiri stepped in closer. "I know. We are taking disciplinary action against the three players. They're suspended for the next game."

"Doc, have you treated people with injuries like these and how did it turn out?" said Staroslav.

"The question is, "Did any of them survive?" Charles said.

There was laughter all around me including the doctor.

"Good one there, Charles," I said.

"Yes, I've been a physician over 20 years. We'll get this closed. He'll recover."

He did his own picking around at the wound on my head then he pulled out a needle. I felt a pinch in my temple; I hate shots. I saw the doctor pull out thread-like sutures from a box. I could feel the picking and pulling of both sides of the skin in that area of my head.

Then he moved onto my elbow and stitched that up, too. When he was done he placed a mirror in my palm.

'Josef, you needed seven stitches to close up the laceration on your eyebrow. And three on your elbow." the doctor said.

I looked in the mirror more carefully so I could see what he did. I looked like a patched-up boxer. White gauze and tape all over my eyebrow. Red skin blotches coming out from the edges of that.

As the medical staff finished up with me, my teammates stayed with me by the table I was lying on, joking with me. I felt great that they were there. These guys were there for me. Maybe I would stay with the team after all.

The nurses brought me to another room to wait. Jiri and I were the only ones left.

The door opened and the doctor was back at my side.

"You are ready to be released, Josef. Any questions?" the doctor said.

"When can he play again? We need him right away," Jiri said, before I could ask anything.

"He needs to let these injuries heal. It's the same problem with the injured glass workers there, too. They don't get paid if they can't work so they go back to the factory. Then they get hurt again and come back here. Is that what you want for Josef?"

"No, I don't. Let's see how he does, Doctor Urbanek," our coach said.

"Can you let him recover and not play for a week? I don't want these to injuries to open again," said the doctor.

"We have few options. With three other players suspended for our next game, against Cesky Budejovice, we need him to play. We don't want to forfeit," Jiri said.

"That's up to you, Coach Hasek. But you know Josef shouldn't play until he's better off," the doctor said.

As we walked to the car in the darkness, I felt a wave of exhaustion sweep over me. I was as tired as the first day I arrived in Svet. Only this wasn't jet lag. I wondered if I could play again. I was in terrible shape. I shuffled toward the car. Eventually I was in the Skoda, but the best I could do was sit there slumped in the passenger seat. Gustav went into the back seat with a towel to wipe off some blood still on the seat from earlier.

"The media will pummel us with questions about this incident, but we are going to get past it. We are going to be down some players, so I hope you play again next game, Josef," Jiri said.

Then I slipped in and out of sleep as Jiri drove back to the glass factory.

CHAPTER SEVENTEEN

BREAKTHROUGH

My eyebrow throbbed and my lower back ached as the warm spray of the shower rained down on my shoulders. The doctor said I should not wet my head.

Just the fact that I was in this space was exceptional. This shower had beautiful blue and white tiles and I poured liquid soap that smelled like spearmint onto a wash cloth. Shower steam swirled up from the floor, rising to the ceiling. I didn't know there was a shower in the factory. There was—in a special wing behind the executive offices. I wondered if any of the players had ever been here. Well, for once I was, and to think it was so close to our player's quarters.

The cubicles of Anton, Vojtech and Kolin adjoined mine in the players' quarters. There was no way I would be able to sleep. Granted, we had a door that we could lock and had a sturdy six-foot high partition that separated us, but that gave me no comfort. I'd seen Anton scramble over the divider and into Charles' room as a practical joke. I didn't want to get thrashed again.

It was a mystery what Anton and the others had against me. To hit me with that much force and repeatedly—I couldn't figure what was behind it. To a degree I could understand why: I was the intruder in their world. But still there was intensity and hate behind his actions that night.

"How are you doing, Josef?" Jiri said, patting me on the back.

"Not so good. Are they here?" I said.

"We're changing things: Zedenik and you are switching rooms."

Jaroslav, Charles, and Milan gathered up everything I had in my compartment.

"Okay, let's go. Let's get this done fast. It's been a long night," Jiri said. Coach Jiri ushered them along as they carried my bags and loose clothes down the aisle. The light of the moon—a full one—streamed through the large windows above.

A few players poked their heads over the partition walls to see the commotion. Pretty soon, it seemed like the whole team was milling around in the aisle to watch the move.

My new room was a cubicle nearest to the front door and next to Jaroslav's space. It felt good to be closer to my second unit teammates. Once all my stuff was in my new space, Anton, Vojtech and Kolin came out.

"Apologize to this player," said Jiri.

They stood in front. Anton tilted his head in defiance and all three slouched. It was the kind of posture you might see on somebody shoved into a police lineup.

They didn't say anything. Their faces wore the universal criminal look—something between a glare and a smirk—just as the flashbulb on the police clerk's camera ignites.

"You three will be suspended for more than the next game, then," said Jiri.

They stood their ground. Then Anton reached out and I shook hands. This made me feel somewhat better about the situation. What struck me was this: Vojtech and Kolin showed no interest in shaking my hand or apologizing. Jiri didn't pursue it either.

"Okay, that's better. A step forward. Anton, Vojtech and Kolin, I'll see you tomorrow morning at 9 a.m. to talk about this," Jiri said.

After our coach left, Anton bad-mouthed Charles, one of the second string players, Charles responded with some name-calling back at Anton. Jaroslav stepped out and held his hand in the air.

"Enough, Charles." Charles turned away and walked back to his room.

Several other players decided to change rooms, too. So after ferrying of bags and other belongings back and forth, the first team was on one side of the players' quarters and the second team was on the other.

Before the lights were dimmed, Jaroslav told me that, had he known, he would have stood shoulder to shoulder with me in that stairwell. I wished Anton had a little more Jaroslav in him. If that were the case, the fight wouldn't have even occurred.

After breakfast, Gustav reexamined the stitches in my eyebrow in the trainer's room. He seemed pleased. Then he looked at my elbow with stitches, too. As I stood there he had me extend my arm and then fold it back in.

"How does that feel? Gustav said.

"It's very sore. Still hurts," I said.

It really did. How was I going to play like this?

"Here, put this on," he said. He handed me an elbow pad. It was very tender as I pulled it toward my elbow. I stopped. Gustav jumped in to help pull it over my elbow and get it snug.

Gustav then walked me to the coach's office. Jiri, who was sitting at his desk, stood up. I went into the office in front of his desk.

"How is it? How does it look, Gustav?"

"He's released to play basketball again today," Gustav said from the doorway.

"Good. Thanks, Gustav. I knew he would be ready. See you later," Jiri said. Gustav left. It felt like some kind of bogus show staged for my sake.

He had a new set of European gym shoes on his desk. I could smell their brand-new scent of rubber.

"Sit down," Jiri said.

So I sunk into the seat in front of Jiri's desk. As I did my sore back pulsed with pain. I feared I wouldn't be able to stand again.

"Those three troublemakers are suspended from all basketball activities," Jiri said

It's the non-basketball activities that worried me more.

"Josef, we need you to return against Cesky Budevoice tomorrow. I want you to have all the resources you need to play again and that starts with today," Jiri said.

"These are for you," he said. He slid the new basketball shoes across his desk toward me.

"The expense for the shoes came out of the paychecks of the three troublemakers. Also, we'll have Gustav tape up your face to protect your eyebrow from reinjury," Jiri said.

"Finally, Pavelosek, the reporter from the *Svet Monitor,* is digging on a story about this incident. Say nothing. I've told the rest of players to follow a strict code of silence on this matter as well. Is that understood?" Jiri said.

"Yes, it is."

"Now go get dressed for practice. Gustav's waiting for you to work on your face"

I tried to stand. A jolt from my lower back hit me. I couldn't stand up. Noticing my situation, Jiri stood up and grabbed my arm.

"Here, let me help you out," he said.

It was slow, but I got to my feet with his help. Anton's kick to my back was one of those hidden injuries that I overlooked. And I knew this one wasn't going away today.

In the locker room, I strained to put my new shoes on. I couldn't even pull my shoes over my feet because of the pain in my back. Jaroslav, who was getting dressed for practice, noticed.

"How are you doing? What's wrong with your back?"

"I can't even put on my shoes tie my shoes, how can I play?"

"Here, extend your leg," he said.

So I did. I outstretched it there on the bench. One by one we got them on, and he tied them for me.

Then I went into in the bathroom. I looked into the mirror at my unprotected face and fingered the stitches. Very tender.

A few moments later I was lying on the training table in the room down the hall from the locker room. Gustav applied some gauze then white tape over that. As the bandage came into contact with my eyebrow, making it throb even more. The tape smelled brand new, just like the rubber of the basketball shoes.

I was all dressed for practice including the tape. As I stood in front of the mirror once again, the starkness of the tape struck me. I had one big white eyebrow that extended from one side to the other. There were several pieces of tape that extended down to the end of my nose to hold the bandage in position. And there was more tape across the center of my face from cheek to cheek.

I looked like a medieval knight wearing a mask that covered the top half of his face to protect it. But I didn't feel very protected. One well-placed elbow to the area above my eye in practice from a first team player or a České Budějovice player would be a disaster. The game would become a gory show with me being the dripping star, blood spurting down my face like Jesus Christ himself. I didn't want that. The tape on my face was now a target. Swing your elbow right here. I needed a plexiglass mask to protect me.

Then I looked in the mirror some more. My hair was ruffled out from the sides like wings. It reminded me of one of the angel statues in the main square of Svet. All I needed to complete the look were some golden stars in a halo over my head.

I walked back up the stairwell where it all occurred the day before. Alone again. I stood at the landing for a moment. The door above opened and shut. My back tightened and I looked up. There was no one there. I grabbed the railing with both hands but this time I didn't look down. Instead, I adjusted the tape a little tighter.

When I arrived upstairs, Pavelosek from the *Svet Monitor* saw me and made a beeline in my direction.

"Josef, how were you injured?" he said.

"I have nothing to say," I said.

"I have copies of your charts from the hospital. You had seven stitches in your eyebrow. Just a few questions?" he said.

"No, I don't have anything for you," I said, picking up a basketball to get some shots in on the side hoop before practice.

"I already know more about you than you think," he said.

I turned toward him to consider what he just said, wondering what else he knew.

Jiri came out of the office and saw the scene. He walked over with some tempo in his step. The keys in his pocket jingled with each stride. Then he came to a stop.

"Just the man I wanted to talk with. Is the team in the state of a meltdown?" the reporter said. He used the Czech word paroucha for meltdown to sensationalize what had happened.

"Nein paroucha. Don't press my players, Mister Pavelosek. We've nothing against our comrades in news-gathering intelligentsia but our practices are strictly closed to the public," Jiri said.

"That's never been the case before," he said.

"Before? You've never come to our practice before," Jiri said.

"Coach, do you have something to hide? Why the secrecy?"

"Nothing, we have rules. Everyone needs to follow them, even you, Mr. Pavelosek," he said, pointing to the door. The reporter left.

As we ran the opening drills there was a new intensity from everyone. I attributed that to what happened the night before. My lower back was sorer than I wanted it to be, but was I was pleased that I was able to keep up with everyone else. The tape would take some getting used to, but I saw that it didn't hinder my ability to perform. Its real test would be the practice scrimmage.

After 45 minutes, Jiri stood in the mid-court and ordered a defensive drill that we did every practice. He blew the whistle and we ran forward. He blew it again and we stopped. He blew it again and we moved laterally, left and then right. When I screeched to a halt and then jolted into overdrive a few seconds later, it felt like a pile driver had been thrust into my lower back. I stopped in my tracks as everyone else kept moving in the direction of the stands. Jiri halted practice and told me to walk it off.

Jiri's understudy, Gustav, worked with me on the sideline. He wanted me to keep it moving but he saw I couldn't. Jiri came over to check and see if I was okay. He empathized, but carried on with the practice shortly after that. When I could move again, I walked out into the hallway to get a drink of water from the fountain. I took the tape off knowing that I wouldn't be putting it on anymore that day and maybe not for the upcoming CB game. As I hunched at the low fountain sipping the icy water, I could hear Jiri's whistle in the distance as practice continued in the gym. My back was hurting, but what pained me the most was what I was missing. I wasn't out there with my teammates.

From a seat in the stands, I watched Jiri call for a five-minute break before the first scrimmage game was to begin. Jiri went back to his office and then walked out in his shorts and a yellow and blue practice jersey. It was as if the Red Sea had parted and Moses stepped out on the wet sand. Everyone watched. Jaroslav looked at me and raised his eyebrows. I wondered what kind of game this middle-aged man with hairless white legs had left in him. Our coach and former Olympian bounced around with the nervous energy of a new player. Jiri played with the first team during the end of practice scrimmage to make it an even four against four.

My second team played well in the scrimmage. It felt odd watching them from the stands, because I had always been on the floor with them.

Our point guard Jaroslav led the onslaught. He played with his typical crispness, but it was the other three that surprised me. They rose from the background in waves, big and small. Milan got moving and didn't stand around. The former Warsaw Pact soldier took chances. During one possession he took the ball down the baseline and did an awkward reverse layup that spun off the backboard and rolled into the basket. Another time he stole the ball and drove hard to the basket. His path was blocked so he spun left and shot a baby hook shot. It was rejected but I was amazed to see him even try it. And then there was Charles. The guy put his doubts on hold and played as a passionate believer. Charles hit every shot he took in the first game. He battled for and *won* rebounds. When I saw that, I knew there was nothing that could beat the second team. By the third game Charles missed a few times in a row and he smiled about it, corn row teeth and all.

The first team was strengthened by Jiri. He had great presence that drew your eye to him whether he had the ball or not. Our coach had moves and craftiness as a passer. He utilized screens set for him then knocked down some nice shots and stole the ball several times in each game on defense. His only drawback was his conditioning. He got winded faster than everyone else but that was understandable because he didn't play every day like we did. The guy was in his late forties and still could be an impact player. His efforts kept the first team in the game and the scores closer than they should have been.

When it was over, the second team had won three games in a row. That had never happened before. Granted, it was a weakened first team without the suspended three. But I felt this new-found dominance was great.

I stopped in a café near the glass factory after practice. I saw a face I recognized looking down reading a book. Shantelina was at a small table along the wall. I tapped her shoulder. She looked up and gasped.

"Josef, what happened?" Shantelina said, as she scanned my face.

"I got in a fight with Anton last night. After practice." I said.

"Why?" she said. "You look terrible."

"Who knows their reasons?" I said, lowering my voice so that the entire pastry shop couldn't overhear our conversation. I felt a twinge of unexpected sadness as I said it.

"Join me for coffee and a pastry," she said.

"Ano," I nodded in agreement.

She closed a book on the table. I caught the title *Trojice* before she swept it aside with a glossy arts magazine and placed both of them them in her black bag on the floor.

"Who's the author of the book?" I said.

"Author? I don't understand," she said

"Who wrote *Trojice?* What's it about?"

She pulled the paperback out of her handbag to look at it.

"Leon Irish, no sorry Leon Uris, It could be Irish; it is story about them. I like so far. I'm halfway through it," she said.

Wow, she's reading the Czech translation of the novel *Trinity*. Impressive.

As we stood in line to order, I glanced at the recipient of my misguided note the week before. Shantelina's hair was gathered in a pony tail by a crimson hair band. Her pale skin and bright eyes caught the light of the gleaming display case.

I peeked back towards our table and saw her white coat on the chair. I was grateful I didn't have to get that tight thing off her again. A repeat of that tangle in this crowded place would be an embarrassing spectacle—like getting hit in the eyebrow in a game.

A passerby must have thought I was looking at him. He walked over.

"Dobry den," he said. I said the same thing back to him. He looked a few years older than I was. We shook hands and he stood there expecting me to say something. I was silent.

Usually I would be my talkative, friendly, midwestern self and start up a conversation. I was an ambassador of the local team that was trying to attract fans. Milos always told us we had the obligation to be model citizens and promoters of the sports club. But this time I didn't want to. My back was too sore for that. Shantelina and I returned to the table.

"So you were hit in face by those three. They are suspended and you play tomorrow night against Cesky Budevoice," Shantelina said, as she cut into her pastry with a fork and a knife at our table.

"They hurt my back, too, and that's what stopped me. I don't know when I'll be able to play again," I said.

She paused to take it in.

"They may have hurt you but they can't beat person inside," she said.

She's giving me the inspirational speech. Who does that remind me of? My mother.

"They did beat me. I can't play now," I said, pointing to my face. I could have lifted my shirt to show her the bruise just above my kidney as well.

"No, only temporarily. They cannot stop you unless you permit," she said.

She had a point there. When my mother said it I wouldn't listen, but in this situation I would.

"But they won't let it go. They haven't apologized," I said.

"They might not ever. Let go. Forgive," she said.

"They don't want my forgiveness and probably wouldn't accept it. It won't work," I said.

"It doesn't matter what they do, only you. Otherwise, you send them more oomph than deserve," she said.

"I can't do that. What they did was wrong," I said.

"Josef, what did you come here for?" She gazed at me intently.

"What do you mean? Here today or here to the Czech Republic?" I said.

"Here to Svet, CR," she said.

"To play basketball, try something different and see a new place," I said. I held back another one: to find a romantic gypsy girl or her Czech equivalent.

"Did you come here to hold onto grudges? Is that what you want to carry with you?" Shantelina said.

"No."

"Then let it go," she said.

"You're right, but it's not that easy. I'm still worried that something like this will happen again. They are not going away," I said.

"Of course. That is natural. Come, I show you Jizera River," she said, pushing back from the table.

We walked out into early evening. The rim of Svet Mountain and the surrounding smaller peaks were cast in a purple light. The trees in the forests below were dark green clusters. Along the street, a sagging lamppost turned on as if someone had flicked a switch.

"If I do play, you might not recognize me. I'll have to wear a mask of tape for this," I said, pointing to my eyebrow.

"They ruin your handsome face," she said. She looked like she meant it. I liked that.

"Did they?' I said.

She squared up to me to consider at my face.

"It might return," she said. She betrayed herself with a slight smile.

We sauntered along the Jizera and sat on a marble slab wall that ran along the water's edge. It was crenulated like battlements from an earlier era but, as I looked closer, it could also have been built as flood control to hold back a swollen river. The river was lower than it had been a few days before when I met Jelina. Cars and an occasional truck passed on the bridge overhead.

"Tell me about Rodina Savek," she said.

I paused for a second. I felt I could trust her. Whatever happened she was on my side.

"My family? I'll start by telling you about my brother and me," I said.

"What is his name?"

"Josef" I said.

"That's your name. I don't understand. Are you both name Josef?"

"No. Let me slow down. I have one brother, he's a year and a half younger, and he received the offer to come to Svet. He got another offer around the same time to play basketball in Australia. He went there. I took his place and his name, Josef. For the opportunity of it. There is only one Josef. My real name is Ferenc or Frank, not Josef."

"You expect me to believe this ridiculous nonsense? What are you telling me?" she said.

"Yes, it's true," I said.

I can't believe I told her. I could turn back and say I was just attempting to be funny.

"I don't believe. I have more faith in you than that," Shantelina said.

Here comes the crash. The end. She'll tell everyone else about this creep, the American fraud. I'll be history in Svet and with the team for sure. But then again, I couldn't go much lower. She had a long-term boyfriend. Jelina and I were a couple or done; I couldn't tell which. Finally, I couldn't play because of my back.

"Shantelina, I'm being honest. I can understand your being upset," I said.

She was speechless. So I filled in the silence.

I told her about my Czech parents, Pilsen where I grew up, the other Eastern European neighborhoods of Chicago, how I came to leave my PR job and even how my father seemed to favor everything my brother did.

I didn't tell her that I never intended to meet her in the first place and that the note I sent her was for Jelina. There was no reason to tell her that. So I didn't.

"Everyone makes mistakes. I don't hold it against you, Ferenc or do you like Frank better?" Shantelina said.

"Call me the English version, Frank. That's the one I like best," I said.

"Yes, I like Frank. That's better than you started with," she said.

I picked a flower near the bottom of the wall and gave it to her. She found a smooth black and white stone and gave it to me. I walked her to her tram stop. We looked into each other's eyes for a moment. I felt like kissing her but held back.

"Since I just learned your name, I can say, Good to meet you, Frank. See you soon," she said. She walked up the steps of a small blue light rail train car. The doors shut a moment later and it accelerated away into the night.

CHAPTER EIGHTEEN

THE CZECH CURANDERA

As I fingered the rotary dial telephone, I decided against calling my father because I didn't want a dose of negativity about my prospects in the Czech Republic. If I told my parents about the incident in the stairwell, it would only intensify my father's doubts and my mother's worries.

Josef was the one person I could talk with about all this. He was my partner in this masquerade and, because of that, I felt closer to him. I pulled out his letter postmarked from Down Under. One sentence stood out: I've gone walkabout from the team in Tasmania and have signed on with a team in Perth. Gone walkabout? Leave it to him to forget about his roots and start talking Australian already.

I scanned his letter but he didn't leave a number. The only way I could get that was through my parents. They might have it. I hung up the phone.

I stepped out from the phone stand into the main square with an insomniac's view. One automobile sped past on the empty streets. Its tail lit the darkness with tracers of red brightness. A few cars were parked nearby, tan little boxes from the socialist era.

Svet looked sad and failing. The brick pavement was dirty and a wrapper from some plastic bag blew around. A good number of the buildings around the square needed updating. My father, the contractor, would prosper in this place. He would have scaffolding up around them and would have his men bring them back to life in no time with some new windows, gates, and tuckpointing.

I didn't know what to make of what I had just done with Shantelina. I hoped I wouldn't regret telling her who I was, because if she turned against me for some reason, I was history. I wondered if I had a planted the seeds of my demise. But she was trustworthy. I had to believe that.

As I sat in the stands the next morning, Jiri said, "What do you think you're doing?" He stood facing me with his legs astride and his feet firmly planted on the varnished wood court.

"My back is still not right," I said.

"Josef, that's a crock of shit. I played in the European Championships with a broken finger when we qualified for the Olympics. My players are the same—tough as nails. Go downstairs and get dressed," he said.

"Jiri, I don't want to make it worse. It's not there yet," I said.

"Where's the there you talk about? This is your chance, your opportunity. It may not come again," he said.

As I changed in the locker room, my rationale for wanting to sit out our morning session was this: our coach's pre-game shoot-around sessions were more like full-blown practices. I wanted to be there to listen to the strategy and tactics for the game that night, but I had deep doubt if I could play then.

When I got back upstairs, Charles was up running bleachers.

"Keep climbing, Charles. We need mental focus. No errant passing coming from you. České Budějovice will eat you up with that kind of mistake," Jiri said.

"Jaroslav, I want 30 push-ups for every minute you were late. Ten minutes late. Give me 300," Gustav said.

Jaroslav got in position and started racking off push-ups. Gustav stood over him. No sooner had I laced up my sneakers than Jiri waved me onto the court. I was running before I could warm up like I usually did.

Yes. Our coach was hard-nosed, disciplined and relentless. But did he have to be an unsympathetic bastard, too? We had no wins and it looked like our winless streak would continue. But I put that out of my mind. So I ran the best I could.

At the end of the session, I took off my sweaty mask of tape and stiffly walked off the court.

"You did it. Not your greatest, but we'll take it," Jiri said. "When I look out there tonight, I'm going to see you moving your feet on defense. I'm going to see you being more active when we have the ball."

Our coach threw the ball off the rim and pulled it down with two hands and cradled it with his elbows extended out.

"You must rebound," he said in English. He rolled the "r" of rebound with emphasis. His voice boomed so the other players could hear.

"It's not the rebounding I worry about. It's whether I can perform at all," I said.

"What are you talking about? You just did," Jiri said. Then he lowered his voice, "I talk to you to this way to set an example. You're coachable, I like that about you."

In this he favored me, and it made me feel apart from the rest. That stuff built resentment from others. And I was having enough trouble with my teammates, especially from the first team group with those three slamming me against the railing and messing up my back.

The doctor came into the waiting room at Svet Hospital.

"Your kidney is functioning well and the x-ray images show no damage besides the contusion to the muscle," he said.

"See, we will have you on the court tonight against České Budějovice," said Jiri.

After the doctor left, Jiri lingered in the consultation room.

"Josef, we didn't just come here to the hospital only for you. My mother's in here too. She's had trouble with her stomach," he said.

"What kind of trouble?" I said.

"The East German doctor that operated on her cut out half her stomach then and did some stapling procedures they wouldn't do today. The real priority wasn't better medical procedures for us, it was those missiles pointed toward the West," Jiri said.

"How is she now?"

"Well enough to go home. She had a short stay. You're going to help me," he said.

I was tired from practice and my face must have showed it.

"Let me slow down. Will you do this with me?" he said.

I gave my answer in both languages. Ano… Yes.

"That's settled. Let's go," he said.

As he and I walked down the corridor, I noticed what I hadn't seen before: the directional signs to the hospital wards were in Cyrillic. I was struck by one monster-sized mural on the wall that touted the virtues of the proletariat and the Soviet state. A remnant of the Czech life just four years before.

"She's in here—this room," Jiri said. He pushed open the gray metal door. There was a mustached guy with burly arms in the bed in traction with his leg and arm suspended above him. He looked like a truck driver.

"My mother was in here. Where is she?" said Jiri.

"Who knows?" said the guy in the bed.

Jiri turned to leave with a puzzled look on his face.

"There was a lady. I came in, they took her out," this new occupant of the room said.

We walked out to a nurse's station but no one was at the desk.

"Stay here," Jiri said, he scratched his head and wandered down the hallway.

Music from *9 to 5* wafted down from the PA system. At first, this translated version sounded odd. But as I stood there longer, this Czech woman was singing it well and brought the dated song to life. To je nádherné.

This country of ten million people had some hope after all.

A short woman with cropped gray hair approached me.

"Are you the American player that got his lights punched out a few days ago?" she said.

"Yes," I said hesitantly, not sure I comprehended her Czech figure of speech. And if it was what I thought it was, I didn't like it.

"I'm Alžběta, Jiri's mother. They moved me over to another room to wait. He's down loading up my clothes so let's go there," she said. I towered over this granny.

Alžběta walked at a slow but steady pace with her shoulders hunched. Her blue eyes didn't have the Germanic or Nordic essence that I'd seen in others since I arrived. They held a hint of the mysticism of the East. When she stood straight up for a moment, her body looked wider and more powerful. These things made me think she was Russian.

When we walked out of the hospital, the afternoon sun illuminated her face. Then we stepped into the shadow of some black birds that flew above.

"Be off with you. Don't get ready for me yet," she said, as she swept her hands through the air.

"Those are crows, not vultures," I said.

"Whatever they are, they're circling," she said.

Alžběta smiled and put her hand on my arm to stop me. She took a deep breath. "A perfect Czech day," she said.

I could see where Jiri got his habit of laying it on thick.

"I see you found my mother," said Jiri. He caught up to us from behind.

When we reached the car, I tried to help her in but she waved me off. Jiri lowered her into the back seat of the black Skoda. She grimaced as he helped her in.

"Help, we need an assist, Josef," Jiri said.

I scurried to the other door and entered the back seat to lower her in.

As Jiri drove, he looked over his shoulder every few minutes to the backseat to make sure Alžběta was comfortable. We went through parts of Svet that I recognized, and then we entered a new stretch of road that had more trees each kilometer we went.

"What direction are we heading? I said.

"What would you guess?" Jiri said.

"We are going north," I said

"Wrong. Josef, we're heading east toward Kivka Pass. That's where I live. It's the lowest pass in the Krkonoše range," he said. We motored up the road through pine forest. I could hear the engine working harder as we climbed. I tried to calculate where we were in relation to Svet Mountain. But I couldn't.

I thought about the trails above Svet. We had run up there three times, but it was the last one I remembered most. He had sent us up there to punish us for bad performance, a lackadaisical effort. That made me think of the tough situation we were in. We hadn't won a game yet. The CB game was a must win.

Jiri drove it like he didn't know the road: fast on the sharp curves and switchbacks, slow on the straightaway sections.

"It doesn't seem very low to me. What's on the other side of this pass?" I said

"Poland. There's a yellow-chested warbler," he said, slapping me on the knee. There was nothing there. He's in high form today, I thought.

"Your driving makes my stomach hurt. I can't take the twisting," said Alžběta.

Jiri slowed, especially on the curves.

An occasional home or two appeared among the trees. Not a bad place to live.

He turned off to an unpaved road that led to a small one-story white cottage. It had alpine-style windows with many small panes in crisscross patterns. A dog that looked like a wolf bounded toward us from some bushes—barking, then running beside of the car as we pulled closer to the house.

"What kind of dog is he?"

"Československý Vlčák. He won't hurt you," Jiri said.

When I opened the door and stepped out, the Czechoslovakian wolfdog sniffed my shoes. Then he brushed up beside of me and let me rub his soft fur coat. He wagged his tail.

Jiri and I helped his mother get out of the car. When we reached the front door, Jiri strolled over to a neatly stacked pile of logs that stood along the clapboard facade. He pulled out two of them and tucked them under his arm.

Once inside, my eyes adjusted to three people standing in line in a narrow hallway.

"I brought home two surprises: the babushka and the American," Jiri said.

His wife Veronika, a young son Karel, and daughter Zuzana gave the old woman a hug. We moved in a caravan to the living room. There was a small daybed with a threadbare quilt on it in the middle.

"Josef, carry in her bags," Jiri said.

When I came back in with them, I was about to place them at the foot of the bed but Veronika shook her head.

"Not there. Bring them to the bedroom," she said.

She ushered me to a back room. Sunlight illuminated a red blanket over a rocking chair. On a small table, there was a bowl of mountain flowers, a pitcher of water, and a burning white candle. Aside from smelling like mothballs, it was the cheeriest room I saw.

On the wall, I saw a color icon of Pope John Paul II, the Polish one. His balding head, charismatic smile, piercing eyes. This was the best one I'd ever seen of him and I'd seen many. Half the Eastern European houses and apartments in Chicago had his picture up on the wall.

Alžběta walked in behind Jiri's wife and me.

"The children will sleep out in the bed in the living room, while you get better," Jiri's wife said.

Veronika had made an early dinner so we ate at the table in the dining room. We had roast pork with bread dumplings (knedlíky), a cold creamy beet soup, sauerkraut *(zelí),* and dark rye.

As we sat at the table, his children focused on everything I did, however ordinary. They watched how I used the spoon. I could never do that without using my other thumb to trap errant food like peas. They laughed at that.

"Would you like a glass of apple juice?" Veronika said.

"Yes. A glass would be great," I said. The kids laughed when I said this.

Veronika brought out a tray of glasses. She placed a large glass in front of each person and put a shot glass in front of me. Then she poured apple juice into them including the little glass near me.

"Okay, I'll drink out of this one. Did you give me this smaller one because I'm the guest or something?" I said.

"You said sklenička. Little glass. I thought that's unusual but if he wants it give it to him," Veronika said.

"No, I'll have one like everyone else. That's what I'll have. That's my Chicago Czech mixing things up again," I said.

I asked the children questions about their school, their friends, and how they liked having their grandmother Alžběta back home. They answered but didn't elaborate like I wanted. I chalked it up to my Czech being different than what they understood.

"My grandchildren are being shy with you. You should see them talk with me," Alžběta said.

I gave them a little background about my own family in Chicago. I told them about my parents and brother there.

"Have you spoken to your parents or your brother about all your adventures here?" Veronika said from the table.

"Which experiences do you mean?" I said.

"Your living in the glass factory, running Svet Mountain, and making the team," she said.

That summed it up pretty well. She forgot to mention getting beat up.

"Not yet but I will. We're pretty close," I said. I lied because my connection to them was not what I wanted. I was feeling slightly closer to my brother. My parents, not so much—although I hoped that my experience in Svet would make us closer as a family.

"You must miss them and the place you are from. Did you have a girlfriend you left back in Chicago?" Veronika said.

"No. My girlfriend and I broke up a few months ago," I said. It hurt saying that.

"A good-looking guy like you will meet a nice Czech girl from Svet. That will make you feel at home here," Veronika said with a wink.

"I don't want him or the others thinking much about that," said Jiri. "Svet players are different. Josef is here to play basketball, unlike those discotheque cads on the Prague and Brno teams. Right, Josef?"

I nodded yes.

I felt my stomach getting queasy. Then I looked at my watch and saw it was only a few hours before game time.

"Don't worry. We have time, Josef. We'll leave soon," Jiri said.

Alžběta excused herself from the table to take a nap.

After we had chai, we said our goodbyes and headed to the car.

Jiri's son Karel ran out to say that the babushka had woken and asked to see me. Jiri and I walked back into her bedroom.

Alžběta waved us in from where she was seated on the side of her bed.

"You can't leave yet. There's more," Alžběta said.

"Right, I thought you were asleep. Sit here, Josef," Jiri said.

So I eased down in a sturdy old rocking chair near her bed. Jiri walked over to a window, then peered through the slats at green pine branches that rubbed the glass. This little woman sat on the edge of her bed. Alžběta and I looked at each other for a few moments that felt like an eternity.

"I wanted to tell you something," Alžběta said.

"About your son, the coach?" I said.

"No, about you."

"Me? What is it?" I said, shifting my weight in the chair.

"I had a dream, the other night when I was in the hospital," said Alžběta, looking at me with clarity. "It was you. I'm certain of it. You were in dark murky waters of a lake. Something grabbed you by the ankles and pulled you under. You fought to get free. Then Jiri reached in and grabbed you by the back of the neck and brought you back up."

Wow, this was unbelievable.

"Jiri was there. I have stitches here in my eyebrow and elbow, and I hurt my back," I said.

She waved her hand impatiently to stop me.

"I know, I know. That fight is done; you're better because of it," Alžběta said.

"She told me this story yesterday. It's identical to the fight the other day," said Jiri

Not exactly identical; I was in a stairwell, not a lake. But there was resonance and insight in the dream. Most of all, the way Alžběta looked at me—eyes wide extra open and deeply focused—made me think she had some kind of radical intuition.

Meanwhile Jiri stood on the other side of the room near the window, taking in the scene as an observer in the middle distance.

"I have a good feeling about where you're heading. And a woman in your life now will be your enduring love. I see you crossing the border with her," Alžběta said.

"Since you are in the fortune-telling mood, do you happen to have a name?"

I really wanted to know that.

"No. There's nothing more," said Alžběta.

Alžběta grabbed my hand. Awkwardly, I began to shake her hand, but she didn't shake back, so I stopped. I wasn't getting it. She just held my hand with a firm grip and wouldn't let go. Then I decided to go with it and squeezed tightly as Alžběta did. Our hands tensely clasped on top of the quilt.

"You know why all this comes about?" she said, looking intently at me.

As I gazed at her, I was lost in the blueness of her eyes. I smiled out of nervousness. Alžběta maintained a neutral face that forced me to pay attention and focus on the moment.

"No. Does it have to be?" I said.

"It doesn't have to happen. But when it does, it's for a reason. You know why? To fulfill your destiny," Alžběta said.

I loved her perspective and the way she thought. Although I had no idea what my destiny was, except to be where I was right there.

"I can't argue against destiny. Do you think the man upstairs can help us against our opponent České Budějovice? We play them soon; we have to leave," Jiri said.

She released my hand. But I could have held her hand for an hour.

"Yes, be off. I tell my son that all the time. If you think you're out here working alone, it's not true, you're being guided from above and below," Alžběta said, waving her hand toward the door.

Jiri bent down and gave her a kiss. Then I did too like she was my own grandmother. I'm happy I did because I would think about her often in the next few weeks. Jiri and I exited from the room to trek back to Svet.

In our blue and yellow uniforms we burst out of the tunnel onto the Svet court. I saw more empty seats than at the first two games. Fans sat in small groups closer to the court. The rafter seats were empty. That's what happens when you open with two losses and three players beat up their own teammate. But then wouldn't that conflict make people more interested in our team? Maybe no one knew about the fight.

The "What a Feeling" song from *Flashdance* boomed across the gym just like the opening night against Pardubice.

"Is this our team song?" I said to Charles running in the line in front of me.

"Yes. It's better than that junk they used to play," he said.

'What kind was that?" I said.

"Every game they played Russian gymnastic music. The same stuff they perform their routines to," Charles said. I remembered that Charles was the veteran of the team who had been in the league since the beginning.

"You're kidding," I said.

"No, I'm not. At least, this is basketball music and American basketball music, at that," he said.

"It must remind you of home and NBA," Jaroslav said, from in front of me.

"Maybe ten years ago, but it's pretty good," I said, not wanting to dampen their enthusiasm.

A dozen years before, music had blared across the Providence St. Mel gym as we ran out onto the court. The *Sun-Times* scribes had already written us off and the home team was the heavily predicted to win. Our mostly white Mendel team warmed up to the rhythm track music. We were tense playing in that all-black-neighborhood and before black spectators. We even went in packs to the bathroom so we wouldn't be jumped.

The home team had not come out yet: their side of court was empty. The music with heavy drum action, electronic energy, and streetwise black girls singing about their men pumped our entire team up.

Then the locker room door blasted open and Providence St. Mel Purple Knights ran out. The crowd that ringed the court stood up and exploded with noise. It was clear in that moment that this music was completely their own. It transformed my inner atmosphere from inspired to intimidated. The music was foreign to me. The naturalness and flow I had moments earlier drained away. I had to regain my composure and play through any jitters. I told myself the music didn't matter; what was inside did. I got used to the music and the intimidation feeling left me.

My Mendel team beat Providence St. Mel, and then my brother and I went on to overcome other teams like St. Mel at North Park.

I reminded myself that Svet was the home team. We weren't going to intimidate with our music, but with our play. My excitement was different than at that first game. Yes, I was overwhelmed in the loss against the Superliga's best team and player in Johann Muller. But I did shut down Darryl Divinity in the last game at Hradec Králové. The biggest challenge I faced was how to play before I was completely recovered.

Our resident announcer on the loudspeaker called us the *Stars.* In the opener it was the Lions our correct name, now this. He said the *Svet Stars* several times with bravado. That made no sense and confused me. The only time I'd ever heard it before was when Koliar used it. He called the first team his Czech All-*Stars,* which never really made sense to me since one of those five, Vojtech, wasn't even Czech at all. He was Bulgarian. I hoped I could play like a star, shooting star, a rebounding star or anything that would help my chances.

When we shifted to the passing drill, I saw the three suspended players in the stands. Anton, Vojtech, and Kolin. They were in their street clothes right next to Milos Koliar. I was bothered that they were sitting with the team owner. I looked up again and they were talking and even laughing with Milos. This guy could be trying to understand them and bring his Czech All-Stars back into the fold. Or maybe he was in on my getting beat up all along. That last possibility darkened my mood as I went through the drill.

I thought it strange how this situation played out. *I* was the one hurt and I likely needed to play more than usual that night, maybe straining my back even more. Those three were being punished with resting.

I put all these thoughts out of my head because I couldn't afford distraction. There was a game to play. We gathered up along the bench. The starters Zedenik, Charles, Jaroslav, Rudenic, and Staroslav sat down on the bench. The rest of us stood in front of them. Jiri stood in the periphery on the court joking with one of the referees, who was wearing a tacky black and white zebra striped shirt and black pants.

While talking to the ref at middle court, Jiri gazed in our direction and then pulled his necktie tighter. He and Gustav were in uniform, too: blue tie, white shirt and gray wool slacks. Then he walked over to give us to some last minute instructions.

With our huddle around him, Jiri said, "We have an undermanned, undersized squad against a České Budějovice team that has height advantages at all positions, a strong bench. This team beat Plzeň and Praha B to start the season. We've never lost to České Budějovice."

Plzeň and Praha B were among best teams in the league and this team had beaten them. What does that say about them?

"They have height with two players at 6'8" and their best player Drabek is 6'6". We are going to have to play better than they do. It's that simple," said Jiri, then sent the team out onto the floor.

The game started with České Budějovice aggressively taking the ball down low. It worked. They raced off to an 18-7 lead. They used their height advantage. I watched carefully. My mind was busy; I thought of the things I could do to counter their opening surge. I saw myself rebounding and scoring. Then I saw them trying to stop me. I worried if I was well enough to perform.

The only bright spot early on was Jaroslav. He was scoring and getting in the face of the four other Svet players to motivate them.

"Are you ready? Get yourself in there for Rudenic," said Jiri.

I told him yes. Then Jiri stood up and signaled to the referee for a time out.

He turned back to me and hit me on the shoulder.

"Focus and just play your game."

I stretched out my tight back. As I ran onto the floor with the others, a louder than usual cheer came up from the crowd. Cheers for me, the guy who got beat up. I didn't want to be known for that.

My head and back hurt as I ran back to set up the offense. Let them go and get into what is happening right now. I went to the free throw line, cut down to set a pick for Charles and another for Jaroslav who used it to drive to the basket. I rolled with him and Jaroslav launched a short jumper. The ball bounced off the rim and into my hands. I shot the ball back up, banking it on the board, and it bounced away. I chased after it, hauled it down and powered it back up and in.

The first miss happened in slow motion, my body and mind reacting at one level and the current of the game flowing faster.

On defense, I blocked a shot from one of their tallest guys and the misdirected ball sailed into Jaroslav's hands. That play started a momentum shift in favor of us. The České Budějovice run was halted. On another procession, I thwarted a CB player's clear look at the basket by putting a hand in his face. He missed his shot. Jaroslav pulled down the rebound. This cluster of plays turned the tide and started our run.

Jaroslav and I worked together as we had countless times before in practice. We put the ball in the basket at a greater clip than České Budějovice. It was as if we were unstoppable. Finally I was just playing the game for itself. The buzzer sounded to signal the half. We led 48-33.

There was jubilation as we ran toward the locker room. Jiri slapped us on the back with extra gusto as we gathered into the empty corner of the cold locker room.

"That last several minutes before half was our best play as a team this year. Keep doing what has gotten you here," Jiri said. He looked in my direction as he said it.

The second half began with the starters going back into the game. Jaroslav hit another reverse layup in traffic. On defense Charles gave up an easy 20 footer to a České Budějovice forward.

"He just let him have that one. That's terrible," Jiri said stamping his foot so hard that the water bottle between Gustav and him fell to the floor. Gustav picked it up. Jiri put his arm around me.

"Josef, give us the same stuff you generated earlier," he said. I couldn't remember what I did to create that greatness. That worried me.

I felt even stiffer, but all I cared about was being able to duplicate the great run we had created at the end of the first half. A České Budějovice player with a short blond Afro and a goatee who looked to be 6'8" reported in from the bench and began to cover me tightly on defense. He had muscular shoulders and long rangy arms. His teammates on the floor greeted him like he was their secret weapon or some kind of fierce lion released from his cage. This could be trouble.

"Sveikas! Jus megaleti suvaidinti krepsinis," he said.

"Can't help you there. Labas to you, too" I said. Labas or hello was the only Lithuanian I knew.

He must have arrived a few minutes earlier because I never saw him on the floor or bench in the first half.

He played me tight on defense; crowding me with his body and slowing my movements under the rim. He screened out hard and made Jaroslav stop throwing anything in my direction. There was no way I could be successful going body to body with him. Even if I wasn't hurting, he was too strong. I decided the only way to beat him was to play into his weakness. Take him outside. Make this big guy chase me through screens.

I was able to take this big České Budějovice threat out of the middle and tire him by running him. I started receiving passes out on the wing and passed to Jaroslav who cut inside for a layup basket. On another possession, I threw the ball to Zedenik for a short open bank shot for two points.

Later, the blond Afro man received the ball on wing and drove to the basket with me at his side. He went up and threw down a monstrous two hand slam dunk. Those were his only points of the day.

A minute later, I received a pass from Jaroslav. I went up to dunk. It went in but to my horror, the glass backboard and rim fell from above. It almost hit me before it crashed to the wood floor. I looked up at the clock. It read 1:26.

The referees gathered on the side to discuss. Then Jiri and Gustav joined them. The CB coaches sauntered over, too. A few times they all looked over at me. They may call a technical foul on me, I thought, or have me thrown out of the game.

Then a 2 meter high metal scaffold was wheeled out to under the basket. They loaded the backboard and rim onto it. Next a janitor and Gustav boarded it and rode it up as Jiri hit a switch operating some kind of pneumatic lift. After 45 minutes, finally it was hoisted back into position. We lost some fans from the bleachers. A few of the CB players lay down on the bench. The Lithuanian player with the Afro threw me a dirty look.

The backboard was back into position. We were allowed to throw up some warm-up shots to insure it was indeed sturdy and stay in place. Then we went back to our benches to talk some strategy. The referee came to our bench to say my dunk didn't count but we would be getting possession of the ball.

The game resumed and České Budějovice immediately fouled Jaroslav. He went to the free throw line and calmly sunk one free throw and then another. České Budějovice furiously raced up the floor and tried to score. And eventually they did, but it wasted too much time. They fouled Charles on the inbound and he marched to the free throw line. He missed the first free throw and hit the second. CB aggressively attacked the basket and their off guard missed an eight-foot jumper in the lane. I pulled down a rebound with 45 seconds remaining, and then I got wacked across the head in their furious attempt to foul. I fell and the whole grid of tape that was on my face did, too. It slid across the floor, coming to a stop near the free throw line. Jaroslav ran to where I laid then turned to face the player that fouled me. After things simmered down, Jaroslav asked if I was okay. Then he reached my hand and pulled me up.

But as I tried to stand back up, my knee buckled. It hurt from falling to the court on the foul.

I didn't like being fouled that hard but wanted to avoid confrontation with the České Budějovice player. Luckily, he missed hitting me across the eyebrow/stitches. As I hobbled around the referee said we would have to keep moving. "Do you want to stay in the game?" I said yes.

So the referee escorted me to the free throw line. I limped over there and hit both free throws before hearing the buzzer. I looked over to see Rudenic was coming in for me.

A smiling Jiri slapped me on the back as I came to the bench.

"Take a seat. Good game Josef," said Jiri.

When the last buzzer echoed out across the court, I looked up to the final score: Svet 77—České Budějovice 67. A Svet win, our first, putting our record at 1-2 since I arrived or 8-9 with the first half of the season included.

The players began to head to the locker room and Gustav was showing the scorebook to Jiri. Our coach studied the book a moment.

"Jaroslav had 28 points tonight to lead the team. I thought you might have broken thirty. Josef had 12 rebounds and 15 points. Good playing, everyone, especially in the first half. We had a lot of energy," said Jiri.

A few minutes later, I heard the reporter in the trench coat Pavelosek from the *Svet Monitor* interviewing Jiri.

"How can you characterize winning tonight with the odds against you and did the fight have anything to do with it?" the reporter said.

"We had something to prove. The American Savek played his best yet. Jaroslav Matura did it all tonight. He may be the most under-rated player in the Superliga."

CHAPTER NINETEEN

A KISS

I made my way on foot, limping slightly, along the narrow streets of Svet. The first snow of the season was falling; new powder on the street and a thin blanket of white gathered on dwarf boxwoods. It was a very early snow even for these elevations.

I discovered a path that led to a green hill. At the top stood a statue of a man on horseback from the Hapsburg era. The Czech writing underneath said he was Karel Havlíček Borovský, one of the fathers of Czech nationalism. It was a lonely, quiet place in a neighborhood of dusty buildings.

When I pulled out a card that had the name and address that Shantelina had written, a small old groundskeeper took notice.

"Be careful. Gypsies are around here," he said.

"Do you know where the *North Bohemia Glass Museum* is?" I said.

"No such thing. What are you looking for? Do you have an address?"

I showed him the index card with Shantelina's writing in red pen.

"I've been caretaker 25 years. No such museum. The only new thing is the statue. It replaced the Czech proletariat worker statue put in after the war."

"Then where is this place?" I said. I showed him the card again. He didn't look at it.

"Good question, comrade, the address is over there. But it must be a mistake," he said. His bony hand pointed further down the street. "You won't find it. Go ahead. Keep your eyes open especially with these Roma near."

Then he picked up a broom and started sweeping the snow off the path.

I walked toward the entrance to the three-story building and noticed its limestone exterior had chisel marks that were the same as those in the corridor of outside our locker room. Then I saw a signhandwritten on cardboard: *Severní Bohémský Sklo Muzeum.*

As I opened the door into the foyer, snowflakes swirled like feathers. I'd entered into what looked like an apartment. Hanging from the ceiling was plastic sheeting used to minimize dust. There were bare drywall partitions and boxes on the floor.

"Ahoj," I said, across the space. It echoed off the bare walls. No one responded, but a light was on.

I walked deeper into the space, then toward an interior stairwell. There was an option of going up and down. I proceeded to take the stairs down where I came upon a brown door. On the wall was a tile with a golden goose—a distinctive family coat of arms. I rapped on the door to this basement apartment but nobody answered. Then I went back to the first floor and stood around restlessly in that space with the construction debris.

After a few minutes, I went up the stairs. And as I did was unsure whether to call her Shantel or Shantelina. But then again she had the same problem with me.

When I reached the top, she was there.

"Come in, player American. You found place. Is snowing, I can see."

"I know we are up here in the mountains. But snowing on September 17? That's amazing," I said.

She dusted snow off my shoulders.

“I read about last night’s game. Are you okay? In fact, here is *Svet Monitor* copy for you,” she said, handing me the Czech newspaper. “In English, this headline would be *Smasher Savek Rips Down Rim*.”

I didn’t like the headline. The backboard never shattered. It just fell.

“I saw that this morning. It just missed hitting me but I wasn’t hurt. Trust me, we needed the win. So where do you need help?” I said.

“You’re notorious now. I show you museum or what will be museum. We open next month,” she said.

She guided me through sparsely furnished second floor rooms. In what looked to be a converted living room, the walls were painted burnished orange and a crystal chandelier hung from the high ceiling. There were no exhibits, just shelves and a few tables here and there.

After seeing the second floor, we walked back down the stairs.

“This first level is the museum space, too but needs work to be complete,” she said.

“I can see. What’s the plan? You say it’s going to open next month. How can that be?” I said.

“It will happen. We pick up these boxes and move them upstairs to main room,” she said. There were maybe 50 boxes.

“What’s in these things?”

“Candlesticks, powder boxes, and covered jars. All made of glass. Czech and Slovakian. Will be permanent part of the exhibit,” she said.

We moved box after box up the stairs.

“Wenceslas will come to help, too,” Shantelina said, before picking up another box.

“Where is he?” I said.

“He’ll be here. The boxes are fragile. Don’t drop especially with your smasher reputation,” she said. We smiled.

“You’re good, Shantelina,” I said.

Our hands mistakenly touched as she handed me a box.

I liked this girl.

Smasher? It was an ironic name for me because I saw myself as creating, not destroying.

About an hour later, I was sweating. And so was she. There were a lot of boxes but we moved them all. Some heavy ones, too. I looked at the fruits of our labor: a sea of boxes across the floor in the room with the chandelier.

"What do you need done now?" I said.

She walked over to the window of that room, parted the curtains and peeked out for a moment. I joined her.

"Wenceslas should have come. We still have more to do. But we rest first."

"Yes, right when we finish the work. Then he'll show," I said.

The window commanded a view of the entrance to the building, the street below, and the snow.

The snow re-constructed the light, bent it, colored it, bounced it. The whole scene was hypnotically arresting.

I spotted a group of what looked like homeless people pushing a cart. They ambled along the path below in a group including some children. They had long dark hair, even the men.

"They're Romies. Don't want trouble from them," she said, whispering the last part.

Shantelina stepped back to stay out of view. I moved back two steps, but not before two of the gypsies looked up at me in the window. Shantelina didn't see that they spotted us.

"Let me get us some water. Stay," she said. She retreated back across the room.

I could still see out from that vantage point.

There was an attached plant box out there. It had only soil in it. Then I noticed the plant box had a frozen stream running down the center. There were little weeds along its banks. A miniature Jizera River running through Svet.

When she came back with two glasses of water, I pulled a wooden bench toward the window. We sat down, drank, and looked out the window together. The silent snow sifted downward. Then a few moments later some snow crystals bounced off the windowpane, landing on the stone ledge. Other flakes hit the glass and melted.

"Let me read what we are going to say in English about this exhibit:

> *From 1850-1900, North Bohemia companies generated export trade and mass-produced colored glass for shipment across Europe and America. This area, later known as Czechoslovakia, was considered to be one of the most important historic centers of glass production. It was the home to over 600 companies creating glass items. Objects in the exhibition show the creativity and technical prowess of Czech and Slovak craftsmen.*

"Tell me what you think," Shantelina said.

"I can see you love this stuff," I said.

"You think so?"

"Yes, it's obvious," I said.

"You're right, I do," she said.

She smiled and looked at me intently.

"You seem happier since you got here," she said.

"What do you mean, I was stuffy?" I said.

"I mean cautious," she said.

Of course, I was. I had to be. And Shantelina was the only one who knew the real me.

Her brown hair had reddish undertones in the light. The fullness of her lips was beautiful. We looked at each with a firm glance.

I leaned in toward her and we kissed. This went on for about 30 seconds until she backed away.

"What's wrong?" I said.

"Sorry, I should not have done that. We have more to do," she said.

We both stood up.

I didn't regret the kiss. The truth is we enjoyed each other and never as evidently as that day.

"What about the words I wrote?" she said, looking back out the window.

"They're very good. It's good you have the Slovakian mentioned in there, too," I said.

We started taking each piece out of the boxes. We heard someone walking up the back stairs. Then Wenceslas appeared.

"Hello, I'm here to help," he said.

"Wenceslas, I knew you would make it. Here is star from paper today. You know Josef?" she said.

"Of course, the American. I read the story about the game. They've made you a hero. Impressive," he said.

His voice was soft and hard at once, like the noise of car tires on wet gravel. Nevertheless, I tried to like the guy.

We shook hands.

"I thought you might be the gypsies," I said.

"No gypsies. I'm just late. I had some calls to make before coming," he said.

The three of us went through the boxes, unwrapping each piece of glass and placing it out on a table for cataloging by the volunteers Shantelina said were coming the next day.

"This is hard work. This can be finished another day. What do you say we stop?" said Wenceslas.

"We have only four more to do. They have to be out and ready for the people tomorrow. We've made good progress. Almost there," she said.

"I want to take my girlfriend to dinner," said Wenceslas.

"That's fine. You two go ahead. I can finish these last four," I said.

"Player American, are you sure?" Shantelina said. She looked at me with full attention.

"Yes, no problem. I'll handle it," I said.

"You are...that is wonderful, thank you. Here is the key to lock this place when you're done," she said.

CHAPTER TWENTY

THE RUSSIANS

I stood in a knot of players outside the Svet gym in the foggy morning air. Everyone had their bags packed for a long stint away from Svet.

Six road games in eight days.

I was happy I kissed Shantelina. She was the person I would miss the most. I realized it at that moment.

Jiri said the trip to Ostrava would take four and a half hours.

"Where's our bus? Coach said to be here at 6:30 and it's past that now," said Anton.

Anton pulled out a cell phone, a bulky flip-down model that looked like a toy, like they all did in 1993. He punched in some numbers but had no luck reaching anyone.

"It's time to get things back to order in this team," said Anton.

"We got the first win without you guys," I said.

"That's true," said Jaroslav in the pack.

"Against České Budějovice? They have never been good in the Superliga. Jaroslav, you've been around long enough to know that," said Anton.

"A win is a win. Jaroslav played great," I said.

"Jaroslav? What is he, your brother or something? You two are back on the bench today. Let the professionals take charge now," he said.

"That's enough from you two. Both of you will be done here if you keep it up," said Jiri as he approached us through the foggy morning air.

"Where is the bus, Coach?" Anton said.

"It's only 6:45, we're fine. Gustav is fueling up, he'll be here soon." Jiri said.

Then out of the darkness the highlight beams flashed. A dark blue bus rolled past us. It had a picture of a lion and a basketball on the side with the words *Svet Lvi Tým Košíkova* or *Svet Lions Basketball Team*. Gustav manuevered the bus in a wide circle so the side with the words *Svet Hrdost* faced us. *Svet Pride*.

Our driver opened the door at the feet of our waiting group. Gustav was grinning from behind an overly large steering wheel like the captain of a royal yacht. Jaroslav and I stepped into the idling bus and looked down its narrow aisle.

We took a seat in the front. The large windows on either side of the bus didn't open, but small slats at the tops slid forward to allow six inches of air to flow in. I opened ours and leaded gasoline exhaust came in.

"Shut that until we get going, Josef," Gustav said.

Jiri sat behind Gustav alone. Anton, Vojtech and Kolin had staked out the best seats near the back.

We were on the road for hours, passing through a dark fir forest. My legs felt like wood. Soon after, we stopped for lunch in a small village outside Olomouc. Our travelling circus of players poured into the restaurant. Jiri knew the proprietor, who seemed happy for the business, passing out plates of kureci prsa, zelene, blond lagers, rolls.

"No beer. Sorry, we have a game in a few hours," Jiri said. The owner plucked away the beer.

The patrons of the restaurant seemed delighted with our arrival. The whole place came alive with conversation and Czech songs that I had never heard before. And that was without the beer for us.

After lunch, the journey continued on through the Czech countryside. Gustav began to pull off to the shoulder of the road every few miles to look at a map. That worried me.

Small black Skodas and semis whistled by us at 160 kilometers per hour. We passed over swollen rivers brown with mud as a light drizzle fell. Eventually we reached the small city of Ostava. We pulled into a parking lot.

ČEZ Aréna.

The stadium looked like a square spaceship painted with the red, white, and blue design that was on the Czech flag.

Getting off the bus, the team went through a side door into the corridor of the gym to the visiting locker room. It was three times the size of our dungeon locker room at Svet.

"I don't have to tell you how important this game is. Ostrava filled their foreign player quota with Russians. If that doesn't raise your ire, nothing will. We were held back by the Soviet Union superpower long enough. We're all Czechs and Vojtech, a Bulgari," said Jiri.

We all put our hands to the center of the circle. Eastern Europeans of the world unite.

We yelled unison: *Svet Hrdost Svet Hrdost Svet Hrdost*

"Let's go out there and beat them with Czech basketball," Jiri said.

Coming out of the tunnel, we took the floor—a rectangular playing surface—that was surrounded by formidable concentric rings for seating. It matched the letter O in Ostrava. I wondered how they did that, especially since the building outside was square. Unlike the Svet gym that had retractable bleachers like the ones in high school gyms, CEZ Arena had concrete stadium seats, maybe thirty rows high.

ČEZ Aréna reminded me of the Rockford Metro Center that held 7,900 back in Illinois. This place looked like it could hold at least 2,000 more than that.

Light streamed through a large window grid from above the court. It was like a glass arboretum. The rims were tight. Bank shots I took in warm-ups clanged off the rim. The same shots kissed off the glass backboard and dropped in at Svet arena. Or at least mine did.

Sizing up the Ostrava team, they weren't at all the wild-haired Russians as I expected. In fact, they looked Czech, although more ugly and mean-looking than any I'd seen to date. Okay, there were two Russians: one was a shooting guard who stood about 6'1" and the other was a big, bony and long-limbed center at 6'8".

The Russian shooting guard tossed up a shot from 15 feet out. The ball wobbled toward the basket after it left his fingertips. Terrible form. But it banked off the glass and in. Later he received feeds on the perimeter from his teammates. Each shot launched was from beyond the FIBA regulation three-point line.

One, two, three.

Three swishes.

Mr. Wobble Shot looked like he would give us plenty of trouble.

We were the first game in a doubleheader. Following us was an exhibition basketball game between the Czech national team battling a team from Moscow.

Jiri walked out onto the floor during our warm-ups and pointed out the Russian players.

"Yes, we know. One of them shoots weird," Anton said.

"But the shots are falling," Jaroslav said.

"We'll see about that. With me on him, it'll be a different story," Anton said.

Our first team Czech all-stars took the floor. Even though Jaroslav and my team had swept all three games in the practice the day before, the first team players were going to start the game. It made no sense.

Ostrava's starting five included the two Russkies. They were tall and muscular, but their tightness or inflexibility gave me hope. We could wear them out with our speed and fast break.

"I have never seen most of these guys before. In the off-season they picked up a lot of new players," said Jiri.

There might have been 700 people tightly ringed around the court. The sheer size of the place made it look like there was nobody watching our game.

Ostrava's muscle men took an early lead. They were very aggressive and kept their bodies on Anton and Vojtech almost at all times. Anton took a shot from four feet out and was hammered. No foul was called.

Jiri stood up.

"That was a foul. Are you calling anything today?" he said to the referee who ran pass our bench. The referee ran past ignoring our coach.

Ostrava used their physical strength to their advantage. I was surprised how quick they were. They were getting fast break points on us and took smart shots. Ostrava passed the ball deliberately on the perimeter. We countered their scoring with baskets of our own.

Several times Ostrava got the ball down low and had a wide path to the basket. But instead of taking the shot, their big players passed back outside. Mr. Wobble Shot hauled in the pass on the perimeter and launched bombs from three point land. The shots went in. The two bombs in row from three point land gave Ostrava a lead of 23-15. Jiri tapped me on the shoulder.

"We need a bigger lineup in there. Go in for Charles," Jiri said. I made sure the tape on my face was tight and ran in. I found my man and was ready for defense.

"What's the mask for?" the player I was defending said.

"Your elbows," I said.

In the first minute I was in the game, Ostrava was passing the ball around us to find an open opportunity to score. But our stiff defense stopped them. As I shadowed my man on defense, one of their muscle men blocked my path with his body. A classic pick. I was ready for it. I slid around it and then another Ostrava player stepped in front of me. A second pick. It stopped me in my tracks and he landed an elbow against my ribs that the referees didn't see. That hurt like hell. Anton stepped up to blunt their drive. I spun around to cover his man on the switch. The forearms of another Ostrava player collided against my back. That pick caught me blind and stopped me from switching. The Ostrava ball handler on the wing dumped into my man, who broke loose from me and scored an easy reverse layup.

Wherever I went, they were a step ahead.

As my time in the game went on, the Ostrava team played us so well it seemed that they had scouted us and put together a great strategy that played into our weaknesses. Their Russian center covering me matched me with physical contact and blocking out on rebounds. As the halftime horn blew, Anton threw up a shot from half court in frustration. The shot grazed the rubber padding on top of the backboard and continued into the bleachers behind the basket.

I looked over at the scoreboard Ostrava 42 Svet 32. With the way we'd played up to that point, we were lucky to be only ten points down.

When we arrived in the locker room, Anton and Zedenik kicked some lockers.

"You need to improve, Savek. You have to get through those picks faster," Anton said.

Jiri and Gustav entered the locker room.

Jiri said, "I know this game means a lot to us. All of us know Czechs sent to Siberia because the people that ruled this country. Suprisingly, they're playing with the emotion. Not us. We have to step it up. Their only true scorer is the Russian guard. Harass him on the perimeter. Slow his movements, Anton. They're disciplined, running a structured offense, passing but not moving much. Take advantage of that."

We gathered up vowing to do better before going out back on the floor. Then Jiri came along side me.

"Josef, you're the key to us getting back into this game. We need your spark when you get in there. Pick up our energy level," said Jiri, and slapped me on the butt.

Five minutes into the second half, Ostrava continued their aggressive and spirited play. Red-shirted Ostrava players were diving for loose balls and matching our points. On one Ostrava procession they missed three times, but each time the ball was tipped into out to red shirted players on the perimeter. We were down 48-38.

"Josef, go in for Kolin and give us what we need," said Jiri.

After I checked in, Jaroslav followed me into the game. Now we are in business, I thought.

Jaroslav looked at me with assurance that our scheme would prevail. He conveyed the most winning look of anyone I had ever played with. He received an inbound pass and bolted into a dribble. I sprinted down court watching his eyes the whole way, then took up a position at the low post. The Russian muscle man defending behind me ground his fist into my lower back. I lowered myself even more.

This guy wanted to assert control from waist level up to the shoulders. I gave them that, then lowered my center of gravity into a ridiculous crouch for a moment. Then I lowered my hands to knee level. A red shirt stepped in front of me. I was sandwiched by defenders so I moved across the lane. One step, two steps, three steps. Then I turned back to retake my original position. The feigned movement across and back to where I had started left me wide open. Jaroslav laid down a bounce pass bullet that I corralled in. I went up and was hammered across the arms. No foul. My shot ricocheted into the arms of an Ostrava rebounder. Play went back the other way on the miss.

Ostrava drove to the basket on the break. I ran hard, angry to get in position. I got to the lane and cleanly blocked the shot. The whistle blew. Foul on 33. My number. As I lined up to watch the red-shirted guard shoot his free throws, I looked up to see fans streaming to the seats. For my North Park College Vikings this would have been a huge crowd. But that was the world of NCAA Division III; this was international basketball against Russians.

I was getting blasted from right to left inside. Jaroslav and I did connect up on a delayed fast break with Jaroslav advancing the ball to me with a beautiful pass when the red shirted defender let down his guard. I scored on a dunk. That's a good outlet for my anger, I thought. The fans liked that one, which told me that the newly arrived fans were lukewarm in their support of Ostrava.

Most of the time Zedenik had the ball at the point, and he never threw that pass to me, but he would to Anton. Every time rebounds came off the glass, two or more Ostrava players were there. I could not battle through their wall. I was getting worn down. As the game continued on, Ostrava's red power kept coming. With three minutes to go in the game, Jiri called a time out. Our Svet squad was on the ropes 63-50. Walking toward the bench I was awed by the attendance boom. At least half the gym had filled up. That's five thousand more fans than were here to start of this game. We were the warm up act.

It was like there were two events going on at one time: the game on the court and the fans arriving. Jiri made a mass substitution, three players at once. He kept me and Jaroslav in. Anton and his Czech all-stars sauntered off the court. They had their chances and couldn't convert. He couldn't tell me, "I told you so." Mostly, the second unit coming in made Anton irate. I was frustrated I could not do more to stop the Svet hemorrhage but was happy for another reason. This was the first time we got the chance to play as one unit in a game.

After ferreting out our defensive coverage, we went to work. I knew that Jaroslav was the best clutch player in this kind of situation. Three minutes was a lot of time. When a loose ball was rolling out near half court I dove upon it and without getting up, I flipped it to Jaroslav streaking up the court. I jumped back to my feet and trailed him to the basket. Jaroslav stalled when he ran into two bigger players. He passed to me. I passed it back to Jaroslav for the give-and go. Our ace shot and missed. I rebounded it underneath and went back up for a score.

Later, Jaroslav drove to the basket and was hit on one side and then the other and fell to the floor. He bounced back to his feet. It was then I learned that Jaroslav was the strongest player I had ever played with.

The only player I could compare him to was Šarūnas Marčiulionis, who played for the USSR National Team and the Golden State Warriors.

Jaroslav stepped up to the free throw line and hit both free throws on the foul. The fans began to get into the game and the arena was electrified. After a time out, we set up a press that led to several more baskets off steals. It looked like we were going to overtake Ostrava and win the game. Momentum was fully with us. Then with thirty seconds to go the Russian player received a pass with the ball on the perimeter. He launched a wobbly shot from long range. It went in for three points. It was like a dagger to the heart. The dream was broken and it stopped our furious comeback.

Even Jaroslav hesitated for a second and then he ran to inbound the ball. We raced back to our basket and he was smothered by two players. He got the pass off to Charles, who hit an eight-footer in the lane. But we couldn't score again.

The final buzzer signaled the muscle men had beaten us. Ostrava 68-Svet 66. We mustered a 17-3 run. The huge crowd was happy with the Svet blood spilled but they seemed more interested in what was coming next: taking Russia to task. Time had breezed past.

"That three minutes was more fun than the rest of the game," I said to Jaroslav as we walked off the floor.

Jiri looked crestfallen. He reluctantly moved out to center court to offer the other coach some words. It had looked so promising after the last game. Something had to change or this was going to be a long season.

CHAPTER TWENTY-ONE

ULTIMATUM

After the game against Ostrava, we all boarded the team bus. Gustav drove into the darkness and Jiri looked down at a list of addresses on a clipboard. Two-by-two we were dropped in different places all around the city that night as the bus emptied until just Jaroslav and I were left. We got off at a home near the city center of Ostrava. Koliar and our coaches stayed at a hotel.

The family we stayed with knew our team owner Koliar. The husband and wife ushered us through the dark brown wood paneled hallways of their Ostrava home. Our room was so small, it was almost a closet. It was almost midnight and we didn't take much time to talk.

The next morning neither us remembered what time the bus was set to leave, so we decided to find out. While Jaroslav went to get a newspaper, I boarded a tram across town to the hotel where our coaches stayed.

When I reached Jiri's hotel room, the door opened abruptly. There I was standing face-to-face with Gustav. I said hello and he smiled and revealed his golden dental work. He pushed past me out of the room.

"It's all right, Josef. Come in," Jiri said.

Milos Koliar was sitting at the desk in the room, smoking a cigarette and fiddling with a glass ashtray on the desk. Jiri stood by the window. The tendrils of smoke from Koliar danced in the sunlight.

Besides the smoke, the air contained a powerful mix of competing colognes.

"Should he remain as coach of this team?" Koliar said to me.

"Yes, he should," I said.

"Have a seat, Josef. I'll be right with you," Jiri said.

I sat on a couch along the wall. Koliar glanced over to me then back to Jiri.

"Milos, let's put this in perspective, we've played 18 games so far," said Jiri.

"And you lost ten of them. Before the American and Bulgari arrived, you finished in sixth place, a second division placing. We're sliding, I'd say. You were expelled from the Party and State Security had you on their list as `politically unreliable,'" Koliar added.

"True. What's that have to do with anything?" Jiri said.

"I saved you, gave you a job when no one else would. Remember that?" Koliar said.

"What do you want?" said Jiri.

"I expect," Koliar said, "you to step down as coach when the team arrives back to Svet. The only thing that will change my mind is if you win the rest of the games on this road trip."

The remainder of our road trip was against Brno, Plzeň, the two Prague teams and Pardubice, the four P teams being the best teams in the Superliga.

"Who do you have in mind as our new coach?" Jiri said.

"The man that I just sent out to get coffee for us. He's wanted the chance."

Gustav as our new coach. He sided with the first team players, so you could predict I would see even less playing time. But then again I wasn't getting the minutes even with Jiri coaching.

Koliar shifted his body behind the desk and inhaled from his cigarette.

"Savek, Savek," he said as if he were ringing a bell. "Where are you from in the United States again?"

"Chicago," Jiri answered for me.

"If you were such a good player, you would still be there," Koliar said.

This is an ambush, I've stepped into.

"You must be really lost to land here. We can't afford you to play like it's your first time out there. I'm not sure why we gave you another chance," he said.

This man liked hitting that nail.

"Why did you?" I asked, genuinely curious.

Koliar stood up. Then he turned his body toward the sidewall that showed his paunchy side profile.

"You're not even two meters tall but we need the height on this team. Coach said you could help us. I took him at his word about you," he said, not looking at me in the eyes. Then he left the room.

After he did, Jiri shook his head in disbelief. He turned and looked out the window.

"Josef, my mother Alžběta is sick," he said.

"I know," I said, then looked at him more carefully.

"She's good at hiding it. I don't know how much longer she has. When I left home yesterday she said, "Thank you for being a good son. I hope I was a good mother, at least I've tried to be," he said.

Alžběta looked pretty good, at least when we had brought her back to the house the week before.

"Sorry to hear that. Alžběta is a great woman, I can see that, Jiri."

I was struck by how empty what I said sounded, but I really felt it. My words couldn't penetrate the deep cavern of thought he was in.

"It's been good to coach you, Josef," Jiri said, shaking my hand.

"Is it over then?" I said.

"You heard Koliar, we need five in a row," he said.

"Any thoughts on how we are going to turn things around?" I said.

"Besides not going back to Svet? Not really. What do you think?" he said.

"I have some ideas. One of them is to have the whole second unit go in as one. We can do more if we have a chance in the games. Keep the two units separate," I said.

"How's that a solution?" he said.

"We have the connection and chemistry, so keep each team together. Revolve us in when Anton's team gets tired. You asked for a suggestion; that's what I would do," I said.

"You have a point there. I saw what you could do together last night. Let me think about it. Josef, the bus leaves at 10," he said.

It was almost as if he read my mind.

As I waited for a tram to the place we were staying, I thought about all I'd heard in the hotel room. Playing on the team coached by someone other than Jiri would be a tragedy. Gustav or even Koliar coaching us would be a disaster for me. And just as I was gaining momentum with Jaroslav—to have it all taken away!

Jaroslav and I had a good European breakfast that morning provided by the Ostrava homeowners where we had spent the night. Besides the ham croquettes, bread, and cheese, we were served was the best yogurt I had ever tasted. It was creamy and a perfect balance of tart and sweet.

I looked at the label on the plastic yogurt container and it said "Made in Slovakia." That reminded me of Shantelina. Her brow, her cheek, her smile came to my mind.

I remembered talking to Shantelina, a few days before the kiss.We walked together to mail a letter to her parents in Slovakia. I loved hearing Shantelina talk about her family and traditions. Shantelina started to drop the envelope into the mailbox, then pulled it back, and kissed it before it dropped into the metal post box.

I was struck by how much that small moment and other interactions with her impacted me. I'd never met a person like her. But I tempered that thought with reality: she had a long-time boyfriend. And she never said, "Forget him; I want you."

But Shantelina had said, "Write me while you are on this trip."

“I’m not exactly the writing type,” I said.

“Yes, you are. You wrote me romantic letter with poem to show me you were interested.”

“Romantic? You joked about it.”

“It was sweet, sentimental. Hard to stop thinking about,” she said.

“I’ll write. But won’t I see you before letters reach you?” I said.

“Not if you write me early in the trip. Mail system is fast and efficient. You drop a letter in mail in Ostrava or Brno, it will be on overnight train to Svet and in my hands the next morning. It will be good for my English to read them,” Shantelina had said.

Overnight mail delivery by train: what a concept. I remembered my mother saying some old Czechs sent letters from the Chicago’s Pilsen to newly arrived relatives in New York City by overnight mail. Back and forth that way. But that was in the 1930s.

We were back on the bus. It was good to get out of Ostrava after the loss. We weren’t scheduled to play that night, but the day after. When we arrived in the suburbs of Brno, the team bus sputtered to a stop along the road. Gustav, who had been driving, and Jiri climbed down from the bus. They opened the hood and smoke poured out. Gustav reached in and tugged something near the engine. A shower of steam and oil exploded out as the two of them recoiled from the hood. Jiri asked a passerby on the street something and the stranger pointed in front of him. Jiri stepped back up into the bus.

“We have an engine problem. Luckily, there is a gas station a half kilometer away, so everybody off the bus. We’re pushing the thing,” Jiri said.

We all got off the bus and Jiri hopped into the driver’s seat. We pushed. He steered. The few cars on the road crept around us, drivers peering out their car windows taking in the scene. A few of them had bemused smiles. In the distance the gas station came into focus. It must have been an impressive sight to see twelve men pushing a bus up the road, because the owner and another man stood in the doorway of an open service bay, watching in amazement. They guided us in.

After the owner looked under the hood for the few minutes, he wiped off his hands on a shop towel.

"Is there any way we can get it fixed today?" Jiri said.

"Impossible, we have to order parts. Two days, that's what we need. In the meantime, follow me," he said.

We walked around to the side of the building to a 26' truck with a tarp on the back.

"You have a whole team here. I'll let you have this until your bus is ready," the owner said.

"We'll take it," Jiri said.

The owner and his employee rolled down the tarp to a flatbed in the back with a gate around it. It looked like a World War II troop transport truck since there were benches along the inside of the truck. We offloaded our bags from the bus and transferred them onto the truck. The twelve of us got in the back and spread out on the benches. As we drove through the streets of Brno, I noticed that everything was flat in the south, unlike the mountainous terrain in the north. The weather in Brno was warmer than in snowy Svet. We came to stop on a street with a line of old buildings on one side and a green city park on the other. We climbed off the truck and it pulled away with Gustav behind the wheel.

"Gustav will take the gear to the hotel where I'll be staying. Of course, you players will stay in homes across the city. But given our situation, we should take our minds off basketball for a while. We'll have lunch and then see some of Brno," Jiri said.

Given our situation? Which one? Jiri was to be removed as our basketball coach if we lost another game. His mother was about to die. Or the more obvious one, that we were going to play tourists in a troop transport truck.

We all marched into an old style Czech restaurant and took seats along the enormous windows that looked out to the park. Jiri ordered all us lunch and a pivo, compliments of the team. As several waiters descended upon us with cold mugs of golden lager, one blew foam of the top and placed the pivo in front of me.

"Have any of you been to Austerlitz?" Jiri said.

"I know the place. But why there?" Anton said.

"It's close only 10 kilometers from here. Napoleon defeated the Russian and Austrian coalition in 1805 to capture the continent. Austerlitz was his most decisive victory," said Jiri. "In fact, we're off to the Austerlitz battlefield after lunch," he added.

The kiss had changed everything with Shantelina. I felt we might have something between us, but I also felt awkward.

Dear Shantelina,

First of all, I want to let you know Jaroslav and I played really well against Ostrava. It was our best stretch of basketball together. We almost won it last night. It was an amazing comeback, and we even were ahead with 30 seconds left, but their guard from Russia beat us on a three-point bomb. Now we have to win every remaining game on this trip because Milos Koliar gave Coach Jiri an ultimatum: win the rest of our games or be dismissed from his coaching duties. That's not going to be easy because we're now facing the best teams in the Superliga.

I write you from the living room of a family we have been assigned to stay with here in Brno. I really like Brno and all it has to offer. There was no practice today, but we took a trip out to Austerlitz and to other landmarks in Brno. Tell you about that later.

I learned that the bell in the town tower here in Brno rings twelve times at 11 a.m. each day. It's an interesting tourist fact. Three hundred years ago, the Swedes were in a war with the Hapsburgs for control of Brno. The Swedes were determined breach the fortress walls and capture the city. The Swedish general had launched several offensives to take it against the Hapsburg defenders and failed. He made up his mind to attack and carry out one last offensive until midday. Amazingly, the bells were so reliable that Swedish soldiers tracked time by the town bell like everyone else. The man that rang the belltower heard about the Swedes' plan. He decided to ring the town bell with twelve chimes when it was only 11 a.m. Upon hearing the twelve bells, the general sent his officers a message to stop and pull back. It's said the invasion was beaten back by the clock in the bell tower. The city was saved.

Shantelina, this is the most interesting city I've ever been to. On to Mendel's monastery tomorrow —you know, the monk whose work with peas led to modern gene theory. A lot of my own genes have a connection to this place. My high school in Chicago was named after Mendel. I can't wait to see you again when I get back to Svet next week.

Yours,

FRANK

I held back sending the note. And questioned whether signing it "Yours" was wise or even true. Was I hers, really? I really did look forward to seeing Shantelina again. And at the same time I wondered who Shantelina was.

The next morning I mailed the letter. Then I lifted weights at a storefront health club with the rest of the guys on the team. My every-other-day practice of lifting weights continued. I hadn't missed once since I got to the country.

After showering in the club's locker room, I dressed near a man whose upper back had a large indentation in the shape of a near perfect square crater. The section looked like he had a small electrical junction box ripped out just below his shoulder blade. The skin around it stretched to fill in and whatever it was, this was no fresh cut; it had happened several years, if not decades, in the past.

He stood to face his locker for a while so I had gotten a good look at his back from behind. He had gray hair on his arms and a balding head. Older than my father and old enough to be in World War II.

"How did you hurt your back?" I said.

He turned around to see who had spoken to him. We faced each other. He looked at me peripherally. Then at Jaroslav nearby.

"Who are you?" he said.

"My name is Savek and this is Jaroslav. The rest of these guys around here are our teammates," I said, gesturing with my hand to the rest of the guys, who were in their own conversations. "We play on the Svet Lions Basketball Sportsclub in the Superliga."

"Jan Weiner's my name. Svet? I didn't even know they had a team and in the Superliga at that," he said.

"A lot of people say that. Yes, Svet has a team. You can see us play tonight against Brno," Jaroslav said.

"As for the injury on my back, the KGB did it. But I don't want to talk about it," the man said.

"Are you sure? I'd like to hear about that," I said. He shook his head to say no.

"See you tonight at the game," the man said. Then he shook my hand to say goodbye. It was a weird handshake like he was escorting or more like pulling me out of the room. We were leaving anyway.

Jaroslav and I went back to the home we were staying in and had breakfast. After breakfast, the husband showed us around his two-story home. He opened up doors to whole rooms that were beautifully decorated but were cold and musty. It seemed that everything was in wood.

"How long have you owned this home?" I said.

"Twenty years. This house was built by a longtime mayor from here. I still have the building plans for this place," he said.

When he came to his study, there were books on the wall and a fire in the fireplace. He pushed away reading glasses and a few law journals that were on the desk in the center.

"Have a seat, gentleman," the man said.

We had talked for a half an hour when there was a knock on the front door.

"I'm a fan of the team. I came to see the American," said someone on the front landing. I could hear that so clearly through the window.

Then the wife and Jelina strode in toward us in the study. "Josef, this woman from Svet asked to see you," his wife said.

Jelina looked great in a solid blue dress and sweeping auburn hair.

"I was in the area. And I work for the team," Jelina said.

She knew how to stretch the truth. She worked for the Glass Factory and Koliar, but this was highly unusual. I couldn't tell if it was official business or what she was there for.

Intrigued. That's what I was. If she came to Brno for me, that was truly impressive. I thought I was done with her.

"She's a supporter from early on," Jaroslav said.

"Jelina, let's talk," I said.

Everyone cleared out. We had the study with law books all around us.

"Are these your parents or something? That woman asked me all these questions before they let me see you," said Jelina, in a quiet voice while glancing at the closed door.

"Jelina, what are you doing here?"

"I'm here to be with you. I've heard you're free today to see Brno," said Jelina. She stood so her hip brushed the edge of the table, near my hand.

"That's true; I'm going to tour the Mendel monastery. Nobody wanted to see it, not even Jaroslav, but I'd like to," I said.

"Most tourists go there. I'll take you to where Mendel lived; he researched the peas there. I know where it's supposed to be and we can walk there together. Let's just spend time together and enjoy it," she said.

She stepped toward me.

Enjoy what? I didn't want to go with her.

A few minutes later, as we walked out of the house together, I knew a better man — a purer spirit would be able to resist Jelina. But then that part of my brain slammed shut.

"Jelina, besides the monastery, where else do you want to go?" I said.

"Anywhere but around here," she said.

She reached for my hand and rested her head on my shoulder as we walked. Here we were, Koliar's model employee and the second string battler from America who had barely made the team.

We arrived at Brno's Abbey of Saint Thomas. It was more museum than monastery. The Mendelianum. Amazingly, everything was written in Czech. No English. Despite being a better speaker of Czech than reader, I read everything about Gregori Mendel, who had lived and worked there. In the garden were the original foundations of the greenhouse, where he had conducted all his work on genetics.

Jelina was way ahead of me. Skimming but not interested. When she reached the end, she circled back to where I was reading.

"That was pretty good, but let's get out of here," Jelina said.

"I'm not done yet, Jelina. Give me some more time," I said.

Afterward, we went to a nearby café, and I ordered us coffee and kolaches. She found us a table.

"If you could go now, would you go back to America? Wouldn't that be great? What I mean to say is this: where will you go after this ends?" she said, sitting across from me.

"I don't know. But I'm not going to think about that now. Plus, I'm not leaving, I just arrived. Why? Do you know something that I don't?"

"No, I don't have a crystal ball. But permit me to read your palm. I know Roma fortune telling." She grabbed my hand and turned it over.

She looked at it, and then suddenly pulled my arm closer to her, tickling me. I looked into her eyes. She was beautiful, and there was no denying that. We were together again in something. Not the uncontrollable hilarity like I'd shared with Shantelina, but laughter.

"I thought you were going to read my palm. Tell me what you see," I said.

"Your heart line shows a passionate romantic life. I see you'll have a long life. A work in progress. That's your fate line here. You have one of those, not everyone has a line like that on their palm. But there's a break in your fate line. That signifies a sudden change made in your life.The bigger question is, what do you want here?"

"I want to play well here. Reach my potential with this opportunity," I said.

I didn't say find true love and have a closer relationship to my family.

A sadness washed over me. I wanted to give the relationship a chance, but I was withholding. If I told her the truth—that I was Frank— then maybe that would be the key to unlock things. That would help me really understand my feelings and maybe she would draw closer if I told her.

"You're interested in Shantelina, too. I can see that. I have my sources beyond your hand," she said. We were still holding hands. I felt the urge to release our grip but didn't.

"I don't want to talk about her. She has a boyfriend," I said. "So there you go, she's a good, lovely person. You just said it, she's taken."

I hated it in the first place that she knew about that there was something between Shantelina and me. I didn't want Jelina to interfere with with Shantelina.

"Nothing's clear right now."

"Okay, enough on that. It makes you uncomfortable. What do you think of us?" Jelina said.

I was going to tell her my real name right then. But I came to my senses, telling myself that, divulging that secret to one person was enough.

"I like you but I'm cautious. Not sure we're right for each other," I said.

"What you mean? What do you expect?"

"We need to learn more about each other. It's too early to tell," I said.

"Not sure I like that. You know it's odd, but I've always cared more for the things I was losing."

Losing? What did the woman want me to say, assign my heart to her right there in the cafe? While I was willing to spend the day with her, I couldn't do that.

CHAPTER TWENTY-TWO

WHAT HAPPENED IN BRNO

Jiri pulled me aside an hour before our game with Brno.

"Josef, I've been thinking about the idea you had yesterday morning. I can see it working. We do have the full complement of players at all positions on each team but eight minutes wouldn't be long enough to get that team into the flow. Ten to twelve minutes at a time and then a switch would work." said Jiri. His brown eyes were alive with the possibility.

"You just need to execute it from your end. Milos may not like it, at first, but if it works, he will," said Jiri.

"What about Anton?" I said.

"I'll handle Anton. Let's win this one," said Jiri, he slapped me on the rump to send me on my way.

Jiri unveiled the new strategy a few minutes later as the team sat in the locker room. Jiri didn't make much eye contact with me as he spoke. Predictably, the starters didn't like it. What I didn't expect was that my own second team players seemed to be hesitant when he spoke about it, too. Jaroslav was shaking his head in disagreement like it was a bad idea, but Zedenik must have seen something valuable in rolling out the plan, as he nodded his head to affirm it. Jiri seemed to be unfazed by any reaction. I took that to mean that the strategy was going to be put in effect no matter what anyone thought.

Coming out of the tunnel onto the floor, I felt some good energy during the warm-ups, feeling decent in spite of the beginnings of a sore throat. That was a good sign. The explosive wild-man energy I had been feeling in the last two practices was not what I had that night. I had to forget about being sick and focus on basketball.

Jiri said I should sit on the end of the bench so I wouldn't give anyone else on the team what I had. Taking the last seat on the bench, I noticed Brno had a black player. Looks pretty good. Maybe 6'7". He was jumping center at mid-court against Vojtech. I looked up at the scoreboard on the wall, scanned the list seeing the name Byron Wallace. He's wearing knee braces on both knees. Bad knees. Looks in his late 30s.

Vojtech won the tip by cheating. Going up a millisecond before it left the referee's hands. Anton came down with the ball and found Zedenik streaking to the basket for a sneaky two. Brno came down and scored when Wallace spun off the baseline into the middle with one big dribble and tossed in a jump hook. Our team played Brno well right from the beginning. Anton got a breakaway dunk. Rudenic began to hit shots from behind the three-point line. When Jiri called for the Big Switch, we had the lead by seven, 25-18.

I went in with my group. Our five in; Anton's five out. Like some circus carnival act. Our ten minutes of fame. Jaroslav dribbled the ball on the perimeter as he held up three fingers. The Stonewall Play. Charles and I came to the right side. I spread my legs and planted my feet. Next I could feel Charles' shoulder graze against mine and knew I was in the right place. Milan popped behind the wall we created; he received a bullet pass from Jaroslav. He went up for the shot and missed a 20-footer. Jaroslav got the long rebound. He drove to the middle and threw a high rainbow that swished in.

With five minutes to go before half, I spied Anton sitting up shaking his head talking animatedly. He loved his new role picking us apart on the bench, I thought. I had my hands full with Wallace, who was not fast but moved around the lane with purpose. More than anything I worked at denying the entry pass into Wallace, and I stayed close to him at all times. And Wallace liked to get offensive rebounds. I concentrated on blocking him out. As the score evened at 40 with 30 seconds remaining before the half, the crowd got into the game. I could see Anton really at it with his ranting. Jiri looked down the bench and waved to Anton to shut up.

We held the basketball for the last shot. The stonewall again. This time Jaroslav was behind the screen. He got the pass from Milan but the Brno defenders were ready for it. They ran around to meet Jaroslav. I broke to the basket and received a high lob from my close friend. I was wide open and went up for a dunk. It bounced off the rim. What an embarrassment to miss that way. Jaroslav chased it down with all he had and came up with the ball. He spotted me and bounced a frantic pass toward me as he fell out of bounds. I drove the baseline and laid it in for two points. A miracle finish. That gave us a narrow two-point lead at the half.

When the second half began, Brno took the lead with early momentum and a deliberate style, finding Wallace inside for an easy two against Anton. He never got an easy one like that on me. It became clear that the only way to stop him was to play total denial defense. The Brno team played only seven players. The two players on the bench didn't look too good. That was going to be a factor late in the game. Anton's five came off the floor with a little over ten minutes to play and a six-point lead.

As our new five took the floor, I could see the looks on the Brno players' faces brighten up. We'll massacre them now, their eyes conveyed. The Brno team didn't respect our second unit. By the end of the night they will be calling us *the finishers* in the newspaper. At least I hoped.

Running up the floor after a made basket by Brno, I never took my eyes off Jaroslav. He sent me his rifle pass. The ball was in my hands before I could believe it. I faked a shot; Wallace jumped. Before he landed, I took a hard dribble around him. I pumped a six-foot bank shot off the board. It dropped in for two.

After a rebound on a miss by Wallace, I launched the ball to Jaroslav on the wing and then ran with abandon to become the third man on the attack against their two guarding the basket. A three on two advantage for us. Jaroslav drew the two taller defenders to him like metal filings to a magnet. He looked directly at me and in a genuine motion did everything but release the ball to me. Next he took to flight. He glided through a narrow opening in the Brno defenders that his fake caused. He laid the ball impossibly high off the glass. It dropped in. Two points.

Looking back, I wished snippets of our games had been filmed for the local news, as I was accustomed to while playing college ball in Chicago. I was sure that that one sequence by Jaroslav would've been featured as the most stellar moment of Czech Superliga that week.

Our Svet five hit a groove; my faster first step and speed took the slower Wallace out of the game. With two minutes remaining, all Brno could do was foul to slow down the clock. The final horn sounded to a Svet victory 84-72.

Our team was invited to a Moravian dance hall and we dined and celebrated our win until 11 p.m. that night.

The next morning the bus was repaired and we shoved off for Plzeň. The victory at Brno brought our record to 9-10. As the bus rambled along to Plzeň near the German border, spirits were high but everyone was tired.

"You danced every dance with Jelina last night and talked to her the whole time we were at that place. Have you given up on Shantelina?" said Jaroslav over the seat to me.

"Jelina and I are done, that's it. We broke up last night for good. As for Shantelina, she's different, I've never met anyone like her."

I pulled out some paper and penned a Dear Shantelina letter with my thoughts on Brno, the game, and everything including Jelina.

CHAPTER TWENTY-THREE

MY BOIL OVER

The high spirits of our days in Brno evaporated as we drove to Plzeň. I had a headache. Only this wasn't a hangover because I only had one lager the night before. This was worse; I was coming down with something.

From the window of the bus I was struck by the beauty of a simple scene: a Moravian field interspersed with bales of rolled hay. Each seemed to capture the wavelengths of the sun differently. After that, nothing we traveled past equaled that although some rugged vineyards came close. For the ride through Bohemia, I was sick as a horse and wanted to lie down.

We crossed a large stretch of the Republic from east to west in three-and-half hours. As we entered the outer section of the city, I could see the factories where, Jiri pointed out, they made the Skoda automobiles. Then I could smell the hops from the lager breweries.

We were set to play our next four games against the best of Czech Republic League against the four P's (Plzeň, Praha A, Praha B, and Pardubice). We pulled into a train station near the city center.

"Why are we stopped, coach?" Anton said.

"Gustav's scouting the Praha teams in Prague. Praha A plays this afternoon against Brno and Praha B plays Pardubice tonight," Coach Jiri said.

Gustav went down the steps of the bus. He opened the compartment on the side of the bus, reached in, and pulled out his bags.

"Jiri, don't get thrown out against Plzeň because we'll be coachless," Gustav said.

Thrown out? Coaches could only be thrown out and asked to leave the gym if they got two technicals in one game. Jiri had his first technical foul called against him in our last game. His only one in five games I'd played with the team to that point. He'd have to be pretty irate to get two in one game.

"I know. These are special circumstances. We need to know everything about these teams," Jiri said.

The whole team knew about Koliar's ultimatum to Jiri. If we lost a game on this road trip, Jiri was done. Gustav would assume the top spot as head coach. That was the last thing I wanted to happen. I'd ride the bench the rest of season in that scenario. The bright side was we had one victory so far! But there were four to go.

"Get moving so you can board the first Prague-bound train. I want to know everything about their strengths and weaknesses," Jiri said.

"Of course," Gustav said, slung his bag over his shoulder, walked to the platform to catch the next Zephyr Train to the capital.

I held my hand against my forehead and it felt boiling. I've got the flu or something, I thought.

We practiced in the Plzeň gym to ready ourselves for the game that night. Jiri called it a light workout. But when it was over, I stripped off my sweaty practice shirt and the rest of my clothes and stepped into a comforting hot shower in the locker room. After I was cleaned up and dressed, I exited the locker room and there was Jiri talking to a gray-haired man alongside a full trophy case.

"Here is our newest foreigner," Jiri said. It felt like I appeared on cue, as if they were just talking about me the moment before. The gray-haired man wore Soviet-issue workout clothes but with one distinguishing feature: he was wearing the newest Nike Air Jordan gym shoes. We shook hands.

"Labas," he said, meaning "hello" in Lithuanian.

"No, he's Czech, he understands. Josef, this is Plzeň's coach Areges Mracek, the longest serving coach in the league. Back then, he had players living in barracks and had them for 11 months of the year. You could really shape them," Jiri said.

"Jiri, you're the only coach left with his players still living like that. How do you like living in a glass factory, son?"

"I'll never get used to it, especially with those floors that shake," I said.

Jiri said, "It's not so bad. That's what you get when you coach in Svet. Areges started in 1981 when the league was smaller. Before the reorganization when the Party ran things."

"Incorrect, coach. It was 1983 when I started. How'd you find him?"

"He's from Chicago by way of England. Milos signed him through a contact up in the U.K. He was one of their top scorers on a team outside London," Jiri said.

"Scoring? That's not what he's doing for you. But I'd say he's the glue to your team here and your wins," the Plzeň coach said.

"It's more than the American. We have a very good team this year," Jiri said.

"Bull, it's your point guard from Plzeň Jaroslav Matura and Josef here. I heard about their effort against Ostrava. You've got depth, that's what you never had before," the Plzeň coach said.

Impressive. The guy's astute. And a trickster, who knows more about us than he's letting on.

"We lost that game against Ostrava," said Jiri.

The Plzeň coach put his finger across his lips like he was holding back saying what he really thought.

Within a few minutes, Jiri and I were walking out to the team bus.

"I've known Areges sometime now," Jiri said.

"He was very good to let us even use his gym to practice, considering they refused us in Ostrava and Brno," I said.

"He's from a different mold than those other coaches. Plzeň doesn't have the market size, certainly smaller than Brno or Prague. The Plzeň organization is well-run. They don't attract the most talented players, but Areges wins," he said.

"Svet's the smallest market in the Czech league and look what we can do. By the way, how come Plzeň's Coach never signed Jaroslav? He's from Plzeň," I said.

"I worked very hard to get him, that's why. Jaroslav wanted a change. For every Jaroslav we signed, we lost many other recruits. Are you okay?" Jiri said.

"I feel awful. Like I've come down with something," I said.

"We need you tonight. Hang in there, Josef."

Before we got on the team bus with most of the team already on it, Jiri pointed across the way to a park. We quickly walked across the road.

"I want to show you this," he said. "Plzeň is a 700 year old town but more modern than the rest. It was heavily targeted by Allied bombers in 1944 and 1945, so many of the old hotels, homes, and churches were destroyed."

I was shuffling my feet as if I was going to pass out.

"I can't make it. I've got to lie down back in the hotel," I said.

"Just a little further. I want you to see this," he said.

We came upon a bronze statue of a soldier that looked familiar.

That's General George Patton. This is odd, why is this here? I thought. I read the plaque that was in both Czech and English.

The citizens of Plzeň are forever indebted to General G. S. Patton. On 6 May 1945, Patton and his American Third Army liberated Plzeň from the Nazi. The original statue installed in 1946 was destroyed by the Soviet authorities with the beginning of 40 years of totalitarian communistic dominion. Reinstalled in 1991 by the American Society of the Friends of Czechoslovakia.

I looked out to the scene beyond where we stood. The white façade of one home was decorated with bold red stenciling that reminded me of the dress that a Czech folk dancer might wear: flowing red ribbon designs on a crisp white background. Plzeň was a town that looked dreary but, at times, beautiful and picturesque.

Being so sick got me thinking crazy. I felt like I was going to die for awhile there. I had a whole life ahead of me. I was only 31.

When we arrived at the hotel, the reporter Pavelosek from the *Svet Monitor* was waiting for us in the lobby. Pavelosek stood there like he knew something but he was trying to hide his motivations. Maybe he knew my true identity.

"What are your basketball aspirations after all this is done?" said Pavelosek.

"I can't answer now," I said.

If he peppered me with questions, I would tell him the whole thing. That's how sick I was. My headache was terrible and the only thing I wanted to do was lie down.

Jaroslav sensed I couldn't go any further because after we checked in, he stepped between Pavelosek and me. Then he escorted me to the elevator so we could check in to our room. It was a small elevator. Only he and I with some of our bags could fit. Before the door could shut, the reporter called out "Josef Savek." He tried to stuff himself, trench coat and all, onto the lift so he could talk to us.

"There was a letter for you at the front desk," he said.

As soon as he handed it to me, the door elevator shut. I looked down at the letter while the lift moved upward and it was in Shantelina's handwriting. When we arrived in our room, I crawled into bed with her letter on my chest. Too sick to open it, I laid there. My head pounded. My throat was so sore it felt as if someone lodged a wood chip in my gullet. I coughed for a while to dislodge what was in my throat. It didn't satisfy. I've never had anything like this. I thought whatever it is, it's damn serious.

Jaroslav left me alone to sleep. After an hour and a half, I awoke with Shantelina's unopened letter still against my chest. I was feeling better but not good enough even to get out of bed. As I opened her letter lying there, I couldn't remember if I had even sent her one letter.

I read her letter:

My dear Frank,

I like that. Wait a minute. I looked at the outside envelope and it said Josef Savek. Good, at least she has good sense to not blow things for me.

How are you doing? I heard on the radio of your win in Brno and know you must have had a big part in that. We look forward to your return to Svet. Hope you are doing well. 26 September cannot come quick enough for me because you'll be back.

There is some big change for me. Svetlana moved out with her boyfriend a few days ago. She's the roommate with the short brown hair with the funny laugh.

The other change occurred today. Jitka, my other roommate, told me that she's moving, too. Jitka always wanted to live in Prague and now she got her wish. She's going to live with her cousins and try to find a secretary job for a bigger company there. It's risky but exciting, don't you think? I'm jealous because Prague is such a great city and it seems to have more of everything than Svet (i.e. more opportunities, etc.) Leave it to Jitka, the tallest and most beautiful of the three of us, to leave for the "Paris" of the Czech Republic first. She leaves next week. I wish she would stay but I know that this is what she always said she wanted.

The good thing is I still see Svetlana at work at the glass factory and we'll remain good close friends. But I know it won't be the same. And for one, I'll miss the late night chats we had.

Meanwhile, that leaves me with this apartment that was too large for the three of us as it is. So when you come back, I'll have the place to myself. I'm going to start looking for a smaller place to live but I'm not optimistic. There isn't a lot of new housing in Svet from what I've heard. An article in the Svet Monitor said that there is a housing shortage across the country so I don't feel too bad. Next month my rent will be incredible with the two of them gone.

On to happier thoughts, hope you are doing well. Please write how it's going. The kilometers between us are great but our friendship for each other bridges the gap. Now, when I look towards the future, I ask what I will be doing. I think of you often. Write me, call me on the phone, I miss speaking in English.

Yours sincerely,

SHANTELINA

I was compelled to call her right then from the black phone on the night stand. Then I picked up the handset; it dropped out of my hands onto the carpeted floor. Too weak to get out of bed and retrieve it. But after a few minutes I could hear a dial tone emitting from the phone.

Then I disconnected the phone cord from the slot on the phone set on the table. That stopped it.

If I survive this, I'll mail her the latest letter I wrote. Then I went back to sleep. When I woke up, I found my shirt was wet around the collar, as if I sweated through whatever ailed me. I felt better but knew it wasn't that simple.

Later, I sat on the bench with the rest of my teammates in the visitors' locker room.

"There is no one spectacular player on the team that we face tonight. They find ways to win. This Plzeň team has only lost one game so far and we are going to have to make it two losses," Jiri said.

As we got close to game time, my throat still had the terrible feeling that a wood chip was lodged in there. I put a water bottle to my lips and drank some water. The pain was excruciating. A boa could ingest a whole rabbit with more ease than I was having with simple H_2O.

We came out of the locker and the Plzeň gym was packed. I looked up into the stands during warm-ups and then again during the Czech anthem. There was no Milos Koliar in the place. It was the first time our owner was not at one of our games, road or home.

The first unit took the floor against an intimidating Plzeň team. They were more like football players with broad shoulders and necks than the rangy slender warriors of the hard-court I was used to. They looked better than the Ostrava team that beat us three days earlier.

This was just a game, I reminded myself. Our goal is to throw this orange sphere through the round hoop ten feet above the floor. Usually, I relished banging the opponents around on the inside.

Overly physical teams could take you out of your game. There is so much body contact that they could wear you down. I was already not at full strength, so I had to save my energy and hope the referees would keep the dirty play to a minimum.

Plzeň jumped to an early lead against Anton's five. From the bench I could see the referees were being fair. They were calling fouls and Plzeň couldn't break the game open. We fell behind 25-15 after ten minutes of play but then just as our second unit stood up to check in, Rudenic threw in a long three point shot. That seemed to swing the momentum in our favor.

We checked into the game, five Svet players in and the first five out. Jaroslav found me with a bullet pass under the basket that went through my hands and out of bounds. Plzeň ball. Bad start. I had to stay alert and focused.

After a Plzeň basket, Jaroslav found me again with another pass off a fast break. This time I hauled it in and scored a layup. That was the thing about Jaroslav: he never quit. He kept coming at the other team. The guy channeled that same determination to those around him. He was relentless with me and demanded the best. I loved that. Their ten-point lead, shrunk to three in a matter of minutes. As much as we tried to move ahead, Plzeň held firm. They scored key baskets to maintain a slight edge. Plzeň 39 - Svet 35 at the half.

In the locker room, Jiri pressed us to play better defense in the second half. We had enough resolve as a team to know that we could beat this team. The crisis of confidence that I had earlier in the season was gone. I knew we could win.

The second half began with Anton powering up a layup in traffic. He was fouled and hit the free throw. Vojtech was now really beginning to rebound with abandon. It was paying off as Svet finally broke into the lead. The Plzeň crowd quieted for the first time that night.

When I checked into the game with my four teammates, the crowd taunted us. The first unit leaving the floor with a lead was a very good sign. I heard someone in the stands say, "Here come the second string bums."

Plzeň's Coach Mracek called a timeout. Plzeň countered by sending in a group of replacements at the same time we entered the floor. Their strategy seemed to work. Their legendary coach had sized us up and now had players on us making us do things we didn't want to do. Jaroslav and I went to work but they were ready for us. A long pass up the floor to me was stolen by a quick Plzeň player. The guy that was defending me began trash talking that I was no good. I pushed him away but luckily the referees missed my shove. When he got the ball on the next Plzeň possession I blocked his shot but they recovered the ball and scored from underneath. Our slender lead evaporated. A Svet turnover and basket by Plzeň put them up by four.

Jiri called a timeout. Eight minutes remained. This was our time to turn it around or lose.

Then Jaroslav drove around the wing and along the baseline for a reverse layup that was blocked by his defender. I recovered it and threw it to Jaroslav and he scored from five feet out. As I ran back on defense I felt great thirst. Jaroslav made a steal at the top of the key and drove hard up the floor but was guarded so closely that he pulled back out to set it up. He passed into me for a layup that I powered in. We were setting the floor on fire. The lead changed back and forth many times in the last minute until I was fouled underneath with 17 seconds to go. Jiri called a timeout. "Why he'd do that?" I thought. The opposing team usually does that to freeze out the free throw shooter.

After the timeout, I stepped up to the line and arched the ball up over the rim and in. The second one I put some more oomph on it and it clanked around on the rim and in.

As we ran back on defense, Jaroslav slapped my back.

"Great job. Two huge points at a crucial moment. You should get sick more often," Jaroslav said. I was too weary to think about what I had just done. Plzeň was bearing down. Their point guard threw down court and worked the ball patiently for a long bank shot that caromed off the rim. I grabbed the ball and smothered it with my two arms at my chest for a moment in the rebound. The buzzer sounded and I hosted the ball up in the air toward the rafters but it only went up about ten feet. Jaroslav and the rest of my teammates gathered close, everyone was slapping each other on the back.

Svet 73, Plzeň 70. My free throws iced it. I felt great on the inside about winning and my contributions to make it happen. Our record returned to winning as many as we lost: three wins and three losses since I arrived, 10-10 overall. Jiri would remain our coach for one more game. We were onto Prague next.

As I walked over to shake the hands of their coach and the other players, my throat was so bad I couldn't speak. I wanted to lie down right there. I ran my hand across my forehead and it felt like I was having a boil-over. It wasn't just the heat of the game: something was really wrong.

Over the next eight hours, I struggled in the darkness with an unyielding headache and barely able to swallow. A night's rest in the Plzeň hotelroom didn't cure me like it had before the game.

As we travelled the next morning to the Czech capital and home of the superliga's most powerful teams, I was in bad shape.

CHAPTER TWENTY-FOUR

THE MAGICAL CITY

Jiri and I stepped into the check-in line at the Cizinecké oddělení or foreigners' clinic on the backside of the Prague Hospital called Nemocnice na Homolce. Here I was in Prague, the city I'd come all this way to see, and I felt worse than I'd felt in years.

"Credit card and passport please," said a receptionist, when we reached the front desk.

That was going to be a problem because I had sent my brother's passport back to him in Australia. I pulled out my passport and handed it over to her. She flipped through it.

"U.S. Citizen, I see. Purpose of your visit?" she said, in English.

"Terrible sore throat. I'm here to have it checked out," I said.

"No, that's not what I'm asking. Why are you in the Czech Republic?" she said.

"I play basketball in the Ceska Republika Superliga with a team from Svet," I said.

"Also, I need a credit card for this. Who's he?" she said, looking at Jiri.

"He's my coach and I don't have a credit card."

I was unable to say another word.

"We don't see foreigners unless they pay up front," she said to Jiri.

Jiri pulled out a wad of Krona notes and gave her some of them.

A few minutes later a nurse came out and called, "Ferenc Savek."

Jiri and I stood up and walked to the nurse.

"Ferenc? His name is Josef," Jiri said to the nurse.

"That's not what his passport states. It's Ferenc Josef Savek," she said.

"What's that all about, Josef?" he said to me as we followed her back to the examination room.

This was it, I thought. My whole identity revealed during my weakest ebb.

"Ferenc Josef Savek is my full name, I use my middle name," I said. He seemed to buy it.

For once, I appreciated my middle name and the fact that it was listed on my passport, too. It got me out of this jam just like my younger brother said it would all those months ago when I agreed to this whole thing. What coach Jiri didn't know was that Josef Savek, the real recruit to the team, was 8,000 miles away in Perth.

A middle-aged man in a white coat entered the examination room. We shook hands and he introduced himself as Doctor Kallman.

"What can I do for you today, Mr. Savek?" the doctor said.

"I have a sore throat, the worst I've ever had. It started with a fever and progressed to this," I said.

He placed both his hands on my neck and massaged the lymph nodes beneath my jaw bone. It hurt when he did that. He looked inside my mouth and depressed by tongue with a stick. He flashed a light into the back of my mouth.

"You have a very inflamed throat, all right. How long have you had this?"

"Two days. I can barely swallow," I said.

"I understand you play basketball in the Czech league. What kind of living situation do you have in Svet?" said the doctor.

"We live in a glass factory," I said, struggling to even say that. I gestured to my throat and turned my hands up and shook my head.

"That's all right. If it hurts that much, don't say anymore," he said. Then he turned to Coach Jiri.

"So the players on your team all live in what, a dormitory? In a factory that makes glass?" said the doctor.

"Yes, they live in the players' quarters on the mezzanine level of the Svet Glass Works. There are eleven on the team and they live together." Jiri said.

What I would have said if I could talk was that the floor shook from the machinery on the first floor, but you get used to it. And there were two factions: the first unit and the second (that I was in), and there was tension and rivalry between the two, and I got my face ripped open in a fight with Anton and two others, so I had to wear a mask of tape to protect when I played basketball after that.

"Okay, that might explain things," the doctor said to Jiri.

He turned back to me.

"You have *Hand, Foot and Mouth Disease*. Extremely uncommon in adults; however, you have all the symptoms. Between one and two days after the onset of fever, painful sores appear in the mouth and/or throat. That's what I'm seeing here," he said.

"Disease?" I said. That was the last word I could say

"That's what it's called, but it's more flu-like than anything else. It occurs in places where people live together and can break out in small epidemics. You don't want anyone else to get it. It will go away in a few days if you take care of yourself," he said.

He wrote out a prescription for some medicine to alleviate the symptoms and handed it to me.

"What about tonight's game against Praha A? Can he play?" Jiri said.

"I recommend not having him play tonight. He needs to get over this," he said.

After picking up the medicine, Jiri and I went back to the hotel where the rest of the team had already checked in. They were already out of their rooms and several of them were spread out drinking chai and reading the paper in lobby.

"There he is. What did the doctor say?" said Jaroslav.

"I've got *Hand, Foot, and Mouth Disease* and he said I shouldn't play tonight," I said. I was struggling to get those words out.

"We need you. This is your moment. They have three Americans on the team," Jaroslav said.

"I can't. But three? I thought you could only have two foreigners per team total," I said, vowing to stop talking. My throat was killing me.

"They got away with it somehow. They asked for special permission from the league office. The league office is situated in Prague, so it's no coincidence," Jaroslav said.

Jiri put out the call to Gustav to gather up the team for a meeting in a small side room off the lobby. Jaroslav and I walked over to the meeting area. It was a round room with a round coffee table in the middle and opaque curtains over the windows. We were the first to arrive and sat down in the chairs around the coffee table. Every time a person entered the hotel through the main door, a draft of frigid air rolled from outside.

"By the way, they have your photo in the English-speaking newspaper, the *Prague Post*," said Jaroslav.

He tossed the paper into my lap. I spread it out on the table and flipped to the sports section. There it was: an action of photo of me under the basket. My arms extended upward and the ball was inches from my finger tips as a Brno player battled for a rebound he wasn't going to get. The caption under the photo was "Svet's American centre Josef Savek." Not a bad photo, I thought.

***Prague Post Sport Preview**: Praha A Titans 21-0 versus the Svet Lions 10-10.*

***What to Watch from Praha A?** In seven contests to open the second half of league play, the vaunted Titans have played to perfection. While they have not played league champion Pardubice, the Titans have put together as unbeatable a team as the Czech League has seen. They could be the first team to go undefeated in league history because their American contingent* *of Darius Longstreet, Escalante Greenfield and David Guse. Longstreet is averaging 20 points per game, Guse 15 per game and Greenfield is the league assist leader with an astonishing 12.3 per game.*

Praha A Coach Tomáš Hochman said, "Before our win last night, we had a five-day layoff so I'm a little concerned how sharp we may be tonight. I stress to them that in this league you can't overlook a Svet or any team. One thing I've never had to worry about is their intensity. They have that. My guys love to play and are just a joy to watch whether in practice or games. We'll be ready."

What to Expect from Svet? *This team is in the middle of six-game road trip and road weariness could play a factor. However, that seems to be mitigated by their coach's utilization of their entire bench in a mass rotation scheme that includes a five in and five out strategy. The Svet 10's gatling gun approach has proven successful including yesterday's 73-70 win against the top-caliber Plzeň club. There is no one star on the Lions, with the exception of Antonin Cermak, who is expected to play for the Czech National Team next year to qualify for the FIBA World Championship. Cermak is Svet's leading scorer averaging 17.5 points per game. Another player to watch is Josef Savek, an American. This newcomer of Czech heritage recently joined Svet's basketball club after a two-year stint playing for Hemmel Hampstead in Britain. If there is anyone to deliver a David and Goliath outcome, the 1.98 meter tall Savek might be the one. He played for the NCAA Division III Champion North Park College of Chicago.*

However, in the end, no one has yet been able to neutralize Praha A's American trio and supporting cast. There is no indication Svet will be able to do that tonight and the only team that has a chance of challenging Praha A is Pardubice. This game is considered a warm-up for next week's contest versus Pardubice.

Prediction on tonight's game: Praha A by 12.

A collector's item.

"I saw it. They're trying to play up the whole American thing with you four. What do you expect? It's an English language paper," said Anton, tossing a copy of the *Post* aside.

Gustav and Jiri walked into the room.

Gustav addressed us, "Both Prague teams are very good. It was good to see them yesterday. Praha A played Brno and won convincingly. Praha B lost by five points to Pardubice but did a lot of things well."

"Talk about Praha A. We want to take one game at a time," said Jiri.

"Praha A plays very aggressively, they never stop coming at you. Longstreet is their star; we want to push him out to the perimeter. He can score everytime on the inside if he wants. But Praha A plays smarter than that. Defensively they take a lot of chances in the backcourt because they have Longstreet defending their basket on their press," Gustav said.

"How tall is this Longstreet?" Jiri said.

"He's 6'7," said Gustav. He looked at me when he said it. I thought it was odd how he singled me out when we had 6'7" player in Vojtech. Jiri and the rest of the team looked at me for a moment.

"Their point guard Greenfield is the quickest player I've ever seen. He harasses and forces turnovers against whoever he's guarding. They do a lot of trapping in the backcourt by throwing presses at you throughout the game. Greenfield gets everyone involved, he's a good passer. Their coach utilizes their strengths very well. They know they can take chances because Longstreet is an eraser back there against even with a 3 on 1 disadvantage. He blocked six shots in the first half alone," said Gustav.

"Coach Tomáš Hochman always traps in the corners and presses full court. He did that last year. That's to be expected," said our head coach.

"Yes, but now they have the personnel to carry it out with the Americans they have. That's their advantage," said Gustav.

Everyone seemed to look at me—their lone American—again for a moment. It was like they wanted me to speak. But I could barely talk and even if I could, what want did they want me to say? I was there and going to play despite being sick. That said enough.

"And their weaknesses? Talk about that," said Anton.

"None that I can see. This team sets the control of the game. Praha A does best when playing at a rapid fire pace. They use speed to break the game open for big leads," he said.

"Gustav, the key is to know our adversary. Know everything about them. Their strengths and weaknesses. How can we force them to do things they don't want to?" Jiri said.

"Slow them down. But what I saw in their game yesterday afternoon and from reports about their earlier games, no one has been able to do that," Gustav said.

"These next three games are going to show what kind of team Svet really is. If we have any pride, we have to show it here," said Jiri.

After our strategy session broke up, I felt terrible. If it was game time, there would be no way I would be able to play.

"Josef, we don't have to leave for the gymnasium for three hours. Sleep for a while and I'll be back to check on you," Jiri said.

As I walked back to my hotel room, I took the medicine. The only thing I wanted to do was lay down. There was no stopping that.

The rest of the team went to Praha 1 and the old town sector with its Astronomical Clock. My parents always talked about the old town tower with the 600 year-old still-working Astronomical Clock, the Pražský orloj, as it was called in Czech. We had two days in the place so I hoped the next day would be my chance to explore this kind-of-Jerusalem I'd come all the way to experience.

I stepped to the window of the room and looked over the street. The view was of a tram line and a park with iron fencing around it. Beyond that, a cemetery and some other architecturally attractive buildings loomed. Visiting Prague was a lifetime objective. It was a shame to be within the city but too sick to venture out.

I closed the curtains to engulf the room in darkness. And lay down under the covers of the bed.

Sometime later, I awoke in the dark. I swallowed and while it still hurt, the cutting pain somewhere just behind my tongue and deeper in my throat was not as bad as it was. I raised my head off the pillow a few inches and the congestion that was clouding my forehead was somewhat better. There was a good sign: I was hungry.

I rolled over and reached for my watch, seeing that it was fifteen minutes before we were to leave for the arena. More time passed in the darkness. Then the door opened and the lights came on.

"Dobry den, Josef. How are you?" coach Jiri said.

"Slightly improved," I said, through it still hurt to talk.

"You look more like your old self, too," said Jaroslav.

Jiri was holding a plate of food covered in tin foil.

"Here, eat this. Good Czech food from downstairs," Jiri said.

He handed me the plate and a fork. Jaroslav went over and opened the curtains. There was still some daylight but a street lamp flicked on. I ate at the table next to the phone and the fine stock paper with the name of the hotel on the top.

"We need to leave in a few minutes," Jiri said. "Assuming you're ready to give us the best of what you have tonight. And you are?"

"Yes, I will," I said, hoping it was true.

A dry-mouth feeling of nervousness came over me as we waited in the tunnel. I took a drink from a fountain. Warm water.

As we took the court to warmup, our players lined up tentatively, and then several in a row missed their first layups. Praha Arena was huge like the arena at Ostrava. Big and boxy. A big scoreboard with a titan on it.

Playing Praha A back at their home was formidable but I thought there was no reason to be intimidated. For all their greatness, the crowd wasn't as large as I expected for an undefeated team like the Titans. There were some empty seats, but still a large enough crowd to be a factor.

The horn sounded and Jiri gave us some last-minute direction. The bench emptied of the starters as Anton's first unit took the floor. The game was close in the beginning because Anton and his Czech all-stars played better than expected. Their group hit a high percentage of shots and hung in there with the Prague Titans. The lead changed hands several times.

I felt tense as my group's moment to check in neared. I hoped that our first group on the floor could continue to score and slow Praha A. But it was as if Longstreet, Greenfield and Guse were playing another game all together. Amazingly we countered their magic, continued to trade baskets, and kept it close.

Two minutes before we were to rotate in, Zedenik was fouled by Greenfield. He stepped up to the line and missed the first free throw and then the one after that. The point of our first squad was practically on automatic when shooting free throws. He and Jaroslav hit 90 percent of their free throws. Missing those wasn't a good sign.

Greenfield wore a headband over his close-clipped Afro and a black patch over one eye like a pirate. It was a real patch that he didn't remove. Greenfield saw the court better than many with vision out of two eyes. He called out a play by raising his fist in the air and yelling out "Scramblers" in English. That set Praha A in motion; it was some sophisticated kind of offensive pick and roll scheme I tried to decipher. Greenfield dribbled between his legs and drove to the basket with lightning speed. Anton stepped up to block him and forced him to pass. He did, and sent the ball to the sandy-blond-haired Guse. The golden boy hit a bank shot that accurately found the sweet spot on the glass and went in for two points.

Over the next few minutes, it was clear that Greenfield was a very good passer and had great court awareness. He threaded some impressive passes to Longstreet and Guse for scores.

On the next series Zedenik had the ball stripped by Greenfield. As Greenfield dribbled up the floor, he had masterful command over the ball. When he arrived at the top of the key, Greenfield stood there for a few seconds, bouncing the ball and heckling Zedenik nearby him and the rest of the Svet defenders. I got a good look at him because there Greenfield stood in plain view from the bench as the ball continued bounce in harmony. He never looked at the ball itself; it seemed to obey him. Rhythmically hitting the wood court. Fingertips, floor. Fingertips, floor. Then he launched a pass to the basket. Longstreet was there to meet it and crammed it down the orange cylinder for two points. That was the greatest play I'd seen against us all season: an NBA move in the Czech league. Longstreet made that dunk look easy. They were now up six against us. Longstreet and Greenfield ran over to each other and interlocked fists for a second.

Jiri called a time out.

'We're a little rattled right now. Okay, he dunked it. Don't be threatened by these guys. Anyone here that thinks we can't beat this team? Anyone? If so, go to the locker room because we don't need that thinking," Jiri said.

No one spoke up.

"Play our game and we can beat them," Jiri said.

"Slow it down. And rebounding is the key. If we outrebound them, we win. Fundamentals, gentlemen," said Gustav before the first team hit the floor.

Our point Zedenik called a play as he dribbled with his forearm out to hold off Greenfield. "Number four," he called.

Anton moved off a pick and Guse jumped out to seal him off. The rest were covered so Zedenik was forced to drive and shoot over the smaller Greenfield. He missed and the smallest guy on the floor, Greenfield, got the rebound; but a red faced Zedenik stole it and passed it to Anton for a fancy reverse layup for a basket. We needed that.

"It's time, Svet #2. Let's go," Jiri said.

Thefive of us stood and reported to the scorer's table. We were checking in, but this time without even wasting a timeout.

"Out. Out. You are in the way," the seated statistician said, with game log book in front of him and a pencil in his hand. He swatted his hand to the side and craned his neck. For the moment he was blocked. We bent down low on our hands and knees with our heads below the level of the table, waiting for a whistle from the referees to stop the play so the big switch could occur.

Vojtech, who was the same height as Longstreet, caught the ball on the right side and turned for a close lay-in. Longstreet exploded off the floor, smacked the ball off the backboard, and left a perfect handprint on the glass.

"Reeeee-jec-tion," said the announcer over the sound system.

Both teams struggled fiercely to come up with the loose ball. Praha A's Guse came away with it.

Both teams turned and raced back to the Praha A end of the floor. Guse dished to Longstreet, who got the ball under the hoop, leaped up and threw down a vicious dunk.

"Did that even go in?" I said, as he ran past.

"Yeah, you got *soaked*, man," Longstreet said, grinning down at me, crouching. "That's how it's done. You next?"

Two Praha A possessions. Two Longstreet dunks. Not a good sign.

The buzzer sounded and officials waved us in. As I stood up, I felt wobbly and not myself from the sickness, but actually better than I felt at Plzeň. We were on the floor. Down by six but lucky to be that.

Longstreet pointed to me from their impromptu huddle. They broke up and found us on defense, Longstreet locating me as his man.

"They couldn't play any defense. You think you'll be better? Your Czech American ass is going to get smoked, too," said Longstreet.

Okay, he knows I'm Czech and from the United States. So? I didn't respond. I felt it was better to be a work of mystery and just play.

I swallowed and my throat hurt like hell. Is this going to work? It better, because it's all I have.

"What do you have to say to that?" Longstreet said, "So you're pleading the fifth. All right, Savek. No difference."

We inbounded the ball at half court. Jaroslav drove hard against Greenfield and threw up a shot from a step in from the free throw line. It grazed the rim and caroomed away. A weak start. Longstreet snatched the ball and whipped it out his go-to guy, pirate-patched, Greenfield. The race was on. I sprinted back alongside Longstreet step-by-step in an effort to thwart their fast break. Greenfield dribbled hard and fast. He dished the ball into Longstreet who muscled past and then finessed it the rest of the way to finish with a lay-up. Two points by my man. Too easy.

On our next play, Jaroslav drove with abandon and was stopped in his tracks near the free throw line. He passed it to Milan who tossed up a desperation hook shot from the right side. Swish. Two points. Then we were able to force Praha A to shoot a long shot that went in, but the referee away from the ball called a foul on a Praha A player who set an illegal pick on Milan.

Jaroslav got the ball and drove again and everyone seemed to key on him. I posted up and had a great position on Longstreet. I felt Longstreet pulling against my jersey and grinding his fist against my tailbone. It was either hidden or ignored by the referees because no whistle stopped play. Jaroslav passed the ball to me and I gave it back to him for a give-and-go. He wanted me to stay with him as he drove to the basket. He forced a twelve-foot shot that bounced high off the rim. I scrambled to get the rebound but Longstreet sealed me off with his outstretched arms. I side-stepped and spun around Longstreet. My maneuver had Longstreet behind me. I snatched the ball for a rebound. As I turned, Guse ripped it from my hands and whipped it out to Greenfield on the wing. I found Longstreet my man. Be awake and get serious. Our second unit was playing tentatively as we began our stint in control—me included.

Jaroslav picked up speed on our possession and drove hard against Greenfield. He passed it to Charles, who threw up an off-balanced eight footer. He missed. As it came off the board, the ball was tipped out to toward center court. Jaroslav raced over and dove on the loose ball. Not bad for a 30-year old. He dished it to Milan and we were back on the attack to shave down their eight-point lead. I was open on the inside and Milan didn't see me. I circled back around and found a new open spot near the basket. Milan wasn't looking in my direction so I didn't know if he saw me. Before I opened my mouth to call for the ball, Milan delivered. A bullet pass inside. He had never thrown me a pass like that before. I powered it up for two and Guse's 6'4" body lunged into me, hitting my arms. The referee's whistle blew against Guse and, amazingly, the ball stayed on course. It went in.

Guse didn't like it and cursed at himself. Then he heckled me as I went to the charity stripe. I dropped in the free throw to complete the three-point play. On the next possession, Praha A patiently worked the ball around with a maturity I didn't think they had. Greenfield took a jump shot as almost a consolation when our defense against Longstreet and Guse thwarted any passes to the inside. Greenfield's shot missed. I checked off Longstreet and snatched the ball away from Guse, who had maneuvered perfectly in front of me. He should have had it, but I got it anyway. The Praha A coach stood up and yelled to the referees that I had fouled Guse.

I looked to pass the ball out, but everyone was covered. After a moment more, I called time out, which the referee granted.

As I walked to our bench a group of fans closest to me yelled at the referee because of the non-call of foul against Guse.

"He's not that good. He fouled him, ref," a fan shouted.

"Savek, you hack," another heckler yelled from further up in the seats.

Jiri diagrammed some plays to get the ball inbounded. He showed us how we could break out of their trapping press. On the inbound, I tried to pass it into our main target, Milan, but he was covered. Jaroslav was covered, too. The sneaky quick Greenfield was looming between our two best ball handlers, looking for a quick steal. There was no way I was throwing it to any of them. For a second, I thought of calling another time out, but knew to avoid that at all costs. So I launched the ball to our other man down the floor near Longstreet. Charles caught it and considered driving toward Longstreet guarding the lane. He wisely dribbled it back out to the perimeter and dished it to Jaroslav to reset the action.

Jaroslav knocked down a jumper off a pick and then another on our next possession. Two plays; two scores. On defense Jaroslav stayed close on Greenfield and denied him making easy passes to the inside. Longstreet didn't score any baskets the rest of the half so I felt like I was doing well against him. It was the scrappy Guse I was worried about as much as Longstreet. While Guse wasn't my man on defense, I knew he had to be contained. For the most part, we prevented Praha A from unleashing their onslaught of speed and chaos.

Jaroslav threw a beautiful pass into me and I was hammered by Guse from the side as I went up to the basket. The ball didn't go in as the referees called the foul on Guse. I stepped up to the line and swished the first free throw as the Praha A fans behind the basket yelled. As I readied for the second one, they yelled and waved their hands more furiously to distract me. My free throw bounced off the rim and clanked in. Guse drove off a pick and roll screen that Longstreet set. He released it just before the buzzer sounded. It swished in. We were down 48-44 at half.

As I walked to the locker room, sweat was pouring down my face and chest. Jiri was walking beside me.

"How do you feel?" Jiri said as he slapped me on the back.

"A little tired but okay so far," I said.

"Good defense on Longstreet there at the end. That's what we needed, but you need to play better on defense overall. Also, shut down their rebounding."

Inside the locker room, we all gathered in the corner to talk.

"So we've closed the gap, that's good. Gustav, what are we doing on the rebounding end?" Jiri said.

"We're even at 19 per team," Gustav said, looking at his notes from the official scorebook. "Refocus on rebounding. That's going to be the key to beating them tonight: we have to shut them off the boards. Our second unit: Jaroslav and Josef you did well but we can't have those lapses like that the pick and roll with Guse at the end. We have to communicate better. Zedenik, you need to slice through that press. Make them pay for their gambling in the back court. And stay on that Escalante Greenfield. Block his line of vision at all times with a hand in his face," Jiri said.

We put our hands into the circle and yelled "Svet" before we broke it up and went back up to start the second half.

As we walked back out of the locker room into the arena, I felt terrible. My throat ached and so did my head. Jaroslav limped along side of me.

"Are you okay?" I said to our point.

"My back is stiffening up and I hurt my hip on that dive to the floor for that loose ball," Jaroslav said.

I realized how broken-down Jaroslav was. He was battered and hurting, but he snatched a ball from the side and took a range of shots on our basket. As he moved, he shuffled awkwardly from right to left. Every one of his shots swished in. Then he missed one and then another. Jaroslav grabbed the ball, pounding it to the floor and determinedly said something to himself and the ball. He dribbled out to the perimeter and launched the ball to the basket. His shot went in and he began a new streak of made shots. One after another tickled the twine in succession. This guy was fiercer and more focused than any I'd ever played with.

The second half began with Anton scoring a nice jumper to make it a two point game. But on the next play Greenfield hit a jumper with Zedenik playing him tight. Moments later Greenfield scored again. Seeing Greenfield achieving a flow was what we couldn't afford. Greenfield was the smallest player on the floor at 5'8" but the best assist man and shooter in the league. He made Longstreet and Guse even more dangerous.

Later Longstreet and Guse started finding shots and hitting them. At least they weren't under the basket, so our inside defense was forcing Praha A to go further out. The difference seemed to be the hustle of Guse. He tried to get offense rebounds on every possession and he played physical. From Longstreet, you expected tremendous plays but Guse was another story. The blond American was surprisingly good for Praha A. With ten minutes to left in the game, we were down 66-58.

"Svet B, you are left with a golden opportunity to pull this out. I know you can do it," Jiri said. He signaled for us to report to the scorer's table.

As I stood up, he came over to me.

"Josef, reach within. Rebound and be alert on defense. This team is ours," he said. He slapped me on the butt. The crazy thing is that I believed we would win and so did Jaroslav.

As we checked in, Guse laughed.

"Are you the one they've sent to do what your other guys couldn't?" Guse said.

"That's right, Czech Man," I said.

"I'm not Czech. Just a mercenary. Like you," he said. Guse reminded me of a California surfer.

I didn't have the energy to banter with Guse. Plus, I thought there must be a reason he was talking to me. Is he trying to soften me up? Of course he was.

Longstreet was my man to contain, so I didn't know why I was seeing Guse all over in the second half.

Jaroslav dribbled the ball at the top of the key. He looked inside as I posted up on Longstreet and was open for a few seconds. We looked straight at each other but he didn't pass throw the ball to me. He passed to Milan, who drove toward the basket. Milan stopped, faked a shot and sent a bounce pass to Jaroslav on the perimeter. Jaroslav wheeled around and fired a pass to me on the baseline. Longstreet sealed me off the second I caught the basketball. I found Jaroslav back near the free throw line. He dribbled the ball toward the basket and shot an eight-foot jumper. The ball swished in for two. A good start.

Praha A advanced the ball but we were ready for them. Longstreet was open a split second but I circled around to seal him off. Then he pushed against my spine with his fist. Greenfield didn't throw it but his eyes opened and widened for a second as if he recognized something. Jaroslav was doing a good job thwarting Greenfield's ability to pass inside. Greenfield passed over the top of me and Longstreet snatched the basketball. An amazing catch of an impossible pass. He went up to dunk but the ball hit the rim and went out of bounds but Charles dove and saved it. Jaroslav got the ball, we ran the break up the court, and this time I got the ball on the wing. I dribbled once in stride, powering it up to the basket for a layup. Two points.

As I ran back on defense with everything I had, I felt the sweat droplets rolling down my face again. I wiped them off and readied for the Praha A attack. Their crowd began to clamor as Greenfield crossed the midcourt with the basketball. They patiently set up a play and Guse eventually shot a jumper with hands from our guards in his face and he missed. Longstreet pushed against me and I fell to the floor and he ended up with the basketball. The referee signaled a foul on Longstreet. Our ball. We scored on a driving layup by Jaroslav on the break. 68-68.

The Prague coach didn't call a timeout as I expected. Neither did Jiri. But I glanced over on the sideline and saw Jiri intently watching and pacing from one end of the bench to the other. Greenfield advanced the ball and called their "X" play. Longstreet leaned against me as he posted up. I leaned against him, feeling tired. But I got a jolt when Greenfield dumped a pass into my man. Longstreet turned and smoothly drove toward the basket. I held my hands up near his head. As he went up for a shot, I tried to block it but missed. He cleanly banked it in for two. We responded with a long shot from Jaroslav on our end but I was able to haul in the offensive rebound. I threw it back out to Jaroslav on the perimeter. I posted on the 6'7" Longstreet and received the entry pass from Jaroslav. As I went up, Guse fouled me across the arm and the ball went flying out of bounds. The referees said it wasn't a shooting foul. We got the ball out on the side. Jaroslav came over and patted me on the shoulder.

"Good job, keep doing that. They can't stop us," Jaroslav said.

We scored on a 12-foot driving jumper by Jaroslav to tie the game. Neither team was able to shake off the other as small leads were erased by a timely basket by Longstreet or Guse or us.

Later, Jaroslav dribbled at full speed never taking his eyes off me on the fast break. He unloaded a hard and accurate pass into my hands while I was a step ahead of Longstreet. This time when I reached the basket, I knew Longstreet and his tremendous shot blocking ability would cram down anything I threw up. I faked that I was going to shoot but Longstreet didn't fall for it. I passed it back to Jaroslav streaking in. Jaroslav shot the ball but missed. But since it was up on the board, I was able to get the rebound. I went back up and missed. I could feel Longstreet pushing against me. I scrambled for the ball and came away with the rebound. I banked it off the board and, miraculously, in. This was huge, our biggest lead of the game. Svet was up by four. The Prague coach called a timeout right then with just over two minutes left in the game. Baskets were flowing our way. I felt we were going to win the thing.

"Good job, unit two. Josef and Milan, you have four fouls. One more from either of you and you're gone," said Jiri, as we sat on the bench in the timeout. Like America, the Czech Republic had a five-foul limit. If you reached that, you have to leave the game; you've fouled out.

"What about them—anyone in foul trouble?" I said.

"Guse has four also," said our assistant coach. That made sense because Guse wasn't taking the risks of pushing and playing as physically as he did earlier. Neither Longstreet nor Greenfield was mentioned as having foul trouble. That would have been really encouraging. Rats!

Praha A came out onto the floor with grins on their faces that conveyed they had secret knowledge and Greenfield and Longstreet exchanged some conversation that included booming laughter. They inbounded the ball and patiently worked the ball around the perimeter. Longstreet posted up in front of me and I nudged him hard from behind. The referee's whistle blew and my heart sunk. Time stood still for a moment. The referee looked right at me but signaled the foul on Milan. Milan shook his head in disappointment and was told to exit the game with his fifth foul. Anton checked into the game for him. Longstreet, whose only weakness seemed to be shooting free throws, hit both his shots from the line.

Praha A's full court press bogged our guards down in the back court. Greenfield picked off a pass from Jaroslav to Anton. Greenfield raced back up the court and everyone followed. It was remarkable that we were able to get back as fast as we did. Greenfield launched a looping shot off the dribble that tied the game with 1:33 left on the clock. Our biggest lead of the night evaporated in a flash. As time continued to tick off the clock, Jaroslav crossed the half court line with the ball. There was no indecision or tentativeness in him. He threw a perfect pass to Anton, who missed a jumper from the wing. Jaroslav, the smallest one on the floor on our side, came away with the rebound and drove the baseline and threw up a reverse layup around me and Longstreet that rolled in for two points.

Longstreet caught the inbounded basketball, cradling the ball with both arms near his chest to thwart any chance of stealing it. Then he finessed a shovel pass to Greenfield off the side. Greenfield raced up floor, then slowed his stride when he reached our side. At the top of the key, he cockily dribbled the basketball and looked inside. He threw a pass over my fingers to my man, Longstreet standing behind me. I harassed Longstreet from the backside but he had me exactly where he wanted me. Longstreet went up and slammed the ball through the rim. The rim continued to shake for a few seconds after that. The game was tied with a minute left. Some Prague fans chanted "Darius, Darius." Then more joined in the chorus. We raced up the floor on a break and Jaroslav threw the ball into me. I was wide open for the easy one. I went up and Longstreet rejected my shot. Greenfield came up with the basketball. I was deeply disappointed and but decided not to dwell. There was plenty of game left.

Praha A had complete control of the game in their hands: the ball and the momentum. Their fans made the most noise of the night. Jiri signalled to us to set up a half-court trap on defense but Greenfield shredded through it until he pulled up his dribble at the free throw line. He was smothered by Anton and Jaroslav. Amazingly they didn't foul him. I danced all around Longstreet, and Greenfield didn't pass it into his favorite target. I saw Guse off to the side and so did Greenfield. He unloaded a bounce pass to Guse. I stepped out and intercepted his pass. I got rid of the ball to Jaroslav, who dribbled to our end of the floor. I sprinted behind him. Guse was with me the whole way. Jaroslav rifled the ball to an open Anton for a lay-up. We were up by two with 40 seconds left. A crucial basket.

Guse drove the ball up and it hit off his shin near half court. Jaroslav came away with the loose ball. He dribbled speedily toward the basket. Guse grabbed him from behind. Intentional foul. Fifth foul on Guse; he was gone. Jaroslav hit the first free throw but the second one clanked off the rim and into Longstreet's hands. We were up by three. Longstreet threw the ball to Greenfield. Prague patiently worked the ball again and then with Anton all over him, Greenfield launched a bomb from the corner from beyond the three point line that went in. The score was tied 81-81. The fans in Praha Arena jumped from their seats unison and screamed.

There was 26 seconds left so I still liked our chances to win. The referees stopped the game momentarily to check the clock at the scorer's table.

"Something is wrong," the blond balding official said to the scorer at the desk. They put one second back on the clock. To make it 27 seconds left. But the score was correct. As we waited on the floor while they worked on it, a wave of exhaustion ran through my shoulders and trembling legs. I was happy this was almost over. I glanced over to our sideline. Jiri waved us forward; there was no timeout signal from him. He was letting us play through.

Jaroslav dribbled up with Greenfield all over him. He passed it up to Anton, who looked more in control of the basketball. Anton dribbled more than he should have and tried to drive into the clogged middle but instead of shooting, he miraculously was able to pass out to Jaroslav off to the side. Jaroslav caught his pass, drove toward the basket and shot a pull-up jumper from eight feet out. The ball caromed off the rim. I came down with the rebound but Greenfield stripped it from me. No call was made. I faked outrage that I was fouled but let it go. It was just a good steal by Greenfield. The fans exploded with excitement. This was break they needed. Instead of being the hero, it looked like I would be the goat that lost the game.

The fans in the noisy gym quieted as Praha A worked the ball around the perimeter. They looked like they were playing to shoot the last shot. It was all happening too fast. Greenfield passed to their other guard near the free throw line, who passed it to my man Longstreet. I covered him the best I could by sealing off his view of the basket. I defended him well but didn't want to foul him. Longstreet shot a five foot leaning shot and it went in. The fans went crazy.

"Timeout," I yelled to the referee.

It was granted by the black and white shirted official nearby. Looking up at the clock, we were down 83-81 with three seconds left.

We came off the floor and took a seat on the bench. My Svet jersey was loaded with sweat and felt heavy on my body like some kind of grimy rag. Whatever happened, I knew I had played the hardest and best basketball game since I'd arrived in the Czech Republic.

"Anton, this play is geared for you. You will be taking the last shot. A two will tie it, a three will win it. Let's have you take a three to win it," Coach Jiri said, his voice straining to be heard over the loudest crowd noise of the night. That was surprising because normally Jiri would play for the conservative two to force overtime. A three felt like insanity in our position. I was too tired to contest anything at that point.

He diagrammed the play on his clipboard. He drew two arrows to indicate Milan and Jaroslav racing in to set screens. The stonewall. Jiri designed a play so that Anton would get the ball in the clear from the right, two feet beyond the three point stripe.

"Josef, we're going to have you near the basket. We want to pull Longstreet out of the shooting area. They'll send him down there with you," he said, looking briefly at me.

The plan looked like it would work, especially if Longstreet actually stayed with me. If he didn't and hung out near half court, he would clog things up and harass the final shot.

Lining up on the floor, the Prague team seemed to instinctively recognize the ball was going to Anton. Escalante Greenfield, the shortest player on the court and another Praha A forward played closer to him on defense.

The referee blew his whistle and then handed Charles the ball. The referee began his count by extending his forearm out for each second that passed. Jaroslav and Milan moved up to set those freeing picks. Anton ran along its axis but was smothered. As I burst to the basket with Longstreet hanging all over me, a sinking feeling came over me. There was no way Anton could get the ball. After four seconds, Charles found the only one who could receive it, Jaroslav. Jaroslav caught the ball in the backcourt near the half court line. The clock began the instant it touched his hand. He advanced one dribble across the Titans crest that brought him a few feet closer to the basket. Still he was about 45 feet out from the basket. The only positive thing that seemed to happen was that Jaroslav released his shot just before the buzzer sounded. His desperation lob, released by an imperfect human, was the sum total of everything at that moment.

It stayed in the air for an eternity. As the ball arched downward, it stayed on target like a missile calibrated with perfect mathematical coordinates. By that point, I was nearly under the basket. The basketball went cleanly through the blue hoop and into my hands like a personalized present from the gods.

The fans that weren't already standing jumped to their feet. I threw the ball up toward the rafters above our basket and yelled. Jaroslav ran to the corner and the whole team followed him there.

Then they mobbed him. *We* mobbed him. Anton, Zedenik, everyone from the Svet organization. Especially our coaches Jiri and Gustav. I was the last one to arrive and dove into the sea of people with my hands up in the air. Somewhere down in the pile was my closest teammate and greatest friend in the Czech Republic, who had just hit the game-winning shot.

For a few moments, the whole gym craned their necks to watch our team celebrate the inconceivable greatness that just occurred. Lost in the moment. Finally there was a small gap in the bodies, through which I could see Jaroslav. He was smiling ecstatically.

I glanced over to see the Praha A players standing and watching the scene. Their faces registered the fact that they had just been beaten by something wholly unexpected but possible within the laws of the universe. They were trapped inside the moment, too. Standing there in amazement, too, were the African-American stars Greenfield and Longstreet.

I'd never experienced anything like this.

Amid my euphoria and the communal witness of greatness, I looked up at the scoreboard to re-confirm the significance of all that just occurred. The red numbers read Svet 84, Praha A 83.

The NCAA Division III Championships I'd won nearly a decade earlier with North Park College with my brother were great, but this win, stands out as the high point of my basketball life. That remarkable moment had moved the team to a middling record of 4-3 since I started in the Superliga.

The *Hand, Foot and Mouth Disease's* symptoms of headache and exhaustion forced me back to the hotel and into bed. The Svet team—coaches and players—went out to a special dinner celebration in Prague. There was no way I could have gone to that. That is, if I wanted to be alive the next morning.

CHAPTER TWENTY-FIVE

GRANDIOSITY IN WENCESLAS LAND

As I slept, key moments from the game replayed. First, I dreamed of the three-point play just before halftime. I shot, a white-skinned arm smashed across my arms, the whistle blew. Meanwhile, the ball traveled like a space rock with a blue aura around it. Completing a single-minded journey and falling through the hoop. A comforting reaffirmation that nothing would thwart what was meant to occur.

That dream replayed. I loved it. That one play turned out to be my favorite individual contribution to the win.

Then it repeated maybe a half dozen times in a row. And in slow motion. I was trapped in a loop. What was tremendous turned into torment.

But somehow I climbed out of that dream. Can people have mastery over their dreams? I did that night.

I was surfing on top of a magic wave of greatness and emotion.

Next, there was a pause in the game. I walked to the bench and looked up at the clock with three seconds left. We were losing by two. My jersey was completely wet through and sticking to my stomach. I had never played so hard in all my life. I told myself that whatever happens next, I've given everything here tonight. It was my only attempt of the night to prepare and protect myself against loss.

Finally, Jaroslav launched *the shot.* The rock left his finger tips. The leather skin stood out like the pores on a beautiful, juicy orange travelling through the air. All sound was muted including the final buzzer, which I knew had just sounded. Instead of spiraling as the real shot did, this ball had no spin on it as it travelled in slow motion toward the target. I watched alongside Longstreet in the post just in front of our basket. As the ball closed in, I stepped back with one large stride to receive it. I was the only one in the whole scene to move. Everyone else was holding their breath. The ball reached the hoop, swished through the net, and fell into my hands. There was a stunned moment of stillness within.

But unlike real life, I didn't throw the ball up in celebration toward the arena ceiling. I held onto to it. In this re-creation, I dashed through the crowds like a football running back that had just broken through into the endzone for a game-winning touchdown.

Next I ran to the corner, jumping onto a pile of my teammates.

This sequence repeated. But eventually the replay stopped after three times. That felt appropriate and even perfect. Then I settled into the comfortable sleep I desperately needed.

As I awoke, feeling better, the next morning, Jaroslav was still under a pile of sheets and blankets in his bed.

"You want to go downstairs for breakfast with me?" I said.

"No, I need more sleep. Keep it down, But go on ahead, I'll see you over there at practice," said Jaroslav.

I crept out of the room, closing the door quietly, and soon I was in the hotel dining area. In Europe, breakfasts are included at most hotels. It was the first and last time this arrangement was provided for us.

I was hungry. I placed my order for a bowl of muesli, a croissant, yogurt, coffee, and an orange juice. There was no way I was going to practice at 9:30 a.m. without a sizeable breakfast.

I wanted to take a week off, take a slow barge down the Danube to Vienna, Bratislava, and Budapest, and just think about key moments in our win the night before.

But life had to move on. We were to practice in the Malastranska gym. After the game, Assistant Coach Gustav gave each of us a slip of paper with directions that routed us through alleys and small streets to get there. He said we always practiced there between the traditional back-to-back games against Prague teams each season. The directions were efficient and correct. But I passed the gym, a small building with plaster chipping off the façade, not thinking it was the final destination. So I walked around the area in a futile attempt to find the gym. About a half an hour later, I recognized I was completely lost. I was in a daze and deep in thought from that what happened the night before. I decided to ask a guy passing out slips of paper to a Handel music performance. He gave me directions to the gym. I followed what he said and it led me right back to where I was earlier.

The only clue was that it said "Malastranska" on the side. I'd seen that the first time, but it was a grammar school and couldn't be the place where the great Svet team was to practice. But it *was* the place.

After dressing in the locker room, I went up stairs to shoot around and stretch. It felt odd that anything so ordinary as practice should follow something as extraordinary as the night before.

Jaroslav came out onto the court with a basketball in his hands. As he walked toward me, he looked like his lower back was giving him some trouble.

"How is that back, Jaroslav?" I said.

"It will be okay. I feel pretty stiff this morning but I'll get it warmed up," he said. He did a few squats to loosen up and stretched against a wall.

"And you, how are you this morning?" he said.

"Better but still tired. I feel like I'm walking on air after a win like that. Jaroslav, that shot was from another world," I said.

We high fived.

"I got lucky. You saved your best work for last night. You helped us hang in there with your good work against Longstreet," he said.

All the players sauntered over to the basket we were shooting at and greeted Jaroslav. Some high-fived him, others patted him on the back, and they all stood near him. We had the whole team loosely gathered around us. We basked in the good feelings that the win produced. Anton playfully punched him in the shoulder.

"You hit the shot. But don't you think that was a little out of your range? If you took that shot again you might hit that maybe one in ten times. Then we have Josef there missing those shots around the basket," said Anton.

Anton threw the ball up to the basket from underneath and it caromed off. He came down the rebound and clutched with his elbows exaggeratedly outstretched for a second. Then he shot again and missed and clutched it in the same way then he went back up to finally score.

That drew laughter from several players standing nearby.

"Josef, that was you last night. Missing your own shots and rebounding them again like crazy. What were you doing? Trying to up your rebounding statistics?" said Anton.

Everyone got a laugh out of Anton's rendition of things. I didn't realize that pattern was what stood out.

"Yes, I did do that a few times last night, but at least I came up with the rebounds off his misses, Anton," I said, elbowing Anton playfully in the ribs.

"And you, Jaroslav, I could have hit that shot, too," said Anton.

"Oh really? Show us now, Anton," Jaroslav said.

Jaroslav tossed Anton the best leather basketball we had.

"Okay, Anton. Take it right now from the same place I did last night," said Jaroslav.

Anton shot from the top of key and missed.

"It was from further out, Anton," said Charles, pointing to the half court line.

"Was it? Not closer?" said Anton.

Before anyone said anything, Anton dribbled across the half court line. He squinted at the basket like it was a kilometer away from there, taking it in. Then he burst across the half court line with one dribble. Anton lofted it up toward the basket in the same motion Jaroslav did the night before. He released it from roughly the exact same spot. It caromed off the backboard. A miss. I threw him another ball.

"Try it again, Anton," I said.

Anton shot again from around where Jaroslav hit the game winner the night before. It fell a few inches short of the rim. Another miss. Then Jaroslav threw Anton another ball.

"One more time, Anton for that easy shot," said Jaroslav.

Anton shot and missed, the ball bouncing off the backboard and falling to the floor.

Within five minutes, the whole team—eleven of us—were on the court ready for practice. This was a first. Usually somebody was late, but not that morning. Jiri gathered us around in the corner court to talk.

"Jaroslav, you did it not just with that shot at the end, but by your overall excellence and leadership out there. Josef, great job last night, too. Your energy is what adds so much to this team. If that's how you play when you're sick, you should get sick more often," said Jiri.

That drew rousing laughter from everyone, it seemed. Even from Gustav. The only time I remember Gustav laughing like that was when I slipped into the mud, running Svet Mountain that one morning before practice.

"Honestly, Josef, you were very good last night. And Anton, your first group rose up and supplied intensity. Keep it up. I thought you all were great last night. A real team win. Can we continue our momentum against Praha B tonight?"

Hearing this analysis was great. It was fun talking about our game the night before.

After our practice and a weight-lifting session, I decided to see the city. Finally I was feeling better enough to venture out. I reached the National Museum on the upper end of Wenceslas Square. What a great place to be standing. I looked down Václavské náměstí from behind the monument of St. Wenceslas on the horseback. From behind the patron saint of the Czech Republic, I peered down the square. Prague's most famous street. Many buildings on both sides of the street still held the gray essence of Communist era but the architecture had character. I walked into the lobby of the building closest to the statue and picked up a telephone. I used a call card to dial my parent's number in Chicago.

"Dobry den Dad, it's your son, calling from Wenceslas Square in Prague," I said. I looked through a window into the lobby and the entrance to a McDonald's. They actually had a McDonald's here and I was going to try it after I got off the phone. I wanted to see if the menu was the same as in the US.

"Hello, Ferenc, I've been there. A lot of trouble has occurred in the place you are standing. How are you?" my father said.

"Our team came in yesterday and we won against one of the best teams in the league. A miracle shot at the buzzer allowed us the beat Praha A. We play Praha B in a few hours," I said.

"Don't tell me, you hit it. You won the game?" my father said.

"No, our point guard Jaroslav from Plzeň won it," I said.

"Do they know that it's you playing there or are they still thinking you are Josef?" he said.

"They think I'm Josef," I said.

"Why couldn't you have done this better? Go on your own as yourself. Find your own situation. This thing you are doing is a farce," he said.

"I don't agree" I said.

"It's not right. They will find out eventually and then it will be worse. I've told your mother that. You don't want to be known as a fraud, do you?" my father said.

"Things are finally starting to really work out," I said.

"Work out? Maybe for now. How could you think this thing would be something you wouldn't regret?" he said.

Maybe the guy had a point—several good points—but I didn't like his methods. I wanted a closer relationship with him and all I got were bad feelings. Calling him was a mistake and I felt like a kid again.

"My call card is running out. Say hello to mom."

"She's out. I'll tell her you called," said my father.

With that, it was over. I was out the door and back on Václavské náměstí to see the rest of Wenceslas Square. Forget my father. But I couldn't. It seemed like whatever I did, he didn't support me.

Then I thought of my mother. This tall Czech woman, who was born in Prague, always talked about Wenceslas Square. The street runs from a high point at the statue of Saint Wenceslas outside the national museum and then slopes down toward a line of buildings that close it on the bottom end. It was more like a rectangle than a square.

As I walked down the street, men were passing out fliers for puppet shows or classical concerts on nearly every corner. One announced a Mozart concert at Prague Castle, another, the music of Smetana at the local concert hall.

"Do you know the balcony where Havel spoke to the crowds when Czechoslovakia became free in 1989?" I said to the most Czech-looking concert hawker in Wenceslas Square.

He said he didn't know. I asked several more people I met, including a woman guiding a tourist group on a walking tour through Wenceslas Square and Prague's Old Town sector. That woman looked around as if to orient herself. In the end, she didn't know. As I walked the square I observed at least a dozen buildings with the same wrought iron balconies on the second floor in the photos I'd seen. It could have been any one of them.

I walked into a bookstore in a building right off the square. Perusing the shelves, I noticed aisle after aisle was in Czech. New books with glossy covers. I'd never seen anything like this. My first all Czech bookstore. Chicago's Cermak Road had a few stores that sold Czech language fiction and non-fiction, but only a small shelf of them, mixed in with other things they sold, such as newspapers, music, Czech groceries and beer. Certainly not a whole store dedicated to books and all in my second language.

The bookstore was an amazing epiphany. The stunning win at the buzzer the night before and finding my first all-Czech bookstore. Two great moments that came to me in less than 24 hours. Then I walked up the stairs to the bookstore's second floor. There were more books in Czech. Then I came upon a small foreign language section. The only books and magazines in that section were in Russian, German and Bulgarian. No English titles at all.

Then I noticed a series of windows. I peeked out the curtain and saw an empty balcony overlooking Wenceslas Square. I opened its French doors and stepped out. I walked to the railing and stood overlooking the square. This could have been the balcony where Vaclav Havel, a priest, and a rock musician stood and spoke during the Velvet Revolution, a little less than four years before. The photos showed Havel standing on the balcony with hundreds of thousands below in the square and streets leading to it. Czech secret police and Russian agents tensely waited on the corners. But they were swept up and powerless to stop Havel's declaration over the loudspeakers that the rock musician had given to the cause. Czechoslovakia was free.

As I looked down the balcony, I realized that this could be the place where they stood. This whole area was sacred. Along the wall of the balcony were potted geraniums and, next to them, a bistro table with black metal chairs around it. I sat down and pulled out some paper and a pen from my bag.

My dear Shantelina,

I'm writing from of a Czech bookstore in Prague. I'm on a second floor balcony where Vaclav Havel looked out over the square and declared Czech-

oslovakia a free country four years ago. Or at least this could have been the place. Nobody seems to know where the exact spot is. It's exciting to be here.

So was last night's win against Praha A. We won at the buzzer on a half court shot by Jaroslav. It was one of the best basketball nights of my career. We haven't lost since we started playing against the P teams and we can't afford to lose now.

I miss you. I've been away on this trip for six days. It feels like a time without end. Last night I dreamed I was floating above Prague with you, your hair flying in the wind. We saw the city together from above the rooftops and across the Vltava River. How beautiful those bridges looked from above. We hovered above Prague Castle, then landed there on one of the bridges, and leaned against the wall, and enjoyed this place together.

This is the first day I'm feeling just a little better from a flu-like illness. Tonight we play Praha B and I'm worried about a teamwide letdown, but the nice thing is that the game comes less than 24 hours since our big victory last night, so there is little time to think about it. We just have to play and play well again against another very good team. Every win from here forward will have these teams gunning for us, because we are kicking up a storm of notoriety in the Prague Post and the radio stations here in the capital. Every win also brings us closer to something. Every win brings me closer to Svet. I'll come to this city again; it would be great to see it with you someday.

Shantelina, I hope you are doing well,

Yours truly,

FRANK

I wrote her address on the envelope and when I reached the street, found a post box and mailed it off. I looked at my watch and decided I might just have enough time to tour Old Town Square, the Astronomical Clock, and the Jan Hus statue.

Sitting in the square, I opened the *Prague Post* to the sports page.

Svet Stunner Deals Titans First Loss

Praha A basketball has been brought back down to planet earth.

It took a remarkable 13-meter shot as time expired from Svet's Jaroslav Matura to hand Praha—their first defeat of the season. The 84-83 victory for the visiting Svet Lions (11-10) over Praha

A (21-1) represents their first win in the series matchup since the Czech Superliga's formation.

The threesome of Americans Darius Longstreet, Escalante Greenfield, and Dave Guse accounted for 52 points between them, but they couldn't tame the Lions, especially Matura. Not only did 1.83 meter tall point guard from Plzeň hit the winning shot, he scored 10 of the final 15 points for Svet. Matura finished with a game-high 28 points and 9 assists on the evening. Svet's only foreign player, Josef Savek, a first-year American centre, had 14 points, 17 rebounds, season highs in both categories.

I'm not the only foreign player on this team. What about the Vojtech? He's a non-Czech foreigner from Bulgaria. They missed that one, or maybe to this reporter, that's not foreign enough.

"They played slightly better than we did in the last half. We had breakdowns that let them stay in the game. I don't think they're the better team. Certainly not. They got lucky on that last basket." said Praha A Coach Tomáš Hochman.

Svet Coach Jiri Hasek uses all of his players each game. His gatling gun lineup includes an intricate scheme of players rotating in and out every fifteen minutes. Svet has won four straight games since its implementation.

When asked how that came about, this is what their Coach Hasek said: "We needed a change. Interposing two lineups has channeled our energy in the right direction. Tonight showed that. But in the end, that shot saved us."

Until last night, Praha A hasn't given up more than 62 points in a game this season, averaging 54 points allowed (a Czech league best). Praha A Coach Hochman was asked if allowing 84 points against this second caliber team amounted to a defensive breakdown.

"I'm disappointed about our performance on defense and the fact that they came in here and outrebounded us. That shouldn't have happened. But Svet played with fire in their hearts and found baskets when it mattered. You can't stop Matura's shot.

You just hope he misses at that point. Also, Savek gives them defensive stability inside like we haven't seen before. Jiri Hasek's teams have never had a combination of scoring firepower and defensive stamina like this one. They are the most improved team in the league. We will be ready for them next time is all I can say."

"We turned up our level of intensity against this great Prague team. These guys I have this year are playing well right now," said Svet Coach Hasek.

This team from the small glass-making town in the Krkonoše Mountains takes on the Czech capital again. Tonight Svet's Gatlin Gun formation plays at 17:30 against the Praha B Flames at the Prague Sport Pavilion.

As the team bus pulled to a halt in the pavilion parking area, Communist-era apartment buildings with graffiti all over them surrounded us. The Pavilion itself was a limestone rectangle. Praha B had two Americans on the team. Jiri said they were Frank Guardino, a 6'3" shooting guard, and Tracy Nicolson, a 6'6" forward. Jiri said these Americans were good players, but it was their Czech players that were most impressive—including a rangy big man named Davey Havelich.

"Earlier this season Praha B beat us twice by 20. I saw them a few nights ago and they do a lot of trapping and had a zone press that created turnovers in the game," said Gustav.

Coach Jiri said, "No one expected much from us—the smallest town in the league. Before, we could surprise them. But that's not going to work anymore. Their all ready for us now. They are going to be in your jockstraps every step of the way. Each of you needs something special tonight."

From the tip-off forward, the Czech all-stars played hard against the very athletic and physical Prague team. Anton had coverage on the wide-shouldered Guardino and had a hard time staying up with him. His crossover dribble and explosive first step enabled him to move around Anton with devastating ease. Anton would catch up but had to play from behind. The result was that Anton picked up two fouls and almost a third that the referees didn't call during the first seven minutes.

Guardino scored several times by driving hard to the basket and putting the ball in on layups off the glass. He hit early jump shots and didn't force it. When Anton closed the gap and Zedenik helped double-team him for a moment, Guardino passed the ball to his big men Nicolson and Havelich. Each was adept at setting screens for Guardino, then slipping behind their defender to accept a pass inside. This Praha B pair had good hands, too.

This team appeared to be even better than the one we faced the night before, if that was possible.

Praha B got their fans into the game, and as hard as the first unit tried, the momentum was all in the home team's corner. We got a few nice shots from Anton to close the gap but we were behind 18-8.

The guy I was going to cover, Havelich, was their tallest player. He looked about 6'7". But I was never quite sure about height until I stood out there next to someone side by side. My chance for that neared. Watching him from the bench, he reminded me a lot of my brother Josef. He was a white guy who could jump and had a real nice court sense against Vojtech. He worked well with his teammates, especially the Americans Guardino and Nicolson, as if they had been playing together for years.

I missed my brother at the moment, especially his offbeat sense of humor and the connection during those years we played together. I wondered how he was doing down there in Australia.

Jiri got Zedenik to signal for a timeout and the players all came back to the bench.

"This Guardino has the hot hand right now. Gustav and I have been watching him. He dribbles between his legs right before he is about to shoot. He does it everytime. Like a signal that he's going to shoot," said Jiri, over the music blaring from the loud speakers.

"Offensively we aren't moving or patient enough like we were last night. The effort's not there and they're taking advantage of that," Jiri said. He drew up some plays on his whiteboard.

"Guardino's the key. We interrupt his flow and his ability to pass and move freely, and we are back in this thing. What do you think, Anton? Do you want to keep covering him or switch?" Gustav said.

"The double teaming—that's not working. The guy's smooth. But I can disrupt what he has going. We need to switch outright if he gets ahead of me. I'll call it out to you if we're switching," said Anton to his teammates on the first unit seated around him.

As much as Anton tried to stop Guardino, he couldn't. Anton did switch a few times when Guardino got out ahead of him on a few occasions, but Praha B continued its roll ahead. But the one positive development: our team started to find baskets against Praha B from a good balance of our starters. Vojtech received a sharp pass from Anton and powered it up and in. He was upended and went down after the shot. The referee signaled foul on Nicolson. Vojtech stepped up and hit the free throw to complete the three-point play. Zedenik's and Anton's shots started to fall from the perimeter. Kolin started to capture offensive rebounds and drew some fouls against the Praha B big men. That was encouraging. When it came to free throws, Kolin was consistent in his pattern. Hit one. Miss one. But he was coming alive and active.

As our second team stood to enter the game, I looked up to the flame scoreboard to see Prague leading 27-20. I hoped that the night before had been the worst point of my sickness. I was mostly over it. As that game ended, I had stood there in a state of delirium from winning at the buzzer, but also exhausted from playing through the sickness. I couldn't shake the fever and extreme tiredness until I lay down for the night. But this was different. I was feeling better when my moment came. We stepped out onto court against Praha B.

"Put a body on Guardino. He'll light you up if you are not on him," said Anton. Sweat was pouring off his face as he walked toward the bench.

"I've got him," I said, motioning to my teammates that I was covering Havelich.

"Who do you have? I thought you had Nicolson," said Havelich. He was trying to add confusion or thought he was funny. It's true that I was covering him, but it was a decoy because we were opening with a diamond zone 1-3-1 to throw them off for a few plays on defense.

Havelich was taller than I thought, maybe about 6'9".

The referee blew the whistle and we began our stint. Praha B inbounded it to Guardino. Guardino patiently dribbled the ball on the point, peering at the whole scene as if reading our defensive setup. We were in our zone with me in the middle and Jaroslav at the top of the key harassing Guardino.

Their point moved around the perimeter and then drove, but I was there to put a hand in his face. He passed it back out to his other guard, a reddish-faced guy that played better than he looked. That guard tried to find Nicolson on the wing but Jaroslav got a piece of his pass. He tipped it and the ball was deflected toward the out of bounds line. Jaroslav raced out to the side and scooped in the rolling loose ball. He moved naturally like he knew all along that the basketball was going there. From there, he dribbled with abandon for our open basket. For a man in his early 30s, he could still play the speed game.

Guardino stayed with him defensively and Jaroslav shot a rushed 10 footer in the lane. The ball weakly grazed the rim. Guardino snatched it and whipped it out to their point on the wing. All that flash and hustle to end like that—it wasn't the best start to our stint in control. I sprinted back to give some help against their fast break. The red-faced Prague player dished a no-look pass to Havelich who trailed from behind. I had Havelich covered, or so I thought. I was right next to him and the pass to him surprised me. Havelich took one dribble to the basket and I closed the gap. All in one motion, he leaned in against me and shot a jumper. It hit the rim and bounced in. As it did, Havelich underscored his dominance by bodying and sealing me off in the lane. He not only did just hit the shot, but he showed me that he had clear ownership of the glass for the hypothetical rebound, too. That was not going to happen to me again—no more lapses like that, I said to myself.

We needed to threaten the nine-point lead of Prague with inside scoring. On the very next possession, I found an opening but Jaroslav, holding the ball on the point, did not see me. I called Jaroslav and circled back around and received a bullet pass inside. Havelich and Nicolson were both there to seal me off. Against my best basketball sense, I ascended and released the ball. I expected a whack across the arm or a rejection but neither came. I did alter my shot in expectation: it dribbled off the rim and back into my hands. Havelich and Nicolson both got their hands on the basketball, too. Maybe my weight training was paying off—especially snatching the 15 pound medicine ball from mid-air twenty times—because I pried it away from both of them and in one motion scooped toward the basket and in. Wow, that was amazing.

When Praha B had the ball, Jaroslav dogged Guardino. I was fronting and circling Havelich. I stood strong and held my ground as I looked into Guardino's eyes a moment. He didn't pass but instead tried to bolt past Jaroslav, but couldn't shake him. Havelich moved out of the lane to the other side as if opening the channel for his point guard. Guardino didn't use the opening, but instead took a jumper with Jaroslav in his face. The shot didn't fall and came off the rim. I was there for it and so was Charles. In fact, my teammate had more of it so I let him have it. Guardino's forced shot with Jaroslav all over him was the first mistake of the night I'd seen that Guardino make. Jaroslav was back to his sharp shooting like the night before. He hit several shots in the row from 10 feet out and a reverse layup. When Praha B tried to double-team him, he found me with crafty passes inside. I was able to convert on a few baskets over Havelich. Praha B's

Guardino didn't stop Jaroslav. Guardino was still scoring off screens but we were able to slow his production enough to close the gap to 48-44 at half.

As we walked toward the locker room, the fans booed us, so I figured we were doing something right. The Prague locker room was freezing because someone had opened all the windows over the bathroom sinks. We slammed them shut and sat on the bench.

"Are there any heaters in here?" Jaroslav said.

"No, not that I can see," I said. It reminded me of playing on the west side of Chicago where the visitor's locker room at St. Mel's had slits in the windows where the snow came in.

"Those pissers did it on purpose," said Anton.

"Maybe, but who cares. Expect it. Use your energy on results, not surroundings," said Jiri as he walked in and took off his sport coat and threw it on the chair. Then he rolled up his sleeves of his white shirt. He paused for a few moments.

"We must rebound. Who owns those back boards? If I'm sitting in the stands I'd say Praha B. They want it, they expect it. That's the difference in this game right now," Jiri said.

"Coach, we just came back. We have them where we want them now," I said.

"No, no, no. We should be leading. Beating them by eight to ten points now. Josef, you've not shown that you can dominate and take over like we need. Where's our defensive and rebounding specialist when we need him? Nobody—first or second team—has shown they understand what I'm talking about or what I've been talking about all season," he said.

The guy's angry. Is he singling me out because I said something? I thought I held my own in there in the first half and we achieved something notable to close the gap to four at half.

Gustav handed him the score book with the first half stats. Jiri looked down at it for a moment.

"Guardino 16 points, Havelich 13 points. Those two are two killing us. Guardino's a solid player but he's not playing like he respects us. We should continue to stop his drive to the basket. Put a body on him. Jaroslav is the only guy playing a lick of good defense on him. Havelich and Nicolson play well together with their picks inside. Havelich is an above average player but not as good as you are making him, Josef. And Vojtech, talk more to your teammates for help when you are out there. We can't have lapses on them. This is anyone's game tonight," Jiri yelled. I noticed that Jiri had white spittle on his lips.

Jiri was wrong on one thing: Havelich was the best big Czech big man I'd faced in the entire league so far. Very skilled, smooth, a good jumper and hard to stop. Right up there with my brother in terms of talent.

Jiri put his sport coat back on. Gustav opened the door that led back to the basketball floor.

"We have them were we want them, but we can't rely on another shot like Jaroslav had last night. Go out there and finish them off," our coach said.

We rushed back to the bench courtside. The halftime clock went down to zero and the buzzer sounded to start the second half.

The first team took the floor and Vojtech lined up against Nicholson in the middle for the opening tip. Nicholson was a better jumper than Vojtech but Vojtech still won the tip. He smacked the ball to Anton. That was a promising sign. He dished it to Zedenik who took the first shot, a 12 foot jumper, and missed. Anton was there for the offensive rebound and went back up for a layup. We were down by only two.

After a tense series of misses on both ends of the floor, Svet's first team evened the score with a reverse lay-up in traffic by Anton. The lead changed hands several times but only by a few points either way. Zedenik was covering the taller Guardino and was doing a good job neutralizing his speed. What amazed me is that they were playing with a kind of consistency they hadn't demonstrated in the first half. They were being patient on offense in a way that showed they were evolving. It was great to see. On defense, they were helping out and working together. The hustle and initiative was there. The rebounds edge went to Svet because of their determination not to let Praha B have the ball after a miss.

The only thing they weren't able to do was haul in offense rebounds, but it doesn't mean they weren't trying. It was just that Praha B's Havelich was there to pull in the basketball. When the Svet first team relinquished the floor to our unit, we had a four point lead, 67-63.

"We've done our job. Close them out," said Anton as he passed Jaroslav and me before going to the bench.

Guardino pushed off against Jaroslav to receive the inbound pass. No foul was called. Then Jaroslav came out a little too aggressive in response and swiped Guardino's outstretched hand. A tit-for-tat move. Jaroslav *was* called for a foul. In the next moment, Guardino stepped toward Jaroslav and drilled a hard chest pass at Jaroslav at point blank range. It hit off Jaroslav's elbow.

"You have nothing tonight and more of that coming," Guardino said.

"Really what are you planning, Guardino?" said Jaroslav as he stepped up to confront Guardino.

Fortunately, Charles who was nearby stepped in front of Jaroslav. The referees did, too. One referee went to talk to Jaroslav and another to Guardino.

"Any more of this and you will be both thrown out of the game. Do you understand?" said the referee to Jaroslav.

No technical fouls were called like I expected.

Jaroslav was irritated and not his usual cool self. I rushed over to talk to him face-to-face for a moment.

"Don't lose your head. They want to provoke you. Don't fall for it," I said.

"Yes, I know, but what a jerk," Jaroslav said.

"He might be, but remember it's a bigger game. Perspective. We need you," I said. My Czech struggling to come forth. He shook his head in agreement that he understood.

The ball was inbounded by Praha B again. This time Guardino didn't push off but still received the pass in tight traffic. Guardino and Jaroslav faced each other for a moment. Then Guardino put the ball down and tried to blow past Jaroslav with his lightning first step. Jaroslav had equal resolve and stayed with him chest to chest. He lobbed the ball up over my head to Havelich, who was behind me. I leaped up but it was a perfect pass over my fingertips and over Havelich, too, and out of bounds. If that were successful as a pass, Havelich would have had an easy two-handed dunk.

We battled back and forth and at one point we had a seven point lead. But Praha B cut that to two points when Havelich hit two free throws with a minute to go in the game.

The Praha Arena fans came alive, yelling and screaming for the first time in the second half. Their Flames had a chance to win this. Havelich saved his monster intensity for the end, it seemed. He was playing flawless, inspired basketball down the stretch. On the play that led to the free-throws, he received the ball on the wing and dribbled right and then left. He penetrated forcefully until he was under the basket and started to go up for a shot that was a sure-thing under the basket. Jaroslav and I fouled him hard across the arms before he could release it. There was no way we were going to let him dunk it. The referees called the foul on Jaroslav. His fifth. The buzzer sounded as the scorekeeper signaled to the referees that Jaroslav was done for the night. Zedenik entered the game his replacement. I was happy to see that because he was truly the only other guy I'd seen that had some success neutralizing Guardino.

Amazingly, no timeouts were called by either coach after Havelich's pair of free throws. I inbounded the ball to Zedenik, who was furiously double teamed in the back court. He had nowhere to go.

Trapped. I ran away from him to create some spacing and he sent a looping pass to me at half court. I caught it near the out of bounds line. I was the last guy in the universe to be handling the ball at that point. Ball handling in the open was my biggest vulnerability. Before I put the ball on the floor, two guys sandwiched me. Nobody open. I called time out. The referees granted it. 51 seconds were left on the scoreboard as we walked to our bench.

"We want to use as much time as possible and then take a smart shot inside. The only reason to shoot now is an open shot inside," said Jiri.

Back on the floor. We successfully inbounded the ball. There was no shot clock so we could use up all the time. Guardino pressured Zedenik who had the ball at the point. Immediately he saw me open inside but didn't pass. Instead, he dribbled hard on the perimeter. After 20 seconds of tense working around, it was obvious that there was no way to rattle Zedenik. But he was playing it safe and playing not to make a mistake.

"Attack the basket. You are playing tentative," yelled out Jiri.

I fronted Havelich under the basket. Zedenik shoveled a bounce pass to me. I faked and Havelich didn't fall for it. Now I was in trouble because Havelich and Nicolson converged on me. Before I could shoot, they knocked the ball from my hands and set me sprawling to the floor in pursuit of it. The ball went out of bounds and the referees said I was the last one to touch it.

Jiri ran to the referee on the floor. Gustav tried to restrain him.

"No foul on that? That's terrible," said Jiri to the referees.

The last thing we needed was a technical. Praha B had possession of the basketball and a chance to win with 25 seconds left. They called a timeout.

"They are going inside with the basketball," said Jiri on the bench during the timeout. It was hard to hear over the noise in the gym. Also, his voice was nearly gone from yelling.

"You've got that guy, Havelich. Also, he can't stop you inside," said Jaroslav as an aside before I went out back on the court.

When Praha B inbounded the ball, Guardino drove quickly into the paint as the area inside the lane lines from the baseline to the free-throw line is known as. I had Havelich covered well and neutralized. Guardino passed the ball to Nicolson, who flashed out in front of his man. Nicolson moved with ease to the basket and laid it in. I couldn't foul him. We were tied with 21 seconds to go. The crowd cheered and all of them were standing.

Charles inbounded the ball to Zedenik, who drove to half court. I looked to the sideline and remembered that we had no more timeouts. Zedenik worked the ball around the perimeter. The crowd continued to stand as they saw we were working for a last shot. Havelich and Nicolson covered me well inside. I had nothing. I couldn't get open for a second. Guardino fouled Zedenik on the perimeter but it was only off the drive. Not a shooting foul, so the referees had us inbound the ball from the side.

The inbound went smoothly and Zedenik had the ball on the point again. He passed to Charles, who passed it back to him. Zedenik took the ball to the basket and was fouled with nine seconds to go.

We went to the free throw line and the crowd booed and hissed as Zedenik shot. His free throw went in. I went over to him and gave him congratulatory high five. We lined back up for his next one. This time he missed but as he shot, I did something crazy. I spun around Havelich and was side-by-side with him when the ball came off. I got the rebound and went back up with it and scored. It reminded me of my overly aggressive moves when playing against my brother Josef. Plus, it's a risk. I could have just as easily picked up a foul on me as I did a basket. But this audacity worked. This time I pulled off the unexpected. We were up by three.

Instead of pondering it any longer I sprinted back to defend Praha B's last attempt. All they might do is tie us if we didn't foul them. I ran alongside Havelich the whole way. Zedenik covered Guardino chest to chest on defense. That slowed him down and forced Guardino to launch a bomb from almost three-fourths the length of the court at the buzzer. It sailed over Havelich and me, the top of the glass, and out of bounds to end the game. Svet was victorious 78-75.

Praha B's players shook my hand like they were in awe of us. Even their coach stood there intently looking at us for a moment after patting us on the back.

Finally, Havelich, Jaroslav and I stood next to each other and talked for a few seconds. We shook hands.

"Great game, big man," Jaroslav said to Havelich.

"You're the best we've faced so far. Savek, you are a lion out there like your team's nickname, I suppose. But you're stupid to come here. To Svet? Come on," Havelich said, looking down at me and then walked away.

CHAPTER TWENTY-SIX

BATTLE AGAINST FINAL "P" TEAM

We arrived in Pardubice before lunch. Near our hotel, there were banners on the lamp posts that announcing a special exhibition of glass-making at the *East Bohemia Museum.* I thought glass manufacturing was Svet's sphere of excellence, but here this town featured it as if they were the center of this trade.

"Have you seen this exhibition before?" I said to Jiri, and pointing to the banner.

"They had that last year. Yes, the East Bohemia Museum is worth seeing," he said. You'll have time after practice and before the game. See it then."

We had come a long way since the Pardubice Stallions club beat us by 15 points several weeks earlier in Svet. We'd won four in a row and beaten the three P teams. The Pardubice Stallions were the league champion and our best test of all.

Later, we walked outside into a misty rain that was starting to wet the sidewalk. Our team bus pulled up in front of the hotel. Gustav, who was behind the wheel, swung open the door. Jaroslav and I were the first players to board.

"Where's Jiri? I said as I stepped up to the top of the stairs.

"He left for Svet. His mother died," Gustav said.

"Will he be coming back for the game tonight?" I said.

"I don't know. I'm running practice. Have a seat, you're blocking the door," said Gustav.

I looked back and there were a number of players waiting to board behind Jaroslav. I took a seat toward the front, as did Jaroslav.

Gustav told everyone the same story: our coach had gone back home to be with his family but would be back for the game.

When we took to the floor in our game uniforms, the Pardubice arena was packed. This was the biggest crowd we had to date. Still no sign of Jiri. We did our pregame warmups. I had come a long way since that first practice when we did this passing weaving drill and I couldn't get it.

Now, Zedenik slapped the ball between his hands to begin the drill. As I passed right and moved left on the drill in Pardubice, I realized I could now practically do it in my sleep.

I looked back toward Gustav on the sidelines. Usually, his game wear was a white shirt, slacks, and tie. But Gustav wore a suit and tie like Jiri did for every game. Gustav looked downright respectable.

The basket we warmed up on should have been familiar to me because I shot on it for twenty minutes that afternoon. It felt great and had some rhythm. But at game time it was different—the rim was tighter—my shots were missing.

On a positive note, I liked the springy floor of the place. You could really jump on the Pardubice court. But then I imagined that might be also helpful to their great white leaper, Johann Muller—the same player that welcomed me to the Czech Republic with a dunk over my head in my first minute of my first game in the superliga.

We had all gathered on the bench and Gustav was going over last-minute instructions. Then, just a few minutes before tipoff, Jiri showed up.

"I drove 200 kilometers per hour to make it here," said Jiri. "Even cut through a barley field and hit a barbed wire fence, but I'm here."

That's all we needed, chaos right before the biggest game of the season against the Pardubice Stallions.

Jiri continued, "Muller's the key. Limit him and we beat this team. We've come a long way to get to this moment."

Muller had won the league's *Best Player* award the year before and I had to wonder if he would again, with the likes of Darius Longstreet now in the league. Not only could Muller consistently hit three point shots, he liked to take the ball inside—my territory. Last time we played them, Muller must have scored half of his 39 points close to the basket.

Even though Muller was from just across the border in Germany, he was their only "foreign player."

I couldn't believe how many fans they had in the arena. Every seat was taken and fans were standing alongside the court and in the aisles leading from the doors into the gym. All this in a gym about the same size as ours. Hockey may have been the number one sport in the new Czech Republic, but at least for that night, basketball was king. One fan held up a cardboard sign that even made a prediction. On the top, it said *Svet Monitor*. That was our town's newspaper. Underneath that was *Tomorrow's Headline: Czech League's Best Crushes Svet, Ending Streak.*

The buzzer sounded and Anton, Zedenik, Vojtech, Rudenic, and Kolin took the floor. Muller won the opening tip. The Pardubice fans, many waving yellow Stallion flags and chanting, soon had plenty to cheer about. They patiently worked the ball around. They scored first when Muller powered a layup off the glass. He made it look easy. Anton fired a pass behind Muller and out of bounds on our first possession.

With each favorable development from Pardubice, their fans became more animated.

Vojtech defended their other inside threat: Sasquatch, the guy I covered the first game and would have to cover in this one, too. This time I noticed his real name on the back of his jersey: Petr Straka. I wondered why he had his full name on his jersey. Then it became clear: another player entered the game a few minutes later and his name was Michal Straka. Brothers. They weren't identical twins because Sasquatch was 6'8" and the other looked to be about 6'5", but they did resemble each other. I thought of Josef and me and how great it would be to have him on my same team again, running the court with him. Having brothers on the same team was impressive.

And Pardubice was impressive, too. They opened up an eight point lead in the first minutes. The highlight was when Muller shot from the far corner with Anton's hand extended a few feet from him. That is probably the hardest shot in basketball. Muller fired the three-point shot with precision and it went in. Later he hit another three-point shot from the top of the key. So Muller was finding our vulnerability on the perimeter. Muller was less effective inside; Anton was defending him well there. Anton rose to the challenge, connecting on a vicious fast break slam dunk on an open basket a few minutes later. That seemed to turn the momentum in our direction. Our defense tightened and Parbubice's scoring run ended. Vojtech owned the backboards and Zedenik even stole the ball from off Muller's blind side. But the first team couldn't capitalize with a streak of baskets to erase Pardubice's lead. Our shots weren't falling and we weren't hauling in the offensive rebounds to get the second scoring opportunities needed. When our turn came to enter the game in the first half, we were behind 27-19. Svet Group B would need to erase that lead before half time.

As I stepped onto the oak plank floor, I found my man, Petr Straka. The guy was huge next to me. I felt short in a way that I had felt against no one else in this league. My earlier self was right to call him "Sasquatch" because in addition to his towering height he had a muscular physique and huge shoulders. He leaned in toward me. I could feel the perspiration that was coming through his gold jersey.

Jaroslav received the inbound pass and drove toward our basket. I came up to the free throw line and he passed me the ball. I pivoted and turned toward our basket. Then I dished it back to him. I flanked to his side and set a screen on the man covering him: Muller. Muller had a five-inch advantage over Jaroslav, so my teammate running the point was going to need all the help he could get. Jaroslav used the pick well and shot a jumper off the board that went in. Sasquatch and Muller both put a body on me so I was completely unable to get in a good position for the offensive rebound. They were ready for me.

Muller and company wasted no time. They passed the ball around until Muller found my man in great position near the front of the basketball. I reached for him and swiped his arm as his half hook shot went in. The referee whistled the foul on me. Straka's brother gave him a congratulatory high five as he stepped up to the free throw line. The ref handed him the ball a moment later and he hit the free throw.

Pardubice had pushed their lead into double digits with that. It was hard to achieve the gains we needed because when we scored during our stint, Pardubice matched it with a basket of their own. Everywhere I went the Sasquatch was on me bodying me, and thwarting passes into me. I did get a few offensive rebounds, but the effort it took was wearing me out. I connected on a few baskets inside, and Jaroslav was struggling to generate the heat we needed. Pardubice gradually extended their lead to 14 at halftime. The Pardubice gym was in full cerebration as we walked to the locker room.

I sat down on the locker room bench to rest for a moment. So did my teammates. I buried my face into a towel to dry the sweat on my face and neck. But I realized that it wasn't a pose I wanted to maintain for long. We waited for Jiri and Gustav. I expected there was a lot they wanted to talk through. We had played under our ability, but that was only one half of basketball. We still had a chance although Pardubice had played a near flawless game to this point. And we had played badly. I tried to figure out how badly. I looked around the locker room at my teammates. No one was saying much.

After several minutes of watching for the door to swing open, I began to wonder what the holdup was. Maybe someone should go out and get Jiri.

"Isn't anyone going to say anything?" I said.

"What is it you want to hear, Josef?" said Anton.

"Jaroslav, what you think? What does anyone think about what just happened?" I said.

"We didn't play well, we're better than that. Let's figure it out and beat this team," Jaroslav said. Gustav did come to tell us to return for the second half of play on the floor. He didn't say anything besides that. Koliar's insistence that our team return to Svet undefeated or else Jiri would be removed as coach weighed heavily in my mind. But worse than that, his mother had died. And she would have expected more from me.

Our coach Jiri never came did come in the locker room at halftime. That was troubling but effective at the same time. The message was clear: whatever had just had happened, we had to work it out and solve our own problem. And start playing the way we were meant to.

Straka and Vojtech lined up for the second half tipoff. Both reached the basketball at the same time but Padubice's big man tapped most of it. He sent the ball into the back court to Muller, who ran to meet it. But Charles anticipated that would happen. He stepped out and deflected the ball. Our point Zedenik scooped up the loose ball. He wasted no time, driving with all his might to our basket. Muller converged on him and looked like he would stuff Zedenik's layup. His defensive presence did alter Zedenik's shot. The ball caromed off the rim, but a trailing Anton arrived, seemingly out of nowhere, to tip it in.

Muller quickly inbounded the basketball to his point guard. Their ability to run a fast break was stopped because our entire team was back on defense. Pardubice's coach called for them to reset and run a play. They worked the ball around until they got the ball where they wanted it: Muller one-on-one against Anton. Muller pulled up for a 12-foot jumper near the free throw line. His shot went in and out. Vojtech snatched the rebound.

Svet's first team worked the ball with amazing skill and patience on their first possession of the second half. I remarked to myself how far they had come. It was a real evolution of their maturity I witnessed. It ended with Vojtech muscling in for two points against Straka. That was great: we had played only a minute of the second half and the momentum was fully in our hands. Over the course of the next nine minutes, Svet's five reversed our situation. We were finding baskets and timely rebounds all over the place. The only scores for Pardubice were Muller's on a few baskets and a pair of free throws by each of the Straka brothers. Jiri was a new man when he called timeout with ten minutes in the game remaining. We had shaved ten points off their lead. The score was 43-39 with Pardubice still in the lead.

"Great job, Anton! Great job all of you. Have a rest now. Our finishers are going to win this for us," Jiri said.

My second unit teammates and I snapped off our warm-up pants. Jiri scripted some plays for us on his clipboard. Then the buzzer sounded and we stood up. Jiri gave me a slap on the rump and we entered for our final push.

Pardubice's point guard held the ball ready to inbound slightly off the side of their basket. We quickly positioned our man-to-man coverage. I extended both hands around their big man Straka. He had such good position on the block that it felt like his man could hand him the basketball. Then he would scoop it up and in with ease without changing his place.

He leaned his sweaty big body against me, giving him even better advantage. I furiously pushed against him but he wouldn't budge. I thought of coming around him and fully fronting him, but then my backside would be vulnerable.

The referee whistled for play to begin. Their point snapped the ball and faked passing into my man Straka. Then he lobbed it up toward the basket. As the ball sailed upward, Muller, who had been behind me, stepped up and leaped up to meet it. He grabbed the ball with his fingertips and slammed it with grace down the rim. It was more audacity that I could believe. The crowd cheered and stood in unison. Their reaction showed me that it was the play of the night for Pardubice at that point. The Stallions had come alive. It was the antidote to the Svet momentum and comeback. I was determined to stop them from building on this. Okay, it was an incredible pass and Muller was an amazing leaper, right up there with Darius Longstreet. But we beat Longstreet's team in Prague, and we would try to find a way to beat this team, too.

Jaroslav quickly received the inbound and I raced up the floor with abandon. I ran out front on the right and Milan on the left. We had a 3 on 2 advantage on the break. I established eye contact with Jaroslav the whole way. He launched a pass to me that reached me right as I neared the basket. I caught it and powered in a layup against the shorter Straka. I slapped hands with Jaroslav as we sprinted back on defense. We did it again and answered with our own audacity in return— nothing as spectacular as Muller's jam, but it worked.

The Stallions worked the ball around on their possession as if they were resting a bit. They didn't drive to the basket with determination. Their passing was tentative. When Muller dribbled around a pick on the perimeter, Jaroslav came up from his blind side and stole the basketball. Muller immediately tried to steal it back and fouled him, sending Jaroslav sprawling on the floor. I helped Jaroslav up. He gingerly walked down toward the free throw line so his hitting the deck had aggravated his back.

"We've come this far. Are you going to make it?" I said to him as we walked.

"It'll be all right," Jaroslav said. He was tough, but I worried for the guy.

Nevertheless, he stepped up to the line and swished both free throws.

On defense, my fronting Straka seemed to work. He did get an offensive rebound on me and scored a few minutes later, but I felt that, for the most part, my defense on him had taken him out of the flow of the offensive game. Even Muller had not generated the magic for a stretch of time. We capitalized on their scoring lull with inside scoring and offensive rebounds that stretched out our possessions.

We tied the game with a driving eight-foot jumper by Jaroslav, and then he hit a three point bomb from the corner for the lead a few minutes later. This guy is a great player, maybe the best guard I ever played with. Here was this six-foot point guard with the black messy hair hitting clutch shots during that stretch. And he was hurting. I looked over to Jiri and he was proud of what he was seeing. He smiled at me and ordered me to get back on defense.

With two minutes to go we held a slight lead of four points. Pardubice called a timeout. They came back out and worked the ball around patiently. Then Muller got the ball on the wing and drove around his man and right into Jaroslav. Jaroslav went flying backward. Muller's lunging shot was perfect; it went in but the referee waved it off. He declared it no good because, he signaled, Muller had committed an offense charge. Muller ran to the referee and shook his head. He put his hands up in the air in disbelief. The referee stood his ground against Muller's rage. Meanwhile, the impact from Muller left Jaroslav hurt. I rushed to Jaroslav, who was still sprawled out on the court.

"Great play. Laugh it off, Jaroslav." I said.

I tried to help him up.

"No. My back is too stiff. Give me a minute," he said.

By that point, Gustav and Jiri were alongside him, too. It was clear that he had to go out and was done for the day. Within a few minutes Gustav and I helped him up to his feet. We had our arms around him to steady him as struggled to walk toward the bench. Luckily, it didn't look like he broke anything.

Anton checked in for him. He was designated to take Jaroslav's free throws. Anton stepped to the line and missed the first free throw but swished the second one. Pardubice inbounded the ball and this time Muller drove to the basket but then passed off to the shorter

Straka brother on the left, who took an accurate shot that banked in. We were up by three, but with Muller's deadly ability to hit a three point shot, it was clear we needed to score. We worked the ball around with Anton leading the attack. Pardubice's pressure was too great and Anton threw up an off-balance jumper that bounded off the rim. I spun and was in front of Petr Straka and grabbed the rebound. He hammered me from behind the instant I had the ball. Foul. The referee handed me the ball at the free throw line. Behind the basket, Pardubice fans waved and screamed in an attempt to get me to miss. I focused with everything I had. It worked, because I banked in the free throw. And for the second one I was better: my shot swished in. I felt confident and proud of myself for doing that under that pressure. Our lead was 5 points with 30 seconds remaining.

Within seconds of inbounding it, Muller broke open and hit a three point shot to close our lead to two points. We inbounded the ball to great defensive pressure in the backcourt. Pardubice's trapping was working and we spent seven seconds to get to the half court mark. As soon as Anton crossed half court on the dribble, I broke to the basket wide open. I heard Jaroslav yell to Anton that I was wide open. Anton unleashed a bullet to me under the basket and as I went up and dropped in a layup off the glass to put our lead back to four. With eight seconds left, Pardubice was able to free Muller on a three point shot, but he missed. In the scramble for the rebound Michal Straka snatched the rebound. He went back up and hit the shot. In the rush, Anton inbounded to Charles who escaped off the dribble to open court. The buzzer sounded, Charles leaped in the air. We had just beaten the Superliga Champion, Pardubice 69-67. Not the prettiest victory, but a win. Svet was 6-3 since I arrived, 13-10 overall.

After the game, we greeted the Pardubice players and coaches.

"Good game, Savek. Whatever happens, we want to talk when you're through with this place. We have more to offer," the Pardubice head coach said.

As he shook my hand, he passed me his business card.

CHAPTER TWENTY-SEVEN

SHANTELINA OF SLOVAKIA

We left Pardubice at eight that morning at Jiri's insistence. He wanted to get back to make arrangements with for his mother's funeral and burial. We had breakfast on the road at a truckstop in a small village. They didn't have enough chairs in the restaurant and were slow about serving us. It was if our group of 13 people that walked in the door was too big of a crowd for them to handle. Jiri had a hard time getting them to give us a bill when it was all over. By the time the bill arrived, everybody on the team, except Jiri, was already out in the parking lot.

As we drove through Pardubice that morning, I wished we had more time to explore it. The place looked interesting with its center square and statues of saints and interesting Bohemian characters. It was smaller than any other place we had played but not as small as our Svet. The building architecture in the neighborhoods was eye-catching, and the restaurants and cafes looked inviting.

Later, we motored through the tunnel and then the canopy of trees on the road just outside of Svet. As we did, small, sharply-pointed brown leaves swept down like confetti across the front window of our bus. We blew in as returning heros but nobody outside the bus acknowledged that.

We crossed the bridge over the river and I thought how simple the bridge's architecture was compared to the Charles Bridge over the Vltava in Prague. Also, Prague had at least ten bridges over that river, but we only had three small ones spanning a much narrower channel. Then we turned up Přední Street. After being away eight days, the town looked empty. Looking out the windows of the team bus, it was as if no one lived in the place.

Svet was still the idyllic little town nestled in the football-shaped canyon with a river running through it. But I also realized that after being away on our road trip, that I had idealized it. In very much in the same way, I was starting to romanticize the place where I grew up. In the midday sun, it looked clean but a little run-down. The buildings were old but less visually interesting than in other parts of the country. I realized why the town hadn't capitalized on drawing tourists: the other cities like Prague or even Pardubice had more to offer. Before the roadtrip I had wondered why more people didn't come to see Svet in northeast Bohemia to experience its glass-making industries. But then it hit me: there was no cluster of large-scale glass factories in Svet. Just ours. Or should I say Milos Koliar's. But there were several glass factories in the other northern towns of our region.

I had mixed feelings about returning to Svet. We were returning as winners of five games in a row including the Superliga's four best teams. No one could take away the great achievement we had just accomplished. That was good. But we were so isolated—who could we celebrate with? Or, more importantly, did anyone care? Also, I was sad that I couldn't be recognized for myself. I was trapped playing under my brother's name. Plus, we lived in a glass factory, not in some nice residence. Most of the time, we couldn't even afford hotels when we traveled, but had to stay at the homes of people in Jiri's black book, or worse, with Koliar's connections who owed him something. But I was enthusiastic about seeing Shantelina. I had someone back in Svet that I connected with and would be excited to see me.

I wondered how our gym would look after being away from it for more than a week. The polished oak floors looked great. The court had been stained several days before and it still smelled of varnish. I reached down and it felt cold. There was no dampness or oil residue on my hand.

We didn't understand the magnitude of what we had just accomplished until we were also greeted by some reporters and photographers. They snapped photos of us and then asked questions of Gustav off to the side. One of the reporters that I didn't recognize showed me a stat sheet on the team. I didn't know anyone had produced such a thing.

I was second on the team in rebounding with 8.9 per game. Vojtech was first with 9.8 rebounds per game. I was averaging 11 points a game. Anton was scoring 19.6 per game. Jaroslav was at 12.1 per game.

We didn't have a game for two days, so our only obligations were practices and weight training. While we were on the road, the weight rooms we had used better equipment than at Svet so I was able to try some new things to strengthen my back and core. It made me think how ancient our weight room was. But it did have a huge assortment of kettlebells. On them it said "Made in Russia." We didn't have a team trainer like I heard the Prague teams did, but we had lists that we followed and signed and turned in after we were done. Earlier in the season, some guys like Anton seemed to be just going through the motions, but I think even Anton started to see the wisdom of achieving the quotas they wanted us to hit. For the next hour we pumped iron in the weight room. I'd come a long way since I began lifting weights to get ready for basketball in the weeks before leaving for Svet. As I looked into the mirror, I noticed that my shoulders, legs and arms were stronger than in years. By the time the workout was over, my shirt was sweated through. Then we had practice that followed that.

Gustav ran practice. Our assistant had a new swagger. We all did. We were returning to Svet a much better team than we started the season. Gustav liked playing the head coach, if only for an afternoon.

We opened practice with running lines on the court. When we finished, he gathered us up on the sideline.

"You're running us like we came back losers. We're the winners of five straight," I said.

His facial expression told me I shouldn't have said that.

"Josef here thinks we have arrived back to Svet as the Best of the Czech Republic. Pardubice and Praha A are way ahead of us in the standings. Praha B and Plzeň are each above us, too. We haven't won anything yet. A hot streak, yes, but we have a long way to go this season," our assistant coach said.

"What have you been hearing about Olmouc?" Anton said.

"They play nearby tonight over at Hradec Králové. Just because we beat them last season doesn't mean anything. They always come in here like they own the place," Gustav said.

Olmouc was the only team we had not faced yet. The league standings in the *Svet Monitor* showed Olmouc was 2-6, 6-17 overall. My teammates didn't listen very attentively as Gustav spoke. I took that to mean that we might have a let-down against this team.

Next Gustav ran a rebounding drill. He had me go to the free throw line. The rest of my teammates lined up along the blocks, simulating a game situation. He handed me the ball to shoot. I hit three in a row.

"These are the only three in a row you have hit in a while, Josef," said Gustav.

It wasn't true. I was a good free throw shooter.

He handed me the ball for the fourth one. I hit that one, too.

"Josef, miss one. That's the point of this drill," Gustav said.

So I deliberately threw it harder off the board and it did miss. When I didn't bolt out toward the basket once, he stopped practice.

"Josef, why didn't you charge the basket after you shot?" he said.

"What kind of confidence does that display if I charge the basket immediately after releasing the ball?" I said.

"Do it. That's the point of this rebounding drill. Everyone rebounds on this team. That's what wins games and sets us apart from every other team in this league. We can't afford anything different. Also, I think this Gatling gun we run has limited days. Other teams are going to figure it out and adjust against it," Gustav said as he formed us to scrimmage at the end of the game.

I had a hard time understanding his Czech because his Bulgarian accent and Czech word choice were unusual.

I was happy he wasn't our head coach because scrapping the Gatling gun formation we ran at games got us to where we were at. There was no way we should to end that.

He set the first team against the second. By that point, Jaroslav tried to play, but his back was too stiff, so he did stretches on the sidelines. Without him, we lost three in a row against the first team. It was like we were back in the beginning of the season. I walked off the court discouraged and headed toward the locker room when it was all over.

"Tomorrow, come prepared to run outdoors. We going up Svet Mountain again," said Gustav.

That's crazy, I thought. Our conditioning was at its peak and we were winning. Now he wants to go back outside to run in that slop and mud. It seemed like overkill.

As I entered the building I saw a sign engraved in stained glass *Severní Bohémský Sklo Muzeum*. Much better than the hand-written one on cardboard from my last visit to the place.

It was impressive to see the transformation of the interior in a little more than a week. There was even a makeshift cafe on the first floor. I could smell dumplings and onion bread.

Then I went upstairs to the gallery.

"We're not open yet," said an older woman, when I got to the top of the stairs.

"I'm here for Shantelina. She asked me to meet her here," I said.

"She's not here. So you can wait," she said.

I scanned the gallery to see how the exhibits were set up. It looked great and was divided into sections. I strolled over to read one the

Czech narrative in the nearest section. Then below was a translation in English. Just two languages: Czech and English. Not German or Russian as I'd seen in Prague and Brno in museums, but English.

I was impressed when I read this:

There are glass factories all over Czech lands and even Czech glass making schools like the Prague School of Applied Arts and the renowned Moser Glass Factory in Karlovy Vary.

But without a doubt, North Bohemia and the Bohemian Forest regions are the capital of Czech glassmaking. Svet and Liberec are the centers of glass trade. Bohemian glass art achieved a prominent position in the world of glassmaking at the '67 World Expo in Montreal, Canada.

I looked up to see the older woman struggling to hang a sign.

"Here, let me help," I said.

"That's thoughtful."

I stepped forward and took one side while she took the other. We hung it into position.

"Let me show you what we've done," she said.

She guided me around. I was impressed. The exhibits looked great. At one point during the tour, I saw a copy on a desk of the *Svet Monitor*. It was folded open to the page with the headline *Smasher Savek Rips Down Rim.*

Then Shantelina strode into the space.

She was in her white coat again; the one I had such a hard time taking off that time we had dinner. We looked at each other. She wore her dark brown hair back in a pony tail.

"Your boyfriend and I are enjoying the moment," the older woman said.

"He's not Wenceslas; he'll be here tonight for the museum opening. Meet Josef. Who looks taller than I remember," she said.

"And princely. You forgot that one," the older woman said.

Shantelina gave her a knowing grin. She bit her lip, then turned to take me in. Her red lips were beautiful and I imagined kissing them, my lips lingering over hers—but put the thought out of my mind.

"Player American, can you bring in more items for opening with me? They are at storehouse a few kilometers away," Shantelina said.

"I'll help, yes."

Soon we were outside in the cold. Neither of us had a car, so we walked.

"Tonight should be good. The museum looks great, Shantelina," I said.

"Hold your estimation, Frank. There's more to be done before then," Shantelina said.

She reached up and touched my eyebrow.

"This has healed up well. Last time I saw you, it was raw," she said.

"Yes, it's better. I don't want to think about that," I said.

I could see my breath floating out in the early evening air. As we walked, a half dozen guys came into view. They were loitering on the side of the square across from the church. Basically, street punks with shaved heads. A few of them had acne on their faces and the backs of their necks. They looked up from breaking green beer bottles against a wall. Our passing seemed to alert their curiosity.

Shantelina put her arm around me for a 90 degree direction change. We maneuvered down a narrow alley and out of their view. Her feigning that we were lovers was a smooth move. But the way one of them looked at me made me think that at any moment they would tear around the corner in pursuit.

"Skinheads," she said.

"Nice. You know this area?"

"I know the short cuts through here. We don't want trouble," she said.

I looked behind us for the skinheads.

"Not there. We've seen the last of them," she said.

We headed down the brick streets that sloped toward the river. A few cars passed us and even a man pushing a cart.

"How do you feel about this winning streak you are on?" she said.

"It's great, we've won five in a row. We're in good position in this league," I said.

"It's because of you, Frank. I can see that. How is your brother? The real Josef?" she said.

I looked around to see if anyone heard that. I didn't like hearing that secret spoken out loud.

"Only you know that," I said.

"I know," she whispered. She looked me in the eyes and patted my shoulder. She was sincere. I felt I could trust her.

"You know me, my secret, more than anyone else here. That's power because now I'm vulnerable. I don't know if I like that," I said. I noticed I was whispering.

"Why? Relax, I won't betray you. That's for real," she said. She came a little closer.

It reminded me of my ex-girlfriend Nancy. One time when we were talking close to each other, and I was talking excitedly. Nancy kissed me to shut me up. That was a good moment.

Instead of moving even closer to kiss, Shantelina spoke next.

"How *is* your brother?"

"He's down there in Australia. It's funny you ask, he's on my mind today," I said.

"That's a sign that you should talk to him. Do that!"

It was a good suggestion to call Josef. I liked this woman's style.

"There's a closeness between you two," she said.

"What about Wenceslas?" I said.

"He's been great. Exactly the person I'm looking for, but we have been living in different places," Shantelina said.

"Is that guy your true love?" I said.

"Explain true love. What is that?"

"It's that your destiny links with another in a deeper way. Is that the case with him? I've always believed you and another person are meant to find each other. It must be an American belief or something," I said.

"This true love, have you ever found it?" she said.

"It'll come for me, I believe that," I said.

"I like that about you. I got your letters—especially the note from Prague and Wenceslas Square," she said.

"We've spent time together. As soon as I'm gone or you're gone, life will return to normal," I said.

"I like all your letters. Is it really possible to feel this true love about someone you've known a short while?" Shantelina said.

"Anything is possible. It's true we've only known each other a short while," I said. I tried to ignore the feeling that I was starting to care for her more than I should.

The tension was high. Darting glances of interest flashed between us.

We were walking arm in arm

"You have a girlfriend. Jelina, yes?"

"We broke up. Jelina's a prize for someone. Just not me," I said.

We reached the storehouse. We retreived some canvas bags with brochures about the museum and glassmaking. She quickly turned out the lights, locked the door, and we headed back.

"We will take another shortcut to avoid the skinheads. We'll cross there," Shantelina said. We were both carrying two bags each. I had the heaviest two.

I'd never been on that stretch of the path before. A dull yellow light brooded on the rooftops of the houses along the river.

Then we saw the same group of skinheads on the path ahead of us.

"Let's turn back and take the other bridge," she said. It was too late. A few of them looked up at us approaching them. It looked like they had surrounded someone.

"Keep going. We're crossing that bridge," I said. We had to pass them to get up the stairs.

Shantelina and I closed in to the spot on the path where the skinheads were. There was a small Vietnamese man in the middle of the pack. One skinhead was questioning the man. They were saying things like What? So! Then one of them elbowed the small man in the chest. Another punched him on the shoulder.

"Let the guy go," I said.

They turned towards Shantelina and me.

"Here is the giant. What do you think you're doing?" one skinhead said.

"Knock it off. What did he do to you?" I said.

"Why do you care? Take your whore and get out," the skinhead said. He looked to be the leader. There was desperation in the Vietnamese man's eyes.

They opened up a narrow path so we could pass through toward the bridge. There was no way I was walking through that ominous opening created. They'd hit us from behind as we walked through.

"Let him go," I said. Shantelina, thankfully, said nothing. One skinhead grasped the bags I held. He had one in each hand and pulled. I held them tight by the canvas straps. Then he ripped one away from me. He ran up the stairs with the bag then took out a brochure.

"Give it back," Shantelina said.

Instead, the whole group of skinheads bolted up the stairs. The Viet man, Shantelina and I followed. They escaped to the middle of the bridge. The one skinhead emptied the bag over the water. They laughed as the brochures poured into the river. Then the skinheads ran off but not before one of them threw a glass bottle toward us that shattered on the pavement in front of us standing there. They crossed to the other side and moved quickly into the town of Svet.

"What a bunch of punks," I said.

The brochures about the glass museum floated under the bridge. We watched together as they fanned out. They took the shape of a cone stretching downriver from bank to bank. One by one the steady current took them away between two rocks in the center of the channel downstream. There was beauty in the image of them widening out across the river.

"Thank you. Do you want me to go down and try to retrieve them?" the Vietnamese man said.

"No. They're ruined now. Are you all right?" Shantelina said.

"Yes, I'm okay now. I must go," the Viet man said. He grasped my hand with two small hands and shook hands with gusto and said, "Thank you, thank you." Then he scampered across the bridge and in the opposite direction of the skinheads.

We stood there looking over the water from the highest rise of the bridge.

"I miss English speaking with you. The Jizera looks great tonight," she said.

"Yes, it does, even with all the brochures floating down it. Are you sure they're sinking?"

It must have been just a few degrees above freezing and I could see my breath.

"It looks like it," she said.

A full moon was rising and the stars that stretched out like eternity across the darkened sky.

"These stars in Svet are incredible. I've never been able to see them like this before," I said.

"That's the way they are in my home village in Slovakia. Svidnik is just across the border from Poland, too. It's in the Carpathian Mountains," Shantelina said.

"Sounds great. I'd love to see it," I said.

"Yes, I'd show you that. We have to get back," she said. There was an awkward pause. At that point I realized that I had overreached.

We had a museum opening to attend, so we quickly walked to the museum building.

"Where's Wenceslas?"

"He should be here. He's just late," she said.

I reached for white coat to help her take it off.

"You don't have to. I had tailored. But I will let you take it from here," she said.

She handed me her coat. I hung it on the rack along the reddish striped wall.

"You don't have to do that. I know you have some kind of some kind of long-hidden admiration for her or something but I've got it from here," Wenceslas said. He looked at me directly in the eyes.

He hitched one hand around her hips and hugged her closer.

"I know it's cold. Your hands are shaking," Shantelina said.

"It's more than that. I wanted to say something. But not in front of this joker," he said.

"What is it?' Shantelina said.

"I know I've been away a lot. It's just great to see you. And I've been away too much but I'll stay and make things better. If..." he said, emphasizing that one word beyond what was necessary, "if you'll marry me."

Shantelina caught her breath. Slowly, to make certain she understood, she said, "You're willing to come here and live in Svet?"

"You'll have much more than Svet and this glass museum. I love you, Shantelina. You can open a glass gallery in Prague. "So will you," he said as he pulled her closer, "marry me sweetheart?"

I noticed he asked her two times.

"Yes," she said. He kissed her, then kissed her again.

Shantelina was so excited she had to go to the restroom.

Before leaving, Wenceslas came to me. I didn't like the smile on his face and intent look into my eyes.

"We can't stay. I'm taking my fiancé to dinner," Wenceslas said.

He stuck out his hand. I stared at it a few seconds. I felt like punching him in the face because he was playing a competitive game with Shantelina as the prize.

CHAPTER TWENTY-EIGHT

WITHOUT HER

The next morning Gustav was true to his word. He came to practice with his stop watch, outdoor hat and clip board. He blew his whistle and stood by the side door.

"Put the basketballs down, guys. Gather up here," Gustav said.

"You got to be kidding me. Outdoor running is preseason stuff," said Anton.

"We're not the best team in the league in the standings. We have to start being the best conditioned. Fitness. Running. Those are going to get us there. Anton and every one, let's go," said Gustav.

The entire team was soon together near the door.

"Loosen up, stretch, we don't want any injuries out there today. Conditioning is everything. It's going to be the key to us winning the Czech League title. So we were doing a timed run up Svet Mountain and back in sixty minutes. Coach Jiri will be back this afternoon," Gustav said.

"Coach Jiri wouldn't have us do this," Anton said.

"I have news for you, Anton. He requested it," said Gustav. There were a few seconds of silence.

"Why sixty minutes? That's insane. This run took an hour and ten minutes in preseason," Anton said.

"You guys are in better shape now. Not as good as you can be, but better. Be back here in sixty minutes," Gustav said.

He opened the door. One by one we progressed out to a concrete pad. Most of us engaged in their own versions of runner stretches. I still couldn't believe it was over with Shantelina. There was an emptiness in me because of that situation.

She meant too much to me to play a game with. I shook Wenceslas' hand before they left. Her "Yes" didn't make sense. What about all those letters she wrote me?

Gustav blew his whistle and we were off. We all hurled our bodies into a 45 degree angle upward. As I ran I thought about how much had changed since I'd run Svet Mountain. Then, it was the second day of practice and I was trying to make the team. Now I was a legitimate and integral team member. We had done great things in the season. We won some incredible games. I didn't want to make a fool out of myself. Still didn't. Sadly, between then and now there were Jelina and Shantelina. Wait a minute, Shantelina and I would talk. I had to turn the situation around. I wasn't going to lose her. It couldn't be the end of us.

Last time it rained while we were running up Svet Mountain. I looked up and there were no clouds. I looked down and my feet were dry. But it was colder now. Around 40 degrees F, I would say.

"It's only 12 kilometers," Jaroslav said.

I took small deliberate steps on the path of dry pine needles and earth. As before, I fell back from the larger group of my teammates. This wasn't a race so much as a battle for survival and avoiding getting hurt. Jaroslav wasn't that much further in front of me. Here was the superstar of this team ambling through the dirt. I watched him in front of me for a moment, struggling to get up this mountain. It was comforting to see him here and gave me renewed confidence to charge ahead.

"What are you going to do when this is over?" I said.

"Take a warm shower and ice my back," he said.

"I mean when the Czech league season is done?"

"You mean after we win the championship? We'll have a beer together and celebrate. I'll return to Plzeň for a few weeks but I'll keep playing basketball. I have to keep my shooting skills going and remain in shape. Let's win this thing," he said.

The trail led to a mountain meadow where we could see the others leading us. The grass along the trail was short-cropped and I had to avoid many cow pies. I heard a moo in the distance.

We kicked into overdrive. The burst helped Jaroslav and me to catch up to Anton and Zedenik, who were running side-by-side. As we passed them, Anton tried to trip me from behind. His shoe hit my shoe, but instead of toppling me he slipped and slid to the ground.

"Nice try, Anton," Jaroslav said, over his shoulder.

Anton was up right away and I thought he would pour it on to catch up to us. But he didn't. He and Zedenik continued to run together but we surged ahead, creating a gap between us.

The trail rose again through the dense spruce. A dozen black cows looked down on us from the hill above. As we crossed a fire road, I peered down it and there was Gustav driving his car with his lights cutting through the shadows of the trees. His engine labored as he began his ascent up the mountain. Now I know his strategy for getting up to the turnaround point.

"We'll beat you up there," I yelled down to him, though I wasn't sure he could hear anything over the distance between us.

We reached the top of the mountain. There was Gustav on the huge boulder there. He called out our times as we passed and wrote them on the clipboard.

"You two are on pace to finish within an hour. Good pace, keep it going," Gustav said.

As Jaroslav and I turned down the trail I remembered we were entering the most treacherous stretch. The way down was where I fell last time. It was a place that could end your season. There was more at stake now. The difference between that time and this one is that I wasn't alone.

Without rain on the trail, the paths were puddle-free. We headed down a dry river bed and stumbled a few times but didn't fall. Jaroslav showed me when to slow down when I was running too fast. We actually gained speed at the end to pass Kolin and Charles. As we ran, I felt great. It was cold out there, the sun and my own heat felt good. Jaroslav and I didn't try to outpace the other as we cruised in to finish.

Last time I was soaked as if I had fallen into a river from the rain, sweat, and falls. This time I was relatively dry.

There was Gustav standing with his clipboard and stopwatch. As we ran in with momentum from the hill outside the gym, we gave it everything we had. I couldn't run any faster. I was tired and had truly reached my limit. We reached the finish side-by-side.

"Your finish is 55:07," Gustav said.

"Has anyone else finished yet?" I said.

Gustav shook his head, no. We were the first.

The *Svet Monitor* featured a story that day saying that no team in the Czech league could beat us with our two-unit in-and-out scheme. The paper predicted we would capture our sixth win in a row, and how the Olmouc team was practically an extension of the town's Palacký University, the largest university in Central Europe. Most of their players came directly from that university.

"Olmouc is battling for respect and is dangerous. You are the league's best team—in the last week that is—so let's keep it up. We can beat this team. But I will tell you, there is nothing that would make Olmouc more happy than leaving here beating Svet tonight," said Jiri in the locker room before the game.

It was great to have our coach back. I really appreciated his influence on our team. Just seeing him there, in his ususal sport coat and tie, was reassuring.

We lined up in the tunnel to make our entrance. As we ran through the door and onto the court to music from *Flashdance*, I adjusted my assessment of what Svet was capable of. Svet fans turned out in large numbers. Not as many as our first game against Pardubice, but almost. Our reception elevated my spirits greatly.

My own mood was low because of Shantelina. We hadn't spoken since the night she said yes to Wenceslas. But what did I expect? She had a boyfriend and she was getting married.

As our first team lined up against Olmouc's five at center court, it looked like we had the definite height advantage. None of their players looked to be over 6'3" in height. On the opening tip, their center out-jumped Vojtech to send the ball to their point guard in the rear court. Olmouc's point drove down the floor quickly with the basketball. He threw a nice pass to his center for a quick two points. They had momentum with that quick score. Anton inbounded the ball to Zedenik. Olmouc's defensive coverage was man to man, and it looked like with our height advantage gave us an edge. Zedenik worked the ball around the perimeter with a series of sharp passes. The first unit was displaying patience on offense. Vojtech received an entry pass on the block, he went up, and was fouled on the shot. Vojtech went to the line and hit the first one but missed the second. Olmouc raced down the court and scored on a fast break layup. Then they threw a full court press on us. The last team to press the entire length of the court was Praha A. In that case, we struggled through their floor-length press but did make Darius Longstreet, Escalante Greenfield and Dave Guse pay for it in the end. We beat them.

"The best thing you can do to solve a press is to score against it. And score against it so much that the opposition calls it off. Let's exploit this press," said Jiri during a time out.

He diagrammed ways we could beat it. He showed how our best ball handler on the first team, Zedenik, would fire a pass to streaking Anton or Rudenic near mid court. For the next 12 minutes of play Olmouc continued to press. We were facing a deficit of 33-29 when we checked into the game for our stretch.

Jaroslav had a confident gait as he walked out onto the floor. He received the inbound pass and immediately Olmouc's point guard and a quick off guard clamped down. Jaroslav drove hard with the basketball to breakout of their trap. But other defenders slowed his progress up court. He threw a long full court pass toward me standing under our basket. It sailed over my fingers and out of bounds.

Later in the half, Jaroslav and I connected when he rifled a long pass to me and I powered it in for two. Every time he threw his long passes, I scored. Eight of ten points in the first half came from his long passes. Our fans got into the game especially off my baskets on the break. Excitement reverberated through our gym. They were right there with me when things happened, good and bad. They motivated me to rebound and score. It was the first time since I arrived in the Czech Republic that our fan base was so active and engaged in the game. They were with us. They were with me. Rebounds were coming my way and it felt like I was hitting every shot I took. A few minutes before half-time, Olmouc called off their press. When the horn went off at the half, Svet was in the lead, 47-40. Olmouc was a tougher team than they looked. The place was cheering at the loudest level as we walked toward the locker room for halftime intermission. An older man burst out of the crowd like an assassin. He blocked my path toward the locker room, he patted me on the back, and said, "Great job, Savek!"

"It's great to be home," I said to Jaroslav nearby after that.

The warmth, connection, and support at that moment *was* great.

"Keep it going for the second half. You are really playing well, Josef," said Jaroslav, and slapped me on the back as we ambled side by side toward the locker room.

I was concerned whether I could sustain it. I was the hero of the moment and didn't want to be the goat in the second half.

Olmouc opened the second half back in their full court press. They stole the ball from Anton on our first possession. As Olmouc's point guard dribbled the ball up the floor in transition, Anton immediately fouled him.

"Don't lose your cool, Anton. Play your game," I said.

I think he heard me because he shook his head yes. He would play his game.

As the second half continued, Olmouc capitalized on the frustration their press caused. They scored a series of baskets and stopped us on defense. The momentum had shifted back to Olmouc. Our team had our chances, but every shot seemed to miss and Olmouc was right there for the rebound. It was painful to watch. I wasn't the only one growing troubled; the Svet crowd was restless, too. In the middle of that run by Olmouc, Zedenik hit a jumper from beyond the three point arc. Our crowd yelled and cheered. I leaped from the bench like a jubilant spectator.

Then there was a lull in which neither team scored. Olmouc scored first to break out of it. Their scrappy point guard and team leader hit a 20-foot bank shot off the glass to even the score at 50-50. The Olmouc bench players were the only ones cheering. Their starters had rattled off a 10-3 run and they were back in the game. As Olmouc quickly fanned out their press, Jiri called out to Anton who was ready to inbound the basketball under their basket.

"Anton, time out. Call for it," Jiri said.

Anton requested and was granted a timeout by the referee who was about to hand him the ball for the inbound.

As the first team strode to the bench, Jiri turned to us on the bench.

"Get ready to go in now," Jiri said.

"It's a little early for them yet. Give us our minutes. A few more minutes at least, coach," Anton said.

"No. Good effort, Anton and first team, but Jaroslav's group is going in. They're playing the best right now," Jiri said.

We checked in at the scorer's table. And the moment we stepped out on the court, Olmouc's coach called timeout.

After a few minutes of going over more strategy with Jiri, we came back to the floor. This time Olmouc was picking us up man-to-man on defense. I thought that was a mistake because their press was working so well. But then again we had broken through it during on our time on the floor in the first half.

Jaroslav dribbled the ball up the floor free and easy until he reached the midcourt line when the Olmouc point guard swarmed him. Their point guard covered him very closely, almost like he was trying to mount a wild horse. An Olmouc player was overplaying me all the way and when I tried to break away from him, another defender was there to make hard contact with me. Eventually, Jaroslav drove into the lane and took a jumper from just inside the free throw line. It missed and I wheeled around to get the rebound, but two Olmouc players were there to seal me off.

Jaroslav's shot caromed over our heads and Jaroslav, our shortest player, got the rebound. He had to snatch it from an Olmouc guard who also had the same idea. Jaroslav dribbled out to the perimeter to reset.

We ran a play called by Jaroslav. I was double-teamed when I stayed near the basket. Then Jaroslav broke through to find another shot from where he had missed just moments before. He lofted the ball up in a looping rainbow. It swished clean through the net. We had the lead, 52-50—and most importantly, some momentum. I ran back on defense and found Jaroslav.

"You're our best sharpshooter. Keep it up, Jaroslav," I said.

"I'm going to keep shooting because they're doubling you so much. But keep eye contact with me on the break. We are going to break this open," he said.

With 1:44 left in the game, we had indeed taken control of the game. Olmouc had to resort to fouling us. The referee handed me the basketball on the free throw line. I breathed in deeply and released the shot toward the basket. It hit the rim and rolled in. My next free throw bounced out. My first missed shot of the night. The scoreboard read Svet 66, Olmouc 58.

Olmouc called time out. Our home crowd gave us a standing ovation as we walked to the bench. Jiri was pleased with our effort. He slapped each of us on the shoulder spiritedly. Then he addressed the whole team as we sat on the bench.

"Great leadership and shooting out there, Jaroslav. And Josef, you have played a dragon of a game on the boards. This game is ours if we continue to play smart," Jiri said

"Hey coach, can we go back in now?" said Anton.

"No. This group has the hot hand. How are you feeling, Jaroslav?" Jiri said.

"We will drive this spike home into their hearts," Jaroslav said.

"Don't go crazy now. Keep active and attack the basket. There is plenty of basketball left," our coach said.

Olmouc did hit two baskets in a row. And furiously tried to force a steal in the backcourt, but Jaroslav launched a risky long court pass to me to break out of the tight defense jam he was caught in. I felt he had audacity to just throw it. I had nothing but open basket between me. I considered slam dunking down from the side off the dribble. But then I didn't want to miss that have it carom off. We needed this basket too much to have me miss it. I decided to lay it in. The ball went in as my defender reached me, but he couldn't stop anything. Olmouc inbounded the ball but Jaroslav stole the pass, and drove to the open basket, and hit a little five-footer over an Olmouc defender. The ball went in and he was fouled across the face. He rubbed off the hit to the face and stepped up to the line and sank the free throw. When the final horn sounded, we had won 71- 64. Our return was successful.

Gustav was out on the court quickly to congratulate us all, but he came to me first.

"Your best game of the season, Josef. Very excellent tonight," Gustav said.

Maybe that run up Svet Mountain helped us after all. All this leading me to either greatness or disaster.

CHAPTER TWENTY-NINE

THE ANTENNA INCIDENT

I looked out through the raindrop-stained windows above our sleeping quarters that early October morning and saw beauty in the gray storm clouds passing overhead. Even the coal soot ensconced in the cracks of the ceiling timbers running above my head didn't bother me. Three days. That was an eternity.

We had just won two more games in succession after the Olomouc game. Night games against České Budějovice_and Hradec Králové. Two more wins. The game against Hradec Králové was especially gratifying because they had beaten us earlier in the season. This time their star player Daryl Divinity couldn't hit the game-winner at the buzzer because we rolled to a 20-point win.

As I packed my bags, I felt like we had just gotten back from being on the road. But it was better not staying around Svet.

I thought of the last time I'd talked to Shantelina. I was heading down the stairs and she was heading up not far from the players' quarters.

I looked into Shantelina's eyes, she looked directly back. But instead of joy, there was sadness.

"Can I talk to you privately?" Shantelina said

"Congratulations. Wenceslas is a lucky man, Shantelina. I'm happy for you."

"I'm sorry I left early that night. He wants to move to Prague and then eventually to Vienna. That's the plan," she said.

"Is that what you want?" I said.

"I said yes. Didn't I, Frank? I love Svet but bigger might be better."

"Take care. Hope everything works out for you," I said.

I was venturing freely into an unknown world.

After having the Czech breakfast of champions, black bread with cherry jam and Slovakian yogurt, we were off. A convoy of cars headed out of the main gate of the factory.

I was certain of these things: for the next three days, there would be no backbreaking picks to fight through, no forearms pounding me from behind, no elbows blasting my chest under the basket during rebounding drills, no free throws or jump shots—no basketball, period. Until Tuesday.

I'd played 12 games; we had won eight in a row and were 9-3 since I arrived. We had two games to go in the regular season, but then there would be the playoffs after that. I held the *Svet Monitor* on my knees as Jaroslav drove. The article said we were a quicker team on both ends of the floor—much quicker than in the beginning of the season and faster than our last game at home. That the second unit won the game and had a tremendous performance.

As I sat in the passenger seat, I realized that I'd played every day since arriving a month before. That's a lot of basketball. Practice was every day, even on game days when we practiced in the morning and played that night. I had a weight lifting streak of 15: every other day for 15 sessions in a row. Those streaks were to end.

As Jaroslav's Fiat motored down the highway, I could see the last of the leaves turning color across the Czech countryside. The smell of horses came to me, reminding me of a dozen things at once, most of them good. There were eleven players on the team, but for the most part, we were going our separate ways during this break. Some like Anton and his part of the first rotation of five players—Vojtech,

Zedenik, Kolin and Rudenic—were going across the checkpoint into the Slovak Republic for merrymaking in Bratislava. I knew I couldn't go because with my passport and visa, I might not get back in. Everything would be exposed just as things were going great.

Jaroslav and I were going to Brno but not crossing over to the Slovak Republic. Two black cars pulled up behind us. Jaroslav pushed the accelerator to the floor. When we reached 90 kilometers per hour, the car began to shake as if it was going to break up into pieces right there on the highway. The first car pulled up alongside us. Anton rolled down the window. He was making a shaking motion with his body in his seat.

"Just like the factory floor, you tall streaks of pelican shit." he said.

Anton knew our car could only go so fast. The game was done. They passed us with Anton holding his middle finger out the window. The second car driven by Zedenik blew past. Jaroslav slowed to less than 90, and the car stopped shaking. I was happy to see them go, which they did until I could no longer see them on the horizon.

Jaroslav's reaction was to shake his head and tell me that he did not like the bastard either, but he was more levelheaded about Anton and his band of followers than I was. All of a sudden, the windshield wipers stopped moving. Lucky for us, the rain was coming to an end. He tried the heat and turn signals, and they also had stopped working.

For the next 72 hours, we rambled across the Brno area in search of dark Bohemian beer and Czech women. We discovered that, for these three days in history, Brno had no shortage of either.

Jaroslav was around 30 years old with dark hair and brown eyes. He was from Plzeň, a working-class industrial city on the other side of the country near the German border. His small-town Czech provincialism seemed to work to his advantage in the big city. He had a real presence and charisma that attracted people to him. We would be sitting in a bar for less than fifteen minutes, and we would be in conversation with small groups of women as the pivo flowed.

The Shantelina loss was still in my mind as I looked into people's eyes and talked. Of course they would notice. The amazing thing was that they were flirting with us. I couldn't believe it. Like Jaroslav, I hadn't shaved or showered for a few days and thought I looked my worst. When I was feeling good and looking sharp, I never got this much attention from women. It truly was a mystery. Two Czech girls, Sofie and Gabina, were sitting with us and asked me to sing the national song of my homeland, so I sang them Jingle Bells. I asked them to sing theirs, and they sang the Czech anthem and another traditional song. Feeling guilty, I sang them the real national anthem, the Star Spangled Banner. Their faces showed they liked my honesty.

Since we didn't have many Krona notes between us, we didn't stay in hotels; we slept in the car. We would have more money for food and drinks that way. During the few times we did go to sleep during the three days, he reclined in his seat, and I reclined in mine. It was uncomfortable, but it was great to be on the loose in the republic's second largest city.

After two days, I realized that I had a low tolerance for strong lager, so I stopped drinking. As the sun was sinking on our last evening on the road, we decided to clean up our act. While searching for the Sezonas Europa Night Klub in the foothills outside Brno, we spotted an alpine lake. The map said it was Husa Lake. The lake was mostly round except it had a peninsula of land that extended into it at one end. Within minutes, we peeled off all our clothes and plunged into the water. I made quick work of soaping and shampooing because these early October waters were frigid. Drying off quickly, we got into our best clothes for our last night.

Winding through a forest, we followed a road through the darkness to Sezonas Europa. We pulled into a crowded parking lot in front of a club. The industrial-sized building was on the end of the peninsula with water on three sides. The route through the forest was the only way in and out by land. The sheer isolation of this place must have made it strategically important to the military or some Communist agency during the Soviet era. The reinforced metal building looked like a converted warehouse.

As Jaroslav and I walked through the parking lot toward the front steps, I saw we were just in time. There must have been thirty people walking behind us toward the line to get in. As we waited on the steps, inching closer to the huge metal doors, the beat of loud German dance music reverberated out. A tough-looking guy with a bandana over his head took our 30 Krona and abruptly stamped our hands. Once inside, we walked around to survey the layout of the place. Purple strobe lights revolved through the darkness over a dance floor that was wall-to-wall bodies. In another big room, the music was quieter, and people were standing around talking near a long bar. That's where we started.

Jaroslav got in a conversation with a short blonde woman dressed up in a sexy white cardigan sweater and a short black leather shirt. He waved me over. The woman said her name was Giselle. She could speak English, but was more interested in talking to Jaroslav than exchanging pleasantries with me. As the two of them were talking closer and closer to each other, I decided to give them some space. Walking around, I felt all my bravado was gone. I was standing around. Standing out. Feeling awkward. I went outside to get some air. Walking down the steps, I bumped into the shoulder of a red-haired woman. I looked into her face and saw she was crying.

"What's wrong?" I asked.

"Nothing." she said, moving away from me toward the parking lot.

I followed and asked her from behind. "No, really, what is it?"

"What are you, English?" she said, stopping.

"No, American."

"It's my boyfriend Marko. I never want to see him again," she said, still crying.

"What did he do?"

"He threw his beer in my face. Then he grabbed my arms—dragged me—I have to get out," she said.

"What's your name?" I said.

"Annika. What's yours?"

"Frank."

As her tears dried, we talked, standing between cars in the parking lot. I found out she'd lived in Brno all her life. She told me about life during the Communist years and said how during those days oranges were like gold. There seemed always to be shortages and food lines. Her boyfriend was a rising official in Brno politics. Annika was cute. Her red hair fell over her face as she talked. She reminded me a little of Jelina but she was friendlier. We must have been out there an hour when Jaroslav and the blonde approached.

"Here, take these keys. Jaroslav and I are going," Giselle said, handing me the car keys.

"Where?"

"To my house." she said with a wink.

"How's he getting back to Svet?"

"I'll take him. He's all mine now."

I looked over to Jaroslav and he was nodding his head in agreement. He had a jovial look in his eyes.

"But wait—" I said as they got in her car, started the engine, and pulled away. Too late. I looked back at Annika with a smile. She had a snickering look on her face. Things were changing fast and I was struggling to keep up. Jaroslav and I guided each other when passions prevailed, reminding each other to keep your head and don't get caught up in the events of the moment, but that was on the basketball court and before a fight was going to occur.

Annika and I walked to the Fiat heap and got in. As I continued to talk nervously, she gave the sign she wanted me to shut up. We put our lips together for a long time. It was a Czech kiss that was more exotic to me than anything before. Her lips came at me from a world away from mine. The windows began to steam up from our breathing. After a few more minutes I thought about her boyfriend, which broke the electric current running through the enclosed space.

"What's wrong?" she asked.

"I can't do this," I said.

Two eyes peered in. Someone was looking in with one hand on each side of his or her face to shield out the light. Then the eyes were gone. We continued to talk but decided to go back into the club. We walked close together, but as we got closer to the door, I could sense she was getting stiff. I saw Anton waiting in line to get in.

"Where are your buddies?" I said.

"They're inside already. Who's the woman?"

"This is Annika," I said moving past him and showing the guy in front our hand stamps. The crowd inside had lessened. I bought Annika a glass of red wine, and we sat in the corner trying to talk over the music. Annika said Marko had left, but she seemed distracted. A group of her friends looked over at her sitting with me. Within a few minutes, they all came around to where we were sitting. Disapproving looks were on her "friends" faces. I could sense something wasn't right. Anton strolled over.

"How long have you been here?" he said with a lager in his hand.

"A few hours."

"Where's Jaroslav?"

"He left a little while ago with somebody he met."

Annika let out a scream and shouted.

"Get away from me," she said as a big, burly, dark-haired guy approached us. The guy took a swing and hit me in the face.

"Get out of here," I said to her. While a whole group of guys were landing punches on Anton and me, I saw Annika break through the crowd and run out the front door. Anton and I were being surrounded.

Some guy grabbed me from behind and then the others pushed me down to the floor. A few seconds later, Anton hit the floor with a thud. Women came over and started kicking us from all sides. We couldn't stand up. Her boyfriend leveled a big kick in my ribs. They were pouring lager down on us. Anton and I scrambled across the floor on our hands and knees to get away from them. This was a drunken mob of at least thirty people against us. Anton started moving toward the front, but I could see they had already sealed the door from us.

"Let's stay together and go back." I said to him as I got kicked again. My teammate and I were united. Instead of going forward, we headed for the back of the club. The boyfriend followed close behind yelling. Somehow we made it to the men's room. We pushed in through the door and shut it quickly with our backs against it—a portal of life or death. Both of us leaned against the door, breathing heavily. I saw no one else in the men's room. The boyfriend was outside the door shouting. The door was battered from the other side, jarring our backs with each blast. We pushed back harder on the door.

"Those guys are going to kill us," I said.

"They're drunk. Who is that guy?"

"Annika's boyfriend. See if there is anything we can put in front of this door."

For a few moments Anton was gone and the pushing outside got more intense. I strained to keep the door from opening. My stomach felt like it was tied in a tight knot. Adrenaline shot up and down the back of my neck.

"Hurry. I can't hold it anymore," I yelled. A few seconds later, Anton was dragging a metal cabinet toward me.

"Move out of the way right when I say so—we are going to make a little switch—Now!" he said. The door opened slightly and we slammed the cabinet against it. All we had insulating us from the horde on the other side was a metal cabinet and a wooden door.

Anton went around the corner and pulled out an old safe with no door on it.

"That thing must weigh a ton. Where are you getting this stuff?" I said.

"There's an old storage closet over there."

We pushed the safe the rest of the way next to the metal cabinet. While he held the door and our accumulated barricade, I ran over to the closet to see what he was talking about. There wasn't much left except a tall hard-backed chair. I dragged it over and lodged it in our barricade. Anton went looking for more.

The safe began to move as the lynch mob pushed harder. I called Anton back from his scavenger hunt. We pushed back against all the stuff in the doorway. The wood on the door began to crack.

"What's that noise?" I said as we looked at each other eye to eye.

"They must be using a table or something as a battering ram to blast it open."

"Where are the other guys from the team right now?" I asked.

"They went back to Svet."

"I thought you said they came inside."

"They dropped me off."

"What about your buddy Jaroslav? You two do everything together. He abandoned you," asked Anton.

"Not really, Jaroslav's good. Did you see the look in Marko's eyes? The boyfriend. Annika is right, he's crazy," I said.

"He really got you with a good round house in the cheek. A few inches up and you'd have a nice shiner," he said, laughing. Hearing his laugh wasn't obnoxious to me now.

I ran over to see if we could go out the windows. I climbed up on top of a sink and pried open the window. The openings were covered outside with metal bars. Beyond that, were the small waves of the Husa Lake hitting the rocks. Looking into the mirror, I saw a big red mark on my cheek. My hand rubbed it and then ran back to my position along the barricade. The pounding on the door intensified.

"Those fuckers aren't going to get me. I'm not going down without a fight," Anton said as his voice got quiet and dangerous. He had an evil look in his eyes that, for once, made me happy we were on the same side.

Anton ran into the middle of the bathroom and leaped up. He grabbed hold of a copper pipe running near the ceiling. He let loose a wild scream and used his body weight to rip off a long section. When he fell to the floor, he got up and threw the pipe toward me.

"That might come in handy for you," he said. He leaped up and ripped down another for himself.

"Where are the security guys for this place? How can this be happening? Aren't there any police we can call?" I said.

"Apparently not. You did say the boyfriend is a politician. That might answer a few things. He might be mayor of this area of Brno."

"This is ridiculous."

He came back to the barricade and waited.

"What time is it?" he asked as I looked at my watch.

"12:55. We're going to have to wait them out."

"Who are you? What's your name?" said Anton.

I wasn't sure he was joking or serious.

"What do you mean by that?" I asked.

"Who are you? I've known all along that you're not who you say you are. I know that you are here under a false identity. Two years ago I played in England against Josef Savek. He's taller than you and a better shooter. I've known all along that you are a fraud. Who are you?"

I didn't know what to say. There was a long silence.

"Who are you?" he said, looking right at me.

"I'm his brother Frank." I said.

"Why haven't you been honest? You came here as a double for him. Where's he?"

"He's playing in Australia. I'm no more of a fraud than anybody really is. I did it because I really wanted to play basketball somewhere," I said.

"When you are not yourself, you're a shell of who you could be. Right now, you're a nobody. Is that the way you want to live your life?"

"No. I can't be him."

"If you're not him then who are you?" Anton said.

"I'm a basketball player lost in the Czech Republic. Looking for my way. I have gotten off the path but I can get back on. A guy trapped in a men's room who is about to die next to the guy I have hated most in the last two months." I said.

"Why hate me? What have I done to you?"Anton said.

"What haven't you done to me?"

"We have been doing it to each other.You have been a guy who comes in here and gets attention, and you're an ugly American, especially with the bruise on your cheek," Anton said.

"Maybe the dead American if we can't find a way out of here real soon." I said, still feeling anxious.

The pounding against the door eventually stopped, but neither of us was confident enough to open the door.

For the next hour, Anton and I talked about our lives and what we were going to do to get out of here. Maybe that punch in the head did something to me, or maybe it was the exposure to some kind of toxins from living above a glass factory, but I was starting to understand Anton.

"What time is it now?" he asked.

"Time to get out of here," I said.

We cautiously removed the chair off our barricade. We tested the door. No movement. We pulled the safe back. Both of us slowly dragged the cabinet away just far enough to open the door. No movement. We both opened the door a crack. The place looked empty. Opening the door wider, we burst out. Purple strobe lights were still spinning around over the empty dance floor. Dance music with German lyrics blasted as we raced across the dance floor. One guy was in the corner picking up empty glasses and emptying ashtrays. A few bartenders were talking near the long bar.

When we got to the front door we stopped. We opened it a crack it to peak out. There were about sixty people standing around out there in small groups in a grassy area in front of the building. I shut the door.

"Is there a back door in this place?" I said, to a man cleaning up near the bar.

"No. That's the only way in and out, even for deliveries."

Anton and I gathered back at the front door.

"What's the plan?' Anton said.

"I'll drive, you ride shotgun," I said.

"I wish I had a shotgun now," Anton said.

"We have to walk out there like everything is normal. No quick movements. Just keep moving and whatever happens we have to stay together."

"Okay, you got us into this mess. You lead," Anton said.

"Hopefully the car will start," I said, running my hand through my hair and wanting to stall for more time behind the protection of the huge door.

"Let's go now," Anton said.

I opened the door and with one step began to lead our exodus toward the car. We walked with a normal gait. I could feel the copper pipe in my back pocket rubbing against my sweaty rear as we moved forward. When we got half way to the car a woman's voice said, "There they are."

Anton and I began running for the Fiat. I reached the door of the car first and jumped into the driver's seat. Anton got in on the passenger side. We locked the doors and three guys jumped on the back of the car as we began to pull out. I swerved hard to shake them off. Two fell off. One continued to hang on. I swerved again. The other guy rolled off the back of the car and into the bushes in the parking lot. We were free.

There was only one road out of that part of Brno and it was through the forest. I saw a group of twenty people gathered on the road leading through the forest. Going 50 kilometers miles an hour I had no other option but to go forward. I drove like a madman into the center of the pack. People began to jump aside as I drove straight at them. They were hitting the car with sticks. One guy holding a tire iron stepped away at the last second. The side window behind me exploded glass like grapeshot into the car, most of it landing in the back seat. I kept driving through the pack until we reached a group in the back of about five people who were not moving aside. I kept moving ahead toward the last of the pack blocking the road. Not slowing down and not speeding up. Just 50 km an hour straight-ahead. All of them stepped aside, except one. The boyfriend. The big burly guy with a mustache stood there looking right at me. From the look on his face, he was not moving. He stood his ground and didn't move. I saw his face change from confident rage to disbelieving anger as I got closer. With a thud I heard him yelling. He was on the hood looking right at me through the glass. We were looking eye to eye through the windshield. That caused me to speed up to 70 km an hour and swerve him off. As I did, the guy grabbed onto the antenna and ripped it off as he fell over the side and onto the road. Out of the rearview mirror, I saw him get up holding his arm. The cabin of the car was filled with Anton's jubilant cheer.

As I floored the accelerator, we continued on through the winding forest road. Lights appeared behind us in the distance. From the rearview mirror, it looked like 5 cars were following us in convoy. We were in more trouble than before. The lights closed in. Then the car began to shake when I reached 90 km on the speedometer.

"This car is a piece of junk. They'll catch us for sure," Anton said.

As I slowed down to stop the shaking, the heater, wipers, and signals that had not worked since we left all came back on. I took it as a good omen that the gods might be on our side.

The road became curvier. It was hard to see anything in the dark. I had to slow down further to go around corners. When the road turned a corner, I spotted a dirt turnoff as we passed a huge rock. At the last second I turned in, narrowly averting the rock. The car smashed through thick hedges that concealed us in darkness. We were trapped. I immediately turned off the lights. I took my foot off the brake as soon as we stopped so they wouldn't see a red brake light. We were stuck. Then along the curve, car after car sped past. Anton and I waited in silence.

"If those guys chasing you don't kill you, Jaroslav will. His car is destroyed," Anton said.

We surveyed the damage to the car. The antenna was gone, the side window was shattered, and the body had some deep scratches from plowing through the hedgerows. That was just our superficial assessment. We didn't know if we could get the thing out of there and, if so, whether it would drive. We could have severed something on the underside.

We waited for two hours until we decided to get out of there. The human eyes begin to work better with light so we had to move before the sun would come up. I put the car in reverse and the gunned the engine. The wheels spun but we didn't move.

"Keep trying," Anton said.

I continued to hit the accelerator but nothing worked. We were stuck in the middle of a tall hedgerow. The wheels spun and smoke and dust rose up around us.

"Stop. It's not working. The smoke will draw attention to us. They'll find us," Anton said.

Anton opened the passenger side window and crawled through. He slid down through the thicket to stand on the front of the car.

"Now reverse the car. Go ahead," Anton said.

The car slipped from side to side on broken branches, green leaves and dirt. It was like driving on snow. Closer and closer we moved to the small opening we came in from. Then Anton ducked down and went through the hole in the brush to the other side.

At that point I couldn't even see him. I just heard his voice,

"If you blast out of here, you'll kill me," Anton said. I hit the accelerator and maneuvered into the opening but heard something crack and then grinding against the metal.

"Stop. Stop. Stop. You're hitting a huge branch. Pull forward a meter where you came from and try again," said Anton. So I did.

This time I drove without incident through the small hole I entered to get us in this mess. We were out of the hedgerow entanglement.

It was still dark and we had to get out of there fast.

Anton jumped back in the car. As soon as he slammed the door, I hit the accelerator, kicking up dust from the shoulder, then hitting the asphalt with speed. We rocketed along the two-lane highway through the last darkness of the night back toward Svet. I flinched a few times as a light appeared from the horizon. It zeroed in on our position. A truck came and went. I did not let down my guard as the lights of a passenger car approached. It looked like some of them coming back to look for us. Even if it was them, they must not have recognized us because they didn't turn back to come after us. We expected some roadblocks but there were none. We had practice at nine o'clock and had four hours of hard driving to get there. We made it back to Svet just twenty minutes before practice was to begin.

"What happened to your face, Savek? You guys have had your break—now let's get moving. Go! I heard about the whole thing." said Jiri.

CHAPTER THIRTY

GAME CHANGER

Anton walked ahead of me into the locker room to get ready for practice. It was empty because everyone on the team was up in the gym. As we both put on our practice gear on the bench, there was silence. Coming back to play this basketball that morning felt trivial and silly compared to the world outside these walls. Basketball. Will I still know how to play? It seemed so long since I have been here. Yet it had only been three days.

I walked up the dark stairs with Anton, awash in the irony of this situation. Anton and I had brawled in that stairwell. Grimy black walls with years of dirt caked in. The two of us trudging up these steps to shuttle us from one world to another. It seemed that all that hate for each other was gone.

We were the last ones in. There was Jaroslav back in the corner shooting around with Charles. We picked up balls to shoot and spotted good ol' Jiri ready to begin. Jiri blew the whistle. We lined up to run.

Standing next to Anton on the base line for line to line sprints, I didn't want to run.

Our morning blastoff was underway. There was no time to think about the weekend any more. No time to go over the antenna incident in my mind, or Shantelina, or my brother. The morning shuffle was on, just like back in Chicago. Work was work. It just depends where you can get it. For me it was in this country town on the edge of civilization. But if the night before in Brno was civilization, then you can forget about it. I will stay here in this little Svet.

"Jaroslav got lucky and made it out of that place with no problems," said Anton.

"What did Jiri mean, he knows the whole thing? Do you think he does?" I said to Anton.

"I don't think so," said Anton.

"Keep it up. Faster, you louts. That will be the last break you get if you come back dogging it this much," Jiri said, as everyone struggled with running. His words were comforting to me after the wildness of the night before.

After running for 20 minutes until we got it right, we picked up basketballs. Jiri never gave us time to rest as we moved on to the next drill. We began our dribbling drills against a defender up the full length of the court. Jiri came up with new ideas to make our drills better.

"We are playing Brno on Wednesday. They copied our strategy and have begun to shift players in and out of the game since we played them last. Gustav saw them play on Saturday and says it is working for them. They have not lost a game since we have played them."

There was a strategy we worked on to counteract the Brno Phalanx. Jiri wanted to keep the rivalry between Anton and me up. When we were talking during a water break he was shocked. He stopped and observed and then moved in closer to hear us. Luckily, we were not talking about the antenna incident or anything closely related.

The practice wound down to the final closing scrimmage. It was then I realized that antagonism was not what fueled the Gatling gun rotation for me. It was the pure love of competition. I didn't have to hate someone to motivate myself into playing well. The second unit struggled in the first game and went down with a loss in the best of three series against Anton's group. Jaroslav and I turned our intensity up a notch. As hard as we played, Jaroslav and I didn't have eye contact like we usually did. He drove up the court as I raced down the floor in front of him. I was covered by Kolin, who knew all our tricks by now. He wasn't letting the long pass beat him this time. But Jaroslav tried it anyway and his bullet pass sailed out of bounds. My chemistry with Jaroslav was not in sync. I couldn't break loose from Kolin. The threat of the pass kept Kolin honest in his coverage of me. We were beaten by Anton's team 24-13 in the second game. Jaroslav drove to the basket before Kolin could get there. Two points. It was one of the bright points in the day, but it was not team basketball. We ran the break hard, but Anton's first unit ran harder.

Usually running out in advance of the other team energized me and brought us baskets. It brought me strength, a wholeness to my game. I played well on defense and rebound even better because of it. But not that day.

Just because Anton and I had a change of heart toward each other, didn't mean others had. Kolin and Vojtech maintained their foul moods toward me. They both elbowed me hard under the basket when I pulled a rebound away from them. We lost three times in a row during the scrimmage and practice was over. This was our darkest day in a while. Standing in the shower I felt exhausted. The sleepless night before caught up with me. From the sound of things, not many others were better rested.

After practice we went to restaurant row in Svet for lunch. It was Starpolska where we met up with the town's biggest supporters our team. They said our team we might be the best Svet team since the team began, just after the wall fell and the borders opened up. There was no news about the antenna incident. That was good.

Before we got to the restaurant, Anton and I told Jaroslav what happened the night before. Then we showed Jaroslav the damage to the car. He didn't appreciate his missing side window.

"I'll pay for the repair of the window and replace the antenna," I said.

"Don't worry about the antenna, Josef. Just get the window taken care of. I can't have that open too long," Jaroslav said.

Of course, Jaroslav was upset that his car was damaged. I felt bad that happened. I would get it fixed.

Jiri drove us hard in practice the next day because he didn't want us to have a letdown against Brno. Brno, of all places, was the last place I wanted to think about. And they were coming to Svet the next day.

We settled back into the routine of practice and life back in Svet. Even the rat hole factory was becoming like home because of the beauty of forests and fields around it. I slept well the night before night. I had more energy after recovering from the weekend.

During our scrimmage, we lost the first one again. We wanted win this next one to maintain our well being and confidence. We'd been pushed too far. Nothing would stop us now. Jaroslav and I re-established eye contact again. We won the next game on a three-point shot from Jaroslav when we were down by two. It was starting to get bad. Jiri was after me about our "losing streak." The final game against the first team we played looser and more in the flow, even though we didn't win.

"That's not good for your unit," said Jiri, looking at me as we began to walk to the locker room. "That is five out of six you have lost in the last two days."

"I don't know what to say, other than the fact that I am disappointed too," I said.

"You have to find the solution because Brno will come in here tomorrow night and exploit our weakness."

I knew that Jiri was right.

We emerged from the tunnel to a packed gym for the Brno. It reminded me of the first night we opened the season or the opening night of the basketball season at Mendel the night before Thanksgiving each year. As I scanned the gym, I could see that there were more people here than I could believe possible. They were looking for our new look formation, the Gatling gun in action. The word about our road trip had traveled around the area. Basketball was alive in Svet like I'd never seen before. But they could be the walkers if we didn't deliver.

Although our second unit played badly the last two days, I had confidence running through me because of how we finished that last game of practice. That was something to build upon against Brno.

The first team took the floor and went to work against Brno. For all their success against us in practice, it was not panning out against a tough Brno squad. We were facing a stronger Brno than the first time we played them. They had a 6'-7" Byron Wallace, an aging American with the bad knees, but a nice shot. Also, they were able to run the fast break very well and took long shots off screens with deadly accuracy. After the first ten minutes, we were losing by three. Stepping onto the floor, I felt our second team had to produce something. The gym came alive with cheering. Our "new look" was weeks old, but many spectators were seeing the configuration for the first time.

Brno's sweaty point guard got the inbound pass and drove right toward the basket. Jaroslav stopped him with his arm. The hard foul sent the Brno guy across the floor. He got up and hit two free throws. After Jaroslav missed a shot on our end, Brno's big center, who stood at least 6'9", got the ball on the rebound over me. The big guy was missing the last time we played and beat them. He ran down the floor and I nudged him as he posted up down below. Their point zipped a bounce pass to him. I timed it perfectly, deflecting it to Charles. He captured the errant ball and ripped off a pass in the opposite direction to Jaroslav. I raced down the floor in front of Jaroslav. He faked like he was passing to me then powered in a short shot with the Brno lead guard right next to him. It was the spark we needed. At least, I hoped it was.

With Jaroslav challenged at the point by a tough defender, our intrepid point guard dug deeper. With explosive speed he drove past the Brno defender at the top of the key. Jaroslav ripped a pass in my direction as I moved towards the basket. It was perfect: I scored a flying two-handed dunk. When I landed and straightened up to play defense, I saw what was happening. We were lighting the floor on fire. All my dunks before in Svet came off the break. This was the first one I scored on a regular setup play with defenders all around.

This was truly the zone that flows beyond any one person. A time of magic. This was the best basketball I ever played, a new high in my basketball journey. And it continued. When two players screened me out with their butts against me, the ball still came into my hands for a rebound. Everything moved in our favor. We went up by eight points at the half-time buzzer. I was floating on air as we ran as a group toward the locker room. The fans weren't in their seats. They were standing. For us.

Even Anton flashed Jaroslav and me a smile like we had achieved something special in our home building. We'd had blown the rafters off the place. The crowd, yelling and still standing up, confirmed we were doing something very right at the moment.

Anton's squad took the floor in the second half and began to produce their own magic. Even Jiri was amazed by the level at which our whole team was performing. We boosted the Svet lead to 15 points. A few minutes before we were to check into the game for our final run, Brno launched a comeback that closed the gap to six points between us. Anton's team couldn't hit a shot and Brno kept scoring. The fans were rapt in disquiet in the seats.

When we came back into the game we were determined to work hard to overwhelm our Brno visitors. It was our time to get to work. The noise and excitement that our home court fans generated was a huge encouragement to continue our inspired play. Our second team *was* able to continue where we left off in the first half. It wasn't just Jaroslav and me. It was Milan and Charles who were sinking shots over the Brno horde. The exceptional play on defense helped us break away with an 11-point lead, 71-60, with 4 minutes remaining.

When Brno called a timeout, we strode over to the bench. The fans lifted us with their cheering. Jiri greeted each of us coming off the floor with a slap on the back as we got near the bench.

"You guys are doing a great job. There's been no one like you guys. Keep it up and we will not just beat Brno. We will be going to the Czech league championship!" Jiri said.

After going back into the game, Brno scored on a three-point shot that settled down the gym. Jaroslav drove hard to the basket and hit a bankshot off the board for two. Later, he got the ball off a steal and drove the ball up court to set it up. Passing it into Milan on the block, Jaroslav got the ball back and sped down the baseline. He was driving on his reverse layup. His best move. I burst down toward the basket to screen the defender hawking him. As he passed me, Jaroslav stepped on my foot. I heard something snap and it wasn't mine. Jaroslav went down to the floor. The ball went in for two points.

I went down with him to my knees.

"Jaroslav, I heard that. Where are you hurt?" I said.

He howled, grasping his ankle with two hands.

The referee placed his hand on my shoulder to move me away.

"Give him some space number 33," the referee said over my shoulder.

"He's my teammate," I said.

From the look on Jaroslav's face and his yell, my best friend in the Czech Republic was badly hurt. He continued to squeeze his ankle.

"Give him some air. Move back Savek," the other referee said.

"No, I'm staying with him," I said.

Within moments, Jiri and Gustav were there to join the circle.

"Can you get to your feet, Jaroslav?" Jiri said.

"No, I can't. It feels like I broke it," Jaroslav said. He rolled on the floor in pain.

Jaroslav started to untie the knot in his shoe.

"No, don't. Keep the shoe on, don't unlace anything," Gustav said. He grabbed the shoe strings from Jaroslav.

I looked up and the spectators across the whole gym were looking toward our little circle with rapt attention. Fans closest to us were on the edge of their seats and others behind them were standing. Then I became aware of myself. I was practically lying on the floor next to our point guard.

"You are going to be okay, Jaroslav. You are going to back playing next game," I said. Gustav and I lifted him by the shoulders and carried him to the sideline. Jiri called a time out. If this guy goes, it's over for me, too. He was everything here, I thought.

As we walked toward the bench, Jiri said, "Zedenik, report in for Jaroslav."

Zedenik calmly strode to the scorer's table and checked in.

Jiri drew up some plays on his clipboard and talked about combating Brno's zone pressure. The buzzer sounded for us to end our time out. The referees came over.

"Let's go, comrades, we have a game to play. Otherwise we'll have a call a technical on you," one referee said into our huddle.

"That's not necessary," Jiri said to the referee. Then Jiri turned back to us. "We can overcome this. Svet B, don't let this change the great momentum you guys have created. You guys have brought us back. We have a game to win, let's get out there and finish it."

Jiri and I spoke one-on-one along the edge of the court for a moment.

"This could change everything," I said to our coach Jiri

"Don't think that way. It's you responding to the things you fear will happen. Play toward it all working out. We want to win this one," Jiri said.

The referee stepped toward us.

"Coach, granted your player is hurt, but any more delays and I'll call a technical on you," the referee said.

"Yeah, okay. Got it," Jiri said to the referee. Then Jiri turned toward me. "Go ahead, Josef. Get out there now." He slapped my butt from behind.

Our reconstituted unit stood up and retook the floor with clock reading 4:01 remaining. Brno was waiting for us.

Brno inbounded the ball. And worked the ball around the perimeter. I was amazed by their sharp passing and strong picks. Their point drove right toward me with the ball. At the very last second he dumped it off to my man alongside me. I maneuvered over with everything I had to harass my 6’9” charge. He missed an easy shot. And he and I leaped up in unison for the rebound. He got a piece of the basketball with his fingertips while his other arm’s elbow blasted me across the face. The ball swished cleanly through the net for two points.

“Take that,” he said. The referees called no foul.

My upper lip was bleeding from its smash against my teeth. I was in bad shape. Our lead was now seven, and it felt like it was going to be a battle to the end.

Zedenik was a very good player but he and I didn’t work well together. He didn’t look up the floor and deliver the big passes with lightning behind them like Jaroslav did. In the remaining time, we struggled.

Jaroslav will be up and ready to play again in a few days, I told myself as I raced up the floor.

With 44 seconds to go, Brno closed the score to 75-73. We were just holding on to the lead. Over the remaining time, our team conducted a furious struggle to score, but we couldn’t. At one timeout, Coach Jiri said don’t play tentatively, attack the basket to score not just run the clock out. So that’s what we did; only the ball wouldn’t drop in.

Then there was the final play: Brno’s point guard took a three point shot at the buzzer. I saw it release from his fingertips as I stood near the basket defending their 6’9” player.

The ball went around the rim and out. I felt like I was running around in a daze those final four minutes without Jaroslav. We were very, very lucky to eke out a 75-73 win.

We were 10 and 3 since I arrived on the team. Our overall record was a respectable 17-10 for the season. Most importantly, Svet had won nine in a row.

The loss of Jaroslav felt like there was a gaping whole that opened up under the basket where he went down. I intuited that that one moment had changed everything. But I said to myself that maybe that wouldn't be the case.

Gustav and I drove Jaroslav toward the hospital in the darkness. Into downtown Svet we drove to the old brick building that I stayed in when I was hurt in the fight with Anton. The very same doctor and emergency room. Lowering a sweaty Jaroslav from the car into a wheel chair, I was amazed how quickly things change. The prognosis, from the doctor that had worked on my head, was that he had broken his ankle. He was done for the season.

When we arrived back to the glass factory at one in the morning, Gustav and I helped Jaroslav climb the stairs toward the players' quarters. Jaroslav was amazingly adept at using the crutches they had given him already. We guided him to bed. Sweat had made my basketball clothes feel stale, so I washed up and went to bed.

Looking up at the ceiling timbers, I fell asleep within minutes. The next morning the noise of the others and the light streaming in the windows told me it was time to get up. We had practice that morning at nine. I grimaced when I remembered what had happened the night before. We won, but in a whole other sense, we lost.

Jaroslav attended practice that morning as a spectator in the bleachers. He sat there with a coffee cup in his hand and his crutches next to him. He was reading the *Svet Monitor.*

We'd all read the front page story with the headline *Lions Win 9th in Row; Matura Injured and Done For Season* article. It was our morning ritual: reading the paper at breakfast. I did that when I lived in Chicago, reading the *Chicago Tribune,* but this was much more meaningful because I was the subject of the articles.

The consequences of losing Jaroslav didn't become fully evident until we ran our usual three scrimmages at the end.

Jiri called everyone to the side.

"I know we lost Jaroslav. That's hard for us, especially you guys on Svet B. But we have to do better: we have Plzeň here tomorrow at 4 p.m. It's an early Friday afternoon game. Let's go out there and win this for Jaroslav," said Jiri.

Jiri sat down next to Jaroslav to watch. The two of them intently followed the action on the court at first; then, moments later, they were immersed in laughter and conversation.

Manioli, our eleventh man, was in Jaroslav's place for our second team unit. He was a 6'1" point guard who never got much playing time all season. Manioli threw me a few sneaky three-quarter length court passes off the fast break. Those were amazing because they were Jaroslav's signature. Later he drove to the basket and scored off a jump shot over the outstretched hand of Anton. I'd never seen Manioli play that well. Our second unit was inspired by Jaroslav's loss. Everything worked as we played on emotion and adrenaline.

We won. But that was just the first scrimmage game.

As scrimmage game two began, I could see no one was going to replace the court presence of Jaroslav. Then Jiri stood up and walked the sidelines watching very carefully. He was in his coach's pose that we were all most familiar with. And Manioli returned to his old self. We struggled as a team and lost badly. The spark of energy I had with Jaroslav was irreplacable. Then we lost the last scrimmage game even worse.

Jaroslav was done for the season. Nothing was going to change that.

CHAPTER THIRTY-ONE

MEETING WITH KOLIAR

The next morning, on the day of our game, the facsimile machine in the glass factory office awoke from its slumber. With quiet efficiency out rolled a document that then fell to the floor. Shantelina reached for it but Jelina picked it up first and read it.

"What is it?" Shantelina said.

"It's a proof of a story that will be running in tomorrow's *Svet Monitor.* Josef Savek's a fraud. I knew it!" Jelina said.

Shantelina read part of it over Jelina's shoulder. But then Jelina spirited it away and moved across the room so Shantelina couldn't read further.

"If that comes out, he'll be ruined here. Jelina, it will hurt the team and the whole town," Shantelina said.

"He deserves it. He should have thought about this before coming here. Milos already knows. We heard from the reporter Pavelosek yesterday that something like this was coming," Jelina said. She continued reading.

"Don't, Jelina," Shantelina said.

"Too late. My hands are tied," Jelina said.

Then she pivoted around and headed to Koliar's office.

"Wait, Jelina," Shantelina said.

"He did it to himself. Do you like him more than you're letting on or something? Don't fall for that," Jelina said.

She knocked on Koliar's door and went in.

I had just arrived back at the player's quarters from breakfast. There was a note on my bed to see Koliar at his office. That was unusual. I thought the outcome of a spontaneous meeting with Koliar would be either really good or really bad.

When I reached Koliar's door, I took a deep breath and stepped in. Koliar was behind his desk and on the phone but then abruptly hung up. He sneered at me for a moment and then gestured for me to sit down. He flashed me a cold smile.

"You lied about your identity, you're not Josef Savek. You deceived us. Can you explain?" Koliar said. He pushed the fax toward me.

I picked it up and read. Koliar shifted his body in his seat uncomfortably as I read. A vein throbbed visibly in his forehead. What the *Svet Monitor* had was mostly on target. Josef Savek was playing in Australia and I was his brother who played under his name, but I was portrayed as a criminal. That angle of the piece was wrong. I put the fax of the newspaper story down.

"Yes, I took his place to come here. It's true. But look, I thought it worked out and I've had success. We've had success. This winning streak has been no fluke. Doesn't that count for anything?" I said.

"Winning streak? Yes. We're going to win a championship but it won't be with you," Koliar.

"What do you mean?" I said.

"We have the option to cut you in the first third of the season according to International Basketball Federation rules. Since you've not played your fourteenth game yet I'm exercising that option. We're not paying your salary for this last week. That's it," Koliar said.

"You can't do that."

"I'm the owner of this team. Yes, I can do it. That's final," he said.

"Even without Jaroslav, we can win a championship. There is something great about our "two team" approach in attacking teams. I've seen how it throws other teams off," I said.

"It has. Even if I didn't agree with it very much. But I appreciate your effort. You gave us a lot, but it's over," Koliar said.

"No, Milos. I've put everything into Svet. My whole life is on the line to play here. Jaroslav is finished here; he and I were a two-part deal. We did great with each other. Without the other one, everything changes. I get it. But not paying me for what I've already done, that's cheap. Where's the integrity in that?"

"Integrity? Where's yours? You said you are someone else. Is that how Czech-Americans do things? That's dishonest. Another thing: I heard about the incident in Brno where you crashed into that official while driving Jaroslav's car. You committed a crime. So don't test me. Finally, if you go to the *Svet Monito*r about the non-pay, you'll come across as sour grapes. If you protest, I'll turn you in to the Czech police authority. Do what you want, but you're off the team here. Gather your stuff up and go," Koliar said.

"Okay, it's done," I said.

I stood up to leave. The way this guy was, I felt I better get out of there. He might very well have already called the Svet police. And some of their men could be waiting outside the door to arrest me.

For the first time, Koliar had some compassion in his eyes. He got what he wanted. He reached out to shake my hand. I didn't want to shake; I wanted to punch him in the face. But I shook his hand anyway.

Then I opened the door into the outer office. When I did, Jelina jumped to her toes when she saw me walking out. She looked like she just won a great victory. What a rival she turned out to be. I was in a daze and steered straight ahead to get out of there. But Shantelina stepped in front of my path before I reached that outer door.

"What happened, Player American?"

"Koliar cut me. My basketball days with the Svet Lions are done. I can't believe it, Shantelina. That's what Koliar just said," I said.

"Come, let's talk," Shanetlina said.

We walked along the railing overlooking the glass factory work area until we stood outside the door of the players' quarters.

"I'm very sorry to hear that. What are you going to do?"

"It feels like I just got here. But the best thing is to go. I'm not going to fight it. I know I can't stick around here very long," I said.

I realized it was risky for her to be talking to me.

"You have more support here than you think. Koliar has nothing to go on," she said.

"No I'm afraid he does. My reputation here is ruined since it's going to appear in the *Svet Monitor* tomorrow. If I stick around too long, he'll have me thrown in jail. Turn me into the Czech authorities. Maybe deport me," I said.

"Think of it this way: you leave today, tomorrow the story comes out, and you're already gone. That looks even worse, don't you think?" she said.

"Yes, you have a point there. But I have to protect myself," I said.

"You cafgvn't go yet," she said.

"What other choice do I have? The only thing I have left is you. And you've made your decision and are moving on. I respect that, so it's time for me to face it," I said.

The next moment, the door to the players' quarters opened and out came Anton and Jaroslav in conversation.

"There he is, our super-rebounder. Here, look at this," Jaroslav said. He handed me the *Svet Monitor*. "Josef Savek, you had 15 points and 17 rebounds the last game. You're second in the league for rebounds with 12.5 per game."

"Guys, I have some bad news. I met with Koliar a few minutes ago. He says I'm off the team and need to pack my bags. Jaroslav, I came here and took my brother's place. My name's Ferenc, not Josef. Josef's my brother. A story will come out in tomorrow's paper. Anton,

Koliar also mentioned the antenna incident. He knows about that, too," I said.

Anton said, "We've won nine in a row. What a time for a shake-up! How much sense does that make? And the Brno thing, what's that have to do with it? Those guys were trying to kill us."

CHAPTER THIRTY-TWO

SAME SUN

A few hours later, I bought a phone card or telekarta at the tobacco shop in Svet. The town's only public phone was in the cobblestone square just off Přední Street. It was a phone booth but it had with no door. I pulled out a note that was postmarked from Perth, Australia. It said:

> *Have left the team in Hobart. Situation didn't work out. The team was no good. The Southerlies, storms that travel up from Antarctica, are fierce. It rained nearly the whole month I was there. Have moved to the other side of Australia. Signed with a state league team in Perth. Call me +61 [0]8 93988737.*

I looked around, making sure no one was watching me, as the phone rang on the other end of the line. Snowflakes began to fall I as stood there. The phone continued to ring. No answer.

These were the grayest days of October, when the sky in Svet felt so close to the ground you could almost step on it.

Fifteen minutes later, I was back at the phone booth. As the phone rang on the other end I looked around me. Clouds scraped against Svet Mountain. It was snowing but the noon sun had anchored itself in the open sky out in front of the clouds. My knees shook uncontrollably from the cold as I waited for someone, even a stranger, on the other end to pick up.

"Hello Josef," I said.

"Frank, you found me."

"What are you up to?"

"I had to get out of that situation in Tasmania. It wasn't even in Hobart; it was out in the country. We lived in the coach's house. I played there a while and now I'm with a new team in Perth. What about you? How are you doing?" he asked.

"I was just kicked off the team. They dumped me this morning when they found out I wasn't you," I said.

"That's not good. What are you going to do?" he said.

"I'm leaving Svet soon. I need to make it to the border and get out of the country. I'll cross later today or tomorrow."

"What do you mean later today…what time is there?" said Josef.

"It's just afternoon, 12:30 p.m. The sun is right above me but snow clouds are coming over the Krkonoše Mountains here in Svet. What time is it there?'" I said, trying to stop my knees from shivering in the cold as I held the phone.

"It's six-thirty at night and 30 degrees Celsius even at this hour. Very unusual to be so warm today. I'm sitting beside a wooden table in the place I live. Trying to keep cool but I'm sweating like crazy. I'm looking out the window at the Indian Ocean," said Josef.

"I'm freezing and you're sweating. We're at different ends of the earth." I said.

"How many miles do you figure it is between Perth and Svet?" said Josef.

"I don't know. Far apart. Hey, I just saw the sun and it's snowing," I said as the clouds closed in.

"The sun here in Perth is sinking like a big red ball into the Indian Ocean." said Josef.

"We're looking at the same thing right now," I said,

"The same what?"

"The sun. It feels like this sun in Svet is different from the one there, but it's not. It's the same," I said.

Krkonoše winds, Freemantle breezes, Czech Republic, Australia. I was moved by the magnificence of this moment. I was further now from my brother than ever before, yet closer.

After we talked a little more, I hung up the phone. There was Jaroslav on crutches outside the phone booth. Over his shoulder, I saw his Fiat on the edge of the square.

Jaroslav promised to give me a lift to where I wanted to go next. He really meant it and I knew he would stand by his word.

But Jaroslav could barely operate the car with the broken ankle. In fact, while driving earlier from the glass factory to Přední Street, he drove with one foot. He almost rammed into a car in front of us making a routine left hand turn.

The question is—where would I go next? One option was to head back through the border checkpoint passing into the Austria. From the border, I could go to Vienna and make arrangements to fly to Chicago. But there were also possibilities of signing on with other teams like Plzeň or Pardubice. Both had expressed interest in me after our last games against them. I had the Pardubice coach's card in my pocket.

We walked to the car. Or should I say, Jaroslav limped on his crutches and I walked. All my stuff was in his trunk. I was thankful the guy was helping me make my escape.

"I appreciate your helping me. But what happened to me isn't your fault," I said.

"Nor has it been yours" said Jaroslav.

"What do you mean? I did take the place of my brother and it finally caught up with me," I said.

"You gave your best here, anyone can see that. Your play made us better. Koliar showed his true nature, that's all. Don't waste a minute thinking you deserved this. You should stay a few more days," he said.

"A few days? That's crazy; I'm getting out of here. It's not safe to stay any longer," I said.

"You'll be fine. There's a festival tonight. Svet Oktoberfest. You should see it," said Jaroslav.

"I don't want a repeat of what happened in that bar in Brno. No, I'd better not," I said.

"It's going to be all right. Trust me, Ferenc—if the police wanted you, they'd already have you," Jaroslav said. I looked at him leaning against his crutch. He had a point there.

"Savek, what if I told you it's mandatory, especially tonight? On orders of Jiri and the rest of the team, they want to see you one last time."

"Yes, I'll do it, but I don't think it's a good idea. I'm not going to today's game, especially after all that's happened with me and Koli-ar," I said.

"Understood, I don't blame you. I'm injured and you're off the team. I'm not going to the game either," Jaroslav said.

"That's good. Let's get some agreement on this, I want to tour Svet one last time—and *not* be killed," I said.

"What do you mean?" Jaroslav said.

"There's no way you're driving with the broken ankle. Let me drive," I said.

He handed me the keys to the Fiat.

CHAPTER THIRTY-THREE

FAREWELL

As Jaroslav and I pulled out, I knew my being behind the wheel of the Fiat was a semi-dangerous enterprise. It was the very car in which I hit the boyfriend in Brno. For that reason, I made sure to avoid Svet's old town sector. The good thing is that I got the car's window fixed.

I motored through the quiet neighborhoods of Svet. Then I passed a cemetery and saw the *Severní Bohémský Sklo Muzeum* sign. I slowed down.

"There it is: the glass museum. Our museum looks great. That's where Shantelina and I had our first kiss," I said.

"That's also the place where Wenceslas asked her to marry him and she said yes. At least, that's what you said," Jaroslav said.

"You're right. Don't remind me," I said. I sped up the car and continued down the street.

After Jaroslav and I stopped for a late lunch, I was restless and so was he. As we walked toward the Fiat, I realized that, at that moment, we would both be running out of the tunnel toward the brightness of the Svet Gymnasium and the cheers of the fans. Soon after, I'd be shooting a basketball that made my hands smell like rubber. Coaches Jiri and Gustav would be pacing back and forth on the side, intently taking it all in amid the blare of music.

It was amazing how quickly things had changed in such a short time. Even with all that had happened to me, I felt a pang of guilt for not being there.

I was behind the wheel again and drove through neighborhoods in the hills. Then the road snaked upward toward the forested lands. Soon we came to a stop sign at a key crossroad.

"This way will take you to Poland, but it's time we head back to Svet," Jaroslav said.

I drove back to Svet. Next, we maneuvered along a street that ran parallel to the river. Every boulevard that led to the old town sector was blocked with police checkpoints.

"We've got to get out of here," I said.

"A Svet bottleneck, I've never seen anything like this here. It's because of the festival," Jaroslav said.

I drove around a curve into a line of cars. About 20 meters ahead were two Svet police officers asking for the IDs of each driver that rolled in front of them. We edged closer.

If I u-turned out of the lineup, the police would take that as suspicious and possibly pursue us. I was driving the very car that hit the boyfriend in Brno. And if that guy filed a report with the Brno police, there could be warrants out for my arrest.

"We're in a world of trouble right now," I said.

"I'd say so," Jaroslav said.

We inched closer to our fate. I saw a solution and turned down onto a dead-end alley, parking along a brick garage. A band of gypsies burning something in a round metal garbage can were nearby. As we exited the car, a woman from their group approached.

"Can you spare some money for a pregnant woman?" she said, holding her back from the extra weight in her stomach and looking me in the eye. I'd heard some gypsy women put pillows under their dresses to make it appear they were pregnant, win your sympathy, and get Korunas.

"Not right now. We're just trying to find our way to the festival," I said.

She cursed at me, then yelled other things in an unrecognizable language. I didn't want her to make a scene so close to the police, so we fled down a narrow passageway past them.

At the end of the alley were several imposing metal cans that emitted smells of rotting cabbage, onions, and ammonia.

"Do you know the way?" I said.

"I thought I did. Now I don't recognize this place," Jaroslav said.

In the darkness, I couldn't tell if my feet were stumbling on old apples or rats. It was worse for Jaroslav, who was on crutches.

"Ahoj. Sorry that person treated you like that back there. We can show you the way," said a gypsy man and his young son, who looked to be around 12.

He guided us through the back quarters. For a while, we traversed an unexpected side of Svet, dark and beautiful.

Soon we weren't alone. Revelers were snaking along the streets that led to the river. Our gypsy guides pointed us toward the river and retreated up the passageway we'd just left. We didn't even get to thank them.

As we reached the church, fireworks illuminated the scene. The bright bursts exposed my face and sadness. Nobody wants cry in front of strangers and friends. But that's what I was about to do. I held back the extra water in my eyes, but moisture lingered for longer than I wanted.

I was reminiscing even though I hadn't gone yet. Being forced to leave felt like excessive punishment. I was playing my best basketball. And Shantelina—I wanted to see her one last time. But chances are I wouldn't. I loved her but she chose someone else.

Then immense blasts exploded 250 meters above the river. The little town looked great. I had to leave it all behind.

Crowds were heading into the church to watch from the bell tower. I'd been up there a few times and knew that the tower offered the best vantage point in town. A man around my age held the side door of the church open for us.

"Here you go. Hey, Jaroslav it's you. I didn't see it, but I heard you lost 63-55 against Plzeň. What happened?"

"As you see, I broke my ankle. And this guy, the American, missed the game, too," Jaroslav said.

"Really? How can that be? I've seen you two play against Hradec Králové. You're good. Come with us Lions to the top to see the fireworks," he said.

He motioned for us to enter. The door was open and I peered in for a moment to see the spiral stairs crammed with people heading up to the tower.

"We appreciate the invitation. Those stairs are going to collapse with that many people going up there. Sorry, we have to meet some people somewhere now," Jaroslav said. We both shook hands with him and kept moving.

We continued through alleys and then a secret passage route. Then we entered a backdoor. While I didn't think it was a good idea, I went in anyway. I was standing in Klas Restaurant.

A whole mass of people were gathered in front of every available window in the restaurant watching the fireworks from the festival. Past their heads, I could see people lined up along the Jizera and throngs on the bridges.

Our teammates, coaches, and fans greeted us but didn't want to lose their vantage points.

"There they are, the men of the hour. All this is for you," Jiri said. He gave us each pat on the back and a stiff hug.

When the fireworks ended, everyone moved to tables. Jaroslav and I sat at a table in the middle of the room. I was surprised at how many people came out to say goodbye. Then the *Svet Monitor* reporter Pavelosek entered the restaurant and sat at my table.

"What you doing here? You're the one that created all the trouble," I said.

"The truth hurts, Savek. I've got some questions for you. Why'd you do it? This whole ruse, that is. Did it get you want you wanted?" the reporter said.

I stood up and so did he, both of our chairs abruptly etching lines on the wood floor in unison. My teammates gathered around us.

"Haven't you done enough harm now? Why would you want to be here? You've hurt our team. You can't be here, this is a private event," Anton said, seizing the reporter's shoulders.

"We're going to have to escort you out," Charles said.

"Take your hands off me," the reporter said.

"He knows how to exploit the situation to his own advantage, especially with this latest stunt. But he's no marauder in the henhouse. We're better than that so let him go, guys. The mayor's here and that makes it a public event," Jiri said.

"Thank you, coach. I have a right to be here and want to see how this ends. My readers deserve to know, too," the reporter said.

So he sat down a few seats from me. Right between Jaroslav and Anton. There was an awkward silence.

We didn't endure too much silence because Jiri stepped up to the podium.

"Thank you all for coming to tonight's farewell dinner for the American Savek," said Jiri. "Josef, or should we say Ferenc? We have only known you a short while. Basketball players bond with each other like family. And as a coach I'm like a father to each player. That's how I see my players: like sons. What can I say about Ferenc? He's like a Rubic's Cube; it's a game invented by a Hungarian named, Ernő Rubik."

Jiri held up a Rubic's Cube for everyone to see. Then clicked it around, and turned the blocks a few times to demonstrate.

"Ferenc's a complex person and it took sometime to figure him out," Jiri said.

He tried to turn the blocks a few more times but he couldn't solve it so it was the same color on all six sides. He held up the unsolved cube for all to see.

"Only this one doesn't seem to be coming together like I planned," Jiri said.

That drew laughter and a few grimaces from the crowd in Klas.

My Svet career was over but maybe I could catch on with another team like my brother did. I had to move on from Svet. Now was the time to find my way home. But maybe home wasn't Chicago.

"My mother, who died a few weeks ago, said this Savek has the soul of a lion and a good heart. She also said he needed someone in his life. Somebody to be with you on the journey ahead. My wife says that, too. I agree. I know there are several nice Czech girls here tonight. I don't know how he did in the love arena, but if he stayed any longer, he wouldn't be single any longer."

I scanned the crowd and the only young Czech women there were restaurant staff. I made eye contact with them to be nice. But everytime the door opened and someone new entered the restaurant; I was hoping it would be Shantelina. And not Koliar or the police.

"His loss combined with Jaroslav's injury hurts us. Today, without these two, we lost against Plzeň. Savek's been an exceptional player. A true spark. I wish we could have kept him, especially as we move into the playoffs. But we'll do well to the end— at least, I hope from here to the championship. This American saved Svet basketball. Here's a guy that gave everything on the court, practices, games—it didn't matter. And Jaroslav, too, but we're not losing Jaroslav, exactly. And not roasting Jaroslav because he'll be back once he heals his ankle. Isn't that right, Jaroslav?"

Jaroslav shook his head yes.

But I knew better. He was done with Svet and was, in fact, heading back to his hometown of Plzeň. Maybe he was going to play with Plzeň team next.

The people in Klas cheered and clapped. Jiri continued his remarks from the podium.

"Tonight we have Juraj Novotny, the Mayor of Svet who would like to say some words," Jiri said before giving up the podium.

The Mayor stepped to the podium. He flipped back the gray hair out of his eyes and straightened his posture. Then he began.

"Ferenc, it's our tradition here in Svet to bestow upon our honored guests a token of our appreciation. For your efforts in bringing the town the Superliga glory, I present you this plaque that recognizes you as honorary citizen of Svet."

He handed it to me. I looked down at it and it had the name *Ferenc Savek* on there. The Mayor and I shook hands as I held the plaque up. A photo was snapped by a woman photographer from the *Svet Monitor*. Then Jiri and Gustav joined in and more pictures were taken.

Later, Jaroslav, Jiri, and I talked in a booth at Klas over a coffee after most of the restaurant patrons were gone.

"Ferenc, we've grown to like you here. You're a great guy. It's clear you've fallen for Shantelina. Where is your sense of fighting for the right thing?" Jaroslav said as we sat there at the table.

"I didn't plan on any of this happening. The right thing is to move on," I said.

"I hope you don't regret that," said Jaroslav.

"That's right, but Ferenc has done everything he could," Jiri said.

Right there at the table we agreed that it was best for Jiri give me a lift to the border the next day. Jaroslav was okay with that. He couldn't drive anyway because of the broken ankle.

"We'll leave in the morning for the border or wherever you're heading next. You can stay in my house tonight," Jiri said.

It was starting to be uncomfortable hanging around so long. I'd written a note for Shantelina earlier that day. We had lingered perhaps longer than we should have. It was time to go.

"Jaroslav, can you bring this note to Shantelina?" I said.

"Yes, I'll do that for you," said Jaroslav.

CHAPTER THIRTY-FOUR

THE BORDER MOVE

I imagined how Jaroslav brought my letter to Shantelina. She ripped it open standing there in the doorway of her empty Svet apartment. This is what she read:

My dear Shantelina,

I've lived a lifetime in Svet. There are many memories of this place that I carry with me but none more than with you.

I've fallen in love with you twice since coming here. The first time was when this amazing Slovakian woman received a letter I sent. We had a magical dinner; I lost track of time and was dancing on clouds that night. Every time I crossed your path, I fell in love with you all over again. I'll have a hard time forgetting your enthusiasm, your love of life, and just you. Your hospitality and friendship etched something on my heart that won't let me go.

I ask these questions:

Does Wenceslas see you as the remarkable woman that you are? Does he know you like I know you? What kind of love will you have?

Shantelina, I wish you the best with everything.

Love,

FRANK

I was standing at an overlook of the Jizera, the same river that ran through Svet 20 kilometers away. Jiri had said it was a good place to visit. Alone. As I leaned along a stone wall looking down at the wild flow, I had many thoughts about leaving. I was sad that there would be no more days with Coach Jiri, Jaroslav, my second team unit, the fans. That was very hard to handle. But the saddest part was leaving Shantelina. I was really going to miss her. How can life be like that? Love is the greatest game of all and I'd lost.

"Ferenc Savek, you forgot something."

I turned at the sound of a voice I never expected to hear again. There was Shantelina. She was holding a bag of food.

"Moravian-style breakfast with roasted potatoes? You should never, ever leave without goodbye."

Shantelina had a beautiful and mischievous smile on her face. The ring that she'd been wearing was not there.

"You forgot the Slovakian yogurt," I said.

"You'll have to come with me to Svidnik, my village in east Slovakia for that."

Then she dropped the bag to the ground. We wrapped our arms around each other and kissed like never before, right there on that overlook of the upper reaches of the Jizera. My time in that town in the little football-shaped canyon up near the Polish border was done, but with this woman as part of my destiny, a greater life was on the horizon.

ACKNOWLEDGMENTS

Deepest gratitude to everyone who helped bring this novel to its final state. I had dazzlingly generous readers, editors, and friends that helped me at key intervals on the journey. That unexpected guidance from above and below was awe inspiring like a gift from the Greek God, Hermes. To my basketball teammates and good friends Dave Buelow, Mike Hauck, Doug Cumming, Mitch Luween, John Doherty and my younger brother Mike Kloak, who was always at my side, on and off the court, very much like the bond between the Savek brothers from Czech-ago. Instrumental angels and guides were Heather Haven, Dr. Amy Ladd, Marjorie Powell, Susan Rojo, Kristen Goldthorpe, Dr. A. John Popp, Ellen O'Neil, Anne O'Shea, Colleen Hogan, Alice Spencer, Maureen Wong, Cindy Manglona, Sheena Bhandari, Rod Searcey, Michael Easley, and Amitabh Sawarte. They always believed. I'm grateful for my teacher Hal Zina Bennett, who gave me the conviction to write from the heart, even when I didn't know how. Thank you to my Stanford writing teachers Julie Orringer, Scott Hutchins, Skip Horack, and especially Doug Dorst, who championed this novel from the very beginning. Two Chicagoans in-exile provided me invaluable support and guidance when I needed it: Holly Brady for her tremendous publishing expertise and strategic accumen and Adrienne Bachleda for her dedication and kindness every step of the way. They understood. My editor Philip Newey from Queensland, Australia, himself an accomplished novelist, provided crucial, late stage feedback on the novel and helped give me the "Australian perspective." I was lucky to have Paul and Marie Highby, a talented husband-and-wife team from Mountain View, play a strong role in the final product. These unassuming stars helped bring things to closure with insightful editing and transforming marketing strategy.

You were amazing. Finally, thank you to my parents George and Therese Kloak, who encouraged my flight from basketball and newspaper journalism to the mysterious world of literary fiction. Same with my brothers Dave, Dick, John, George, Bob, and Mike and my sister Mary, who threw herself into early stages of the cover design with outstanding art work. Most especially my wife Teofila, who traveled to the Czech Republic with me to research this book, supported my early morning writing, and tried to thrive along the seemingly unrelenting drive into the unknown.

A NOTE ABOUT THE AUTHOR

Andrew Kloak studied Creative Writing – Fiction at Stanford University and at the Writers' Loft, Chicago's top writing workshop. A longtime resident of Chicago, he now lives in Mountain View, California, where he is researching a new novel.

www.ingramcontent.com/pod-product-compliance
Lightning Source LLC
Chambersburg PA
CBHW060541310726
48982CB00009B/1335/J
9780997027808